ALSO BY LORRAINE ADAMS

Harbor

THE ROOM AND THE CHAIR

THE ROOM AND THE CHAIR

A NOVEL

LORRAINE ADAMS

 ALFRED A. KNOPF NEW YORK 2010

THIS IS A BORZOI BOOK
PUBLISHED BY ALFRED A. KNOPF

Published in the United States by Alfred A. Knopf,
a division of Random House, Inc., New York,
and in Canada by Random House of Canada Limited, Toronto.

www.aaknopf.com

Knopf, Borzoi Books, and the colophon are registered
trademarks of Random House, Inc.

Grateful acknowledgment is made to Hal Leonard Corporation for permission
to reprint an excerpt from "I Don't Know How to Love Him" and "I Only Want to
Say (Gethsemane)" from *Jesus Christ Superstar,* words by Tim Rice, music by
Andrew Lloyd Webber, copyright © 1971 by Universal/MCA Music Ltd. Copyright renewed. All rights for the U.S. and Canada controlled and administered
by Universal Music Corp. All rights reserved. Reprinted by permission of Hal
Leonard Corporation.

Library of Congress Cataloging-in-Publication Data
Adams, Lorraine.
    The room and the chair : a novel / by Lorraine Adams.—1st ed.
        p.   cm.
    ISBN 978-0-307-27241-6
    1. War on Terrorism, 2001–Fiction.   2. War on Terrorism, 2001–Press
Coverage–Fiction.   3. War on Terrorism, 2001–Social aspects–Fiction.
4. Political fiction. I. Title.
    PS3601.D38R66 2010
    813'.6–dc22   2009024009

Manufactured in the United States of America
First Edition

For Zoe Adams

The Infinite does not burn the eyes that are lifted to him.

EMMANUEL LEVINAS

CONTENTS

POTOMAC SEPTEMBER

1. WE ARE SHADOW

She heard the air. It sounded like her Mustang on the Interstate. She'd push its tat engine hard for the on-ramp. Dash would vibrate. She'd check mirrors. Trucks were there, scaring her sideways to the shoulder. She'd strain up to speed in the slow lane, flip the blinker to join the faster ones, relax into the drive, and only then would she realize the radio was a ruffle of lost words because the windshield was whistling on high. Air that loud was normal on the ground. Here in the cockpit, it was a sign.

Solar bands, raw dawn beauty, were hours away. Clouds blocked stars. Moon was gone. As for her visor, its night vision just fine on the ground, it'd frizzed out. Green light had gloomed to black. This night, Mary had no horizon.

She checked the head-up display. It said she was at thirty-five thousand feet with her nose tilted two degrees down. So what was the noise?

She toggled up attitude detection. She was pointed to ground at seven hundred miles per hour.

They couldn't both be right. She moved the stick.

Head-up stayed; attitude changed. She was an arrow straight for earth at the speed reserved for sound.

Her forgetting hands went to the grips to eject.

Some checklist came in time to save her. Gloves: she took them off. Helmet. Second was the helmet. Wait. Should she take her helmet off? She strained. Helmet was on, wasn't it? No. Hadn't somebody got a face sheared because the helmet was on? Off, would something she'd forgotten to batten blind her? Faceless or blind. Faceless or blind? Blind. Helmet stayed. She pulled out the oxygen, held on to her breath. Store it, store it. Into the compartment under the seat, she shoved and locked tubes. She released the survival gear in the seat kit. That would have broken her back.

She could not find the four-line release for the chute. Fingers and palms were mumbling all over the surfaces near where the release should have been. It was here. It has been here. Here. Here. She was at twenty-five thousand feet. Belts were flapping all over her chest. She hooked. Another she pulled off, couldn't, and tied it down instead. She tightened the Koch fittings.

If she couldn't get the four-line to deploy she would never make it. No, sometimes you make it. The odds were just bad. You *could* make it. Flailing, that was the thing that could kill you.

She pulled down on the grips.

The windblast threw the helmet from her head. Her earplugs disintegrated and flew like buckshot out a shotgun. Two pens in her pocket became stilettos that scored her chin. Her wallet fired through the bottom of her G-suit, along with a water bottle that busted out of a zippered pocket—missiles both. The laces on her boots plastered into the leather; one of them got through to her ankle, making an arabesque wound. Her watch sank into her wrist until the wind whipped it, and her skin, away and into the atmosphere.

One leg was twisting out of its socket in her right hip. Tendons snapped, one, two; another held. She could not feel any of it. In minutes she saw the city below, old houses in rows, the bowed Potomac, memorial stairs lit white beside it.

There was a crash. The night editor saw it at the top of his screen. Before he could open that story, another story arrived.

The first story said inhabitants of the Watergate heard something in the Potomac *like the sound of a ship running aground.* The second story said a bus smashed a truck in Potomac, the Maryland suburb. *An explosion heard for miles wracked this affluent enclave of the nation's capital just after midnight.* Stanley remembered how he had edited a story the night before last, removed *enclave.* Someone else had excised it from his copy when he was just starting, the youngest reporter of all. Back then he thought the word couldn't be used because it sounded like "clavicle," or collarbone, a long bone curved like the italic letter *f*. Some editors let *enclave* stand. He'd built a vocabulary without such chiffons. It was a language of straight timber.

It hadn't made him a newsman. With more than four decades behind him, he was instead a repository, the memory of the newspaper that had judged him wanting. He knew on which Washington street one murder unfolded and another almost did, which lobbyist's first partner was someone else's third, how the vote on appropriations changed something in conference when someone was Speaker. He had accumulated, first on spiral-bound paper, then in steel-case Rolodexes, and later on peach index cards in oak recipe boxes, a way of finding who to ask and what had happened and where they'd been and when they'd mattered. The city-states and principalities he'd chronicled knew nothing of him, but his enlarged understanding had made him their defender. Sometimes, he felt like moat and parapet. The attackers were hyperactive reporters, seasoned editors with tin-cup recollections, the paper itself— an organism sensitive to status, especially its own, but deaf to smaller bells.

The final edition had just closed. The last papers were furling out of warehouses many highways from downtown, where he and the copy chief, the last two working, sat tilted to terminals. From his desk his colleague was distant, featureless across a shaken board of careless desks. The air conditioning, a constant in September Washington, was the one sound. Stanley wore a suit vest over a Mexican shirt. His hair was gray tufts—a sun-scuffed baseball cap was on his head.

Stanley felt as if he sat by the sea. His computer screen, where the newswires sent their stories and bulletins and advisories, was his estuary. He spent his nights judging movement on this inlet. He had become, he thought, an honest estimator of depths. To be sure, there were reporters, the best of them fearless divers; he had to admit even the most middling of them reached an underwater he only imagined. But Stanley liked to think he knew more than they. He had learned to see how the actual of the world sometimes became known, and how, most often, disappeared from told life.

He felt those losses, some he even mourned. He relished that the night editor was one of the countable few who decided what was important enough to discuss publicly. Granted, he signified only in those hours after the last edition closed and before the newsroom—the Room—came to its senses, sometime after ten in the morning. Things at night appeared different in morning; night editors were constantly corrected, and it all rushed into the infinite light stream of amending and shading that continued day-in and day-out to give shape to what the outside world called factual. His contribution was not even a fleck of light in the sun blast of that constant making and unmaking of what might be true.

He looked at his screen again. He Googled to see if blogs had it. Nothing came up but pilot video games. He switched back. Now the wire was saying there was a helicopter accident near the Watergate. A noise like a ship in a river had become a bus in a suburb, an explosion in an enclave, and now a helicopter in the Potomac. This time, "aboard were government employees." He sent the copy chief a message—*See the wire on Watergate crash?* She messaged—*????* Then added—*No bodies.* As if answering her thought, Stanley saw the wire had sent another take—"Pilot presumed dead."

She landed in a tree. From it, Mary could see her Viper—now a fire in the river. In the Washington thrillers she had read so many of as a teenager, she would be a saucy woman. And she would not be in a tree. She would have landed in the water, clung to an outcropping of rocks after being battered by the rapids, and somehow managed to get her mirror, the one in the survival gear she had, in truth, jettisoned, and, flicking its light to the sky, been rescued by a sailor. She'd have been piloting a secret mission, but ultimately, because of dirty politicians, nosy reporters, and heart-of-gold detectives, the reader would see she was not what she seemed.

The Coast Guard was a few minutes away. There were automatic relays that brought them when an F-16 went down. She felt her face—slashed but not too deep to fix. Leg felt numb. She looked down. Her heel was where her toes should be.

For as long as she could remember, the only thing she knew was to do what frightened her the most. She was not aggressive, not technically proficient, not physically self-possessed. So she ran to the military, to the men who didn't want her there, to the women who were nothing like her, to trials that strafed her nature. She wanted to grow out of herself. She wanted to take the coat of appearances given her by birth and burn it away by will. She had a picture of herself in her mind. All that was left of the cloth shawl of circumstance was smoke. She was a naked figure in its haze, coming out of the soft focus to let the storm come hard as it may.

The walls glowed raspberry, the woodwork gleamed cream. At the base of the broad stone mantel was a collection of frayed bellows. Nearby was a Japanese screen hand-painted with rocks and trees. There were easy chairs in celery with a brushed-silk sheen. On the rumpled linen sofa were pillows made from canary damask, a salvaged Colonial quilt, and, needlepointed on the largest pillow, in a russet explosion, a cascade of begonias. One lamp was a royally yellow Chinese jar touched with jade, on top of which sat a pleated ivory shade. For fun, there was a leopard-print ottoman finished with heavy silk-twisted fringe, some strands of which were a little too long, on purpose, to create a sumptuous sensation as they draped on an antique rug the color of dried bamboo.

The dinner party of Mabel Cannon and Don Grady had gotten as far as the first drink. The guests were people known to be known. They presumed they were on the written-about-but-not-actual A-list. It was not called the *Social Register*. In conversation, if spoken about at all, its peripheral aspirants thought it was called "the circuit." These guests were lavishly parodied. Unknown to their diagnosticians, they were also people who knew they were satirized. It felt fine to them. Mockery was the living sign of envy.

Mabel had come to see that her husband was almost the last of a time past. No one else was in his rank. He had promoted his home as the place most important conversations occurred, more than in any official location. One guest, whose wife was out of town, had been attending dinner parties here since he was a somewhat young man. Yet he, a historian, had come to think of Mabel Cannon and Don Grady, who'd been so reliantly welcoming to him over the years, as not unlike the European aristocracy before the First World War. It was all crumbling around them. It would never be as it was. It had to end, it would end, and no one believed it ever could end.

But people—having faith in what they had read of power, or had seen of it onscreen, or, most often, believed through the sanction of asides describing it—still came. They averted their eyes and drank up, spoke of things that reinforced what was supposed, wore smiles, stayed late.

The conversation this night was when one war would end and another begin. Don Grady, working on a national-security book, could not speak of events as they unfolded, but only when they were completed. Interest in any event was highest when it was unknown but presumed to be knowable. That was one of the privileges of dining at Mabel Cannon and Don Grady's: you might be able to divine, through observation of Don's reaction to a guest's proffered scenario, what was going on—in that worn expression—behind the scenes. Someone could then say, I was at Grady's, and when someone said war was coming next week, Grady winced. If war came next week, this moment would be remembered and recounted, proof of Grady's unimpeachable access to power's highest balconies. If war did not come next week, the wince would be interpreted as his tut-tutting at the wrong many who could only guess, and badly, the future. As for Don, he was constantly bewildered and had made a profitable art out of masking his confusion. His books were best-selling. He felt despicably lucky. He acted like a bishop.

The copy chief said the wire was reporting casualties on the ground. The body count could be high.—*fuck,* she messaged Stanley, picking up her phone. Stanley turned to look at his fingernails. The cuticles were thick, and the one on his right thumb was bloody from tearing. He pressed on a flap of skin to stop himself from picking at it. He looked back at the screen. The copy chief had messaged—*Adam's coming in.*

Stanley messaged—*please*—and dialed Adam's number. Adam's wife answered. "Oh, hi, Stan," she said. Stanley had always liked the executive editor's wife.

"Adam doesn't need to come in," he said quickly. There was no need to go slow; Joan grasped events. You couldn't rile her. She taught damaged children how to hold a fork.

Just as he said the words, the copy chief was messaging—*POTUS on board.* President of the United States. That acronym was pretension Stanley deplored. Next—*Donovan called Adam at home.* Donovan, the president's chief of staff.

"Did Donovan really call?" he asked Adam's wife.

"Donovan? No," she said. Her voiced sounded far away.

"Let me talk to Adam," Stanley said.

"Hold on."

Stanley waited. He messaged the copy chief—*Donovan didn't call.* He typed—*take it easy*—but let it hang there without sending it.

"Stanley, you still there?" Joan asked. Stanley nodded, forgetting to speak. He had been waiting a long time for Joan to get back to him. She and Adam had been talking much longer than the time it would have taken for Joan to fetch Adam.

"He says he'll talk to you when he gets there," she said.

"Right," he answered. A drama had begun. Stanley couldn't stop it. He felt winded.

The night editor was, in the ordering of daily journalism, pitied. Stanley Belson, Adam Sanger, and Don Grady had been interns together in the summer of '71. Adam and Don had risen; Stanley's dinghy caught a little wind and sank. Stanley's demise had come because he had been deemed not tough. Stanley's eyes were blue and delicate and, more often than not, moist. He felt tears were nearby, almost always. His first days as a reporter, alongside Adam and Don, were lessons in facing that nothing mattered as much as he felt it did. Adam was his brother in this—he was not like the others they encountered, reporters or editors made of steel wool, obdurate, abrasive, and useful. Don was one of these others, but, unlike all others, his name, Grady, became a household word. It had always tickled Stanley that the ultimate ring, the outermost circle of achievement, required possessing a name as recognizable as household appliances, brands, or habits. Like Maytag or Hoover, Kleenex or Clorox, tooth brushing or napping, the celebrity was a common, almost comfortable item. Somehow it had come to pass that, in reaching the pinnacle, one entered the domesticated.

Stanley also knew that Don's aspect had helped his role in life—eyes low on spark, paternal gravel in his voice, his expression a permanent implacability. Stanley had never ceased to be amazed at how looking the part contributed as much as meriting the position. Adam's eyes were dry as old sand in a corner. He had a look like a crag. The only way anyone might have been able to tell his heart was in a state of pretty much perpetual torment was the way he put his chin in the air. Even that was a bad signal, because it seemed to broadcast self-righteousness. Stanley knew it for what it was. Adam was a conscientious man.

Stanley signed off—they would after all not need him, what with Adam, the White House reporter, and whoever else the copy chief had telephoned. As he got up from his chair, he realized his finger was still staunching his thumb. The pressure was too much, and he'd restarted the seep of blood along the base of the nail. He reached for a tissue on his desk. As he did, he saw that Adam had just appeared in the Room. He was walking toward Stanley. But then the White House reporter waved from the National Desk, and so did the copy chief, and so Adam raised his index finger and scrunched his eyes toward Stanley's, saying, *With you in one minute.*

What we think we are, we're just not," said Mabel. It was late in the party, a glass of spilled red mopped with white napkins, the cork popping for another bottle.

"How so?" asked an editor at a weekly news magazine. His cheeks were boyish, his skin smooth, his hair—an indistinction of brown—receding. He was, if he stayed in the right company, somewhat feared.

"This is a new time," Don said. Mabel couldn't help considering his jaw. "Stolid" was the word for it. When she saw Don, her husband of the last twenty-two years, father of their three sons, her mind went to "jaw" and "stolid" on a conveyor belt. She wondered which words his mind automated toward when he saw her.

"There have been new times before," the historian had to say.

"So what are we?" asked the editor, rhetorically, through his malaise. How many times could this conversation be had?

"Imperialists. I think that's obvious to everyone. We don't even need to talk about it." This was from a thin woman who played second cello in a chamber ensemble. Mabel thought she was a flipper, a goose, a kumquat of a person.

"You can't be serious," said the woman's husband. He was an economist.

"Partly, partly I am," the cellist continued. "The CIA is constantly going into other countries, and people die mysteriously because of what we do."

"You're so caught up in the details," her husband said, sounding too kind, as if he had wiped clean the contempt just before he got the gibe spoken. He had to be careful. He could not seem to get ready, even a little, for divorce. A golfer, he was tapping his sun-damaged fingers on a side table. They were mottled, and it wounded him to see it.

It had been too long since the historian had heard anyone with a command of the grand sweep argue the particulars. Mabel had become little more than a provocateur. She used to have thoughts he wanted to hear. He shivered. They had the air conditioning on the highest setting.

They always did. It wasn't even a hot night. It was September, just past Labor Day. His lips felt scaly. His left arm was numb.

"Every day, the paper says who is dying and how many," said a small lawyer with an exact voice. "But it's a trickle. Not like Vietnam."

"A trickle," the economist agreed. "And all volunteers. No draft."

"Any number is too much," said his wife.

"More would have died," Don was saying to another conversation farther down the table. "The prisoner-of-war camps the Japanese ran during the war—I know a dear friend, a terrific woman, she and her parents were liberated. The *Enola Gay* was their savior."

"Our Japanese camps—those, what that was—there was an exhibit by a son of one of the internees. Installation art. I found it powerful," offered a guest; Mabel thought he was from Los Angeles. He couldn't seem to get his bearings, even this late in the evening.

"Have you seen the new Holocaust museum in Berlin?" asked the cellist, sensing his constant tottering.

"It's actually a museum of Jewish history," said the architect. He felt better.

"Photographs of the GIs liberating the camps," Don began.

"Remember the *St. Louis*," said a smart young writer.

"Roosevelt turned away that ship with ease," said the historian. "To very little outcry."

"What ship?" asked the cellist.

"Four hundred thousand Africans," said the editor, who had not heard the cellist's question. "Our ambassador to the UN, the grandson of Holocaust victims, did nothing to stop it."

"I saw the movie, that one about the hotel keeper," said the architect.

"What about this, this report that came out of Sissy?" Mabel decided to ask. SSCI, the Senate Select Committee on Intelligence. She needed someone to tell her something about it. Her jibberjash of a column was due tomorrow. "I have calls out all over town about that report. I'm told it's remarkable."

"So much of the report is classified," Don said.

An expectant quiet cleared the frowsy din. During the time before conversation, to remain polite would have had to restart, the prevalent surmise was that Don had seen—may have even had a copy in the house in which they were sitting—the report his wife had been reduced to making calls about, and not told her. What had been a lolling dénouement, an evening tending to a reclining, sat up. Some had always thought little of Mabel for her lack of what everyone called sources, even though they knew sources were just and only people. (Sources, even so, had dominion; a person had a job.) Some had thought Mabel a wisp-weight. But now even they wondered why Don had to expose his wife at dinner in their home. Don looked innocent; yet maybe not entirely.

If she could just put her toes down, she would get solid again. The tree that had Mary was large, a branch as wide as her waist was near her backward foot. A rumpus and a fall—the lines of her chute settled, depositing her . . . where? She blinked the Watergate's lit curve into focus around the river. Farther, the columns were straight and white. They always saw her as the goody-goody. With a name like Mary, with a last name like Goodwin—what could she be but Girl Scout and dear daughter and no trouble at all? She had a baby face. Or did have, before flight school. Sixteen and not quite kissed. And that photograph in the yearbook, somehow they'd shot it with a halo. Way before that, playground boys tried to find a way to snap her bra against her back. They just couldn't. She wore what they wore—T-shirt, Fruit of the Loom, they thought. She had an appliqué rose on the scoop neck they couldn't see. One ninth-grader thumped her sternum, said, "You don't have what I want."

There. Her swaying had slowed. She could almost hold on to a branch.

The writer looked impassive. It was important to be unimpressed with Don's coup on the report. He also made sure he was not searching the faces of the others for their reaction. Not so the young pretty with mascara eyes, a type who came to Mabel's parties over the years, usually not more than once, and then disappeared into the private agony of discovering whom to marry. The pretty was looking at faces; she was also wondering why a balding man with a long chin and high cheeks like radishes looked so happy.

The writer considered whether this man, who had been so invisible the rest of the evening, had seen the report in full and knew—what?—that its blacked-out paragraphs contained nothing of significance? That Don had seen it and been meant to see it, so that a certain line of story might be more convincing to Don than another? Or was the radish-cheeked man gratified that Don had managed to find out, with a thoroughness born of the slow accumulation of detail he was famous for, what no one wanted him to know?

The room was butterflies of beating questions. Someone, a substantial woman in a blunderbuss of a suit, wore an expression of gravity; she looked as if she were on a witness stand, waiting for the cross-examination to begin. Mabel's old best friend, now just an acquaintance, with luxuriantly long hair and a longer dupatta, had lips puckered as if to pull a face of intelligent concentration together from the disarray of her features. An ambassador from Eastern Europe with his closely cut hair and padded face, the smart writer with his tightened lips, Don with his merchant-banking gaze—all looked watered down, diluted somehow, to the pretty young woman. She was an English major now in law school. Her date had called the morning of the dinner to invite her. He talked fast. His confidence was overheated. It curdled her. Other men here were composed, and they were interesting to her.

"I don't know. The report comes at a time when there is almost no debate inside the administration." This came from the young writer, who had broken the silence, but with a tone that sought to suggest he hadn't noticed it.

"Oh, there's debate," Don said. "Alliances are forming around smaller and smaller gradations in policy. Do we turn this bolt an eighth of an inch or a sixteenth?"

The historian looked at the young woman no one knew. He saw she was open to life. He wanted to get her away. He unrolled a scene in which he showed her Don's study on some pretense and disabused her in a series of paragraphs, astonishments of concision, of the most pernicious soul-stealing misconceptions. Her tenacity of mind and a pliancy she implied with her posture—they tricked him into thinking he could tutor her.

Below her backward foot, the thinning of leaves made sounds so familiar Mary used them to relax, to go to Greenland cold in Death Valley heat. The Lincoln Memorial, she could see it. His eyes sunk in, his eyes trying, trying to be closer—to what? Brain, inside, soul, pith? Cheeks hollowed, and the reflecting pool not far from her, they were connected—no, that trivialized; no, that redeemed; no, that was the president, she thought, our president really, really liked to put on that he was his wife's creation. It was the First Lady he feared, not any man. It was a lady who knew what he couldn't quite see. Running everything, someone had to run him. It was too much against the science of things that any one man could have no real master. Mary had been crying, a nose-wet sobbing. Her chin was cold with her phlegm, and her nose dripping weepy. Eyes were swollen. The medics would treat, the gurney would carry, but she wanted rescue postponed, delayed until she began the shivering. Shock—a best remedy for hysteria. Shock came some time after tears. Shock sobered. The whooshing leaves were whooshing. Greenland was crystal. Death Valley was dead. Don't bring help, not yet. There were so many things she had to do.

It's a bear of a report, I think," said the lawyer. "Tough to summarize. I don't believe, to be honest, there is just one author. They say parts of it are not yet written."

"I think it's fair to say," said a man with white-dusted brows who had waited out the conversation, "that this is an example of something that was written not to be leaked. It reads like something cooked on a long night with a head on fire." He picked up his glass with exaggerated fatigue and drank his wine. No one spoke. They were waiting for him to continue. He knew who the author was—they felt it.

"If I may," he started, after putting down his glass on the long cherry table, "we cannot start another war until one war ends. From a practical standpoint, we are overextended. One memo in this compendium of a report says what has been said here tonight. It is all there—the inconsistencies in policy, problems with allies, and the scimitar of mass destruction."

Mabel stared at the top of his head. Above him in a gold frame was a seascape; its ocean grayed to flat violet, its horizon a tint of shrimp, its sky a light-robbed wash of almost blue. He had solemnized the obvious, purpled a synopsis—of all they had said before he spoke. It was not new. Mabel wondered—did only she see it? If they respected his take, what had done it? The word "scimitar"? The timing of his weariness? Perhaps, wiser than she, they knew that there was nothing more to know, that the scenes backstage were identical to the scenes any audience saw.

They sat, wondering. The writer, for example, knew he had command of only two of the four languages on his résumé. For him, much of the world felt less than half authentic. He thought the former secretary of state, whose papers he owned but hadn't read, had missed something. The writer also loved his grandfather, a man who'd never shamed him, as his mother had, and his father had impotently permitted her to do. So, for the writer, the former secretary of state was a wise totem most likely more right about the report than wrong.

There were, inside all of them, filters similar to the writer's, filters made from histories as intricate as quantum equations on the blackboards of exceptional scientists. What poet could make sense of such formulas? Who could see the lens living had made for them? And who was the person who could pluck their cornea out, behold all it was, study it, worry it, map its quadrants with the precision of microscopes or telescopes? Only the blind could, but not all of the blind—just those that learned to see by some other means. The kind of person who gave up everything, to gain nothing, and, by some grace, survived to describe his ordeal.

Mabel's gray eyes were dulling. She thought they were bright, because when she looked in the mirror she saw her face transformed by the wish she brought to checking how time had played with her. She was a fighter for her vitality. Yet, lately, she was becoming less interested in the battle. For so long, she had camouflaged her higher wisdom—to let him shine brightest. She did it again tonight. Another wife would have been piqued by Don's knowledge of the report. He could have provided her with a scoop for her column. He knew she didn't know how to dig up a scoop. He knew she had never had a scoop. But scoops— Mabel shrugged—they lasted for a day, two at most. Breaking a story was a cork trophy in an evanescent sport.

From impact Will Holmes knew all there was to know about what got called "Potomac Pilot." It was his idea to get the White House involved. Donovan, White House chief of staff, put out conflicting versions, none of them too right. Will had noticed that reporters took anything the White House said. Still, he was curious to see how they wrote it. It amused him to see the stories, *well sourced* and *well written*.

Will avoided book learning. He was high-school degree and Ohio son. He had a face like a thumb: drab eyes the color of grotty hair not much different from dingy skin. Now, after years of being high and tight, he could wear his hair so long it needed aerosol. He looked like a failed rocker, sober after touching death, once, twice, more. He'd been part of so much *peligro* that there was something of rigor, as in mortis, about him. A few operators had Will's look, and many had his capacity for control. He thought his came from the same place as his eidetic memory, his crypto talent.

The mining of data, analyzing media, digitized logic—he was glad for them. This night's test run was different, a program with duper avionics that would stop suicide pilots from smashing into buildings. It was a war-boffin special from the Defense Advanced Research Projects Agency. The DARPA prototype could, from the ground, control a plane without a pilot knowing it. It was in the beta stage. It was buggy. He'd made the decision to test it—too soon. So, when he got to the crash site, his mind shorted out—to Panama and the rescue mission he'd flubbed. That was, in '89, his first kill ever. Later, they told him: He'd gotten stinked-up intelligence. He'd taken out the wrong man. Days of grief-sick wouldn't end, so he put the gun to his own teenage head, debating, debating. His CO said, "Gotta kill the captor to rescue the captive." And if the killed man wasn't, it turned out, the captor? "You can't always be right."

Until this crash, he'd been happy there was no more Pablo, not Pancrace, Kibungo, Mogadishu, or Rome. No corpses his eye could see, none of the sounds thousands dead didn't make and yet did. Now that he was the Chair, he directed the action: no more making it. He could switch it on and off. Standing beneath this pilot in a tree, he tried to remember why that was better. By morning, some of it came to him. He could control what he heard.

2. AFTER SOME ILLIMITABLE SATISFACTION

Stanley went to the two o'clock meeting. No one else nightside did. He knew that day editors—if they thought of him at all—could not remember his name. Still, even among the always changing up-and-comers at the *Washington Spectator* there were editors with gentleness for any breathing soul; they were the ones who said, "Hello, how are you?" and looked at him with fellow feeling. Most others could not risk a greeting. He was dull as foot soles, a man with nothing to share about how to get where they were going. Unaccountably, Stanley felt for all of them, his tribe of avoiders. He saw even the marauding ambitionists were bashful. Lately, their anxiety was higher than usual: the managing editor had stepped aside to write a column; the competition to replace him had begun. His vying successors all attended the two o'clock. They played to Adam, the *Spec*'s executive editor.

Stanley thought this as he sat on the wall bench that ringed the conference room, never at the table. He possessed none of the appurtenances of power: slots, working reporters in those slots, stories by those reporters, space for those stories. In the daily debate over the front page, Stanley was rabble, not player.

Adam, last to arrive, took a seat. Stanley saw Martina Welk, the National editor, move her hair with the smallest jut of her shoulder. He was not sure if it was a crush, a bloodbath of unfinished father-need, or the actual article of falling and being felled by love, but Martina was subject to one of them—and Adam the cause. All this, and she wanted to be Managing Editor. She was interesting to look at, Stanley thought, with her knotted intensity of a face, not much to speak of in the way of eyebrows or eyelashes, long thin hair always ponytailed and gray, and those hands, such hands Martina had. Long fingers that ended in hard-driving nail-bitten slimness, knuckles and joints oversized compared with narrow digits, and all of it attached to wrists so see-through he felt sure if he got close enough he would be able to watch her pulse.

He thought about the pilot from last night. His mental pictures of pilots were from movies. There were unshaven actors from World War II films, disgraced motorcyclists from Vietnam cinema—those were all he could summon. Had he ever interviewed one on the phone? He had many plane crashes in his clip file. Yet none were military. The Delta crash one winter—in the Potomac. One in a field, maybe United, he thought in Maryland. An editor had sent him to the airport to find relatives arriving from somewhere to identify the dead. The editor told him to stake out the gate, interview them. He had hurried away, hidden his notebook, given off an air of waiting for a flight to Orlando, and, after watching the grieving arrive and disperse, called his editor to say he'd asked all of them if they'd wanted to talk, but none had. Keep trying, the editor told him. So the next flight of grievers came, and, notebook in hand, he approached a woman in a raincoat. Before he could speak, she shook her head and looked away. He couldn't try another. He watched the other reporters to see whether any of the relatives talked to them. If they did, he promised himself he too would crowd around the talkative ones and switch on his tape recorder. But no one did, not that he saw. The next day, the other papers had the interviews with grieving loved ones. His editors saw the other stories, and they said, in meetings— Stanley didn't get one interview. They didn't berate him. He feared that would happen. What happened was someone else was assigned to do the next-day story on relatives.

But airline pilots—had any survived a crash he'd covered? He couldn't call one to mind. The pilot was usually dead on impact. Stanley recalled the voices of aviators recovered from the black box, which was always hard to find, a dear prize of a laborious search, more than a few times never found. The words recovered from this throttlehold reminded him of those said in the confessional booth or the psychiatrist's office—sanctified into a privacy only calamity could sometimes breach. To his sorrow, the transcripts were startling in their brevity.

There was little of moment or portent said, just the exigencies of a present like any other. They spoke as if an unremarkable outcome was not just possible—it was likely. He, too often aching, wanted, "I loved Miranda!" Or, "I'll never see my son again—God help him." Or, "I have felt lost a lifetime."

But no. They said, "Palm 90 contact departure control." Or, "Forward, forward, easy. We only want five hundred." The best he ever heard was, "Stalling, we're falling." "Larry, we're going down, Larry. . . ." And what did Larry say? "I know it."

When they played the black-box recording on television, Stanley was wretched to hear the tones of the pilots: stunted, unreadable, the opposite of the burning music he imagined.

No doubt this pilot too—the one who ejected—was as disembodied, as untouched by grandeur or longing as all the others he had never interviewed or known.

Yet he hoped. He hoped that there was a place where the real transcript could be found. And there, where he and others of his trade had no windows, there was the dialogue that made living a sacred, felt thing. There would be, somewhere, a marveling—wouldn't there?

Somewhere, perhaps, but not in the Room. There, last night's pilot, if found dead, would have become someone whose military records were requested; someone whose commanding officers, if they were retired, would be called; someone who would have had to fit either into the story of a brave pilot, beloved by all, cruelly and ironically unlucky, or the story of the headed-for-trouble pilot whose superiors were too overburdened or negligent to have stopped him. Sometime later, there might be a feature writer who craved writing for magazines and would consider writing a longer, more nuanced story, but who would decide after a few weeks that a fall into a river in the nation's capital from a great wasp of a warplane was a singularity upon which no writer, no matter how great, could improve. But the caracara reporter, that bird would not rest. He would run to the doors of those who didn't want to talk at first but might finally. He would database and dial neighbors, flight-school classmates, lost spouses, half-siblings, math teachers, aunts, and, if bitingly lucky, poach the sweetest morsel: parents. He would compose a story that would be too long—Stanley had never seen one less than seventy-five column inches, the height of a tall man. Unless there was something in the pilot's past—criminal record, too many accidents, a supervisor who wrote him up as unbalanced—editors would cut the story. It would run inside Metro, not even on the front of Metro, and certainly not, as erroneously dreamed by the keenest striver, on the newspaper's front page. Stanley was often called upon to edit these remnants of moxie; big editors edited big stories, less-so editors edited stories that found neither the usual nor the unusual.

It was time for the day's budget. Foreign had a roundup of battles—the assault on Mosul, ambushes in Kandahar—one dead, two wounded. Sports had a track star testing positive for drugs. Business had regulators charging a high tech with fraud and a brite on Facebook. Metro had a shooting that wounded three at Edgewood Terrace and a raid on a money-wiring business moving cash to Pakistan. National had the first day of a gay-marriage package—news lede-all from the religion reporter, A1 Features with a portrait of a lesbian couple. Style was pushing a scene story for the front.

Stanley scanned the budget for the crash. The story, if you could call it that, had made it only into the last few thousand copies of the paper; and it was only a few inches long. But the front-page photograph, of the fire in the river, was four columns wide across the top. The photographer had shot at water level from the Virginia side of the Potomac. That angle put the Watergate in the background. It looked as if war had come—to Washington.

The top said a pilot had experienced mechanical difficulties in a warplane and ejected prior to the crash. The aircraft had taken off from Andrews Air Force Base. It was part of the fighter wing flying combat air-patrol missions over the capital. The wing commander said a preliminary finding would be finished in about six weeks. A more thorough inquiry was expected to take four to six months. The name and condition of the pilot were not released.

"Adam," Martina was saying, the skin on her forehead like her wrists, thinned to transparency, "as you know from last night, this was not the story we had thought." She looked around the room to see if anyone needed an explanation. "Training crash," someone said non-committally. Stanley craned to see who it was. It must have been the Foreign editor, who continued, "Nice photo."

"It was more than a photo for the folks living in the Watergate," said the Metro editor. He was jauntily disrespectful to the solemn echelons of National and Foreign. Always jiving, is how he would have been referred to in Stanley's time.

"I think you have a point," Adam said. "Three inches got into, what, a few thousand copies? Is Mitch working on it?"

"He's moved to the Foreign Desk," Martina said of the Pentagon correspondent, past retirement age, a resistor of all buyouts. He pre-dated even the summer of '71. That year, Mitch had been the National editor when Adam was an intern. "Last night the White House had it as a helicopter," Martina continued. "They had the president on board. Ground casualties. You know this better than anyone, Adam. But it was an F-16, actually. The president was asleep in the White House. No one injured or dead on the ground. The pilot survived."

"Do we feel confident we know why the first take had it as a helicopter and the president in it?" Adam asked.

"We all know these training missions are routine," Martina said. As they all had, she long ago mastered the art of not answering when replying.

"They're not training exercises," said Martina's deputy, who had been the Pentagon correspondent once. "This is a combat patrol. After the Pentagon and World Trade Center, it was continuous; now it's random and abridged."

"Readers don't know about the first takes," Martina said, getting back to Adam's question without, still, answering it.

"It's curious," Adam said, looking preoccupied.

"What did Donovan say to you?" Martina asked Adam. That was a good question, maybe the first one of the meeting. Stanley leaned forward to hear.

"Donovan did not call me," Adam said. That sounded off to Stanley, even though Joan had told him the same thing over the phone. He had believed her then. He was doubting now. "Let's do a follow—Photo can get something on the clean-up," Adam was saying. "Metro—have someone talk to Watergate residents. See if we get any calls on far afield debris. Business—percentage of accidents with the F-16 compared to other warplanes, Lockheed's response. If you can get the pilot's name and anything on his record, I'll consider it for the front." The segue, effortless, to the tributaries of worn streams—Stanley never failed to be disappointed to watch Adam steer there.

In the Walter Reed emergency room, doctors manipulated the knob of Mary's femur into her hip. Toes went back to the front, and heels went back to the back. Nerves were unhurt.

Her blood vessels were supple things. Veins and arteries had twirled around without breaking. She had, the chief of orthopedic trauma told her, a musculoskeletal system they wanted to study.

Doctors drove past the shorn grass alongside the walnut-shaded drive into the military hospital. Medical pilgrims came to her bed, disbelieving at first. One doctor asked her about the crash and tape-recorded what she said. Another touched her pelvis and hip and thigh with concentration, questioning her at pauses, looking at her face as he did as if he could read in it something more than what she said. Every so often, another doctor in the room would add a question. Her nurse, a young man with red sideburns and a bird face, interrupted from time to time, bringing up whatever he thought was important. He liked to use Latin words—"acetabulum" was one—that excluded Mary. She learned that the acetabulum connects the pelvis to the femur, the body's longest and strongest bone. The acetabulum was a socket. A capsule. In her—they discovered after scans and tests and analysis of childhood records—there was an unusual genetic mutation. It was like being born with six fingers or webbed toes. Her acetabulum was malformed in such a way as to make what would have been a cataclysmic injury into something less. It was a holy abnormality. One morning, the bird-faced nurse with his love of Latin handwrote *Mary Mirabilis* with a broad-tipped Sharpie on an envelope. He taped it above her bed.

That afternoon, Will Holmes walked through the ward. No one was nearby. He was glad he could stare, that she was alone with eyes closed. He heard voices, an emergency of problems, in a room two doors down. It had drawn everyone on the floor into the crisis.

So he looked at his crisis. It was a woman in a bed. His reaction was different than expected. He'd hoped that by now he'd feel relieved she had survived. He checked the inventory of his emotions, trying to kick out the guilt. Would he have felt the same had it been a male pilot? He believed women had no place in combat. He was convinced that the innate response to the female, which study after study found to be difficult to train out of the healthy adult male, was protective. And he failed to understand how most men could command individuals they wanted to safeguard. You had to send soldiers to hell. As he stood there, he changed the scenario. He'd sent an object into harm. The object was an F-16 Viper, one that everyone who signed off on Potomac Pilot agreed was the best guinea pig. An airliner couldn't be used. How would it be if an empty airliner fell? No, a Viper had to be the pig, and it never occurred to him to check the gender of its pilot. Yet, as he looked at her cracked lip, he thought he could have. Just then an orderly in white streaked brown—his latex-gloved hands trying to roll a crackling paper gown into a ball—rushed past Will.

And there Will was, his ass up against the sand pit he'd dug with his hands, taking a shit with his pants down just enough. The memory had almost disappeared. But he sensed it perfectly now: His team had taken cover for an hour, up to necks in the trenches, been surprised by a convoy, but stayed undetected as they realized this convoy meant to spend the night. The only choice was to keep still and buried. He remembered scooping his own shit away from his backside, pushing it into the sand as far as his arm would reach.

It hadn't bothered him. His own ills didn't much. Now, looking at Captain Mary "Extra" Goodwin—narrow shoulders, high curved forehead—he saw why he was stuck in remorse. He thought about fighting out from it. *On average* the *majority* of men sheltered women. A selection of men, small but resolute, broke free. Wasn't he one of them? Wasn't exceptionalism his post-Panama creed?

He took a step into her room. The orderly had disappeared again, into the consternation down the hall. He knew she had no family—there'd be no guests. He knew without really knowing that she had to be a loner. He recognized his own kind. He moved to the foot of the bed, thinking he might just get a closer look. She was bundled, though the top of her head was uncovered. Just above it he saw the envelope taped to the wall with her name, *Mary,* and a word—what did it mean?—after it. *Mirabilis.* Oh, it had to be her last name. He thought for one false moment she had gotten married—was Mirabilis her new surname?—but he shook that away, confused. He backed out of the room, through the doorway, aware of his surroundings, and the new quiet where the noise had been down the hall. Someone would be coming.

A dam."
   "Don."

"Thanks for doing this," said Don Grady, who was distracted. He had missed the two o'clock. Really, he didn't need to go. No, he forgot to go.

Adam couldn't tell what Don meant. He gave his automatic response. "Not a problem."

"I really appreciate it," Don said, pushing the two o'clock away. He had to get Adam solo, and the best time for that was after the two o'clock, though not exactly as it closed. Adam was always waylaid then. It was the time when someone could buttonhole Adam and avoid the public walk to his office, the glass wall that showed the someone in the office, the expressions on Adam's face in the office, and the transmittal of these particulars to the Room. Don, who was used to being watched, cared nothing about these visuals. He just wanted no one to hear.

"So," Adam began. He waited. Nothing. He tried, "How can I help?"

"I just want to go over the weekend first, if that's okay with you."

"Happy to," Adam said, realizing for the umpteenth time he had never had a feel for what Don was thinking.

"Have you had a chance to read this Metro project, what, is it slugged . . . ?" Don looked down at his budget.

"The northern-Virginia highway project."

"ROADS1," Don said. "It's, what, four parts?"

"Yes."

"Has anyone given any thought to tightening the lede?"

"Let me see," Adam said genially, motioning to a printout of the story Don had marked.

"The lede is anecdotal, and I think that's a problem," Don said. "Sure, sitting in traffic is awful. I mean, this reads like any bad-commute story. And there're some facts way down that I think need to be brought up higher. And the context—how does this compare to other regional traffic dilemmas? But I guess the deeper question I have is, we seem to be saying this is the fault of the governor, and I'm having trouble seeing how we lay this on his doorstep."

Adam put his glasses back on his nose and looked over them at Don. He gestured for the printout so that Don might hand it to him.

"I mean, can you help me with that?" Don said, unaware of Adam's hand moving toward his.

"Have you talked this over with Metro?" Adam took his glasses off again.

"No one seems to be over there."

"I know there was some discussion as to why the top was the way it was, and I don't remember exactly, so I can't tell you as much as I'd like."

"The nut graph. It's vague," Don said. "Who was in charge of this?"

"The Metro projects editor. Tom. Tom Simon."

"No, I mean who really edited this."

"He did."

"Not Hank?"

"Steve edited the version from Tom."

"So Hank was fine with this?"

"Don, I was fine with this. Maybe I could just take a look at your printout."

"Sorry. I'm sorry." Don handed the story to Adam. Before Adam could look at it, Don said, "I'm not myself."

Adam put the printout down and folded his glasses beside it on his desk. "What's on your mind?"

"It's Mabel." Don shook his head. "Can we close this?" he said, going toward Adam's door.

"Sure. Sure." Adam looked at the Room out the glass that was the fourth wall of his office. It was Thursday. Maybe it would be better to go with the roads project next weekend, when it was Adam's turn in the weekend rotation. Don, who came on the rotation once every ten weeks, had not been part of the discussions and rewriting. A network of asterisks and arrows crisscrossed Don's copy of the story.

"As I may have mentioned on the phone—she wants to throw her hat in for the managing-editor job," Don began.

"Good. Good."

Don opened his mouth, and then closed it. He hadn't expected that response.

Adam raised his eyebrows and nodded. He looked at Don's printout of the story. "You know," Adam said after a short time, "I think you may be right about this top."

"The nut graph, I really think it needs to be punched up," Don said, still wanting to talk about Mabel, but willing to be agreed with on ROADS1.

"It really does," Adam said, still reading. "This is going to take a lot more time than I'd realized," he continued, tapping the printout. "I'm going to talk to Hank, put this into the hopper for next weekend."

"I think we could get it in shape by tomorrow."

"We could, but we don't have to. This has been in the works for seven months. No sense in rushing it in at this stage."

"I tend to agree," Don said, although he didn't. Adam was always trying to push him away from the paper. You're the big shot. I'm the real guy. That was the message.

"Good. And on the other thing, why don't you have Mabel give me a call, and we'll get rolling." Adam needed to get Don away from the series. Five or more editors had edited the reporting team. Some had wanted contrary approaches, ordered rewrites, seen the rewrites, and then realized the rewrite was not quite right. The top of the first day had been written more ways than Adam could recall. In the end, to keep the peace, Adam had typed out a lede that was serviceable.

It was war, first in Afghanistan, always against terror, then Iraq, then not Iraq, then Iraq forever, now Afghanistan again. It made so much, even northern-Virginia roads, into, at the least, a set-to, and, all too often, sloppy arguments, sometimes loud, in the glass offices lining the Room. The usual reasonable discussions were harder to have, and the ones the Room did have couldn't settle things. It meant Adam usually had to write the tops of important stories. But maybe it had always been that way. Adam was beginning to forget—so electric was any given day. So much, he felt, was at stake. Stories were no longer about gradations of the appearance of wrongdoing, the most visible theme of decades past. Lives, young ones lost in combat, upset him. They could say what they wanted about the body count being low. They could tell him the world wars outclassed this global war on terror. And while it wasn't the first era the government had asked his kind not to publish, now it was happening to *him*. The case of that pilot crashing was only one of many instances when someone at the White House or Pentagon told Adam that blood and treasure—how he despised the words—would be lost if he didn't hide information that might or might not have been factual. It overloaded him. He'd blown a circuit, and although he'd managed some alternate wiring, the makeshift machine that was left couldn't roar to life the way it once had, just after the first attacks. Even they were starting to blink on and off unpredictably. When the images reappeared for discussion on the wearisome anniversaries, he had no interest in revisiting the emotion of the day—he always vetoed suggestions to rerun the towers collapsing. They were now like postage stamps to him, and, like the Statue of Liberty, a profile of George Washington, or the looped ribbon in the fight against cancer, they were everywhere and invisible, easily summoned, the exact opposite of news.

"It's been hard for her," Don said. And suddenly Adam thought: Her? Who was her?

"Hard?" Adam decided to ask. He felt as if a weak fan somewhere in his left-brain was the only thing available for marshaling the energy required to interpret this new sentence from Don.

"Being away from the Room."

"I didn't know." Adam almost smiled, so often and so easily had he resorted to this sentence in his years running the paper. It was truly the most important sentence he knew.

"Well, it has been."

"And that's been hard on you." The fan had whirred to high. Mabel. It was hard for Mabel to be away from the Room. An unhappy Mabel, Adam had to assume, meant an unhappy Don.

"I've gotten some concessions from the administration, Adam; I need to talk to you about this over lunch at some point. It's unusual. I want to coordinate." Don paused, not remembering how he had gotten to lunch and coordinate. He looked at Adam, who leaned forward and opened his eyes a little more to invite elaboration.

"Mabel," Adam finally said.

"Mabel," Don said. "Right. Mabel. I don't want to characterize this in a way that could be misinterpreted."

"Take your time."

"It's not that she is unhappy per se. It's more that she has some misgivings, nothing as strong as regrets. You know, married to me all these years—how should I put it?—she's had to adjust. And I see, and I think she sees, that my book, on this administration, it's important. Important. And once again, Mabel Cannon will be overshadowed. It's inevitable. She knows it. I know it. It's there."

Adam nodded. These intimacies from Don—it was more than a little strange to him. He felt uncomfortable, badly so. Adam picked the mask of concern—the least convincing in his collection—and tried to put it on his face.

"I, uh, I want to put this out there," Don continued, "that I in no way expect any special treatment, no mulligans, no practice shots. Mabel Cannon has got to be the best managing editor for this newspaper, bar none. Absolutely no hands on the scale. I mean that."

"I know you wouldn't want it any other way." Adam got this sentence out with difficulty. That last warning from Don had ticked him off. It was, of course, on its face preposterous that Mabel, after fifteen years or more as a columnist, would be a viable candidate anyone would propose for the job of managing editor unless he was the great Don Grady and she was the great Don Grady's wife. But that was to be expected. It was ever thus. The wives of such men as Grady were often offered up for consideration and often accepted. He recalled with not enough guilt that he had volunteered his first wife for an op-ed piece on socially conscious vacations. (She had written it. They had run it.) Maybe his pique came from Grady's use of what Adam called power clichés—the manure of mulligans, hands on the scale, practice shots— formulaics that Adam surmised Grady had heard at his dinner parties. He hoped he never talked that way. He hoped his humility never failed him. He hoped that Stanley, its best guardian, would forgive him for the other night. He could have taken the time to talk to him. Why didn't he? He, affable Adam, had been only a little better than grating Grady.

"And she wouldn't either," Don said, moving toward Adam's door. "I'll let her know you're looking forward to her call," he said, opening the door.

"I am." Adam gave Don a smile. Don gave his and pushed out the door.

It was beautiful in the garden—magnolia leaves plattered over-head, frills of white impatiens between hostas in shade. Mabel was furious. She counted ten, nine, eight, seven, six, five, four, three, two, and one. She repeated banalities heard in passing. Parking is horren-dous. It's the hottest September on record. She about-faced to her own facts. She was thirsty. She was sweating. She was not nice. She was sweat-wet tits in a sundress. There was that inner voice, an impersonal gibbeting, "Sweaters make sweat. Sweat makes sweaters. I sweat in my sweater. My sweater sweats on me." She was dressed for summery Sep-tember in white cotton. Ten, nine, eight—she heard the phone ring. She should answer it. She was expecting a call-back. *Call me, don't be afraid, you can call me/ tell me and I'll be around.* Pop lyrics organized emotions. *Take this cup away from me/ For I don't want to drink its poison/ Feel it burn me.* Was that Gospel, or 1970s Broadway skunk Jesus Christ Superstore? *I don't know how to love him./ What to do, how to move him./ He's a man. He's just a man./ And I've had so many men before,/ In very many ways,/ He's just one more.* Mary Magdalene. She washed his feet.

Mabel didn't want to have the evening she was about to have. She knew exactly which pleasures were within the range of the possible, which pleasures would be near the borders of what was possible that she needed most to have but received least frequently, and which pleas-ures she acutely needed that were mostly impossible. She saw long rows of legal filings, need entries, and opposing possibility entries in a docket so long it reached to the graves of Mars.

To be a righteous woman of the night who loved the son of God—that, Mabel ventured, was a way to live. Upstairs were her babies, three of them, grown into talking, living, thinking outcomes of all she had ever wished dead in her polluted bogs of despair. They were Leonard, George, and Robert, adorable blastocysts now livered, kidneyed, lunged, fully neuronal sentients who saw right smack through her.

Instead of the promised consolation of three sons, she had produced three low-aiming critics of preternatural acuity. Of course they were right—they were moleculed to be right. You couldn't deny their mastery, try as you might through the agency of the usual appurtenances—the extramarital affair for love, the extramarital affair for sex, the extramarital affair born of opportunity, the extramarital affair because the extramarital affair for love had been transforming. Seated, in underwear, in a basement real or imaginary, the self had nothing but nothing to excuse itself. It saw what her sacred once-seedlings saw.

What those boys didn't see, they sensed.

And talked about. Even their guesses were educational.

There, the ringing stopped.

Leonard opened his bedroom window and shouted, "It's for you."

She kept quiet. She heard his window close.

When you edited the night, you could think of words as stars. Stanley tried. There were a finite number of constellations—eighty-eight. Twelve of the eighty-eight made the zodiac. Such a formula might be enough for a system of personality. But the night couldn't be built out of eighty-eight sentences. There were other problems. When he stared at the night sky, walking home from work, he never recognized the supposed-to-be-there shapes. How did Pisces resemble a fish? In none of his neck turnings could he find a crab for Cancer or a bull for Taurus in the stars that were said to be there, right there, in front of his eyes. When he went online and studied the animal shapes superimposed on the astronomical photographs, he became convinced that it was all a scam of a most childlike sort. These fish, crab, and bull were little more than wishes. Someone wanted the stars to look like something familiar. It was the same way other editors wanted the remnants of moxie to look. They were never content with the glittering agglomerations of reality. They had to have them look like something—panda bears, trusty steeds, Easter bonnets, pythons. Touching stories. Inspiring stories. Frothy stories. Cautionary tales.

He was more interested in galaxies. They contained trillions of stars, but their mass—almost 90 percent—was dark matter. He'd amended his earliest suppositions. He wanted to edit a galaxy into being. He wanted to find the reporter who could see the dark of it. He had faith, these days, in one new hire named Vera Hastings, a night-cops reporter on the Metro staff, the only one who reported directly to him.

She was someone who saw him clearly. Wasn't that how it usually started? Stanley scolded himself. His conviction about a person's notability was too often proportionate to that person's understanding of him in the way he wanted to be understood. All right, then, he continued, walking down the street to the alley where he'd lived so much of his life. So that's so. That doesn't mean she couldn't be special.

He found himself wanting to fit her into the Room's abiding legend. It was Don Grady's story, how he as a young, lowly Metro reporter assigned to cover a simple break-in saw more than was there. Through late-night door-knocking, unappealing bird-dogging, sideways and sliding begging, persistent talking to little-known men instead of highly placed chieftains, Don prevailed. He shamed the Room's White House reporters. He deposed a noxious president. Stanley knew it could be done, or something like it, again. It was always a small thing—a break-in, a plane crash—that bumped through the surface. Underneath that hump in the continuum were white dwarfs and red giants.

But Vera was so new. Just yesterday he'd had to acquaint her with the oldest of saws. In Washington, he'd explained to her, there were pretty much two ways to find out things: people and paper. People, he warned, could fudge. Paper, made by government—courts, agencies, committees—was worse. You had to use both, flawed as they were, and find where they met, where there was some kind of coinciding about what might possibly have actually happened. But even that wasn't enough. You had to be more than the young Don Grady—who was basically a busy scrambler. You had to take time to feel your way along the edges back to the center, and to wonder, past the point of patience, what it was you still couldn't quite believe.

He climbed the steps of his wooden frame house, one of only a few left in this part of the city. It had finally cooled down, after a hot day for September. He heard the approaching wave of a car on the next street, then its braking near what he could now see was a late-model Impala speeding without stopping past the intersection's blinking red light.

Inside, his old house cracked underfoot, planks reminding him of unseen others who'd tried to live here. It had a history before him of hosting more than a few kinds of runaways. He'd once spent quite some time researching the slave owners who'd chased runaways here and how some of the chased ended up owning a homestead a few doors down. It had been a busy conflux, this alley. Now, in its probably not even final quasi-gentrification, this piece of it was his. He opened a window to let in what he hoped was the first of the fall air, and with it came, just within the range of what he could hear, an airplane, gone almost as soon as he thought he heard it.

The pilot's crash was still a National story. He would not be able to suggest Vera work it on the side, as Don had worked his break-in those many years past, until the Pentagon reporter on the National staff was done with any reporting Adam, the executive editor, and Martina, the National editor, deemed necessary. So far, the military had withheld the name of the pilot. The Pentagon reporter was too busy with Iraq and Afghanistan. So the Follow to the first story had been on the Metro cover. It got some residents of the Watergate who said they saw the crash. It was mostly heard-a-noise quotes. The after-the-boomboom talk was a hash. Each contradicted each. In Stanley's estimation, they had seen something on television about the crash and mashed it into a memory they called their own. Time had taught him that eyewitnesses had bad eyes and made even worse witnesses.

Mary always said if she got to Walter Reed she'd quit. She was on the floor with them now, losing sleep with the gimps who had the positive outlook, the innocents pure wounded, the wise alecks shut up. She could hear them at night, the amputees especially. She dreamed about a man with phantom arms reaching for her, chasing her, but her crutches, which they said she needed and she had to agree she did, crunched in half like they were made of candy brittle.

She woke from it. Listened, felt maybe she should investigate. Just walk down the hall and see what she thought was a whisper, whether it really was. Because she swore she heard the boy she'd met in her therapeutic walks with her intravenous piping on its jerkily rolling frame.

The guy had no right leg. Right, the leg on her that was mutated, space-age, supernatural. She could see him, this new unfortunate, coming at her in the hallway. She and he had crutches, a pair apiece. And they had to stilt themselves toward each other, facing each other, he watching her right leg, she watching his one leg.

And their eyes, what else to do with their eyes? Whenever she saw him in the hallway, she could feel him feeling that question. Once, he tripped, not really falling, because he was in some harness with an aide on either side of him. Tonight, lying in her bed, she remembered how from a distance in the hallway her special amputee had been roughened sexy, the guy who could take you in his arms standing straight and hold your ass in his hands with the studied attention you saw in movies. So the first time he got close enough, her thoughts were tending that way, and without trying she was the one who tripped. It got her piping pulled out and the top of her hand jam-red, the itchy little needles popping out. Their eyes met. Better that they meet when she was vulnerable and bloody. Because they both knew she was the stronger.

She lay there in the dark remembering. There it was again. The whisper like someone in grade school, when the teacher's back was turned. She could see her crutches, propped on a chair. She was well enough to drag her IV to them.

She rose up some, babying her left hand's crochet of piping, taking a careful, firm grasp on a point beyond the needles, so they wouldn't, even if she slipped some, come free.

She hopped. It felt good. Fun, even. Pull, pull—nicely she tugged the intravenous tangles. She reached the crutches and gingerly let go of the lacing tubes of her left hand. Got the first crutch. Wished she could have twirled it like a majorette. She used it to retrieve the second one, bring its padded top to her left hand. She stood there for a moment. She'd not thought about how to bring along the IV mechanicals with both hands occupied with crutches.

A whisper was not enough to tell anything. She just wanted. She needed to go see him. He was twenty-two, the ten years she had on him felt like a generation and, given the facts of her life, were probably more. Mothering? Not quite right. Confiding? Could be. Or maybe she craved touch that wasn't medical—night kisses.

She thought again and decided she could put her arm around the intravenous walker and still keep the crutch in hand. It was a slower-than-slow hobble, and, naturally, once she got it figured out, the whispering was gone. She also made more than a little noise herself, and when she turned the corner of her door into the hall, the arrangement didn't quite follow. It was the crutch for the left leg, the good one. It hit the hall with a muffle, thanks to the sheepskin on its armrest.

Looking in his room, she saw the monitors blinking, the night-lights making sure of his vitals, and she saw instantly he was awake. He was looking at the window, at the closed shade, as if it were open. She paused. She probably hadn't heard him whispering, yet here he was.

It was just like her to think she could save him. He was a pull, so gravitational she couldn't quite turn around, so forceful she guessed there was some trouble here. Quietly she put the other crutch on the floor. She walked with pain, but not enough to matter. They'd be mad at her for this in the morning. But now she was concentrating on his line of vision, wondering why he couldn't sense her, and then, when the IV's wheels made their rubberized whistles, and he still didn't turn, even though she was right up against the bed, she froze.

He had to sense her breathing. Her inhaling was like a thudding drum. Blood was a cascade in her ears. The sound of the air in the cockpit that night: she could hear it. Not the specifics, just the intestinal, cochlear register. The sensation that what she was hearing was wrong. Yet the instruments, they'd reinforced the sensation. And what else did you have but intuition or component? The alive, and hence flawed. The inert, and so impartial. "Tell me something else to believe," she said out loud. The kid should have heard. She'd assumed only the leg got taken. He might be deaf; an explosive under a convoy did that. She was lassoed, the sweat beading in the crooks of both elbows. There was something artificial with him. She put her hand on his forearm.

It was a mistake. She saw that the minute both of his arms came up in the jujitsu she had no training to counter. All that saved her this time was her size. Small, always the smallest in any military setting, Mary hoped she registered harmless in this guy's gut. So much time spent alone in the cockpit—she'd forgotten it was way dumb to touch a soldier. Even lying down, he picked her up off her feet like a scarecrow. His monitors started dinging right away. The nurses were there before he put her down. When she fought back to push him away, all she did was realize he was blind.

Mabel saw him at the bookshelves. Jonathan Strasser was reading spines—oh, he pulled on one. It wouldn't come out. He put his wineglass on the floor and tried with both hands. Would he go to the author photo? Would he go to the blurbs, or the jacket flap? The index, to look for his own name? Perhaps the dedication, scoping for marital status. He did none of these—he opened the book and rubbed one of the pages between his fingers and a thumb. He put his nose to it for a moment. He took off the jacket carefully and moved his palm across the hardback as if it was soothing—to him, to it, hard to say. Then he wrapped the flap around the front board, closed it, and eased it back into the tight shelf. She chose the pause after it was lodged to make herself known.

"I didn't know you were a bookbinder."

He lost his balance in surprise and knocked over the wineglass with his foot. Oh holy mother, she said to herself, now others will come. She and Strasser were standing in a hallway apart from the dinner party. He had probably just come from a bathroom. These were Don's books. His home office was the next door down. But no, her masterfully uptight help was otherwise busy. They hadn't heard the glass on the limestone. She hated limestone. She had chosen it, and now it looked like the floor of a bank lobby or a museum fountain. Here was something lucky. The glass had only tipped over, not broken. She picked it up and poured some wine from her own glass into his.

"I didn't see you there," he said.

Well, at least he wasn't a bumbler in all ways. He said that with calm.

"I didn't want you to," she said.

He shrugged. She appraised the shrug and straightened up.

"I often look at bookshelves at dinner parties," she said. "They're usually more interesting."

"Oh well, this is a marquee evening. I don't need to tell Mabel Cannon that."

"I'm curious," she said, moving stiffly, not flirtatiously, toward him—it was important to know when to pull back hard on the reins. Her one hand tugged out the book he'd just had in his both. She had a feeling it was a book by a woman he wanted to seduce. Or one he'd had and lost. She looked. *Getting to Parity: Balancing Subsidies in the New World Order* by Frances Strasser.

"It was her first," he said.

She looked at Jonathan Strasser pleasantly. She nodded and smiled.

"A difficult, complex subject—she must be brilliant."

"I love her so much."

His wife's first book—pawing it. Don had told her Jonathan Strasser was married, yes, but she had heard—who was it?—hell if she could remember—that it was a first marriage, a marriage made when too young, that there had been problems, something about a mood disorder, or maybe even hospitalization. Pain relievers. She had not heard that the wife had a book. Or books. Don's researchers read these books. Writers of wonk and tank—that was how she thought of the good women and men who penned these unoffending, useful volumes. They were the only honest Abes she ever saw. They were on the streets in affordable khakis carrying fabric briefcases. She had half hoped one of her sons would become one of them.

"I'm so sorry she couldn't come tonight," Mabel said.

"That would be difficult. She's on her honeymoon."

Mabel looked at her wineglass, which was now damnably empty. Telepathic, one of her Missusmabels had entered the hallway with an open bottle. She walked to Mabel and poured.

"Congratulations," Mabel said after a swallow. There was not one straw of comprehension in her. She wondered, Could he and his now healed wife be divorced, and this ex-wife was now newly, very newly remarried, while he, heartbroken, was caressing the talisman of their gone shared years at a dinner party. Congratulations—not the best response.

"It's funny you would say that," he said.

Dear tortured martyrs.

"No, no. I'm sorry; it's of course the right thing to say," he said, smiling, and for the first time she felt him thinking she was a little better than a jerk.

"Well. I don't mean to intrude," she began, feeling, no matter his warming to her, this was a disaster not much ready for rescue.

"No man is good enough for my daughter."

"Your daughter," she couldn't help saying. Frances Strasser was his *daughter.* She'd assumed it was his wife.

"She's sensitive, she's special, she's, well, she's just a terrific human being."

There was Don. He was in the hallway and clanking his glass against Jonathan Strasser's before Mabel could lift herself back into the conversation. "I am in your debt," Don said to him in a manner Mabel found off somehow. It was strange—her husband's mouth looked unnatural. It always looked unnatural, but it looked different from his usual unnatural mouth.

Mary was the lead. Her wingman was an 0–2 first lieutenant with a skinny frame that earned him no end of ribbing and the call sign

"T-Knee." Like any wingman, he flew behind and outside. He had her back.

When a girl was a lead and a boy her wing, it could go sour. Frank "T-Knee" Partnoy didn't let it. He more than covered for her, not just in the air, during OEF—Operation Enduring Freedom—the military moniker for the Afghanistan war after 9/11. He protected her from her own mistakes, made his own and let her see them, resisted the running joke on her among male confrères, the one that went, she was surely slut or mostly dyke.

Anaconda, the father of Afghanistan operations, was their first meeting. To one and all, the poetry of code names was not bard-made, but to Mary, spy in the barracks of men, the song of it always amazed. How could it be that military males made such descriptors? They punched them out fast, Mary knew that much. They most likely never unpacked a word's ancestry, but Mary opened the suitcases and pulled out all the scarves. Anaconda was originally a Sri Lankan snake, an unexplained alteration of Latin *anacandaia,* for "python," yet still from Sinhalese *henakandaya,* for "whipsnake," itself being from *hena,* for "lightning," and *kanda,* for "stem."

So Mary and Frank had first met in a lightning stem, situated in the Shahi-Kot Valley of Afghanistan, back in the late winter of 2002. Anaconda was also (geographically speaking) eight by eight square miles of (militarily speaking) sloppy intelligence—i.e., "slop intel"—but the blame went to CAS, close air support, or, as Frank called it, Aunt Cassie, which consisted of Frank and Mary and all their fellow airmen. Frank faulted the rules of engagement and the worst confliction stew Mary had ever seen. A small air-support command at Bagram thought they were in charge; a larger command, in Doha, thought they were. Frank complained and was completely right, that both—Bagram and Doha—had to have Tampa's okay to drop a thumbtack.

She and Frank always said it made no sense that Florida controlled their wings in Afghanistan. Yet she and Frank, like all the militaries of all the worlds, had been taught to do, not think. This was the thesis. It was absolutely the job. Most important, they had, after all, *chosen* to do these things, these flyings and smokings. It all came back to her first solo flight—feeling in bones the cudgeling roar she commanded, craving the angle she could have, and then the loft, up to up, up to up, hovering like frozen smoke, flightless for that one instant before blading through air. Ground, the death trap, falling off, and none of it comparing to the vault of crying sky, the flume of speed. She had been so long small, so often overpowered, she would never forget getting her steel at last. She felt it every flight.

Until Anaconda. And the worst of Anaconda was Neil Roberts, a Navy SEAL. He had carrot hair and a pink face. Three days into the operation, she was hovering in her Viper, one of many birds trying to bomb the right target. Neil was below, on a Chinook's ramp, when three Taliban RPGs hit his chopper, shredded its hydraulics, spilling liquids. He slipped off, into the Qaeda enemy. He had a pistol and two grenades. She watched him run out of ammunition. She watched three men drag him behind rocks. She couldn't see what came next. Later, a team recovered the body. He'd been shot in the back of the neck.

"Although I sacrificed personal freedom and many other things, I got just as much as I gave," he wrote his wife in his open-in-the-event-of-my-death letter. "For all the times I was cold, wet, tired, sore, scared, hungry and angry, I had a blast." Mary revised her open-in-the-event. Bravado, she realized after Neil's, served up bogus.

Bluster was nothing like what she felt. First came vengeance. She worked harder to lay waste. She itched to press the pickle button, the one her thumb hit to release projectiles. Next came choking up. It didn't always happen in private, and it went on much longer. Third came numbing out, which outlasted avenging or weeping. As for Frank, he seemed, from what she could see, stuck in payback.

But even that came to an end when, after a year in Afghanistan, both of them posted back to Andrews. They flew random patrols, awaiting their next assignment, which everyone said would be Iraq. She was grateful to survey D.C. She wanted to stay. She told herself she was guardian, not an angel, but at least sentry. She definitely and only flew. She began, on certain days, to get back to the blooming soar of it. As for Frank, he was bored.

Her crash revved him back. That night, he got to Walter Reed before the rest of the squadron. He was, after all, the only kind of family she had. He motored up Sixteenth Street Northwest, the White House in his rearview, wheels fast into the old hospital drive, his cell phone on speaker, begging for the duty nurse.

Frank, Mary guessed, was thinking of Neil. Neil, to Frank, wasn't carrot curls and pink chin. Neil was gonzo made of kryptonite, he-man of phys-ed stats and training-day glories. To Frank, Neil's slide off the Chinook was proof that no one was safe, not even kings. And on this particular day at Walter Reed, he had more evidence—here was Mary, trussed in bandages. A medical miracle—alleged—though Frank never believed military pronouncements. Her crash made no sense, that much made sense. He tried with her, more than once, to hear the story. She told him each step, more than once, as if it were a logical story. But each time that he looked at her and she looked at him, the final expression in each tense eye was this: Frank and Mary were in the dark. Something, somewhere, in some inch of some infinity, was hidden.

Adam saw her by accident. When he looked up from a small map he was studying at his desk, he saw Mabel Cannon on her knees picking up her overturned purse. She was just outside his glass wall.

He looked back fast. She didn't see him. He hoped.

Adam tried with his peripheral vision, but couldn't catch a glimpse of her. What was she doing here?

Adam's secretary, Tabitha, knocked softly and put her head inside the doorframe.

"Mabel Cannon's here," she whispered, as if announcing a descent from the rafters of the importunate batty aunt. Adam got up, forgot why he had, sat down, remembered, got up, forgot again, and sat down. Tabitha kindly ignored the entire procedure.

"She came up with Don," Tabitha said in a normal voice. "He wants to see you too. But first he has an interview."

"Quite a news day. I think that we . . . There's also . . . Let me see how . . ." Adam stalled out. He stood there. Tabitha walked forward a step and closed the door. "Adam Aaron, let me call that young woman from NPR, let her know that you need to set up another time." Tabitha always called him by his first and middle names. She had not known his mother, but she was old enough. Tabitha's son was also named Adam. Adam Rebander Collins.

"Thank you. And show Mabel in."

Mabel had never called. It was two weeks, maybe three, since Don Grady had had weekend duty and told Adam that Mabel wanted to try for managing editor. Now here she was, no call, no appointment, no warning. To Adam's dismay, he was nervous.

When she walked in, he realized he had never taken a good look at Mabel Cannon. Back before they were who they were now, she had been not good-looking, or at least not anyone he thought was good-looking, though many others, as he could just recall, thought she was. As he looked at her now, it occurred to him that he didn't really have much of a definition of good-looking. He was something of a duffer when it came to a woman. His first wife had been the first girl he'd kissed. His second wife had been the grade-school teacher of his youngest daughter, who had special needs. He had fallen in love with Joan, instantly and illicitly, because she had been so painlessly under-standing, so calm, as he wasn't, and so unworried, as his first wife, Carol, couldn't be, about their irreparable child. It didn't feel like his life to have been married twice; he was shocked by it on the most regular basis. Yet his chief fantasy lately, unaccountably, was walking away from Joan, from this office, from what was by any reckoning a full life. The thought of it was like a clarinet playing in an empty street.

Mabel had been the one everyone wanted. Adam was the one who hadn't bothered to look. Her hair was brown, long. Brown eyes, he thought, looking quickly.

"Adam," Mabel began, "this is just ridiculous."

"Mabel," he said. "Good to see you. You look wonderful." Sometimes when he blushed he could feel it, but he didn't appear red to the casual observer. Maybe now it was that way.

"I am so sorry that Don made up this bullshit."

"He said you would be calling," Adam said, trying, from under his warm cheeks and absent frown, to get back his sentences. Why had he said she looked wonderful? He never said that to women in the Room. She wasn't in the Room, though, was she? She was a columnist for Editorial. They were on another floor. She never went there. She was on contract, worked from home. They took her ID years ago. He was still talking, and he said something he often said, "I didn't hear," along with the pause that was taken for thoughtfulness, an introspective nature. He had a sense that he had to talk some more. "And I thought that maybe—it's a big decision. Well, here you are. Have a seat."

"I don't need to stay," she said. "I just wanted to let you know in person how sorry I am."

She stood there, a tornado.

"Sit. I have some time."

"No, you don't," she said. "Look, it's close to five."

"Hard to know what's going on over there."

"In the Room?"

"The White House."

"I'll tell you what's going on over there. Maybe five or seven hopeful nudniks are sitting around a table trying to figure out how to stop the rest of the world from knowing they don't know what the fuck they're doing. The ones who know what's up in their corner of the universe are the loyal toilers thinking about baby-stroller safety regulations or propane-gas subsidies or our nation's lakes and streams or, more likely, a flowchart. That's what. That's all that's ever going on over there."

She had a sweating bottle of cold spring water in her hand. Without a hitch, she came close and pressed it to his cheeks, one at a time, for all the Room to see. "Here, you need this," she said. Then she put the bottle on his desk and sat down in a chair.

"I will sit down," she said. "I'm tired."

She kicked off her shoes.

"Do you know how many times I've lost my balance on those things?" She held one by its long thin heel and watched it twiddle in the air. "I landed on my ass right outside your office. I'm surprised you didn't see me, what with these gerbil aquariums. People in glass houses. Editors in glass cages."

"They let me out, though." He surprised himself, managing a witticism. He hadn't recovered from the thought of how the Room was processing his scene with her.

Oblivious, she laughed. He reached for the bottled water. What the hell. He wasn't thirsty, but he had no idea what to say to her next. He drank a long swig.

As quick as that, she was shod and standing again. "Hey, you don't know what to say to me," she said cheerily. "And I don't want to take up your time. I just didn't want this hoax about me wanting to be managing editor to go on much longer. You've always been such a great guy."

With that, she was opening the door and gone.

Just on the rim of the Room, in the space between Adam's office and his secretary's desk, Mabel came to a full stop. For some reason, whatever had propelled her out his door had evaporated. Tabitha turned to look at her, her eyes brightening. She was about to begin her motherly blandishments when her phone rang. Mabel touched her shoulder and smiled, mouthing a goodbye. What Tabitha knew! The Washington secretary, Mabel mused, was the Sibyl of all realms. No reporter, naturally, spoke to her. Instead, they spoke to "men in power." As if such a man would hand his safe box of failings to the watchman.

She sighed. Her eye traveled from one end of the Room to the other. To most people it would have looked like any other office bullpen. It started with the afterthought that would always be the Business section; the identical cubiculum of the National staff, looking to the unschooled like other cubicles but actually a prancing ground that peacocks sought; the horseshoe of the National Desk, where assistant National editors rested on their climb to the risers; the ovoid orbit of Copy Desk cynics; the small outpost of Photo editors, always nicer, crazier, and more honest than everyone else; the plentiful underdogs of Metro; the wall of clocks—New York, London, Moscow, Tel Aviv, New Delhi, Beijing, and Tokyo—announcing the glamorized zones of the Foreign staff; the too many Metro editors of Virginia, Maryland, and the District, cruelly seated beside their international betters; the mange of police-beat desks; the introverted clinic of obit writers, and their adjunct in rank, the harmless night editor, one Stanley Belson, whom she'd once known so well.

He was no fool. Though everyone long ago judged he had to be. In the Room, only a chump would notice any ache of loss. She saw the objection: a journalist who cried at unfairness was like a surgeon made dizzy by blood. But, standing there, looking at his jiminy cap and his concentrated bearing, she stood newly lit with an old feeling. They were wrong about him.

She wanted to kick off her silly shoes again and stride over there like an actress on an orchestral surge, but she picked her way with dignity so as not to fall off her heels among the e-mailing enviers. They hated coveting her, she thought as she overlooked some of the climbers hoping she would recognize them. They angled for seats at her dinner table. If they knew how little was had there! She should address them posthaste, on that chair conveniently empty and so easily stood upon. You wish to be me? You wish to find status, its guarantee of contentment? My fellow newsmen, my sad girl reporters, beware of this, my listing ship.

"Stanley Belson," she said joyously. She was behind his shoulder. Getting in front of him would have meant sitting on his keyboard. He was devouring the computer screen. For a moment she thought he might not turn from it. He probably didn't remember her voice.

But he did. "Mabel Cannon," he said, his fingers clacking a few last words.

She couldn't help it. She swooped to him and put her arms around his neck.

"You remember," she said in his ear. She could feel him laughing. She snuffled. "Just think," he said back to her, "what everyone watching is thinking." She unclamped him, and they turned to smile at each other.

"It's always been a stage, hasn't it?" she said, motioning to the Room.

"Yes, but one whose spotlight has yet to find me," Stanley said. "Until now."

"How have you been?" She really wanted to know. But the words weren't out before she felt the gully between them and wished she hadn't asked.

"Mabel, I've been terrible," he said, fixing her unease.

They laughed again. And he added, "You too?"

"How did you know!?"

"I have instincts," Stanley said. "If nothing else."

For a few more moments, they were silent, just smiling at each other. Items pouring through their heads were too different in color and shape to seem similar. They were fundamentally the same, nonetheless. She felt it.

"Do you take a drink now and then?" she asked. Maybe he would make this second gambit feel natural as well.

"I do. Smoking still too, I'm afraid."

She crouched quickly, removed the painful high heels, and said, "Here." She scribbled her mobile number on a paper she pulled from the trash can under his desk. "I'm around tomorrow and the next day and the next day. I want to talk, really talk. Stanley, it's, well . . ." she almost forgot what her convictions were. "We're old enough to do this!" She whispered this conspiratorially, energetically. His eyes crinkled, and he cocked his head.

"We are," he said. "I will call you."

"Promise."

"I promise."

"Okay, then," she said, reluctantly standing up again, toes slowly finding the infernal shoes.

On the way out, she passed the place where the receptionist used to sit. This was their den mother back before voice or e-mail. Mabel remembered confessing to her that she had a crush on Don. The day was right there, it was April, the first new hyacinths out, he had definitely smiled at her in the elevator for no reason, and Mabel had floated into the Room in a buttercup of a dress, drifting to the receptionist's counter for telephone messages, and Treena had looked over the tops of her tortoiseshell glasses and guessed—*somebody's in love*. Mabel had gushed awful, stupid longing to her until the next message retriever appeared—Don. Of course—he was right with her on the elevator. But someone had stopped him to talk. Now here he was. Mabel saw his hand reach into her line of vision to pull out his stack of messages. How long had he been standing there? Had he heard? Mabel could still feel how he had touched her elbow. He guided her, his palm on the small of her back, away from Treena, into the Room. Thinking about it, she remembered. There was such a thing as a princess.

Dozer Garcia the flight surgeon walked along the wall through a hallway at Andrews Air Force Base. It was a few days since Mary's discharge from Walter Reed. She stopped Dozer when he saw her. She wanted to pump him about her crash.

"Your psych evaluation was always wooly," he announced before she had a chance to say anything. "Now you're a sleepwalker with a statistically impossible mishap on your record."

Dozer was case manager on the Aircraft Mishap Board investigation into her crash. He was grumpy and had a curl on his forehead. He looked like a butcher. Dozer was hard to budge. Character consistency— the sunny team quipping that went well everywhere—made him sullen. He liked to sit in his car at lunch and eat chocolate frosting out of a can.

"How's that fleabag?" Dozer was the only one who knew about Mary's father. So he was the only one who asked.

"Locked up."

"Parole not given," Dozer said. "No chance at mercy."

He was twenty years into a life sentence for first-degree murder. After school, Mary, age twelve and an only child, had found her mother face-down in the tub, floating in blood and bathwater. Her father, an F-4 Phantom pilot, was gone. The hunting knife he'd used was in the sink. Mary remembered it. She'd watched him skin game with it. The grip was indented, he'd often told her, so it wasn't slippery when wet.

"They sent him back to Graterford," Mary told Dozer. It was Pennsylvania's largest maximum-security facility.

Dozer looked as if he'd been socked in the mouth. "Good," he said, his lips messed. "Good," he said again. He was looking down too, embarrassed, as if it were his father.

"So—can I have the photos of the tree strike?" she asking, changing the subject. She regretted telling Dozer about the penitentiaries of her childhood, thousands of different shadings of shame for each moment, an impossible clarity of disgraces, as if each blade in a yard were separate and visible from cloud cover.

"Can't," Dozer muttered, as she expected.

"What did it look like, then?" She didn't much care how the tree she landed in looked—she wanted Dozer to remember duty, the regulations, not her father.

"Like a Guard Baby loose with luck tore off some mighty oak's crown."

She laughed. He called her Guard Baby because she had only ever flown for the Air National Guard, which trained her. Dozer came to the military after flying United and a midlife medical degree.

"Loose with luck," she said.

"The joints, you know," he said, speaking of her miracle hip, "when you're lucky, they're loose."

"An oak tree," she said. "Huh."

"Acorns everywhere."

"Wild."

"For squirrels, yeah. But, Mary . . ." Dozer started.

"I know," she said, "we're getting close to thirty days after the crash."

She dreaded this part of the timeline. It meant she had to see the psychiatrist. It meant the preliminary finding would follow a month after the session. It meant they might take flying away from her. Was it even feasible that so much went so wrong? How could night vision have malfunctioned, the sky gone dumb black, the onboard computer massively failed—because that's what a Viper was, flying by wire—how could so many impossible wrongs have busted that one ride on that one night? Frank was right. It made no sense.

What would the session with the shrink dredge out of her? She knew her father was in there somewhere. The rancid smudge of her progenitor—it had shown through the bleached sheet. Because of him, she'd always been double-checked and triple-questioned. She was used to X-rays. This time, though, she needed more than heavy lead to keep them guessing.

Later in the week, the session came and went. It was as perfunctory as buttonholes. Worked up as she was, she could barely pay attention to the shrink's questions, which came in far less insinuating tones than she'd expected. She was beginning to think she'd come through it with no nicks or cuts. But then she heard from Frank, who insisted they talk.

The bar he chose was Apehangers. It was a good hour from the base. He said he didn't want to bump into anyone from the squadron. He lived only a mile from this dive, down a country road in Bel Alton, far deep into NASCAR, Mary Kay, poker runs, and taxidermy. The waitresses wore *Freedom Isn't Free* shirts, and the music was rockabilly. This was a locale Mary found less than easy to fake her way through, but she was working up her acting and getting herself less silent. Frank often said Mary was one of his favorite females because she spoke so little. But about the crash, he wanted more from her. Where was her outrage? What about curiosity?

They sat at a corner table. It was just before Halloween. Skeletons and pumpkins were taped to the ceiling. Orange glitter dusted the place, and Mary was picking it up too. She tried to rub some off a fingertip and just got more on her palm.

"So you kept things zippered up good with the head twister," Frank said. The base shrink was a woman Mary might have been close to in the life she would have led outside the military. In this life, this woman was outside the squadron's trust. She was sensitive. She expected that others were too and just wouldn't admit it. That was why the word on her was negative. She was always looking for what just wasn't there. Mary always feared being assigned to that suspect category. She tried to think, right now, how to act in this bar to avoid it. Luckily, sitting still was sometimes enough.

"Sure," Mary replied, hoping she'd been inscrutable with the shrink, but not too much so. It hit her, sitting there, that she would have been happy for this crazycrash to have any origin, just so it wasn't her doing. And no one, to her great relief, seemed to be saying it was, at least not yet. Could it be that now, despite how roughly it'd first housed her, military had turned into home?

"Anything funny go on?" Frank had an investigatory tone.

"Like?" She barely said it. She was worrying Frank could sense the dependency she'd just recognized in herself. He knew he was kin. That was personal. Taking the armed forces for Ma and Pa—that was dumb.

"Like did she poke around as to whether you knew something was flat-out wrong with the bird?"

Mary considered. There'd been the usual canned questions to gauge paranoia. She'd had those before, on her other psych evaluations. Apparently, she'd passed okay. She couldn't tell if some of the questions from the shrink were different. She'd been so cramped with anxiety her memories were mostly about feelings, the chief one being panic and how to contain it.

"Nothing about the Viper," she finally told Frank. She wasn't really positive about that. But she didn't want to get him going any faster than he already was. Lately, he couldn't seem to stop jumping to theories, most of them far-fetched.

"What about the rescue? She grill you on—what?—the welcoming committee? I mean, who *were* those guys?"

"I was massively turned around," Mary reminded him. "Could have been hallucinating."

"Yeah, I know," Frank said.

She thought about it one more time. She remembered the trees on fire. She could feel the heat from them. But not her tree, the tree she was in—that was whole and cool. She thought she must have lost her sense of hearing. Maybe she'd gotten too close to the engine. But the thing that worried her most was the paramedic squad. She remembered them, clearly, wearing black. No, some of them were in jeans and T-shirts. That was the thing she had to believe she could have imagined. They wore white, right? That was the uniform. Well, maybe not. Could be black. Could be casual. Could be, definitely.

Frank was talking about how he had found the last guy on the maintenance crew just this morning. He told Frank that Mary's engine had spent its usual time the week before the crash in the Hush House. They'd taken it apart, put it back together, stuck it back in the Viper as usual. It went to the blocks in perfect shape. Crew loved Mary, Frank reported. "You're the only pilot in the squadron who doesn't leave used piddle packs tucked back in the corner by the flicsip," he said.

Piddle packs by the flight-control-systems panel. It was like leaving the toilet seat up. No, more like piss on the rim. Mary recalled how she'd befriended her first crew chief, asked him, What drives you nuts? Piddle packs in tight spots topped the list. He gave her runners-up, and she remembered them: pilots who left fuel master switches in off, Alt Flaps in extend, DED bright turned all the way down, Air Source in off. Frank was a regular offender on each. Mary wondered how honest anyone from Maintenance would be with him.

She was most curious about the weapons loaders. Frank said none of them would speak to him. That baffled her. She wasn't permitted to ask them anything until the investigation was concluded. But she would then.

Frank had made the rounds with pilots in the squadron weeks ago, asking if they'd experienced a portion of what she did. No one had. They didn't believe Mary's story. She must have left something out, they said. The cockpit couldn't have given her the readouts she described. This morning he'd overheard a pilot from another squadron, some captain from Albuquerque, with mitts for hands and a smirk instead of a smile. Call sign was Roughhouse. Someone told Roughhouse that

Mary'd fouled up ejection. She had. But who told him? How'd that word get out?

"And then," Frank said, continuing, "they clamped down hard on him, put a letter in his file. Almost like they wanted to put out it was your fault, and then decided against it."

"Maybe," Mary said, looking down, focusing on the black glitter she'd just noticed on her sneakers. It was everywhere. Her eye went to the bar and the razzmatazz of dancing skeletons.

"It's just like dogfights," Frank said.

"What?"

"You don't see it?"

"See what?" She honestly didn't.

"Like, how it's all related."

Well, she could try to see it. "Uh—there's no more dogfights. I mean, yeah. Yeah."

"And basically, like, they trained us for that."

"Sure did."

"Chinese got—what—a dozen J-10s."

"About, maybe."

"So—that's a ways off. Dogfights with J-10s."

"Too late for us," Mary said, genuinely sad about it, though still in the dark about what all this had to do with her crash.

"So we, like, best of best, drop fire."

"Uh-huh." They could drop ordnance on a pin. It wasn't what Mary would have liked to do. It was definitely what Frank hated doing.

"Instead of what we, allegedly, um, by our training, should, should do . . ."

". . . which is aerial combat, aka the dogfight." She tried not to sound impatient. "And?"

"They're trying to have us do something else."

She couldn't help it. She was exasperated.

"Like, make us into projectiles. Ourselves," he said, leaning close to her conspiratorially. She groaned. She had to.

"Listen up," he said, still level with her ear. "See, we got technology so advanced, Haj can't compete. So what does Haj do? Takes up darts. A suicide bomb isn't even a slingshot. It's the tactical equivalent of a peashooter. But, practically speaking, strategically speaking, it works better than a fighter jet."

"I know, but, but . . ." She still didn't see.

His expression lit up. Wait, something else had his attention. She turned to see what—how could it be, but it was—Blue, as in Airman Mike "Blue" Schuyler, ordering from the bartender.

"This can't be happening," she said.

It was Blue all right. They'd gone a ways to avoid the squadron, and here the squadron's loudmouth had found them. Well, he hadn't seen them yet. He was squarely facing the mirrored wall of liquor bottles. Mary surveyed the exits. Frank saw her and shook his head.

"No," he said. "Unless you want to set off the emergency alarm. 'Course, we'd be through the door by then."

"But also most likely dragged back and questioned," she said, teasing.

"Never seen him here," Frank complained.

"He looks comfortable," Mary said.

"He does," Frank said, smooching his lips together.

"He lives down here."

"He does not live down here." Frank was irritated.

Oh, now, there she was, the lady Blue was meeting. She was built—there was no other way to put it—butch. But the hairdo was feminine—a curly ponytail with a feathery scrunchie.

"Are those earrings?" Frank peered.

"Not sure," Mary said, trying to see in the light that had gotten much dimmer.

"Biker chick," Frank said.

"I think so."

"Hmm."

"Know what, I think he's married," Mary said. She tried to pinpoint the story on Blue. He wasn't one of her favorite people. Still, she was of such an order of oddity herself, she kept a constant track on who was what and did what for which reason.

"Is he?"

"Yeah," Mary said. "And that's not his wife."

"Hmm."

"Might explain," Mary said, "the distance he's traveled to meet this lady."

"Hard to know," Frank said. Frank, the reputed carouser, enjoyed listening to Mary's thought process on the mechanics of deception.

"Well, what should we do?" she asked.

"Put out a hand, shake his, and ask why he's here," Frank said. "Give-over-your-secrets type of thing. You know, as in, can't keep a secret from your flyboys."

"Okay."

They got up. Just then, the sweetie pushed back from the bar and left. In a huff too. Frank and Mary looked at each other with eyes narrowed. They relaxed their expressions when they got to him.

"Blue," Frank said, his hand, as he promised, outstretched.

"T-Knee, what the fuck," blurted Blue.

"Hi," Mary said. She kept her hand to herself. Blue ignored her. Which was fine.

"Love trouble?" Frank said, still pumping Blue's hand.

"Afterburner, I guess."

"Hot and heavy," Frank said, winking.

"Was," Blue said, glancing nervously, for the first time, at Mary. "Hello, Extra," he mumbled in her direction.

"Hi," she said again.

At least he was too flustered at being discovered to give a shred of thought to what they were doing here. She was always afraid Squadron would misinterpret her closeness with Frank.

"I'm around the corner; want to take up with Extra and me and put some burgers on my grill?" Frank had made their being here right. If there were something going on between them, inviting Mary over to see the wife, daughter, bambino, and patio would not be in the offing. And inviting Blue wouldn't be either.

"You live down this way?" Blue looked horrified.

"Sure do."

"Nice area."

Mary felt bad for the guy. He looked trapped. After a few more awkward pauses and a loop of non-sequiturs, they said their goodbyes.

Love grew better, she often thought, in hidden soil. She'd lost her virginity to the boy everyone said was gay. Yet Tim wouldn't hang with gays. Trying to toughen up, he was a before-school smoker in the parking lot, usually solo. He had one friend, a girl. She came to Mary. Look, he likes you. Mary stared across the cafeteria, where this girl was pointing. He was sitting at a table by a window, earbuds dangling down, black knit cap on a warm day, skin glue white, bony everything— shoulders, arms, chest.

She didn't want Tim, but she wasn't afraid of him either. That was the main thing. They were sixteen. It hurt her, but not too much. Mostly, it was over with. It was his idea to keep on with it, trying to get it to feel a little more like what all the noise about it said it was. She'd gone along. They kept all of it secret. When she passed him in the parking lot before class, she put her hair behind her ears and looked down, their private hello. She felt more for him in that gesture than anywhere else they'd been.

3. THE LAST LIGHTS OFF THE BLACK WEST

There'd been five stories. All said pretty much the same thing. Apparently, repeating the same things—that was allowed. The pilot had crashed due to technical difficulties. That was, as far as it went, true. It was much better than the story Donovan went for first. Simple and likely, covering bases, that was the storyline these writers wanted. Will knew that much.

They're not writers. How many times had one of his men said that? Will didn't care to understand the distinctions. These writers, reporters, whatever you wanted to call them, wrote about what Will lived. That was true. Anything else was class and status. Neither affected him.

So the stories didn't mention some things he would have mentioned if he'd been writing them. He would have said planes crashing into buildings had been a recent big event. He would have said this was a plane crash too. He would have said this crash might be related to someone trying to fix the big event of planes crashing into things they shouldn't.

It never got to that. They wrote five stories, total. He kept saying that to himself. Five. Five. Five. For weeks he waited. Soon it got to be possible that they, the writers, were done.

Mabel," Adam was saying. "Mabel."

Stanley couldn't decide whether to tell Adam of their snip of a talk, of Mabel gracing Stanley with a visit. He decided to say nothing yet. It had meant too much to him.

Adam smoothed a pew with his hand. They were meeting in the Metropolitan African Methodist Episcopal Church. As they had for years, they met in the last pew around four in the afternoon. Church people, few at that hour, assumed they were involved in government work. The back of the Russian Embassy abutted the church's crepe-myrtle courtyard. Other white men over the years had spent unexplained time at Metropolitan AME. This pair at least nodded to religious belief. One or two times they looked to be praying together. They spoke softly. They bothered no one. Stanley and Adam had become as welcome and unnoticed as the smells that lingered from Sunday worship—wood polish, hymnals, carnations.

With his aqua eyes, Stanley was considered white by just about everyone except Adam, who knew from their starting days at the paper that Stanley's father, Reverend Henry Payne, was a son of one of the founding AME bishops. Kay Belson met Henry Payne during the Depression. He was husband to a gifted pianist, and father to four girls. Kay was a reader of biographies and had finished one on Clara Barton. Barton propelled her—to the thought of battlefields, or some accessible sacrifice, and the nearest of either in her protected conscience were soup kitchens. Oddly, for a woman of her fold, it worried her that she'd never seen a dark face in any of them. Who was taking care of the colored? For a while, she imagined they had no havens. When she learned otherwise, she began searching for a way to volunteer somewhere on the other side of Rock Creek Park, but no one seemed to know how to do this uncommon, strange thing. Finally, she was sent to Reverend Payne, who informed her that soup kitchens did exist for his race, but funding, not ladling, was needed. A philanthropic partnership began, its efforts furthered by the best of LeDroit Park, many of whom disliked this woman, with her overexposed magnanimity, but endured her for the greater good. At Henry's urging, Kay gave enough to restore the True Reformers Hall, created the Home for Friendless Colored Girls, kept doctors on staff at the Old Folks Home for Aged and Infirm Colored People, ensured the continuation of the Howard University Mandolin and Glee Club, and other causes necessary, but to the wider Washington, the one that figured in history, immaterial.

Stanley was born during the war, in the generation that produced

Frederick Gregory, the first Negro spaceman, as they anointed him, and Hugh Price, lawyer and activist for his own. But Stanley was not among them. His mother was past youth when he was conceived; Reverend Payne, a grandfather. Kay's husband was a diplomat in love with a man, and then another man—he'd never been able to turn his longing to Kay.

She kept the fact of Stanley a secret from Reverend Payne, and her legal, closeted husband agreed to give the infant his name. Kay, Norwegian, produced a ginger baby with convincingly blue eyes. She saw no way to raise him in between—one half of him had to sleep. His putative father was delighted with his not-actual offspring. Stanley was raised with unexpected love—he often thought it was the only lasting kind— by two people who had dreaded his arrival. It was only later that he wished he had grown up in LeDroit Park. This was why he now lived in Blagden Alley.

All this only Adam had pulled from him over many years. Adam had persisted—been eager, even—to learn Stanley's past. It wasn't clean for Stanley. Adam first knew him when these people, no longer Negroes or colored and suddenly black, were chic to a certain kind of man; he wondered whether Adam's friendship grew from that spume, and even at times, whether it had reached sturdy places anywhere along the way.

Stanley sensed, rightly, wrongly, his mind flitted always, that Adam would not have listened to Stanley's newsroom impressions if not for Stanley's parentage. Stanley saw he was maybe not more than that old trope—the mammy who knew better than Scarlett, the Remus to Bobby Driscoll. He felt sure Adam was dead to this. In his worst moments, Stanley saw himself using Adam. It was then that he most hated his own ornate manipulation of his more powerful confidant—all done for Stanley's own private grandiosity, for the tempting of Stanley's ego into believing it was he, not Adam, who ran the Room. From not very far away, Stanley saw himself too clearly.

"To dismiss her, to say no," Adam said, "to say . . . Well, it wasn't me, it was her who said no. Do you think she meant yes?"

Stanley tried to see past this frazzle. He was surprised that something had vibrated in Adam about Mabel. Mabel was a woman Adam should dislike. No, Stanley thought, nothing that active. Adam should be indifferent to a Mabel.

But then, Adam shouldn't have had the thoughts he shared with Stanley. Anyone in the Room who'd had a peephole on their conversations all these years would have been flabbergasted at the Adam who sat in these pews. Thinking of it reminded Stanley of the surprise—for a completely opposite reason—at the foul-mouthed Cabinet of the Watergate tapes. The president, who in public said he spoke for the silent majority, spoke in private like a longshoreman, the figure most of the silent majority had climbed out of their family histories to leave behind. Although Don proved the president a crook, it was the way the commander in chief talked that made him sound like a crook. If he had been just a little more baffled and evil than nasty and evil, he could have been forgiven. Or perhaps Stanley could have absolved him. What had his mother taught him? *It's not what you say, it's how you say it.*

Adam was nervous in these pews. His anxieties were a betrayal of an idea of newspapering that had—until the Internet began stealing readers from the print edition, whose advertising made profits—prospered. Adam knew he could not appear in public as he did at church with Stanley. The newspaper was authoritative. The executive editor was the exemplar of this impossible fiction, a fantasy that was dissolving into gossamer and dust with each reportorial scandal, every blogging tiddly-bit, each of the millions upon millions of disaffected subscribers busy with the abandon of leaving the world to others.

"The obvious thing to think is, she's not qualified," Adam said. "She's not. Not qualified at all."

"If qualified is what you want," Stanley offered.

"Exactly. Do we want that?"

"In the past, you always did."

"That's just it. The past is no good, don't you see?"

Stanley objected to this. But he said nothing.

Adam took Stanley's silence for assent and continued, "Change. I'm looking for change. More couldn't possibly be at stake at a time when fewer and fewer readers are turning to us."

"In the paper," Stanley reminded him. "Online, we have more readers than we ever did." Adam constantly forgot this, possibly because advertising dollars online hadn't yet caught up with readership online. It distressed managers. You couldn't get advertisers to pay top money for online ads, the way they'd always paid for display ads in newsprint. Stanley had tried to convince Adam to mount a public-service campaign on the subject. Let's talk about advertisers' obligations to democracy. "Democracy" was one of Adam's sweet words. It got him going. But he'd rejected the campaign idea as self-serving.

"We focus our resources on accountability reporting," Adam was saying. Stanley realized he hadn't been listening very well.

"The paper's also a place where you can be different and quirky," Adam continued.

Stanley stifled a sigh. Different and quirky—to the summer of '71. Here, in a new century, he'd hoped, he'd yearned, he had waited so long—

"The focus on good, in-depth coverage is the first priority," Adam said, lifting his face, feeling certain. "You know, hiring reasonably well, enabling talent to thrive, and having a newsroom that's not top-down. I'm not seeking any particular outcomes, and I don't necessarily expect any cataclysmic outcome from this managing editor choice. We're existing at a very complicated time right now. The threat of terrorism is ongoing. The occupation and leaving of Iraq is going to last a long time and be very difficult. I think we're in very uncertain waters politically here, and so the . . . the fate of this paper's management will depend on lots of factors, and this choice may or may not turn out to be one of them."

"Adam."

"Yes. We've had lots of time. . . ."

"Adam."

"Wait . . . do you know, I just thought . . ."

"Adam. I know what you say—out there."

Adam looked abashed. He glanced around him as if to check

whether anyone but Stanley had earshot on his pat reversion to the tape in his head.

"Christ," Adam muttered.

"Yes."

"I have to stop that."

"It's easier."

"Infinitely."

They were quiet. They both took what they could from the surroundings. Stanley had never met his birth father; he liked that this church had been his. Adam liked that no one ever bumped into them here. It was almost theirs and no one else's. Stanley jumped into thinking of Mabel, sitting here, beside them. In his mind, she would fit.

"Can you imagine Mabel here?" he asked Adam.

Adam had to think. "No," he finally said.

"I think she'd get it," he said.

"Get?"

"Our coming here."

"Oh."

"Don't you think?"

"Possibly."

"You know, Adam," he said, after another silence, "I have a feeling about something."

"Oh?" Adam sat up and stopped tracing the whorls of wood in the pew.

"I know there's really nothing to back this up," Stanley continued. "And I feel it's one of my least reliable hunches, in terms of surface facts, you know, meriting it. But the feeling is stronger than I've had in years." Stanley paused, worried that he had overstated. "It's about that crash, that one early in the month, the one we thought was a helicopter, or the president was aboard."

"Huh." Adam was interested. He put his hands on his knees, a move for him signaling seriousness.

"I think there's more to it."

"You do."

"I don't know what. But I just feel there's more there."

"The beginning of it was strange," Adam said. He realized he wanted to tell Stanley what had happened. He thought about how he should begin.

"That night?" Stanley whispered as a woman with prayer cards bobbed past their pew.

"Yes," Adam said. "You know, Donovan did call."

"And?"

"And I didn't think much of it at the time, but he—oh, now I remember, he said, of course he said this, he said it was 'strictly between the two of us.' I said, 'You know that's not something I ever agree to.' And he, let me see, oh, now I know, he said, 'Lives are at stake.' And—"

"Still hard for me to believe he says that," Stanley murmured.

"Yes, yes, me too," Adam said. "So I humored him, said something I often say to him, which was along the lines, 'Oh, Van, you know I've always taken great care with anything you've been able to share with me.' "

"Careers are at stake," Stanley added quickly.

"Most likely, yes. Lives. I'm not sure Donovan has any say-so where lives are concerned."

"By the time he's involved and he's calling you—that's, it's, well, damage control. Is that still the phrase?"

"Possibly," Adam said softly. "Oh, have you noticed how 'the way forward' is everywhere?"

"Yes, yes. I don't know why, since no one has a way and most are going backward. But Donovan."

"Donovan, yes. So he said, 'We can't have anyone writing about this tonight. Can you hold it off for one night, two at the most?' 'Why?' He says, 'Can't say at this time.' You know, last year, Stanley, I would have . . . that, that would have stopped me for two days. But since these other things, the way they've happened—the wiretaps, the warrants— I wasn't prepared to agree. Told him that. He argued. Then he said, 'If anyone learns we have this capability, having the capability will be meaningless.' "

"What capability?"

"I asked him that. He never said."

"They said it was a helicopter. I wonder . . . if it was?"

"We never saw the crash site up close, did we?"

"No," Stanley said.

"What kind of capability is that—that . . . that takes down a war plane?"

"Funny enough, in Iraq, in Afghanistan, Al Qaeda doesn't have fighter jets. *We* have them. So why do we want to take our own people down?"

They sat silently for a few moments, thinking of capabilities. The church was getting colder, and it occurred to Stanley that the sun was setting, they'd been talking too long, and it was time to get back to the Room.

The crash was gone—first from print, then from milblogs. Will Holmes looked lucky. He knew luck wasn't luck. It was preparation and follow-through. He'd bungled the planning on Potomac Pilot, so the back end had to be rulebook. He did some last-minute tinkering to make sure the mishap report was clean. He got ahead on arranging for the National Guard to move the pilot out of Andrews but not to Balad. He couldn't have her in Iraq. He thought Bagram should be the assignment. If she was detailed there to Special Operations Forces for close air support under a classified program, she'd be insulated. There weren't any land-launched missiles in Afghanistan that could so much as smudge a fighter jet. Plus, Special Forces was using so many drones, they might never need her.

He told himself he'd looked out for men under his command. So what if she wasn't under his command. He had an interest in making sure she didn't find out how the crash happened, didn't he? Keeping tabs was nothing more than insurance. He got notes from her doctor visits sent automatically. She was repairing fine. He got her file, read about the fuck of a father, the dead mother. He got a full rundown from the shrink session. He saw that her wingman and his wife were the ones on her Notify List. Her in-the-event-of-my-death went to them too. So he made sure the wingman also got a Bagram assignment. The guy was too curious about the crash for Will's taste, but the pilot, she was stand-up. Having the wingman at Bagram would shut down his scratching around Washington for answers. It would also keep him from going to a reporter if he got hold of anything he shouldn't. Yeah, the fire was out. Pretty soon the embers would dampen.

Another blaze had a headwind. Senate Select Committee on Intelligence had voted on and approved the creation of, and then regular updating of, a report from every known Intelligence Community component. Committee members tried to tell Will they needed it because the Iraq prewar intelligence didn't pan out—to Will it had; Baathists had moved the WMD and hidden them in Syria. (He was putting together a covert team to find them. The way it was lately, he might have to lead the thing in-country himself.)

This report from SSCI—always pronounced "sissy"—was bigger than the Family Jewels, the post-Watergate review that listed every CIA activity in conflict with the National Security Act. Sissy wanted details not just of the CIA's sensitive activities but also of *every* IC agency's. Some of these were ongoing operations. Any disclosure would be bad. And he couldn't keep Potomac Pilot out of the next quarterly update.

Long before Potomac Pilot, he'd told Sissy staff that if any of them leaked, quarterly accounting of special-access programs would end. For over a year, no one squawked. But as often happens, someone somewhere passed along the report, in this case, from what Will had learned, to the National Security Council staff. He didn't know how or when.

It hadn't shown in papers or television. The report was so messy, any reporter who got it would probably get lost in it. He liked to think of it as censorship by inundation. It was working, but it wasn't intentional, and it certainly wasn't a plan. So Will was chasing this thing. He couldn't quite catch it. He had someone on the NSC he almost trusted. He needed to see if anyone on his own staff knew anyone on the NSC staff.

Yet none of it—not Potomac Pilot, not the Sissy report—compared to one leftover from his pre-Chair days. Like any case officer, Will had recruited agents inside foreign governments willing to sell info. The Pentagon handed them off after he became Chair, but one, Hoseyn, he kept. Yet Will had seen him only once these last years.

Recruitment between any officer and agent was dirt seduction masquerading as coincidental friendship, but in Hoseyn's case, Will's first recruitment, it had turned a newer bend. The Pentagon agreed that Hoseyn, a scientist in Iran's nuclear program, was too valuable to risk to another officer's handling. That was true. The gnawing in Will was of another type. He missed Hoseyn.

Vera Hastings walked with Jesus, but pacing herself was a forever problem. She prayed staccato, wouldn't kneel, and praise of His name was lighthearted and doubt-dipped. "Faith of our Fathers" sped in her rendition. She wanted to belt it. Ruined it, according to the choir. (She'd quit last March.) As for God's will—her mother's surety—Vera was waiting to see it.

She wasn't Southern Baptist, neither extra-strength nor hundred-proof improved, as born-agains seemed to want to be, with their wavy hands and hoodoo Amens. She was raised Catholic in Northeast D.C., so it was catechism, not Sunday school; priests, not reverends. Baptism came once, to *babies,* not after adultery or thug life, and *never* in a swimming pool, pond, fountain, or fake river. The Lord's Prayer did not end with Luther's kingdom, power, or glory, but the Catholic word Vera understood—*evil.*

This September night, only a month or two since she'd been hired, she looked to see who was left in the Room. She still felt uncomfortable, noticeable. She was grateful no one was near; it was after ten. She didn't like anyone to see her spraying Windex. Her beat-mate, the day cops-reporter, slavered. A corkboard hung above and beside their shared desk. Her side was empty. His was triple layered in snaps and reminders, dirtied by malt balls, caramel bites, Lipton bags, burnt coffee. As she worked, she saw she wasn't alone after all. Stanley Belson, the night editor, her boss, was walking her way. She put down the spray bottle.

He was a short-waisted man with house-help posture and a wide collection of international shirtwear. He was colorfully polite. Whenever he conferred with Vera, he sat lightly on the nearby empty chair of Marcus, who covered the mayor and regularly tried to interest her in a drink after work. Vera didn't drink. She didn't much like the taste or the feeling. Marcus couldn't believe that. His working premise seemed to be: I'm the mayor, you're night cops. You should want to date, or at least, once or twice, bed down. She told him one day that she liked women. No more drink invitations came. You could never tell what a person would accept as fact.

"Miss Vera," Stanley said when he was in earshot.

"Hey, Boss Man," she called.

"You keeping up with your dancing?" he asked.

Vera had been close to ballerina star-life. She'd moved to Manhattan for training, made the corps at seventeen. By nineteen, she was finished, grown too tall and hotted-up curvalicious. She enrolled at Howard University, but her grades were uninspired C's. After freshman year, her parents sent her south, to Knoxville, for a summer of healing with grandmother, aunts, and cousins. Vera hid what she was in tracksuits, tainted all she saw with resentful bale. Looking for trouble, according to her mama's mama.

She found something else that summer. It started with Nola Waters, who lived alone across the street from Vera's aunt. In the wee hours, Miss Waters made out burglars at her own window. Vera heard little of it that night—not the shots, only some of the sirens. Vera got the official story the next morning on WKHT. *Officers responding to a burglary in progress shot and killed Nola Waters, an eighty-five-year-old woman in the 3700 block of Catalpa Avenue in East Knoxville after she charged them with a loaded .22 from her front porch.*

After Vera heard that, she walked out the front door to see uniformed and suited men ambling through Miss Waters's bungalow. She watched for a time. Then she friended up a man unscrewing the hinges of Miss Waters's screen door. He worked for the County Medical Examiner's Office. After their chat, Vera sneaked under the tape around the back yard, looked for a window, and listened in on men dusting jams and sills. That night, she sat on the porch the police claimed Miss Waters had charged across. She tried to see what this lady saw. She stood where officers saw this lady. She remembered Miss Waters's metal cane, the silvery stick she needed to walk.

We call for help and we get killed. A few days after the shooting, the rally whooped and umphed down the boulevard near Vera's aunt's house. Vera didn't join. She was sidelined by fascination, caught up for the first time ever with something not herself. It was the only relief she'd gotten since her dancing career evaporated.

What really happened to Nola Waters? How could it? Maybe even: why?

Vera called the county medical examiner. She left message after message. Finally, the Examiner's assistant got back to Vera, after a grand jury exonerated the cops.

The assistant told Vera it came down to the screen and the cane. He said when they autopsied Nola Waters they found pieces of the screen in her chest. The bullets pushed the screen bits into her. The screen door was between her and the bullets. That meant Nola Waters was behind her screen door when police shot her. She may have charged across the porch *before* they shot her. But at the moment they shot her, she was in her house. That wasn't conjecture. The police had lied when they said she was charging across the porch at the moment they fired.

He told Vera that even though the cane was crucial it wasn't enough to explain every last thing. You could say that at night the cane could have glinted. You could say Nola Waters usually used the cane. You could say the glinting cane might not have been under Nola Waters's bed, as police said it was. You could say Nola Waters's .22 was black, which was hard to see at night. You could say that such a dark gun wouldn't have glinted. You could say Nola Waters might have left the dark gun in the drawer where it always was, and she didn't bring it to the door to greet the police. You could say the police shot her because they saw a glinting cane and mistook it for a gun, which normally does glint, but the police claimed Nola Waters had a gun in her hand, because then she was a fatal threat to them. Shooting an old lady brandishing a cane was embarrassing. But you couldn't prove any of these things. They were conjecture.

That fall at Howard, Vera had a new calling. Counselors insisted her timing was off; she'd picked "an industry in its death throes." But she landed an internship for gifted urban minorities at D.C.'s alternative weekly the following summer, then another at the *Washington Monthly* magazine the next. After graduation and a tryout, this paper, one of the best papers, hired her full-time. She got assigned to Stanley Belson.

Vera couldn't imagine there was a black person on the paper's staff who didn't know Stanley was one of them. But, yes, she had to admit, not one of them seemed to get it, just as he'd told her. To her eye, he was a raisin through and through. She'd confirmed this in the paper's basement smoking room, because both of them were offenders in that regard. The smoking ballerina, Stanley called her. Tonight he looked at her patiently, waiting for an answer to his question. He always wanted, for some reason, to make sure she was still dancing. Why, she wasn't sure. There were many things about Stanley she didn't completely understand.

"I've been dancing," she said.

"And smoking too," Stanley said. She promised each morning to quit. Each noontime, she relented. She had some kinds of discipline, but not all.

They went to the elevator and walked down the long cement hallway. On the way to the smoking room, he began to tell her about the pilot.

HORMUZ   OCTOBER

4. NO PLACE FOR ME OUTSIDE OF PERSIS

Few knew the history of Hoseyn's Samsonite, bought for five euros in the crap souk of Dubai. It had traversed millions of kilometers, becoming the color of a donkey asleep in the shade. He had made it a visitor of each inch of his motherland and any country unafraid of Iranian passports. "Tell me what I didn't understand and didn't notice," he implored his bag in private. Bungee-corded to the roof of his Peugeot, sealed against rain, impervious to heat, the Samsonite waited. It would speak one day. Everything eventually speaks.

But this sweltering day, Hoseyn drove to work with the Samsonite in the trunk, pills in the folds of his ears. They were flesh-colored, the two tablets. He'd already swallowed the first part of the chemical cocktail. He had a half-hour to take the second part, those pills, or his death would fail. When he reached the gate, the guard who waved him through each morning stopped him.

"*Sobh beh'khayr,*" Hoseyn said, rolling down his window. He frowned.

The problem was a routine one, the guard explained. The computer system was down. The electronic eye on the gate could not read the bar code on his windshield. "We must have your badge," he said politely.

Hoseyn produced it and watched the man disappear into his air-conditioned booth. The heat was so scorching Hoseyn rolled the window back up. He turned the fan to high. The chill blast from the vents found his moist face. The relief of it made him think how much easier it would be to do it here, to die in front of this guard. But his cohorts in the *Ahva Pesarah* said one witness to his death was not enough. He must die in a crowded place.

A tap on the window broke his reverie. The guard was gone. In his place were three men, his *Pesarah* helpmates. Two of them were dragging the guard by his feet from the booth into a waiting sedan. The window tapper nodded, and Hoseyn rolled down the window enough to take back his badge. He glided through the now open gate. The asphalt drive, straight across baked ground, shimmered. The common illusion of glassy water on the surface beckoned, then disappeared as he neared. It reminded him of the salt basins left from the drained lakes of his country's interior. When you saw them from the hills, they looked like hardened sugar.

Concrete walls surrounding the corporate campus appeared in the distance. Razor wire glinted. He saw the Iranian flag on its pole, drooped to full vertical. The wind had died weeks ago. The only movement in Tehran air was the upswell of smog. Here in the suburbs, it should have been cooler. The usual breezes should have helped. But there were none.

Aban, the month his American handlers called October or November, was his last at the nuclear facility. The weather had pinned him down. He had suffered much under the arm of this overlong summer. He wanted his Samsonite aloft, Europe-bound on a jet. Instead, it would bump over land, toss onto boats, offload to sand—he paused.

He picked up speed to get a little closer.

It was smoke. It rested like a gray shelf, unnaturally low, just above the western roof of the lab building. Had there been an explosion? How he hated the clogged river of incompetence that pushed through everything. It was curious, this muck in the air. Maybe it was industrial exhaust. The temperatures and stillness were no doubt a factor. He should check.

He opened his mobile. Soon he had Ali.

"What the fuck is that shit in the sky?" He was inching along as if squeezing through traffic.

"Where are you?" The connection was weak. Ali's voice was small.

"Right outside the inner complex."

"There was a problem at the wind tunnel last night. Nothing serious."

"That's almost two kilometers." The wind tunnel? It couldn't be.

"It took this funny drift. The fire sprinklers got broken. Look, you're going to be on time. So don't fuck it up. Just get over here."

Hoseyn hung up and picked up speed. Soon he was at the wall. He waved at the guard. The guy didn't wave. He never did. So that was normal. Hoseyn made the right to his numbered spot, watching for the guard in his rearview. He was taking a drink from a thermos. That was okay.

After he parked, he made sure he'd left the trunk in the unlocked position, so his Samsonite could be retrieved and sent to him. His crepe soles slowed into the heated macadam. Ahead, the cooking air rippled. His collar was sopped by the time he paused under the awning and pulled out his badge for the guard behind the window. This was the last one.

This guard was a type you didn't often see anymore—burly. His biceps were thick. His beard was dense and black. He looked young, but not new. Most guards Hoseyn saw looked malnourished. They weren't unlucky to have these jobs; they paid well, for Iran. The country was looking underfed. It didn't have enough, even for those who were *khodi*. Hoseyn had been "one of us," reviled by 85 percent, protected by 15. That would be over. His wife was as yet uninformed about this switch, which was—he looked at his watch—less than a few minutes away.

"You look at your watch, not the clock," the guard said.

A suspicion had arrived. Hoseyn put his wrist forward so the guard could see the gift from his in-laws, high-priced. The guard had felt something was wrong. He'd fished. And found an eel. Now the Rolex was distracting him. He asked questions about the self-winding Cosmograph, the delicate moons at three, six, and nine. Any man would consult such a timepiece instead of a wall clock. The guard was satisfied. Hoseyn passed through the metal detector with a briefcase in hand. It was the object of last resort. If the cocktail failed, he could make the case ignite with the right number of clicks.

He walked down the hallway. A technician from the just-built calutron, holding tea, raised the beverage and said, "To your father." He did this to mock the hardliners who tried to compel the use of Bedouin phrases in the facility.

"Honor the Prophet, peace be upon him," Hoseyn returned. They laughed. This was their daily greeting. He would miss that guy.

The air conditioning was excellent, and his damp shirtsleeves flopped against his skin. He hoped he got to keep his watch. It would sadden his in-laws were it to disappear permanently. He imagined them at the gravesite, how inflamed they'd be by driving past the Khomeini mausoleum and shrine—the only way to get to the cemetery. They'd spend the ride home exclaiming against the lavish waste of public funds, the repellent architecture, the deluded pilgrims. He might miss them the most.

Not that he wouldn't miss their beloved daughter, his wife. She was stubborn outside of his bed. It was a good thing. This was only one of the many lessons marriage had taught him. And he clung to them. He was certain that most in his trade were incapable of learning much outside isotopes, superheavies, and the f-block. A willing wife—most of his friends longed for one. But the extremely few who had them, rued. They complained they were exhausted. They worried that she wandered. There were doctors some consulted. Why? It was a habit of human nature to see only to the nose.

Iran's greatest topic—the bedding of the wife—was an absorbing one. It branched far and drew in much. He would be, in his new country with his new identity, sorry not to know its latest fluctuations. He had to pity the Americans and the Europeans, with their pornography and tabloids. They missed out on shared confidences—not only of fetish, though the confidences included that—about the quintillion naked acts for which most men lived. He wouldn't trade the entertainment of those conversations for rampant free expression. In his experience, liberty dulled minds.

Pfaw. The cafeteria smelled of sulfur. The venting was broken. Ineptitude was in full flower. Not once did he get to praise the homeland without its displaying its blooming idiocy. He shook the briefcase a little. Out came the reliable click. At least someone in the garden had a sharp hoe.

He ordered his tasteless coffee from the little woman in the schoolgirl veil. He looked frankly into her eyes, letting her see he wanted her, a definite no-no, but she ate it up today, as she did every morning. He stopped his lingering look with a respectful smile, which delighted her most. No harm from their daily indiscretion would come to her, or him, the smile said. So she smiled too, as she always did. He shook the brief-case the second time, felt the four clicks, waved his badge past the armed cashier, and picked a table close to the door.

The cafeteria was full, and that was good. He put his coffee down, unfolded the paper, and started to read. One of his favorite stories was on the front page. *President Says Iranians Men of Dialogue, Logic.* Only in China could a news agency publish such a fable. A week ago, he had read, *China's Top Legislator Calls on Members to Learn Exten-sively.* He memorized it, it was so charming. Countries in which such kindnesses could be termed news were in short supply. His American friends wanted these supportive tales. They tried so hard to seed their newspapers with them. A rare achievement, they didn't quite realize, a society so amiably informed. He decided to tear this one out and tuck it in his pocket. That might be a nice touch when his body was found.

But he was interrupted. He had taken the last empty table, and a stranger, a ladder of a man in a brown suit, pulled out a free chair. He placed a plate of bread and yogurt on the table and sat down. They exchanged good-mornings. Pockmarks rippled the man's skin. He jabbed the dry bread in the runny *mast* with impatience. Hoseyn had never been able to get down the cafeteria lavash. The yogurt was always too soupy. This man was hungry.

"What you want you can't have, and what you have you don't want," the man said.

Hoseyn tensed in his chair. The guy was romping through the yogurt; he hadn't even looked up. Maybe I'm hearing things, Hoseyn thought.

"Pardon?" Hoseyn said.

The man looked up. He nodded to the paper. Hoseyn looked at the front page again. He sped through the headlines. What you want you can't have—there was nothing. What you have you don't want. He searched.

"I didn't hear you, my friend," Hoseyn said.

The man's mouth was full. He was chewing. He put one hand on the paper. Hoseyn looked again. The man's thumb was rocking back and forth on the newsprint underneath a quote from the president. Hoseyn squinted. "Wait until I leave," the sentence began.

The man pushed back his chair and picked up his plate.

Hoseyn's mind felt overcrowded.

The man had read his thoughts.

He had listened to his inner talk of wives. How had he heard it?

Could the first part of the cocktail have already begun disrupting his thinking? They said it might have side effects. He'd taken it earlier, with orange juice. One of the doctors seemed uneasy. Water, he kept saying, water is better.

Hoseyn stirred his coffee. When the mind wavers, return to the familiar. The spoon circled the cup's bottom. The cafeteria was subdued. A table of women to his left, the only female scientists, were at their usual spot by the window. They were whispering. He had once worked closely with Zarah. A project of importance had been a disaster when they arrived, the two of them, to fix it. Her work was meticulous. She was his mother's age.

It was now almost five years. He heard of his mother, but not often, and usually through an uncle. She lived in Dallas with his sister. His brother was in Michigan, a town called Ann Arbor. He didn't blame them for their silence. He had disappointed them. He was sorry, but naturally it wasn't enough. He had the love of his in-laws. They didn't know what his family knew. Thanks to God, his wife did. She was his lifeline.

Here was the little woman in the veil. She seemed upset. She looked around the cafeteria nervously and tugged at her eyeglasses, fussed with her hair, scratched her ears. Who would pour the coffee if she were over here at his table? He'd never seen anyone but her work beverages for the cafeteria line. He glanced around, hoping no one was watching her behavior.

But some were. A group of low-level managers—mannequins, he always called them—had noticed. They did no work. They stood around for others to ogle and be impressed at their skill sets. Only engineers did work immune to fakery or finesse. It offended him. He would tell them. He stood up.

The little woman was not having any of it. She put her hand on his right shoulder, and he could have told her that would not fly. It was completely unlike her. There were no Basiji in here, but even so. Though they might not pack her up in a van this minute, it would be noted. What else did those mannequins have to do with their time but waste it on something like that? He needed to set them straight. He was not someone they could afford to ignore.

Had the floor gotten hot? He looked and saw he'd spilled his coffee in his rush to get to the mannequins. Maybe the little woman had come by to put sugar in his coffee. She'd never done that before, but it would explain how the coffee got so sticky. It was a little difficult to walk. And now Ali had gotten mixed up, because he was coming through the cafeteria doorway, carrying the Samsonite. Just behind him was the man in the brown suit, running in the opposite direction, toward the parking lot.

The little woman was licking Hoseyn's ears. She had lost her mind. Now she was kissing him, her tongue in his mouth, and the pills were coming with it, but did he want that? It had all been a gentle game, didn't she know that? She had known it for months. Why today had she chosen to break their unspoken agreement? He hoped his wife would never hear of this. He tried to embrace his wife, but she broke away from him and walked to the table where his mother was sitting. He picked up his briefcase. He would go even that far. He could not let his mother speak to his wife. She would tell her. There was the one thing he had kept from her. He had made the mistake of pretending it wasn't there, even to himself, but it was there, it had happened. There was one way to get rid of it, though, and he was not afraid to take the step. He raised the briefcase above his mother's head, and down it went, bashing, bashing, bashing. But the explosion didn't follow. His mother had escaped. All he was doing was hitting a chair, and it had skittered across the cafeteria to the doorway. People were running to right it, several of them, with their hands in the air like kites without strings. The briefcase, for all its clicks, had failed. It was useless. The gardener was sick, the hoe was dull, a broken river had found him, and he would never get past the burning chair in this room of rain.

5. EDITED SCENES OF ADVENTURE

Hosyen's wife had mailed photographs of his funeral to him at his hotel in Dubai. Every so often he would get up from the muffin softness of his king bed to look at them. He would arrange them by time stamp on the floor of his suite. He usually waited until sleep overtook his orderly and nurse—paid for by the Sacred Sons who orchestrated his death. He was their secret prize possession. He also belonged to their allies, a self-righteous satrapy officially known as the National Council of Resistance of Iran, but one, he was gratified to see from this seven-star suite, with money. Outsiders said the cash from these Iranians in exile came from Americans, but his new friends inside this particular finger of the opposition told him, Oh no, we are free. We are pure Persians, here for the overthrow of mullahs *and* Western lies. Inside Iran, they were known as *Ahva Pesarah Persis,* the Sacred Sons of Persia.

These holy offspring, even now, knew nothing of his work for Washington. He hoped his American case officer, Will Holmes, knew nothing of these Sacred Sons.

Ten years ago, before Hoseyn had met Will, Will had tried to recruit other nuclear scientists, and, suspicious, these scientists tracked down his story, and his real name, which some of them believed was Will Holmes. Will had tried to befriend many of them—taking each separately to dinner, pretending to enjoy each one's hobby, professing connoisseurship of drink or delicacy impossible to obtain in Iran. They saw through it; they had been recruited before. The British, the French, the Israelis, the Germans—all were busy to know Iran's nuclear fathers.

But Hoseyn, the youngest of his colleagues, had not been recruited before Will Holmes. It smelled sweet to him. He liked the steps. The coincidental drink at a conference in China. The stories Will fashioned about a life he had not lived. The exchange of confidences about personal tribulations that had not happened, though maybe some of them had. Its convolutions occupied Hoseyn's brain in a way only certain pleasures of the mind, such as theoretical physics, could. The gifts—liquor his favorite, but not the most enticing—could be elicited from Will by Hoseyn's slightest hint. He made out once that he liked the meat of yak. It came to him vacuum-packed in a box through the mail.

For a year, maybe more, not one thing was required of Hoseyn. By the time he shared information that might be judged treasonous, it felt as if he were telling a story about someone else's work, in a facility wholly imagined. He was convinced of only one thing—the attachment Will Holmes had for him. He knew it was false, but, like a woman who needs to hear she is loved before she will succumb to seduction, he believed.

He thought of that metaphor often. Strangely, dwelling on it did little. For years, he told Will where the nuclear program stood, how it was failing, when it was succeeding. Sometimes, relishing his own power, he told him nothing resembling the truth. Often, he returned to it—yet usually when he wanted to, not when Will challenged him. He guessed that Will couldn't tell when he lied and when he didn't, though sometimes Hoseyn tried to ascertain if he could. It was spirals on glass ladders in mirrored nests of possibilities. It was ravishing.

Their relationship changed only after 9/11; he assumed that some shift in Will's assignment had made his contacts less frequent. Hoseyn had seen him once—right after Ahmadinejad took office. The midget, as many called him, revamped the state-security apparatus. Hoseyn judged it would discover his dead drops for Will. He stopped them. He moved the gain from his betrayals—American dollars for spying—to New York accounts controlled by his mother, now a naturalized American.

Their rift had complicated matters. She insisted some of his assets were rightfully hers. A family real-estate deal—his Ann Arbor brother financed a strip shopping mall—had ended badly for everyone concerned. Hoseyn had pledged to put his money in, but never had. Now his mother said his seditious profits should cover her losses. They had argued bitterly, and then she refused to discuss it. It had been years since they had spoken. Hoseyn was not even sure how much of the money was left. He consoled himself that its loss meant that no sign of high living could come to the attention of Iranian counterintelligence. He had never craved the money. His chief hunger was for the psychological maneuvering with Will. He could not, even after the danger the midget posed, give it up.

It might have been well enough. And was, until the reception. Such events never happened before the midget. He thought if he shook your hand you were a sure friend. The colossus of his naïveté shadowed everything. At the event, there were men the small leader invited from IranAir, the favored cover for the Ministry of Intelligence and Security, called MOIS; and nuclear men, among them Hoseyn and many of his colleagues. It was a jamboree for foxes among chickens. There were wolves too. One of the MOIS men noticed Hoseyn's wife. This animal displayed and rutted and sniffed at her, and then, as weeks went by, pursued and played her. The insult, the fear, the knowing that she could not definitively refuse him—for months they shuttled in smothering despair past each relay and switch in the monstrous machine that enclosed them as their tormentor called and manipulated and bumped into her or caught her in an excuse. His wife, defiant, silkily difficult, said she could fend him off. But Hoseyn knew. They were at the mercy of this man.

They would move. They could flee. But the regime would leave no nuclear scientist in peaceful exile; he knew of men in car accidents or sudden terminal illness in Paris and Sydney, perhaps Los Angeles. He tried to seek Will's help. Will was busy. He set up a meeting, then canceled at the last minute. Finally, he was available. During their one meeting, in Tirana, Albania, on a blasting cold sun of a morning, nothing moved Will's digit of a face. He made promises; that he did do. But he was, after all they had shared, useless to Hoseyn. It chewed at him. The regime nut still lusted, Will delayed. His wife, finally, properly, as it should have always been, was dead center.

It was her idea to seek out the Sacred Sons. The *Pesarah* always needed nuclear defectors who could tell of Iranian progress on the bomb and push Washington into an Iranian invasion to topple the regime. Hoseyn countered that they would want him to say the nuclear program was further along than it was. His wife didn't care what they wanted, she wanted out. And eventually Hoseyn saw it was their only choice.

At first he scoffed at the *Pesarah*'s idea to stage his death. No one would believe it. That is why, they told him, it is believable. He recalled his early faith in Will's need for him, and he thought maybe, okay, yes. After the death trick, Hoseyn would leave Iran. His wife argued it would neatly end his relationship with Will. Will would hear of Hoseyn's death, assume Hoseyn dead, there would be nothing else. Yet he brooded. Would Will be deceived? Wouldn't the Americans learn he was alive?

At the least, this life after death would be an involuted existence. And that interested him. After studying the photographs of his funeral one night in the suite, he realized the nurse and the orderly wouldn't be able to tell from looking at them that it was his funeral. His hired care-takers didn't know of his faked demise. They thought he was a more usual kind of defector, one made ill by regime abuse—poisoning, drug sadism, the reputed enfeeblements.

He was missing from the photographs, wasn't he? So he left the pictures on display, ordered neatly on the floor. It saved energy, something he still lacked. It had taken too much time to put them down and gather them afterward.

Still, he felt a need to explain to them. He decided to tell the orderly they were from his mother's funeral. His poor condition, he said, stopped him from going. But then his recovering mind finally pieced together that the orderly or nurse had never met his mother. She could have been any of the older women in the photographs from the funeral. They wailed, as was the Iranian way, as if their own sons had died. Perhaps the orderly and the nurse were suspicious. The more he worried it, the less he could see clearly through his fears.

He was not quite recovered enough to enjoy his new deceptions. It was easier to find comfort in pettiness. The orderly insisted on wearing white, even though Hoseyn told him it was unnecessary. It made him feel like an invalid. The orderly was fidgety, a bossy African. That was a strange joining right there. Most bwanas were implacable. This one was irritable. He was squat, calling to mind a circus performer. Because he was wall-eyed, Hoseyn had to fight feeling embarrassed in his presence. He wondered if this was a residue of the drug that had made him appear dead, because usually he'd tease and mock such a defect to make it okay. Maybe he was just too tired. It had only been a week.

The nurse warned Hoseyn that he would have personality changes, but they were temporary. There was a list of potential medical issues, and every so often Hoseyn felt the nurse checking him for them. The guy meant to be unobtrusive. He was obvious. At least that part of Hoseyn's brain was untouched.

The nurse wore blue jeans and the kind of belt most Iranian men wore, made of lacquered leather clasped behind a rectangular plate of chrome. Hoseyn hated it. He wasn't sure why. He thought that perhaps the origin of this belt's supreme irritation might be solved during his convalescence. It must have had some association that was unpleasant. He couldn't remember what it might have been. The nurse also wore a fitted dress shirt with his blue jeans. It was hard to determine which infuriated Hoseyn more, the belt or the shirt. Perhaps it was because, worn together, they made a man look like he was in a disco. He had wanted to tell many men that this style was American and from the 1970s. They were dressed like American men when the Shah was in power. They thought they were being anti-Western. They were so long inside Iran that their own appearance said things they didn't understand.

The funeral included religious and social events at various locations. He was most curious about those at the cemetery. His family managed to do the grave interrogation. It surprised him. If it wasn't done the evening of the day of death, it had no efficacy. His wife couldn't have wanted it. Certainly his brother, the Ann Arbor pizza manager, wouldn't have asked for it. Who, then? He'd not spoken to his wife on the phone. She might have put a note in with the photographs. It wasn't there when he got them.

He studied the pate of his uncle as he stood in the grave. The camera was pointed down, so only the top and back of his head were visible. Hoseyn remembered how it had irked Will when Iranians buried their dead standing up.

His uncle faced the dead man. Where had they found this corpse? And who was he? In the customary *kafan push,* it could have been anyone.

His uncle had his hands on the shoulders of this cadaver. He was shaking it, but not much. This was supposed to be the rehearsal before the actual questioning at the gates of hell. The male relative, basically, played Allah. If the dead man gave the right answers, he might make it to heaven. It was an entrenched custom of Tehran; nowhere else did such apostasy survive. The hardliners didn't stop it, but they didn't approve of it. For once, he agreed with them.

Some harassed the dead, pushed and pulled; they took out their anger under the cover of grief. Hoseyn wished he could have heard his uncle's questions. Most times he'd seen the interrogation, he'd heard rote queries: Did you make the haj? Did you keep the fast? A few times it was: Did you lie? Did you kick a man in need? One time, winter, plow blades were scraping snow, and he stood in the wet air with a big family. Did you seduce her? Did you kill him? One brother tried to drag and lift his sibling out of the ground, pulling hair to get a grip. Hoseyn just walked away from that, stood talking to the snowplow operator down at the mouth of the martyrs' section.

He was in it now. Or his surrogate was. Since Hoseyn had lived and died in the nuclear program, any death of his, even a natural one manmade and false, qualified. His slotting among martyrs offended him. In Iran's war with Iraq, waves of men fell to muzzles. They died so fast in such numbers, the military had to put four to a grave. Stood them up and poured in the cement. The martyr section grew like bacteria through crud water. He, the planner, wasn't worthy of a place with the unquestioning.

He walked to the windows. Walls of them, glass from top to bottom. He was on the twenty-third floor. He peered down at calcined lime and clay, churning in drums below. Construction stretched to the horizon. Haze never lifted. When he first came to Dubai, he thought it was the earthworks. He guessed that digging and cratering made filmy air. Back then, there weren't many structures to show for it. Different now. From his room in the sail of the Burj, the icon hotel, the sailboat building, he saw lanyards of skyscrapers. Highways—five lanes each direction, traffic-jam free—carved around and over and down to the Gulf. They were ready for everyone.

He had to lie down. The orderly followed his movements. He hated being annotated. Clinical as he was, he rejected the need for it. Either he would be well or he wouldn't. Notes couldn't make anything what it wouldn't be. His progress was like an audio transmission on a two-dimensional graph. The serrated up and down on the x line would flatten and rise, and no watching would affect it. This gorp of a nurse didn't get it.

By the second week, the orderly and the nurse were tranquilized by Hoseyn's lack of visible symptoms. His watchers mostly watched television. Hoseyn kept close to them but managed forays. After several trips to various corners of the suite, each for longer absences, he went to the closet where they'd stored his Samsonite. He pulled out a sweater for help against the air conditioning. The day after, he yanked down an extra pillow from a high shelf.

Then, one morning, he opened the door and fell to his knees. He crept to the suitcase gingerly. When he reached its vinyl, it smelled like a baby's neck. Had they washed it in talc? Maybe his imagination was still overworking, as it had in the cafeteria. He tugged it from the recess in crab motions. Near the closet door, he put his ear to the combination lock. It was a seashell. For a while he was content, listening to nothing.

Later, he pulled credit cards from the Ziploc packed beside his coffee-blotched shoes. Their embossed numerals shone like mercury. Their surfaces were mirrors. The rough back strips awaited his signatures. With these he could elude his medicalized protectors. He slipped the cards in the pocket of his old sports jacket. He had worn it with Will in Moscow.

Still crawling, he found the suite door's handle with his hand. He pulled it down and liked its well-oiled torsion. He nudged the door into the hall. He waited. There was nothing from nurse or orderly. The television droned. He crept forward and out. After his breathing settled, he positioned himself correctly. With care, he pushed the door back. Then he let it settle into the frame. He released, second by second, the latch into the jamb.

He was free. He bolted upright and loped down the hall.

Once in the elevator, he looked in its high-gloss panels and smoothed his hair. He hadn't quite trusted the suite mirrors. He looked good enough. There'd been no bruising. He had not one cut.

He felt enthusiastic. He decided to hire a car from the concierge. Given the medical worries, driving was less than wise. There were three guys behind the desk. They were European. They had small noses. One of them asked for room number and passport. He gave both. Hands flickered over the keyboard, confirmations surfaced. Soon he was in a honey Benz, seated on its august leather, his Mumbai driver coasting one of the five lanes of a shimmying highway.

He used to talk to the drivers. It was taxis back then. Now he knew every story they had to tell. All were sad. None had remedy. He wanted something. He looked around at the bottled water, the maps, the magazines.

"A satellite phone," Hoseyn said in Hindi. "Where can I buy one?"

The driver took the next exit.

After a trip to an ATM, they wound their way around a number of warehouse districts until they reached an import-export business owned by a friend of the driver. Hoseyn doubted the guy's phones would be what he wanted, but, then again, no one he knew would be there, and that was good. Most conventionally available sat phones were terrible appliances anyway. But this would be his—all his. He made sure the service provider would not display his number as private for anyone with Caller ID. Then he asked the driver if he would mind registering it in his name instead of Hoseyn's. They agreed on a payment for this favor, and as they backed out of the warehouse lot, Hoseyn cradled the device like a boy at Nowruz.

They drove to the desert. It heaved before them, fabulous curtains of sand, ridged into heavy ripples. Their color was ecru, and the air so still they seemed fixed, like resin. The driver sped the rolling roads these Dubai emirs had just made, up and down, making calls to get the right elevation and latitude for the satellite phone, adjusting position based on how well he could hear a man on the other end. His brother, he said. It took at least twenty minutes. Hoseyn would have waited twenty hours.

When the driver finally parked, turned off the engine, and handed the phone back, Hoseyn couldn't summon his own phone number to mind. It felt as if he had a dowel in his cortex. It was like choking, only worse. Then he remembered. He pushed down on the numbers deliberately. They were precious to him.

He listened to the ringing. On the fourth one, he heard his wife say hello as if it were anyone, and when she heard nothing on the other end, she said hello a few more times and then hung up. He called her immediately after, heard her hello again, but this time the tone of her voice was hopeful, and just that made him weak. He almost said her name. He pushed the end-call button reluctantly. The third time, she didn't pick up. He stopped calling, put the phone in his lap, and waited.

He looked out the car window. The flaxen sand was undisturbed, the air still unmoving, just as Tehran's had been. He must be living through some kind of record for windless weather. He looked at the driver. He should worry more about him. He should think about who he might be. He shouldn't lean on a hired man. Yet he wasn't strong enough to care, though he was improving—thinking about what he should be thinking. Hoseyn sighed.

The driver didn't glance back at him. The guy was lost in his own thoughts, no doubt ten thousand troubles. Past this desert there were ten million more.

The *brrr* of the sat phone's ring crashed through to them. Hoseyn pushed the talk button.

"*Joahn,*" his wife said. My soul.

"*Joahn,*" he said.

"You're good," she said. She didn't sound as if she were asking.

"I am." He decided to answer.

He could hear the fast intake of her breath. He should be fucking around with her. It would worry her that he wasn't.

"How's the cookie?"

She laughed, but not for long.

She didn't seem ready to say anything.

"So my uncle, what did he ask?"

He could hear her thinking. Her mind wasn't graveside.

She finally got it.

"Of that mummy?" She was trying to laugh again.

"Yeah."

"Did you fuck your mother. Did you betray your country. Those were two things."

Hoseyn laughed, his first time since getting to Dubai. It quickly went to tears.

"The asshole," he said, trying to keep it to laughter.

"The asshole," she said. She wasn't crying or laughing.

They were quiet. He remembered her voice. He could almost hear the way it sounded when she wasn't on the phone.

"Some more time," he said to her. That was because he'd be gone a long time.

"Some more time," she said.

"Okay, then." He didn't want to hang up.

"Okay," she said.

He heard her hang up. He didn't hang up. He sat there, the receiver at his cheek. He wondered if he could just hold it there for a while and not hang up, if the driver would notice. He didn't want his talking to his wife to end yet. It was over, yes, it was over. But if he didn't push the end-call button, it wasn't over *for him*.

He listened to the phizzing from the phone on his ear.

Maybe it was adjusting to that sound that did it. But he realized in a matter of seconds that the driver was talking. He was also not talking to him.

Hoseyn didn't move. He nodded and said, noncommittally, "Okay."

The driver paused. Then he began to talk again. He didn't have a cell phone to his ear. There were no earbuds. There were no wires. There were no clips. Hoseyn saw at the edge of his just-about-thinking mind an outline of an unknown shape. He struggled to focus. He bore down. He pushed himself. And there it was. This driver's talking meant someone, either the Americans or the Iranian regime, had discovered that Hoseyn's death had been faked. A panic almost encircled him. He forced it away and considered. What was the best way to read this particular reality? Here was a driver talking on a phone that was not a visible phone, but something, no doubt, implanted in him, like a veterinarian's computer chip in the neck of a pet.

Hoseyn decided to say okay again. He made the tone lazy this time. He wanted the driver to think he was still talking to his wife in wistful tones. The driver kept talking. Hoseyn said okay once again, reaching now into his blazer, the same one he'd worn with Will in China. He drew out the kukri.

He jimmied fast to make a fatal wound at the base of the driver's head.

He dug out a transistor from under the tongue. After he put it in his pocket, he opened the trunk, took out a bucket, and ladled sand over the body. Now he liked the lack of wind.

He drove back to Dubai carefully. He dropped the satellite phone in the creek between a pair of dhows. He boarded a flight on Emirates for Iran. He wasn't sure anyone, not even Will, would understand what it took for him to leave the Samsonite behind.

Ahwaz was a sink. You couldn't get clean in it. It collected dirty things needing a wash. After a while, you were one of them. The city's best hotel, the one overlooking the river, was dank. It had bath towels as thin as sheets, and sheets as rough as washcloths. The mini-fridge verged on tepid and was empty except for a faded red pitcher of water. Would anyone drink such a mystery? Hoseyn wanted to take it to the front desk and demand it be tested. That would have been conspicuous. That was what he couldn't be.

Here in Iran, he couldn't call anyone. He had to avoid the windows. He couldn't leave the room. He couldn't eat room-service food. He couldn't open the door to anyone. He was no longer sick. It would have been better to be sick. It would have been better not to have called his wife from Dubai. It would have helped if he'd rented a car on his own. All of his outfoxing had cornered him. He could try to blame someone not himself. But he didn't bother. He had made this purgatory. He would have to sit down in it.

He had come to Iran for one reason: to see, precisely, who came for him. He chose this loo of a city to control how he met whoever followed the transistor. Here he could tell friend from foe before actually laying eyes on either. If the Dubai driver worked for foe, for Tehran, someone would arrive quickly. If the Dubai driver worked for former friend, the Americans, no one would show. Or it would take them a while. They couldn't get into Iran quickly. They could rejigger an identity fast enough, send a muscled spook on a tourist visa, but even that visa, the easiest one, took a minimum of a month for approval. The Iraq border was sealed to casual travel. There were parachutes, and ironmen who could land them on dimes, but then what? Walk. Turkey, same. Armenia too. Turkmenistan, Pakistan, and Afghanistan borders were sieves, but from each an American would have to *walk* or, most likely, most desirable, fastest, *drive* across the length of Iran to Ahwaz without any Farsi. It was at least three days of travel.

Anyone would rather fly, but commercial flights had to stop in Tehran to connect with a flight to Ahwaz. Mehrabad and Khomeini airports were impossible to slink in and out of undetected. An American rent a car at an Iranian airport? Stealing one would be easier. For the right guy, even that would be easy. But once you were on the road, then distance was so great you'd have to get gas. With rationing now, government-printed vouchers were required. How do you buy a voucher on the black market without Farsi? You'd have to steal even gasoline.

Hoseyn scaled these decision trees his first afternoon. He concluded that anyone commando enough to overpower or steal wouldn't be linguistic enough to master Farsi or technical enough to finesse his way out of the gaps he had in both. Sir James Bond was Sir Unrealistic Trash. Yet he had to remind himself that the unrealistic and unlikely had happened and could happen. That's what got him in Ahwaz.

After spending the night thinking, sleepless and overheated, he concluded once again that if he'd stayed in Dubai, whoever came looking for the transistor could be either American or Iranian. To look at the person, he might not be able to tell who was what.

Getting out of bed, he felt hyperactive, like a first-grader. Not sleeping always made his thoughts race. There was nonsense mixing through the competing fragments of ideas. He tried to silence the pinging. Maybe sitting down on the side of the bed would help. He put his head in his hands. Protect me. He repeated that a few times. Even a nonbeliever could pray, and he always had.

When he lifted his head, he noticed that the curtain on the room's one window was loose from the rod in places, letting in weak triangles of light. It must be overcast. That was calming, for some reason. He went to the bathroom and turned on the cold tap. The water was warm and cloudy. He let it run and was about to walk back into the room when he heard voices in the hallway. He put his ear flush with the door.

It was a German and a Japanese, two men. Neither spoke English well, but they were trying to pass pleasantries back and forth. They moved down the hall to the elevator bank, and he lost their voices. He looked at the watch his in-laws gave him—fortunately, still with him. It was a Monday, and it was before seven. The maids should be in the hallway by now. He listened carefully, but there was nothing. Perhaps they were at the other end of the hall.

He examined the tap water he'd poured into the bathroom glass. It was still cloudy after he'd let it sit. So the cloudiness wasn't trapped air. He'd have to take his chances. It could just be chalk. As he drank, tasting nothing unusual, he picked through the bag of food he'd bought at the airport. He ate some chips. He started prying apart pistachios to store up the nuts for later, when he was too hungry to wait.

The shelling steadied him. He should, he realized half jokingly, take up knitting. Occupied hands were therapeutic. It was a discovery made rather late in his career of risk taking, though perhaps one he hadn't had to arrive at sooner because his Samsonite had been his lucky charm. Now that he thought of it, the bag had little to do with good fortune. Its meaning to him was outside any measurable purpose. "It is still *here*," he used to think gratefully when he saw it. For all that, still *this*. He looked around the hotel room, as if searching for another way of seeing things—at the board-hard bed he'd lain down on but not slept in, at the loafers he remembered sinking into the macadam the day he'd played dying, the plastic sack from the airport that held his stash of rip-top food, his once-compressed wallet bulging with new cards, and beside it, the sharp-cornered smoke-green passport of a man who didn't exist. It was a scene many like him had evaluated over the years in many hotel rooms.

Most often, when possessions were at this minimum, in a hotel of this dreadful condition, his kind were thinking—systematically if they were good, and intestinally if they thought they were good—about what would happen next. What next? he thought. What next? He pictured it: everywhere in hotel rooms, men asking, What next? He took a red pen through all of them. He would not think of what next. He would refrain.

It came to him in moments. It was possible no one sent the driver. It was possible the driver had been involved in some other assignation. Unlike the Americans, who assumed so all the time, he, Hoseyn, wasn't the protagonist of every story. He could have walked onto the wrong stage in the wrong theater. He could have parachuted into the field of potatoes when it was in the onions where he'd been supposed to land.

And if no one sent the driver for *him,* for Hoseyn, then what was he, Hoseyn, doing, exactly, in this hotel room? He was waiting for someone with motives he couldn't guess at. He would react to this visitor's arrival assuming motives unconnected to him.

He didn't have to wait to see if it was Tehran or Americans who sent the driver.

He thought of jumping up and throwing the pistachio shells in the air like confetti.

He was not ready to trust his own breakthrough.

He listened to the sound of a shell fall on the small dune of shells he'd made. It was a tendril of a sound, and there was, strictly speaking, no word exactly for it. See, he told himself, you had to use a strand of hair to approximate the uniqueness of its sound, and even that, he said, listening to the drop of another shell, had not conveyed it.

There was a knock at the door. It was a columnar noise. It seemed to push him back from where he sat. One hand dropped into the shells. Then he moved. He got up and made his way on the balls of his feet to the door. He was going to apply his ear to it when a female voice—it sounded like a girl's—said, "Maid service," in Farsi. No time for decision trees now. The knock came again, and then he could hear jingling and a metal sound progressing into the grooves of the keyhole.

He opened the door.

She was a teenager, he judged. She had thin lips and a too-pointed nose, and in another person they would have been witchy, but on her they looked delicate. He could tell she wasn't stupid. She was saying her "sorry"s, she would come back later, and he saw over her shoulder the older supervisor, with another girl facing another man at *his* door. Hosyen put his index finger to his lip, breathed out his most fatherly expression, and opened the door. To his great joy, she followed, wheeling a small case of cleaning supplies with her.

He put his arms across his chest but didn't entwine them; he just held his own arms. "I need your help," he said.

She still had her hand on the handle that steered her bucket. He looked at her fingers, and when he did, she adjusted her grip but didn't let go. He saw her eyes take in the room, the pile of pistachios and their shells, the bed not slept in, the one plastic bag, his wallet.

"How many rooms on this floor?"

"Twenty," she said. Her voice was gentle, but only a little afraid.

"How many with guests?"

"Four."

"On either side of me?"

She shook her head. "There is no one."

"Not for tonight?"

"None are coming."

"How long does she stay?"

"All day." She knew he meant her supervisor.

"No lunch?"

"She eats it—in the room by the elevator. She has her eye, always on this hallway."

"Except when she uses the restroom."

"Yes."

"Can you get me into the room next to mine?"

"You don't like this room? You can call the front. I will—" She thought she had entirely misunderstood. Then he could read in her face that she was not sure what she understood.

"No. No. I need the front desk to think I am in this room."

"You have a friend? A lady friend?"

"Not necessarily. Though it could be a lady. But it could also be a man. And, yes, a visitor. But I don't want to be in my room when this person arrives. I want to put some of my things in another room. I want some of them to stay in this room. And I want to go to a third room. Can you help me do that?"

"And that is all? That is all you want?"

"That's all I want."

He could see she was puzzled but relieved. She had no doubt been asked many things, and her supervisor prohibited all of them, but this one she had not been asked. This one, he could see in her eyes, intrigued her. He had happened on a girl with imagination. He saw her hand was no longer on the supplies, and she had moved a little to the left of the case.

"There is a way," she said. "I will come for you, but you must leave this door open. I cannot knock, or she may hear."

He remembered the knock—it was loud. But the door unlocked? He didn't like that either.

"A slip of paper?" He said it without moving. He had a sense that if he did she might change her mind.

She looked over at the hotel pad, skinny, only a few pages. She took a step and scooped it into a pocket of her long apron.

"Slide it under the door. I'll watch, right here," he said, slowly pulling the chair out from the desk that segued into a credenza.

"It won't be too long."

"Good."

"You must give me the things for the other room now."

He suppressed a smile. She had entered into the plot with complete fidelity. He would hold a special place in his memories for this girl.

"There's a sports jacket in the closet," he said. She turned and guided the warped door to the left. The transistor was in its breast pocket. Whoever had planted the transistor in that driver's mouth, whoever had followed its progress as he'd carried it with him from Dubai to Ahwaz, whoever intended to trap him, to harm him, to find him—they would find the transistor in a room Hoseyn was not inside. "Take that to the room on my right. If you don't mind, it would be better if you didn't look in the pockets. Can you promise me you won't do that?"

"Yes," she said, but he couldn't tell if she would obey. She would at least know that she was to leave the transistor there. And what girl would fish a pocket for a transistor wafer? What would she want with taking it?

"It's nothing of importance. It's not money," he said, turning to his wallet and taking out new bills. "I know this is risky for you, and I know, if something happens that we don't expect, they'll look for this on you. So I'm going to put it here," he said, walking slowly to the curtain, lifting the ragged hem of it, and pushing the currency into the space between the lining and the heavier fabric. "It'll be here for you, later."

She smiled, a shy look, but he could tell she was pleased.

"When are you expecting your visitor?"

"I may find that no visitor comes."

She studied him closely, wanting him to say more.

He stood there. That was enough.

"*Balay?*" he finally said.

"*Balay,*" she said.

The supervisor used the toilet just before lunch. As Hoseyn saw the paper come under the door, he hoped his co-conspirator had the sense to keep the other maid out of the plot. He opened the door a fraction. His maid was standing just outside.

"Now," she said. "Don't wait."

He looked left and right down the humid hall. It was empty and perfect. Sometimes a miracle could be achieved through no effort at all. They moved silently to the next room's door, and she opened it with a single key hanging from a belt loop at her waist. She joined him inside.

"There is a switch for the hall cameras," she told him. "I turned them off. But I must hurry and turn them back on."

He hadn't worried about them, counting on the front-desk employees' being too incompetent to watch them in this dilapidation of an establishment, but he was flooded with affection for this girl soldier he'd found.

"It is a hotel with foreigners," she added.

"Yes, you're right about that," he said.

"So they watch," she said.

"They want you to think that," he said, trying not to sound harsh or knowing. What did he know? He almost laughed. He had an adolescent maid helping him conduct a crap-assed experiment for finding a granule of truth.

Now she was looking disappointed. She had imagined an importance to her chores in these halls and rooms. Being watched might have been the only thing that could have conferred it on her. He almost wanted to comfort her.

"You cannot turn on the television," she said.

"I know," he said.

"The supervisor might hear you. She does walk by."

"Yes, the doors hide nothing," he said.

"How long . . . do you want this, this arrangement?" she asked. "For the night?"

"Yes." He wanted to tell her he would be leaving in the morning, but it wasn't necessary. He felt a sensation like heartache for her; he was sorry to see this excitement, his appearance in her life, drain away without a sincere leavetaking.

"Thank you," he said, meaning it to be his goodbye to her.

She hesitated.

"If there is something wrong, if something . . . I will put the paper under the door. With writing," she said, fumbling her words.

He didn't want her near the rooms.

"Not safe," he said.

He could feel her wanting to know more, but he looked impatient, and she left.

.   .   .

For a while, Hoseyn amused himself with if-then-else statements, writing them in columns like software code along the borders of the three-ring hotel directory. His hand ached a little from holding the pen too tightly. His anxiety had gotten the better of him. He shook his hand a few times. There was an abraded feeling on the roof of his mouth, probably from eating too many chips. He was thirsty, and his bathroom glass empty. He looked at his watch. It was almost eight in the evening.

He unfolded himself from the desk chair, trying to stretch out his hamstrings and lower back, toggling his neck. He was too thirsty to put his ear to the door when he passed it on the way to the bathroom. He turned on the tap.

He would remember it later, how in the next moments the building downshifted, as if a scalding hand had pushed down at the point where the next room began. The tiles of the tub flew away. The showerhead twisted into a straight line. Clouds that smelled of drywall held him. Pelting bricks and the groaning of wood casings continued, until a quiet came that was followed by back-flipping beds, tumbling chairs, some floor reaching a breaking point not far from the sloping floor on which he stood, clinging to a towel bar. His pursuers had found the transistor in the pocket in the next room. They had wanted him dead. He was, once again, not dead. As the crumbling resumed and a new settling threatened, he came out of his stupor to understand that the Americans were not his hunters and that the guns for him pointed from home.

TIBER CREEK NOVEMBER

7. O MY DOVE, LET ME SEE

Adam believed Martina Welk was the best candidate for managing editor. The most stressful night he remembered, she was the calmest. No embarrassment fell on her watch. No slippery favorite had ever conned her into accepting fake copy. No news outlet challenged reporting she'd edited. All he ever heard, from editors outside the building, was this: Martina Welk was sound. Inside, she'd rarely ticked off anyone, except those ticked off by most everyone. She could disappoint a rookie with a crummy assignment, or ease out a veteran with a plum one. She had the coldness to lead, but, unlike most who did, she took care to make herself available and look them in the eye. She was only slightly humorless. She confided in no one—if she did, he couldn't tell who it might be—a feat in a pen of magpies. She was outwardly fair to other editors, many of whom were rivals. She delivered criticism without venom. She read the paper. It had become depressingly clear to Adam that not everyone did. The reporters—so be it. But there were too many editors he could tell were off the page.

Most of all, he liked her plebeian background—state school, not Ivy; high school, not prep; Midwest, not coast. She was Jewish, which felt familiar. She was married, which kept things simple. Best of all, she was unattractive, which crossed out unwanted tension. Still, he couldn't bring himself to make the final decision.

Maybe it was because she had not been his first choice. Gordon had been—and Gordon had refused to even apply for the job. Gordon Bray didn't like to manage, didn't like to edit, and his current job, as foreign editor, was the exception he claimed he could stomach. His attention span was short, his energy—what did one of his reporters call it?—oh, it was kinetic. He'd authored two books—on the fall of the Berlin wall, and China's new economy. He was born in London, the son of a Foreign Service officer. He'd been a precocious young man in Germany, Japan, and Hong Kong. He had an undergraduate degree from Stanford in political science, and a master's from Harvard in economics. Unlike Martina, who had joined the paper as a suburban court reporter and hoisted her way up, Gordon arrived at the paper not a full year ago from the competing paper, where he'd been posted in Beijing. He'd been coaxed away after his wife imposed a fiat. She'd leave him if he didn't find a nontraveling Stateside job that paid enough for her to stop working and have children. The other paper couldn't put together the right package, so Gordon came aboard, at the highest level, no dreary dues-paying, with a salary twice Martina's. His wife had recently delivered twin boys.

Gordon had all of Martina's good qualities—cool under haranguing, ruthless but affable, collegial yet commanding. His platinum education and worldliness complemented Adam's brass upbringing. Gordon was compelling. Adam was steady. Was Adam strong enough to highlight a comparison that left him looking rustic? Could he risk being goat to Gordon's ermine? Adam believed he could. Adam felt so self-congratulatory about his confidence that it never occurred to him that Gordon wouldn't want to apply for the job. That was a few months ago.

Adam worried. If he simply offered it to him, no applying or vetting, would Gordon bite? Adam knew how he had felt after his own first son arrived. The more time he could spend at the paper, the better. No one would have guessed it of Adam Sanger the mensch. But Gordon Bray the cosmopolitan—surely he wanted a break from squalling times two.

Adam walked into the Room. He took a look in the glass box that was Gordon's office. Gordon was talking with his deputy. Adam looked up at the clock; it was eleven. He glanced guiltily over at Martina's desk. She was sitting behind her screen, the owlish doyenne. No, she looked a little funny. He tried to see her face better. Oh, there were flowers on her desk. White roses—an expensive, oversized bunch of them. It must have been her birthday, or maybe anniversary—but she looked awful. Even for Martina she looked terrible. Was she embarrassed by the flowers?

Surely not. Though they were rather—much—for work, to have at work, to have them seen. They looked as if they were made for a debutante. It occurred to him that maybe she and her husband had had a nasty fight. The apology bouquet—Adam had sent more than a few. White, the color of mortification, his first wife had said. He'd always chosen yellow. But he'd once tried red, and it had worked far better. What had she said? Oh, that yellow roses were for funerals. Red was for passion. He'd been a dud in that department. He was a yellow husband, through and through. The white-roses husband—he couldn't decide how to see such a man.

He turned around to see if Gordon was done with his deputy. He walked a few steps, got interrupted by a copy aide with a press release. As he was beginning to read, he saw Martina approaching, just about even with his secretary's desk. She looked like she had the flu. He'd tell her to go home—that way he could talk with Gordon, maybe even risk a walk outside. It was a bright autumn morning. Poor Martina, she looked gray, not healthy at all. He was set to be solicitous when he saw Gordon coming, his meeting with the deputy abruptly over, from the opposite direction.

Damn, Adam thought. Damn. When Martina and Gordon converged, Adam's face was a mix of bedside doctoring and exasperation. Martina took this to mean he already knew what she was about to tell him. Gordon gave not a quid for Adam Sanger's inner state—he didn't bother to check its facial tint. All he wanted was to get his wife soothed about his year-ago affair with the Burmese dissident in hiding. There'd been a flare-up; his wife was on the phone, with newly discovered old correspondence he'd entirely forgotten he'd stashed; over and over the phone ringing, his secretary exhibiting the tact of a spliff-smoking scourge. She was a bit of fluff, except when she fancied him. As he'd not fancied her back, it would be all over the Room if he didn't head home directly. Telling Adam of an unexpected truncation of the workday was the smallest of his problems. He'd had the mistaken idea that his wife would be rendered placid by breast-feeding and that his agreement to serve time on the intellectual tundra of a daily newspaper would suffice.

Not so—her abuse was tenacious of life. Worse, he couldn't figure out how to slip through his fate: he loved the twins, was just besotted with them. He'd fallen for his wife's long red hair all those years back, and for that mane, that limited desiring, well, it certainly looked as if he'd be paying until the twins were men.

"Adam, urgent at the house," he said before Martina could get more than the word "we" out of what Gordon considered to be her pained and therefore sensual lips.

". . . have a problem," Martina finished, with Adam riveted on the word urgent, especially since it came from Gordon. The executive editor ignored the national editor and said to the foreign editor, "The twins."

"Yes," said Gordon hoarsely, warming to the Broadway of it all. "No time to explain." He had already turned his back and was walking, but Adam was following him, and saying, "Call if you need anything." Should Gordon amplify? He paused and turned, allowing Adam to place his hand on his forearm. Somewhere in his ear, Adam heard someone saying, ". . . beat us." He prickled. Gordon began to blur in Adam's mind; he was connecting Martina's "problem," and "beat us," when Gordon said, "You'll be the first I call."

"Good. Good," Adam hurried. His back was all Gordon saw.

Martina hoped she had Adam's attention, but with Adam you often couldn't tell—was that the basis for her longing? Her therapist believed this. Martina resisted that interpretation. Martina did, however, practice some of the techniques they'd talked about for getting past obsessive attachment when important work on the job was at hand. She thought of Adam's wife, Joan, most particularly of a kind of angelic connotation around her eyes; then considered Adam's discolored teeth, and in particular the left canine, which was practically sepia. She completed the cognitive refocusing by dwelling on his rocky mannerisms. Her feelings cratered just enough so she could say without emotion, "We have a problem."

Adam sensed it. The other paper had broken a story his paper should have.

"The report. They have a story on it," Martina said. "Story's on their site; the wire already has a story; CNN just cut away from regular programming to tease it. They're saying DOD, some military-intelligence component, has had the White House under surveillance."

"The report?"

"IC updates to the Senate Select Committee on Intelligence."

Adam stared into the near distance with determination. Martina waited for him to remember.

"Family Jewels II," she said. They had been discussing it in a few meetings. Still she waited.

Don. It was always about Don. Family Jewels was his triumph. But what was Jewels II?

"Did you say someone is spying on the White House?"

"Not exactly," she said. "The wire is hedging. There may be legal precedent for it."

"Have you talked to Kim?" Kim was the longtime Justice Department reporter.

"Well, she thinks it would be the general counsel at the CIA we need to get with—but I was hoping we'd have someone on the Hill who had somebody on Sissy they could—"

"Sissy? The Sissy report?" Adam didn't let his voice rise.

Martina thought her therapist would have something to say about this slowness in Adam, would compare it to her father, would—but wait, she—

Adam looked away from Martina. He found himself looking at the flowers on her desk.

"Yes," she said, noticing him on the flowers.

"Where's Mitch?"

"Mitch? I think the question is, where's Tom." Martina spoke of the man who covered the Senate, where the Senate Select Committee on Intelligence could be found and from which the report—Martina believed, her deputy asserted, and, unbeknown to Martina, Mabel Cannon at her dinner party had assumed—originated.

"Tom?" Adam searched around for that name in his head. In a see-saw of almost commensurate justice, Adam's reporters did not read the paper, and he did not know those who wrote it.

"Tom Romero. We just hired him from Metro to cover the Senate," Martina said, happy that Adam had displayed one of his least appealing traits—acting like a rhinoceros.

"What's Mitch working on?" Adam said.

"Adam, he's on the desk," Martina whispered. Adam had forgotten days ago in the two o'clock, and here he was, forgetting again.

"The desk?"

"Foreign Desk."

"Right. Right."

"I want him on this."

"But there's Anne—and Harriet."

"He worked the Pentagon longer than anyone in this city. I want him on it."

Martina wanted to ask why they'd hired Anne, in the midst of buy-outs, with a special dispensation from the publisher, if Anne was not to be brought in on a drubbing like this. But she didn't.

"I don't want Harriet off the secret-prisons story," Adam said.

Given that Harriet was in Poland, this was hardly visionary of Adam. Martina fumed into expressionless rancor.

"I will get with Mitch," she said, trying to slow her clipped words into plain flat.

"I don't want him on anything else but this report."

Now the Foreign editor was coming for Adam.

"We've got an Iranian nuclear scientist committing suicide," he said. "Wire has him doing it in the bathroom on board a flight to Dubai. Guardian says he hung himself in some hotel in southwestern Iran. Our stringer's on vacation. Should we try to get Harriet in Dubai? Or run wire?"

"Harriet is in Poland," Martina said. The Foreign editor refused to remember where she was. He'd been told twice this morning.

"Glenn in London," Adam said crisply. "Have him make some calls, add in wire, leave it at that."

Mabel was grateful to feel anything. So, when she did, she ran to the instigator. The man in question was not a type. She had no types. She did not have phases. She tasted from all cups. It was enough to find that falling for someone was always possible if one waited for the first sensations, if one was neither too picky nor too slattern. When it came to success, the stud had nothing on the woman who appeared restrained but had few compunctions, the she who could take to her bed the hopeless Brazilian with smoke eyes and Mabel's garden to manage, or the black Marine with the thickest snake who placed an ad looking for his white damsel, or the married Methodist manufacturer closing on sixty who'd never fallen in love, not once, until Mabel. She took them, not for sport, and always one at a time—she was extravagantly monogamous, passionately attached. She never saw them as lovers. They were all serious candidates to be her undeniable love, the one for whom she would leave Don Grady. Their improbability only signified hope. Hope that she had turned wrong when she chose Don and that another way waited.

Jonathan Strasser, for whom lesser things were planned, things such as merely staunching Mabel's ennui, was committed to his wife, she of the less-than-right immune system. Mabel was more relieved than disappointed when the gossip came back to her. She'd cooled right down on Strasser after the communion he'd had in her hallway with his daughter's book. She liked what he might have brought, which was— was it too much to ask?—distraction. Anything was better than this torpor, this mortuary of the spirit.

Her enthusiasms were leaching out of her. Like the rest of her bimonthly arriving dinner-party guests, she leafed through the contents and read the last pages—of the War Cabinet group portrait, the fired advisers' tarantula accounts in hardback, the four fat magazines, the famished opinion journals, policy soft-bounds sent gratis. She and her kind checked the top lines and bylines of the same three op-ed pages, one of which Mabel contributed to every third Sunday. She was the woman's voice, the diversion from the trade imbalance, election reform, judicial nomination, and corruption columns.

She found daytime the hardest but welcomed November. Avoiding her dauphins Leonard, George, and Robert was no longer her chief occupation. They had moved to dormitories at distinguished schools. Robert, the youngest, had lectured her on drinking the September morning he left, noting with begrudging deference that she'd not imposed one major embarrassment on the family for three entire months, and he had downgraded her condition to alcohol abuser from incipient alcoholic. George, the proto-environmentalist, informed her she'd cut back on dishonesty this summer—keep it up, don't backslide, yoga helps, and other such whimsies. Leonard, in his second or third chapter of not speaking to her, broke his silence to say he would not be coming home for Thanksgiving or Christmas.

Yet their absence emptied her. Today, Don was away from the home. He had gone to the Hill. She couldn't quite believe he went to the Hill. It was a place for miscellaneous yearners—coastal summa graduates, Southerners proud of accents, aides in awe at the process, crimson suits on pantyhose legs making the case for moneyed perspectives, bloggers spearing mice. They were all fine people. They were, she insisted. What could be more understandable than going to the Dairy Queen if it was soft ice cream you craved? What was the harm in it? Were these places meant to be Jefferson and Hamilton's laboratories, workshops for great experiments on the capacities of mankind? They were dance halls. They were bulletin boards. Their doings were Parcheesi.

So be it, and grandly too. Yearners more than deserved their time. Time, after Darwin, was the only munificence left to anyone. With no heaven to behave for, if a girl wanted to strut through chambers past panoramas of idealized national loft, it was her birthright. Mabel remembered her smooth days on the Hill—how senators perused her, how staffers maneuvered her, how women hated and talked, and a few desired. It had all been a shock, and now it was sentiment and nostalgia of old tulle veils.

Don, on the Hill—it made her fond, almost, toward him. His memories, she said to herself with a bullhorn. His memories! Could he go up to the Hill to relive them? That, *that* was unseemly. If he could have managed ill-advised, caution-exhausted love with a woman in no way at all resembling her—that she could respect. Then again, he might just be doing just that. The thought of it cheered her immeasurably. It might be possible to finish her column a day early. She climbed the stairs to her office, listening to the creaking of the old wood beneath the Persian runners. She decided to step back down one step and replay the creaking. Then up one she went, listening. Then back down, comparing. She pivoted there for a while and realized she could reproduce the sound, but not always. This old house was mined with diversion. She put a hand on the wall. There was a herringbone pattern beneath the lacquered white, as if someone had painted over indented wallpaper. It was only here, on the stairs. The rest of the rooms were smooth. Her fingernail bumped down the angled grooves in a crazy-cat way. What a marquise of dawdle she was! She hurried now, down the hall to her second-floor office, lined with books.

At the keyboard, lassitude arrived. She was injected with it; her bloodstream had slowed to algae in jelly. It was the column. There on her laptop it was—the dreaded, half-written, beseechingly awfully conceived latest proof of her fraudulence, of her incapacity to craft anything more than a few hundred words, to reach any farther than a cocktail napkin, to focus any longer than the time it took to shower and shampoo. The column was about the peregrination of grown children to college campuses in the fall, the complexity of expectations and the inevitability of loss, the affirmations retrievable despite the complexities, and the ways in which these personal reflections were actually political reflections, parables about the way we live now.

If only she could lance her eyes. Blindness would be preferable to finishing and filing. She peeked at it, just a little, but enough to catch, "On a personal level and as a matter of social policy . . ." Oh, it stung. To this pass she had come. No, that was wrong. She had been at this malingering stretch every three weeks for the last many years. This column was no worse than any other. The use of her children, the summoning of the bittersweet, the unrepentant manufacturing of a personal drama or two—she'd done it all before, happily, breezily, as indefatigably as a pompom float with televised mummers. The paper put up with her—at first she thought it was because of Don, but then she decided it was because they needed a woman, and it was only quite recently she had realized that they quite honestly believed she was good. Not just that, but that she was in possession, as the editorial-page editor informed her over lunch, of an instinctive understanding of human nature and the nature of power. Her moral impecuniousness and vice-caked stratagems had left her happy, healthy, and wise, afloat in coin and praise.

She pushed away from the desk. It was late morning. There was nothing to do but nap. She curled into a sofa, held a pillow, and knew that sleep, so recently just finished, would still come.

Vera watched Mitch walk across the Room to his desk when he'd been, at least as of 1:15 p.m., trounced. A story about the report was on CNN, and CNN was on every television screen, angling downward from ceiling-high shelves across the Room. Reporters and editors were standing around the screen in their vicinity, engrossed, nodding with lips pressed, performing the head tilt that signified dismay to be working at the chump paper of the moment combined with the anticipation that came from knowing someone's hindquarters, not their own, were soon to be on carving wood. Rejoicing detractors were bouncing e-mails back and forth like overamped chimps. Since no one dayside ever e-mailed Vera, she knew of this the way she knew of everything, through Stanley. *Mitch, the old sock, is in trouble.* A little later, Stanley added, *Be nice to him if you can.*

Vera saw Adam glued to the TV, not far from her marooned desk, and now Martina Welk, the National editor, who never came to this part of the Room, was approaching. Mitch, newly transferred to the Foreign Desk, had a seat right next to Vera. Her desk was at the border between Metro and Foreign.

Why didn't they use the new Pentagon hire on this? The rationale of most decisions was a mystery to her. But she was pleased too. She had not yet seen such a big story up close, to get a feel for how the Room really worked.

"What do you have?" Martina asked Mitch when she got to him. Adam had left the television, making his way to Mitch. Vera couldn't imagine withstanding such pressure. Her inner scolding was bad enough.

"I'll be able to advance it," Mitch told Martina. Vera couldn't read anything from his delivery of this sentence. She vowed to practice that kind of presentation in front of the mirror in her dance studio. It seemed an all-body performance—a full exploration in physical terms of self-assured boredom.

She watched Martina intercept Adam and say, "He can match it and advance it." Vera wondered why Martina's attitude—an extravagantly unflappable mirthlessness—was extolled. It was almost like Mitch's, but it had less impatience in it. Vera added it into her poses to practice.

"Good," Adam said. "Good." His version of the tone was different yet again. It popped a question into Vera's head: had he ever been in love? It was impossible, given the temperature of his voice. This was a big story, wasn't it? Vera looked around. She could feel excitement. But she couldn't, as Stanley often instructed her to, find the details that conveyed it. You can't just say it was exciting, he often advised. Were eyes open wide? Were feet tapping? What did you *see*?

Vera watched Mitch closely. He disconnected his headset. He signed on. Vera twisted a little to read. There was already a message, Martina saying, *Can you have a top for me for the 2 o'clock?* He messaged, *Yes.* He looked at his watch. He opened a file with phone numbers and contacts.

The calls went poorly. One contact was out of the office for two weeks, checking in for messages; Mitch left one. Another was hospitalized with elective surgery. Mitch called all three major hospitals, found the room number, called, and got no answer. A third was in a meeting. The fourth was on the other line. The fifth took the call and commiserated but couldn't contribute. The sixth was swamped, in the middle of markups, couldn't talk until five. The seventh gave him the name of someone in an attorney's office who knew someone on the committee who'd boasted about the report. The eighth gave him the name of a man she'd hired whom the committee had interviewed just last night, and they'd brought up the report; she was sure the guy was listed. Fifteen minutes: gone. He had only twenty minutes until the two o'clock meeting. Vera couldn't actually see his anxiety. Maybe her pulse was too quick.

Mabel was talking with Jonathan Strasser. That was what her ears told her. Her mouth also seemed to be participating. He was saying words. She was hearing them. She said something, but he kept saying something, and more than once. What? What? She tried to pull herself upright, but her arm or her hand was numb. Well, she did have a phone in this hand. What? Had he said that or had she?

"Are you asleep?" Oh, that was him. Mother Teresa, she'd been napping. Her column. The algae.

"No," said her newly arriving pride. "I just got back from the dentist."

"The dentist?"

"Novocain." She had to get away from this pillow and off the sofa. "Hold on."

She uncoiled herself and looked for the clock. Not there. She pulled herself over to the computer and looked in the lower right corner. It was one-forty. "Yes, can you please come back in about five minutes? I have a call," she said to the empty air. "Right. Absolutely." She drew out some silence, moving some papers on her desk, giving herself a ten-second count.

"Jonathan!" she finally said into the phone, and remembering her Novocain ruse, she added a left cheek of marbles to her voice.

"I'm so sorry. Look, you sound terrible. Maybe—"

"I'm fine. Fine. It wasn't root canal. Just a filling."

"That's good."

"I should be talking normally any minute now," she said, losing interest precipitously in her acting foray. She looked at the clock.

"So how are you?"

The rumors of loyalty to ill wife were wrong, and look: she'd napped herself into a baffle.

"Good. Good. Say, listen," Jonathan Strasser said.

"Say, listen"? That was not the locution of a man tempted to reinterpret vows. "Uh-huh," Mabel tried.

"This may sound strange."

"Nothing sounds strange to me," she said.

"I guess you've heard—from Don, I mean—if . . ." began Jonathan Strasser.

She could feel her lungs puncture, a sewing needle opening her chest. A sound like air leaking from inner tubes came to her.

". . . about my problem." She gasped, stunted, impaired into meekness. He continued, "The report. That I gave to Don."

No love walked here. No desire. Her radar was antique. It picked up caterwauls and train whistles.

As if on a sickening carousel, she remembered talking to him by the bookcase at the dinner party. What night was it? What month of the summer? Was it hot enough for air conditioning? No, it was fall, it was September—yes, it was two months ago, hot enough for summer, but Labor Day past. She slowly remembered how most of what he had said that night fell outside recognizable channels of thinking. It was happening again. Maybe this meant something of import. That he could so rearrange her senses—it had to mean something.

"Have you been watching television?" he asked. She flapped around, only with less strength. This was utterly nonsensical. Television? He rushed to fill the shortest of silences, saying, "No. Of course not. That was dumb of me."

It wasn't as dumb as she. She thought again—Don told her; *on television*. She looked around her study for the remote. There, it was on the floor. She picked it up. CNN lit the room, muted. Headline News was on sports. No help there.

"It's all over television," Jonathan Strasser said. He sounded excited. Was he panting? "It's—well, I guess I'm to blame, because I went to the other paper, I was frustrated, Don kept saying he would use it, early, you know, before the book, and then, when he didn't, and I felt I had no options, and I went to him, and he said, It's your decision, I would like it if you didn't, it's not part of our agreement—we never had an agreement. He only mentioned an 'agreement' when I was dissatisfied. Not dissatisfied, that's too strong, when I was worried. Worried that it was just not soon enough. I learned, I talked to some people, his book is not on any fast track, and then I heard from some friends of mine at OMB that he might have finagled sitting in on principals meetings, a rumor, nothing more, and I thought, My God, and what I said to my wife, I said, 'This thing has gone on too long,' and today, today, when it finally got moving, it was not at all what I expected."

Mabel switched channels on the remote. Soap operas, cooking class, *This Old House*—there, there it was. It had gone beyond CNN. It was on one channel. It was on the next channel. And the next. She didn't even bother to turn up the sound.

It was the Sissy report. The report her white-browed former secretary of state had opined about—the report she had casually wanted and forgotten about since. But Strasser had not been at that dinner party. He had come to another dinner party, a later party. With quavering clarity, she saw the scene anew: she was by the bookcases, and she had tried to understand Strasser's fondling of the agricultural-policy book, only gradually understanding it was his daughter's, not his wife's, and Don had come, and his mouth—something looked funny about her husband's way of talking.

Don's mouth, she remembered now. She had taken it for a new awkwardness. But it was something else altogether. Don had been grateful. And Jonathan Strasser was the object of his obeisance.

"So you're looking for Don," Mabel said. "I'm afraid I'll have to take a message, because he's up on the Hill." Her talking was problematic, but now its clotting had nothing to do with play-acting.

"Mabel, I was looking for you."

．　．　．

Will Holmes, walking, glanced at his office door, on which was Scotch-taped the white piece of paper that gave his title, *Director of Information Technology*. It was contrived to mean almost anything. As was the name of the key component where he worked—Media Exploitation Component Services, or MECS. In another time, it would have been called his cover. In this time, it was a fundamentally functioning job. He legitimately had oversight for at least a hundred information technologies. The cover of the past—professor or consultant—contributed too little. And these days a code-word job, even the choicest of those jobs—Chair—was not enough of a contribution to the infinite war. He was two men in one place. One thing stood. This person, this Will Holmes, inhabited a Virginia office building with an Applebee's in the basement.

MECS occupied one floor. It was not listed in the front-lobby directory. In the elevator, its floor's button was key-activated. Once out of the elevator, there was no logo on a wall. There was a reception area, but there were no magazines in it, no seats for waiting visitors, and no receptionist, only an armed guard. To his right was a door with two combination locks, two key locks, and, behind it, two doors with their locks and combinations—but the guard possessed none of the keys and none of the combinations. Past the doors were cubicles and the warren of semi-padded passages they created in any office. A sign reminded employees that they were transitioning from a nonclassified area to a classified area. It was in this interregnum that the onset of lying began.

At his desk, Will put his landline's receiver back in its cradle. He did it the way he used to put his son down. He remembered studying infant skin, so recently in the world, and wondering. When would this one die? And how? And whose loved one would have to die so Will's might live? It was hard for him to see anything without reckoning the sacrifice needed for its existence. He looked at the phone with a similar sobriety, not directly at it, but at its news—that Hoseyn was gone. Dead, of course, although some of Will's colleagues, friends, associates, buddies—what could he call the only people in his life who knew pieces of the truth of his life?—disappeared. Some of them were in compartments he was not permitted to understand or hear about, even after the compartments had been folded down and taken away.

What had always struck him was that the laws of nature disallowed destruction. The wood, burning in the beaker, became gas and carbon. In the laboratory, form changed, but essence, if the right instruments measured the right matter, remained. Even in the black world, the disintegrated programs and operations eventually gave way to some one or two or more things. No thing, living or dead, could escape leaving its mark. Yet didn't his superiors try to make out as if it didn't?

Hoseyn was Iranian. He was thirty-eight, Will's age, and the age at which, Will had begun to notice, so many in his world died. Hoseyn was not a soldier, far from it. He was a nuclear engineer. He lived without conjecture or speculation. A thing worked or it did not work. If one could predict that a thing worked, one had wisdom, which for Hoseyn meant the legitimate possession of power. Will remembered a conversation with him four years ago in Vienna. Hoseyn explained that his faith was Persian, older than the Israelites; his people were called Zoroastrians. *Hear the best with your ears and ponder with a bright mind.* It was Hoseyn's favorite, a proverb his mother had taught him.

Hoseyn now was calcium and oxygen and dioxide, bodiless and exploded, still wet, not close to dust. Hoseyn's family would hear, but they would be told he died in a way that was not the way he died, in a place he had not been, on a day different from the day when he was killed, and for reasons not the reasons someone had killed him.

Will accepted. He didn't thrash. He only just grieved. He could mourn, but he knew that conscious loss would take away from the time, so brief, that he had in which to try to help the still-living. It was they, the not yet dead, who haunted him. Each time he drank a beer, or went to a movie, or washed his car, or sent an e-mail, or bought a tie, or fell asleep, he knew, because of his distractions, that someone would die—perhaps horribly, like the hostages of beheaders; or accidentally, like the mother whose path a bomb from the sky found; or haplessly, like the Polish secret agent speeding through a checkpoint with a hostage, who had notified the armed young Americans, except for the one soldier preoccupied during the briefing about his stillborn baby born to his lonely wife.

Information—to no one's surprise, ever—could kill. Information—in this new time—accomplished more. When a bad guy made a beheading video, his ski mask didn't hide him. His video encoded the ambient light from which an electrical grid could be traced. If the United States had F-16s, then the ground, on which walked children, supplied ammunition more lethal than the F-16s': the story of how the United States killed innocents, however unintentionally. If an ally joined a convoy, if a daughter died in a raid—then communicating was more important than readiness, than mastery, than firepower. Killing allies and daughters crippled the United States. Mistaking them for enemy stole moral ground. Forgiveness was in short supply if America was mightiest. Perhaps that was why to understand and be understood, the province of intimacy, kitchen, bedroom, and nursery, had migrated to combat, and across a short bridge to power. Will had realized this long ago and so became the person men in charge needed. He was one of the many crucial specialists modern life required. He'd never been able to apply his mother's genius for closeness to his personal life, where it belonged. He brought it to the battlefield.

He'd gotten so far from her that he often repeated to himself—usually before he phoned her—the links that joined and now separated them. He became a soldier because he was a sliding student. It was the army or joining his father in a field, his classmates in the factory. Farmhand or machinist couldn't whisk her to Paris, her fantasy. He was a middling recruit. (She didn't care.) He would never have lasted, he knew, in the regular corps. That was *her*, dabbed tight in him. He was an army hater during the Gulf War. They even talked about it when he got back, how dumb moves got yellow ribbons, how it was all heroes, no matter how it went. His father overhead them, didn't agree. That was a fine war, he said.

He'd seen his father as a slow moe, a get-along. She was the one who wanted to heat up ambition in Will like mother love in biscuits. Or maybe it was army softcore, its pamby acceptance of mediocrity, that made him bleed for the special unit. Kidnaps, hijacks, rescues, kills. Best, the unit was isolated; whether you fucked up or did well, no one knew. That, for Will, fit. Only two men a year got in. Women weren't welcome. It had no name, until, sometime after the Pablo Escobar capture or Noriega's seizure, the Pentagon called it Special Operations Forces Detachment Delta.

At first, Will wasn't much. His first kill was a muff. He stayed, undistinguished and dipshit, through places: Lebanon, Somalia, Rwanda, Kosovo. It wasn't until code names—Knight Fist, Quiet Night, Gray Fox, others—that he stood up, looked around, and saw he was often in the running, but didn't have the last push in him, was more comfortable in reverse. Blend in—that was the masculine Holmes agenda.

He had to act like Mom, or someone who, like his, longed for a little more. It went down from there. He was still a teammate, but not quite a team player. Jokes, joshes, and games with the guys lost charm. He made the Blue Angels—the corps of jumpers who dived from aircraft and landed feet-first on a nickel in a field. He grew into a geek—detailed on and off to the National Security Agency, HQ for intercepts and surveillance. He got pushed to be spook-trained at the Farm with college boys bound for the CIA.

You think you can do it all? He heard that. Lucky enough, the fog of war, over Will's career, got replaced by the All Source Analysis System. It rapidly correlated large volumes of combat information and sensor reports to produce a composite, nearly real-time picture of the multi-dimensional battlespace. All a field commander needed was temporary information dominance: something to allow him to distinguish between a bus of children and a line of tanks. It didn't always work but not because the enemy had figured out how to foil it.

One of Will's inventions had been tested and proved in Iraq. They called it the Prophet system. Prophet allowed commanders not only to understand their battlespace but to paint it. It gave them a comprehensive picture of electronic emitters—on a portable computer screen that hacked surreptitiously into enemy satellite software. But above and beyond all-source analysis, it also let commanders locate, select, and *interfere* from that screen with emitters that aerial reconnaissance couldn't penetrate fast enough. (Prophet was a dedicated, dynamically retaskable asset with the capability to look wide, as well as deep. That's how he told generals about it.) Prophet could electronically attack a signal to stop its transmittal. It could replace a signal with the signal of a field commander's choice. Enemy would think he heard his own side. Enemy would be hearing foolery. Reality, because of Will, had become fungible.

Fewer died. That meant the dead came individually. To those who didn't know them—the sentimental, suggestible public—these dead were anonymous and overlooked. The dead were wholly unlike the black wall of names weighted enough to sink in ground, the monument for the war that stood watch over this one and every one he'd fought. So these, in this war, could keep dying. Protest stayed at that minimum that reflected badly on an ungrateful few. Only those who wanted to serve took bullets. The coffins were sequestered, secluded in the name of reverence, hard to photograph. The widows and mothers lived everywhere, and nowhere near each other. They took comfort in the flag.

Prophet didn't get him promoted. It was multitasking. The Twin Towers and the Pentagon showed him off. Here was the Joe who would have infiltrated the plot, intercepted the planes, parachuted the roof with wire ladders to choppers to save doomed bankers. If the Chair at the time had only known how to use Will. What if Will were the Chair? He'd know. He'd stop. He'd show.

So Pentagon made Will Chair. He went from being an operator in one compartmented program at a time to seeing all programs at all times. It felt glory and guts to him at first. Then he saw he didn't care for politicians; he could stand only a little more their appointees. They were his mornings and afternoons. All they wanted was for the press to get better. They didn't care if a man or a nurse or a dog bone got left dead in-country. As for secret ops, they only wanted to know everything about the ones that failed. They only asked after their own pet ideas. They didn't feel like knowing the big secret picture. That was left to him.

He looked at the phone on his desk. For the first time since he had sat in this office without characteristics, Will felt its impersonality like a presence. He wished for a photograph of anyone he knew on a wall. Oh, there were photographs—of a group of men golfing, of an official dinner with handshaking, a family picnic. Will had been digitized into the jolly golfers and into a center seat at the banquet table. The children at the picnic—they were not his.

The fakery goaded him. Who could get into this sanctum? He knew that anyone good enough to reach this far would not have come to find Will Holmes's mementos.

He had to stand. He walked over to the window, made of a refracting glass that jumbled the room's interior to outside viewers. He thought of punching it. If he did, there would be a wail, the alarm for the component. It would bring the director, weapon in hand. Others would follow—Will's secretary, who was not a civilian; his deputy, who had orders to fire if a breach sounded; and the linguists on his staff, who were armed. Will imagined standing there, feeling the outdoors on his offending hand. He'd say, "This is for Hoseyn." It wasn't a suicide wish. He wanted more than a trace, readable only to a few, to note Hoseyn's passing. He wanted a detonation so unlikely, so out of the regimented order of his own life, that it would reach, if only for the least minimum of measurable time, out of the black world. Black, the unclassified representation of a code word.

He looked out the window at the suburban reality—minivan at his building's entrance, cars in traffic to the east, Pier 1 Imports across the roadway. Nature was a squirrel in a nursery-grown tree.

Where were the lions? Flies had chased them off. Flies had built a bomb that was Pebbles and Bamm-Bamm—the improvised explosive device. High gadgetry couldn't find an IED, let alone paint it. When someone, not him, wrote the words that lasted, IED would be one of them. They would say a great nation was felled by acronym. They would say Prophet won and so soon later lost. They would want to know why a people of ingenuity, who could minimize their dead, who caused more dead to their enemies, could not write themselves as victors, and still be hated for being victors.

Mabel felt sure the phone jumped in her hand. She must have misheard Jonathan Strasser. She wanted to shout "What?" or ask him to repeat what he'd said, but she was as stiff as a Laplander.

"In your column, I think there's a way that you could write this thing, the way it will matter, the way it will have the right impact," Strasser said. He was talking with the forward motion of a cartoon cannonball. "I'm asking you to do something that, frankly, I think you'd be crazy to do, and if someone asked me to betray my husband—or, I mean, my wife—of course, I'd be plenty offended, and normally, of course, I wouldn't ask anyone, let alone Mabel Cannon. But I had this funny feeling—I can't believe I am actually saying this, but at this point it really doesn't matter—that you were, I don't know, trying to tell me something that night by the bookcase. You've probably long ago forgotten."

"I haven't forgotten," she said.

"Really. Well. Okay. Did Don—he must have mentioned that I gave him the report."

"He didn't."

"Okay. That's—well, I suppose, with both of you in the same line of work . . ."

"Jonathan, where do you work?"

"Me? You mean you don't honestly know?"

"No. I really don't know."

"The Normal State of Consciousness."

"The what?" Her hearing was a problem. Christ and saints.

"Oh, sorry. That's just what my wife and I call it. The NSC."

The National Security Council. Don and she did not make up such things. She tried to imagine a marriage where such conspiracies and pet names were hatched. It was monks and nuns at the Grady household, where government was concerned. At least, it was for Don. She'd gone along. Not entirely. But more entirely than she'd realized. She chewed on her lip. "Oh. Oh. Okay. So you wrote the report, the one that's all over the news?"

"Oh no. I didn't write it. I just got it. Or—someone got it to me. It wouldn't have been something I would be able to see. It was outside my area."

"What is your area?"

"Former Soviet Union states. Ukraine. Georgia."

"So why would someone give the report to you?"

"One of the mysteries. I can't believe Don didn't tell you all this."

"Well, he didn't."

This Strasser—who enjoyed his wife, a woman who was an authentic mate to him—Mabel had never bothered to imagine. But he, Strasser, he did imagine. And he imagined more for her than she had for herself. He imagined her in a marriage of shared confidences. He imagined her work to be useful.

"Uh, Mabel, are you listening?"

"What, what do you want to do about all this—I mean, today?"

"I'd like to give you the report. I'd like to talk to you about it. I was hoping you could get something in tomorrow's paper. Not a column, obviously."

"I don't do that kind of thing. That's not opinion. It's . . ." She remembered when she had done that kind of thing. It occurred to her, just then, that she had not even been curious what the report said. Or what the other paper said that it said.

"What's the other paper saying that you don't like, Jonathan? Are they wrong? I mean, just a little bit, or completely wrong?"

"It's not wrong—it's just, they've seized on one little thing, this thing about the president being under surveillance, a thing that doesn't matter, that happens all the time anyway, but isn't widely—well—

appreciated, and the things that do matter, the new things, they've ignored them."

"Where are you right now?"

"I'm at work."

"Let's meet at a bar, it's called Stoney's. It's on L, around Thirteenth Street Northwest."

"I've never heard of it," Strasser said.

"That's why we're going there," Mabel explained. "No one we know would go there."

"I could be there in twenty minutes."

"How long is this thing?"

"The executive summary is several hundred pages. The whole thing, we're talking about boxes. But I have it on DVDs."

"They probably didn't even read it—at the other paper. When did you give it to them?"

"Yesterday."

"My husband's had it all summer."

"I know that!"

"He doesn't put these things in the paper. You must know that. It's for his book," Mabel said.

"He must have read it."

"He has a lot of assistants."

"He wouldn't fob this off on one of them."

"He would have had to—anything that long. People give him records, documents, downloads all the time. It's not humanly possible to read it all."

"But I told him what was important. He didn't have to read the whole thing."

"For whatever reason, my husband thought your take on the important parts was off-base. And, from a news standpoint, he could be right. So could the other paper. What looks like news to you, inside, isn't always news to newspapers. You know that. Come on."

"We'll see if you think that after you read it."

He couldn't explain anything to her anymore. His mother was a liberal, although Will saw her trying to hide it. Sometimes negative things would come out, and she would have liked to ask about them. His father must have stopped her. Or something inside her did, something in her that appreciated the trip to Paris he'd given her, a week of glum for him. Did she see that? It was hard to know what got grasped, even between two people who should have known each other better than anyone.

Used to be, she'd cut out the newspaper stories that ran anything about intelligence. Soon enough, she had so many, and there was so much of it unread, she couldn't make sense of what he'd try to remind her was his part. Electronics, any story about electronics—that was about all she could say she retained.

He realized in this new time that if Sissy got updates on *everything* that was sensitive and compartmented, they'd read through next to none of it. Staffers in the past would be up all night with reports like that, but he'd noticed since 9/11 that more and more didn't stay up to speed. He could mention something in one of the Sissy updates, and he could tell they were *pretending* to have read about it.

It was better to give out the whole shebang. So he did that. And instead of trying to find the NSC guy who'd gotten his hands on the Sissy updates, Will gave them to another NSC guy. This guy gave them to one of the papers. But he told them what the Sissy updates *meant*. And they believed him. The interpretation of the report was the reality. No one at a news organization had time to read the full report and think it through.

They'd had the stuff for over a week, and here, today, they were writing about White House surveillance, just as Will had wanted them to. And though they had everything about Will's Potomac Pilot fuckup— they weren't writing about it. Like his mother, they could only remember so much. They were mostly interested in Recognizable Place-Names, like the White House.

The old way—telling editors not to publish—was a limping strategy. Ultimately, they published. Maybe not right away but sooner than he'd ever wanted. White House surveillance sounded like scandal, and it would take time to sort out if it were, and even if it were, it would drift aside, just as his mother forgot about his work. They lived in a fuzzed-over way.

It was five to two. Vera had done some checking in Mitch's public queue, where he stored computer files anyone could access. He had no top.

She had seen the message from Martina: *I really need you to take the top out of your private queue.*

She had watched him message back: *I need more time.*

Suddenly Mitch picked up his phone as if he had just gotten a call. But it hadn't rung. He waited a few seconds, then messaged, *On fone.* Vera detected a cringe as he sent it. What if Martina come over to his desk, put her hands on Mitch's keyboard, and started typing the commands to take the top of the story out of his private queue? The Metro editor had done it once to Vera—and, yes, Martina was getting up and walking toward his desk, where she would quickly see that the lights on his phone indicated he was not on the phone at all.

Vera feared for him. She watched as Mitch opened a file and began typing nonsense strings of words into it with the phone wedged between his ear and his right shoulder. This would mean Martina would have to push him away from the keyboard and might, if she typed the commands, erase Mitch's "notes." That's what the Metro editor had done to Vera.

But then it happened. Mitch's phone *did* ring. He was so unprepared for it that he banged his elbow against the desk. He quickly pressed the second-line button, and Vera watched it light up a welcome green.

"Mitch?" The voice was so loud Vera could hear it exactly.

"Yes," Mitch said.

"It's Eugene."

"Thanks for calling. I appreciate it."

"You should know something," this Eugene said. "This is personal. I'm not talking to you officially."

"Understood."

"Are you taking notes? Because, if you are, I want you to stop."

Mitch let his fingers rest on the keyboard.

"They're wrong," Eugene said.

"Who is?"

"The other paper."

"Have you seen the report?"

"That's all I'm going to say."

"That doesn't help me."

"That's all I'm going to say to you, Mitch. As a friend."

"You've read the paper's Web site?"

That created a pause.

"You're trying to get me to say more."

"Eugene. You can't do this to me."

"I have read the paper's Web site."

"Can I use this off the record?"

"What does that mean in this situation?"

"I would say an intelligence official said the account of the report published in the other paper was incorrect."

"No, you can't use it off the record."

"On background?"

"And your definition of that today is?"

"I can use it, but I can't attribute it to anyone, not even a military official. I have to get more people besides you to say that."

"That's fair-minded of you."

"Eugene. You know that's how it works."

"So you pressure other people, get them to say the other paper's account of the report is wrong."

"What's with you? Pressure? Pressure? I ask them."

"Do you say to them, I have this from someone on background?"

"Yes."

"You can't use it that way, then."

"Then there's really no point in telling me," Mitch said. Vera felt he was angry now. He needed Eugene to tell him. Eugene held the jack for Mitch's oh-so-flat tire. It was nothing to Eugene to tell him. Please, please, please, Vera was saying to herself, please, tell him.

"At least you'll know. That's the best I can do. Bye for now."

Vera looked at Mitch. She felt her nose tingle, her eyes burning. Mitch was screwed. Totally, totally screwed. He was blinking an awful lot. It was as if he couldn't believe what his ears told him.

Everyone in the Room was phoning—after two o'clock, the racing that was putting stories together had begun. Anyone who didn't have a story was feeling antsy about being lazy. Vera did. Her colleagues were byline counters, almost all of them. The more you had, the more valuable you were. The more stories, the more praise, the more good, good, good, everything is good.

She cared more for Mitch than for measuring up. And wait, Martina—she was—where? Vera stretched to see. She looked at the clock. It was almost ten after two. Could it be? Yes, Martina had gone to the meeting without stopping by Mitch's desk. This was reprieve and relief. It might even get him through the next hour.

Stoney's served wine in juice glasses. At three-fifteen, Jonathan and Mabel were the only customers. Strasser put two stacks of DVDs on their table.

"This is the Sissy report," he said.

He was muscular, a rarity among White House staffers. Was he broad-shouldered? She wondered what the suit jacket was doing to her impression of him. Most likely exaggerating it. That was the point of it.

"I Googled you," he said. "You were a reporter before you married Don."

He was drinking tap water. She'd ordered Coca-Cola.

"Right, that's right," she got out.

"Don doesn't give things like this to the paper?"

This again.

"No," she said. "Sometimes, yes. Yes."

"It's newsworthy."

"Have *you* ever been a reporter?"

"Not a possibility." He looked slightly—yes—offended. "But my wife—my wife is. For a Tokyo newspaper."

A Japanese wife. Mabel—large eyes and plush lips—would never appeal to Jonathan Strasser. She went slack. The afternoon stretched ahead. There was little for it.

"Why doesn't Don give," Strasser said, "something, something of this magnitude—the paper, the paper he works for, doesn't get it? I guess I don't. I don't get it."

"He wants to save it for the book. To make it, you know, revelatory."

"And they let him? I mean, the paper does?"

"They don't like it. But he's Don Grady, so"—she shrugged—"he can." A plenitude of boredom began its dinging. She would always be asked to speak of Don Grady. She was the dwarf satellite of Don Grady. She would never not fuck Don Grady.

"He controls what we hear."

"Um. Not really. Look. What is it the other paper is missing? I mean, why, or what, do you want me to—like you said earlier—write about? Just, just, why?"

"Because the other paper believes everything the administration tells them."

The consensus. Common knowledge. She swam in it. "And?"

"And because it describes Media Exploitation Component Services, and the guy who runs their information technology. That's one thing. One thing he does. By far the least important thing he does."

The bartender had put her cola on the Formica station, and the waitress was picking it up.

"You know—hold on," she said. "Hold on, Jonathan, if you could."

She got up and walked toward the waitress with her cola on a tray. "Restroom?" she asked. She knew where it was. But Strasser didn't know that. Then, closer in, near the girl's ear, she whispered, "Could you get me a larger glass, less ice, and a shot or two of vodka?" The waitress didn't even nod, just put up her eyebrows and turned around. Mabel returned to the table in time to realize she should have gone to the restroom.

"It can't really be called that," she said, flustered, hoping to cover with impatience. She added disbelief. "What did you say? 'Media Exploitation Services'?"

Strasser was pleased, smiling for some reason. "Media Exploitation Component Services," he said. "It's called that. Exactly that. You can find it online."

"But that's ridiculous. They wouldn't, not even now, they wouldn't go *that* far."

"They're not exploiting your paper. Or any media outlet. 'Media' is military-speak for any kind of, well, media—DVDs, videotape, hard drives, photographs, government documents, legal records, I guess even newspapers. But that's not what they're picking up in Iraq, Afghanistan, or Pakistan, basically wherever. Soldiers find hard drives, suicide videos, that type of thing. It has to go somewhere for analysis. Before, it was haphazard, went to whichever service found it—army, navy—and, like, you know, got lost and never used right. And the vice-president insisted on this centralized center, and the secretary of defense wanted it too, and Sissy—the Senate Select Committee on Intelligence—listened. They recommended it. They got a budget appropriation. It exists. It 'exploits' the stuff soldiers find."

"Reasonable. Perfectly reasonable."

"It is."

The spiked cola had arrived. Mabel felt Strasser looking at her, not casually. She pushed the glass a few inches. She didn't have to drink it.

"So," she said.

"So." He seemed undecided about something.

"What?" She would just ask.

"You're not a reporter anymore."

"Right."

"A columnist."

She took the cola now and drank it.

"The people who stay in it, the people who don't become columnists," Strasser began.

She drank another sip. Smiled at him. She'd been told she had a phenomenal mouth, and maybe even for this uxorious hare of a man she did.

"This guy, he's one of the ones who stay in it," he continued, not looking at her, moving his hand to the side of the table. He held it and said, "He becomes a manager. Not because he wants to, but because it works out that way."

"A manager of videos? Analyzing videos?"

"No, no. That's just his public job. This guy was an operator."

Her mind went to pop music, *Smooth operator, he's a smooth operator.* And down to Washington melodeon—mailbox drops, trench coats on a bench at the Lincoln, parking-garage meetings, one foxy assassin. People in love with unnecessary circumspection fostered it, and one of them was her husband. But had he encouraged it? Or been the one true one who fell into it? Maybe she was the skulking impostor, the derivative. She chose this dive.

"He's an operator," she said. "He works for—unclear. A novel could say he's a spy."

"He started as a soldier."

"They often do. Does he have a name?"

"In the Sissy report? No."

"He's just information-technology director."

"Of Media Exploitation Component Services," Strasser said. He sipped his water.

"He's an iron major—not a political appointee."

"An operational person. A creative person. But this guy, from what I've picked up, he looks up to the graybeards—some people call them Knights of Malta."

Purple bookers, iron majors, invisibles, operators, graybeards, Knights of Malta were pirouetting and skywalking across her smut and pearled brain. She'd wanted love, the engulfing kind. Instead, it was

Ludlum and Paterson and airport Bantam books; she could see that spry little rooster on the spine.

"Anyway," Strasser was saying. "I don't know his name. The Sissy report doesn't give it. Except there's something, a little, small window. In one part of the updates, there's a series of e-mails, and in one of them, no, it may be two—you have to check this—he's called 'the Chair.' "

"What does this have to do with the other paper?"

"They don't care about this guy. But they should."

"And Don didn't either." Now she *was* impatient. Her glass was empty.

She heard someone hit a nail into the wall. The bartender was gone. Waitress was too. Something banged again.

"You've been drinking Coke—and vodka," he said. He looked amused. But maybe like one of her sons. She stared at him.

"I have," she said, her expression uncharitable, maybe hostile. Yes, she felt mean. "So this guy—he screwed you over, didn't he?" she said. She knew this tale. The origin of all leakage: wounded pride, the career sidelined.

"Never met him."

"You don't need to, not in this town."

"Do you and Don talk? At all?" He murmured this—a little sadly, she thought.

Mabel, annoyed, said rather loudly, "What do you think?"

Strasser was as still as a stick. She looked around. Waitress had vanished. But no, there was the bartender. He waved.

Mabel signaled back. She wanted another. What did she expect? Agricultural subsidies—that's what Strasser was skipping proud about that night in her hallway.

"Can you hang on? Don't lose that thought," Mabel said, getting up and going to the bar as the bartender moved in their direction. He had an apron on and was clicking the channel changer; he muted the television and turned her way.

"You believe this shit?" He shook his head.

"Can I have one of your rum-and-Cokes?" That took her back. She used to come here before she married Don and order these with a gang of reporters who had wanted to change the world and didn't work at the paper anymore.

"I mean, they put the White House under surveillance," the bartender said. "The president called the head of the CIA a marionette. Some general said something to the effect that he would talk to the puppet master."

Mabel tilted her head. "What?"

"It's unreal. Just when you think you've heard it all."

"That's what they're focusing on," said Strasser, suddenly beside her at the bar. "The story's developed into a hunt for the origin of the surveillance, the identity of the puppet master, and other important government figures described in colorful code words in the Oval Office conversations. It's a roman à clef."

Writing, Adam didn't give a flip for writing. Being first, that was what he knew. News was fresh. If it wasn't, it wasn't news. It was history, the lazy man's way. He read history, naturally. But when he thought of all the time a historian had to look into an event—it just didn't impress Adam that a well-funded, highly educated, universally esteemed individual found out something much closer to the truth than a daily newspaperman did. The historian examined a reality about which memoirs had been written, archives opened, stakes lowered. All it took was patience. To Adam, it didn't matter by the time the adjective "painstaking" was a word of praise. It wouldn't change policy. It wouldn't have impact.

When anyone wrote a letter for a prize entry, which he used to do but now delegated, "impact" was the word. The trick was to get the investigative work done early in a year, so there would be observable impact before year's end. Impact after that—it couldn't be included in the letter accompanying the work, and so it was good, excellent, in fact, but less excellent than impact during the calendar year. You needed indictments, a congressional hearing, a regulation revision, a protest outside an institution that led to the beginning of talk of reform. He did not speak about this. He would not want to be accused of prize chasing.

But being first, it had meaning. He had stopped examining the assumption. It would have to be enough.

So, when he didn't see a top for the story about the report, and when he asked Martina after the two o'clock where it was, and she said Mitch was busy on the phone continuously, he worried. Actually, he was suspicious. He'd presided over enough pastings in his career to know the signs of being whipped by the competition. It often began with the top not materializing by three o'clock.

So here it was four-thirty in the afternoon, and still no top. Adam could not sit at his desk. He tried to see if Stanley was out there. He couldn't see past the first line of desks. Why did everyone seem to be standing at this hour? They should be on the phone, or better, out on the streets, in the field, anywhere but here. Phoning a story in, that was the way it was done when he'd started. You were out in the world. Today, they sat at desks in the Room, attached to headsets attached to phones. They were all wordsmiths now, looking for book contracts.

He was grouchy. Very grouchy. The phone rang. He let Tabitha take it.

Now she was buzzing him. She was out of step. She had no use for messaging. She was badly in need of retraining.

He picked up, annoyed.

"Adam Aaron," came her voice. How had he settled for Tabitha? She should be in the book-review section, what was left of it.

"Yes."

"Security is calling from the front lobby. They say Mabel Cannon's down there, forgot her ID, and she wants to come up. To see you. Says it's urgent."

"It's too close to deadline."

"I told them that. They just say she's causing 'a commotion.' 'Couldn't somebody please come down to the lobby and escort her to the fifth floor?' And such."

"Go down there and tell her I can't see her."

"All right, then."

The phone rang again.

"Mr. Sanger, this is Security in the front lobby. We have a situation down here."

"A situation."

"Yes, sir."

Just then his other line rang. And there was no Tabitha.

"You're going to have to hold on," Adam said. He picked up the other line.

"Adam, this is Mabel. I'm on my cell in the lobby. Would you please tell this man to let me take the elevator upstairs?"

"Mabel, this is not a good time."

"I know that. Why do you think I'm here?"

Adam couldn't quite grasp that. She was nuts. But she was Don Grady's wife.

"Put him on the line. The guard. Give him your cell phone."

"He's on the phone."

Adam was incensed. He pushed the other button for the other line.

"Let Mabel Cannon go upstairs," he said.

"Sir, I can't do that. You're going to have to come down here."

"Mabel Cannon is Don Grady's wife."

"That doesn't matter to me."

Vera went to the ladies' and splashed her face to break the nausea. She'd already had to take a walk and a smoke when Mitch busted the first-edition deadline. She'd always had a crazy stomach, but this was probably the worst case of empathy ever. It was too bad the scanner was routine and every precinct was tomblike. If she'd had one brief, even a weekender she should be starting, she might get distracted. All she had was a pile of clips to read about F-16 crashes that News Research had put together for her. Stanley thought the clips were a waste of time. Walk around the crash site, he told her. She didn't have altogether that much faith in Stanley's reporting suggestions. Plus, he couldn't seem to remember that so far not one official had been willing to tell her where the site was.

So maybe she wasn't sick for Mitch. Maybe she was queasy thinking about the pilot story. From Stanley's first assigning it to her, she hadn't been too jumped up about it. She had vague ideas how to go about it, but not many. This minute she felt failure coming for her. Look at Mitch—with decades in service, a reporter with sources as deep as earth's core; he was lost. Stanley would pish that observation. He'd say she didn't have much in the way of visible signs to prove Mitch was sinking. That gut of hers, though, it told all of her all she needed to know about Mitch's state of mind. You couldn't put that in a story though, could you? *I could feel the desperation of Mitch because my stomach was flipping.* Stanley would hit delete. He liked concrete writing. Tell it clear, like glass, he said to her once.

It was simple when you had a dead body—dissect the corpse. But here, in the fields, how to get at secrets? How to put your hand into the dirt and pull out the root? It could be twenty feet down, or twenty miles at a diagonal. And this thing that had confounded Mitch—it was a report! It was fourth-hand, fifth-hand, ten-hands, and more. A way to defer a decision. A study to make a recommendation to craft a proposal to consider a conclusion.

Before this day, Vera would have disdained getting a report. Getting a report someone else got first—like tap dancing a talent show. But she saw from watching Mitch that he would be considered less-than for this failure. She wondered how the other paper had gotten this report. Why would someone leak to one paper and not the other? If she had more experience, she might understand this government curlicue.

The number *1* flashed on Mitch's screen, announcing a new message. Vera felt woozy. Mitch pushed enter, but slowly, Vera thought, as if a gentler touch might bring a kinder message.

Any luck?

It was from the executive editor. At first she didn't recognize it as him. SANGER was his sign-on. He was, after all, just a person with a last name, like any of them. Though he was hired so long ago, only his last name was used. Did they even have computers then? Today, new hires had their first name's initial automatically attached to their last name. Vera was HASTINGSV.

Mitch pushed *n* and *o,* then enter. Vera would have put her head in her hands. Mitch remained upright.

He suppressed a burp. So he was aware he was not alone. She balked at this. He had seemed *so* unaware of the Room. She watched him reach for a can of Diet Coke that had to be warm by now. He was taking a sip—

Whoa. Adam was walking toward Mitch's desk. So was Martina, from a huddle of assistant National editors in another part of the Room. Adam's and Martina's faces looked inanimate. Their cheeks seemed stuffed with sawdust.

It was almost eight. Mitch didn't turn his head; perhaps he didn't see them. Yet his peripheral vision had to have them. He was unwilling to let anyone read his face or movements. All of Mitch would, when Adam and Martina arrived at his desk, be organized into rebuffing their disapproval. This aging, corpulent man would display this detachment with more virtuosity than any emotive dancer she'd ever admired. She saw something else. In the Room, in full sight, people like Mitch had perfected hiding the most revealing details not only in their writing but also of their own lives. It was what dance had trained out of her. She had been taught to divulge.

A whore named Baby said the pilot was a woman. Baby had been working a corner no one else worked, by the boathouse, behind the Watergate. She told Vera she'd seen men cut the pilot out of a tree and put her in an ambulance. Trying to get Baby to remember anything about the ambulance didn't work. Vera went to the Amoco at the on-ramp for I-66 more than once, sat with Baby, smoked with Baby, hoped with Baby that the same ambulance would come to get another patient. It didn't.

Even so, the breakthrough pumped Vera. What had at first been an unwelcome assignment become an engrossing quest. She called to find out which engine company had that part of the city and went down there. The guys told her they'd had nothing to do with it. When she wasn't looking, one of them took her purse and hid it in a locker. It took her a few hours to figure out that her purse was gone and Engine Company 23 was responsible and to convince one of the firefighters to tell her which locker it was and trick the prankster in such a way as to get her purse back. During the back and forth, one paramedic said that the Coast Guard was part of the pilot's rescue. He said to ask for a guy named Bert Banks at the Rescue Coordination Center. Vera drove to Norfolk, because that's where Bert was, and he didn't take her calls or return them. When she showed up at his office at seven-thirty in the morning, having had her third cup of coffee since five, when she started driving, he told her that he would have been happy to help over the phone and he was sorry she had driven all this way. So Vera got her hopes up. They went into his office, and she told him what she knew about the crash—the date, the time, that it was somewhere along the Potomac River, maybe across from the Watergate or behind the Thompson Boat Center. He tried every different way there was to search in his computer, but the crash didn't show up. She asked him what he would do if he were her, and he started asking all these questions about what she knew about the crash, until finally, when she mentioned that the pilot had been cut down from a tree, he said, "That means it wouldn't be us, because she wasn't in the water." That would be the Parks Service. U.S. Park Police, he spelled out for her. "A bit of history trivia," he said. "George Washington himself created the park police. In 1791."

Vera went to the Park Police Aviation Unit at Anacostia Park after the Park Police public-affairs commander told her it was true that the unit's mission included aviation support for law enforcement, medevac, search and rescue, high-risk prisoner transport, and presidential and dignitary security, but they had no record of responding to a crash on Roosevelt Island, directly across from the Thompson Boat Center and the Watergate, which had to be where the pilot would have been found in a tree if the Park Police had jurisdiction.

She tried Andrews Public Affairs again, this being the fifth time, to see if, now that the crash had faded pretty far out of the news, one of their flacks might tell her what kind of ambulance carried the pilot. Can you tell me it wasn't a District ambulance? No, the flack said. Can you tell me it was a military ambulance? No. So she tried Walter Reed Public Affairs again, just to make sure they hadn't had a change of heart, since she'd been awfully respectful to the flack there, but the flack there said that ambulance information was not something she could make public, even though, "if there were anyone I could make it public for, it would be you, Vera."

The last thing she could try again was Baby. So Vera decided to try Baby again. It was close to two in the morning when she found her at the Amoco. She was wearing a white pinafore, high-tops, and nothing else. Her pimp had sent her to the I-66 ramp and showed her how to hide in the woods near the boathouse.

They walked across Rock Creek Parkway to the bike path. Not too far down the parkway, the path ran close to the river. They went in the opposite direction, which ran into the woods. Vera had her flashlight, but they didn't really need it. Vera, working night cops for at least a year now, had noticed a while back that the night sky always stayed mauve, never reached true black. They took a turn away from the bike path toward the boathouse. It wasn't cold; in fact, it was warm for November. They could hear crickets.

Vera wondered how Baby had seen anything from her vantage at the Amoco. Vera couldn't see the street at all from where they were, let alone the gas station. But she kept quiet. Her idea to find the paramedics had gone everywhere but where she wanted it to go. She wasn't exactly sure what she was hoping to find on this expedition with Baby. More than anything, Vera wanted to see the tree. She wanted to put her hand on it.

Baby wasn't chatty. She looked dirty. On closer inspection, Vera could see that her pinafore was actually two aprons tied together so her backside was in view, along with a tattoo that said *Ram Me*. Baby must have caught Vera looking, because she said, "Ain't real. Comes off in the wash." It pained Vera that Baby even gave a thought to her disapproving of a permanent tattoo.

They heard a bird's wings flapping hard, then another joining it.

"They have ducks back here," Baby said. "I seen them a lot."

"Ducks. Well, this is a national park. Or part of one."

"Real ducks. No cartoon ducks."

Vera nodded. "Daffy Duck," she said.

"These are my first ducks, these ducks back here, that I seen, you know, alive and walking."

"Well, that's good. I mean, that you've gotten a chance to see them."

"Not real friendly, ducks. They run off."

"Pecked to death by ducks."

"Say what?"

"It's a saying. You know, like 'A stitch in time saves nine.' 'Look before you leap.' 'Early bird catches the worm.' "

"Bitty duck peck to kill?"

"Wouldn't mean to. Like a pin jabbing and jabbing."

It was getting harder to see. Vera switched on her flashlight. They were in a place that was fully wooded, as if the city had disappeared. The air had a damp stillness.

Baby thought a while. "I need to better myself," she finally said. The temperature had dropped. They couldn't hear crickets anymore.

Baby stopped walking.

"It's around here," she said after a moment.

Vera shone the beam into the dark in front of her. She couldn't see anything more than the worn dirt path cutting through more trees.

"We gotta go off this," Baby said.

"Here?" Vera looked at the trees on either side of them. There was nothing that set apart one side of the path from the other—no old stump, no big rock, no white birch.

"Shit," Baby said. She took the flashlight from Vera and pointed it around, stopping here and there.

"You looking for something?" Vera whispered.

"Ain't the feeling," Baby whispered back. She seemed to be concentrating.

"What kind of feeling?"

Baby was pointing at some trees that looked no different to Vera from the other trees. "Let's go back in that mess."

Vera hesitated. And she wondered—did she need to see this tree? She lit a cigarette and handed it to Baby, then lit one for herself. They stood there smoking for a while. Then Baby shone the flashlight on Vera's watch. It was two-thirty. They needed to get going. Vera ground out her cigarette beneath her foot and gave Baby's an extra stomp. She shouldn't be smoking out here at all. And this, this off-the-path part, was slowgoing. They had to push back low limbs, curve around bushes, push away ivy that had turned into long vines. Vera's face hurt from a taut stem that sprang her way after Baby passed it. She tripped on a rock. Her hands felt cold, almost numb. Finally, Baby said, "Fuck this shit."

Vera felt herself expecting this and dreading it and hating it. "Uh. You sure?" she managed to say.

"Not really. But—like, this far, I just can't . . ." She trailed off.

"Why were you here? I mean . . ." Vera stopped herself. She sank more when she recalled how Baby had not wanted to show her this tree. She'd been saying things like "Dun know if I can find it." To which Vera had said, "You can. I know you can." Baby protesting, Vera pushing— she should have just backed off. It was so hard to know when people were afraid, when they couldn't be bothered, when they wanted to please you, when they really didn't know.

To distract himself from Hoseyn, Will went to see how the recent downloads from Mosul were going. They came from five computers that were intact and three partially restored hard drives. There were already so many terabytes from other exploitation teams; Forensics was drowning in media. He offered to take a look at some. There were boxes labeled with address, time recovered, unit that made the retrieval, schematic on how it was found. Some boxes had a report in a slipcase on top. Most of them, he noticed, Forensics hadn't touched.

He pulled on a new pair of gloves and took the thick archival lid off a stiff box not yet opened. He reached for the first plasticized envelope, so new it smelled a chemical lilac. He unhooked and unzipped the top and took out a disc the size of a matchbook. He signed his name to a log on the envelope.

The image came up. He could tell it was natural light. The air had a grain only sun could cause. No. There was a lamp in the foreground. Wait. Was it on? He squinted. Four figures were out of focus. Then the cameraman adjusted the lens, and they came out of the blur dressed in the black knit—ski mask, turtleneck, trousers—the kidnapper's uniform. He'd seen more than one of their handmade movies. He almost ejected the disc, but he needed to consider the light. The execution house in Falluja, where the first cavalry had picked up the last behead-ing video, was shot in electric light. He'd watched it more than once. It triggered a discovery. Coalition controlled the electrical grid. Army Corps of Engineers could modulate the current, block by block, for the city. The next time, the next video, examined by software programmed to pick up modulations invisible to the eye, would be like a fingerprint. There would only be so many blocks where it could have been made. So what if they moved the hostage? There was always a trail.

They had not as yet put the power-grid changes into effect. It could be a coincidence there were no electric bulbs in this new video. But if it wasn't a coincidence, it could mean that someone, perhaps inside, definitely someone supposedly on the good side, had shared secrets.

There was something else bothering him. The beheading movies he'd seen—they were particularly valuable because the participants were unmasked. The producers of these scenes sent the masked versions to television and Web outlets. What soldiers found and intelligence sent back were the outtakes.

This time the leading men were masked from the start. Could be they removed the ski wear at the end for a war dance. He sat back a little. He watched in order, from the beginning. It was a wait. For one minute, two minutes, three minutes, four minutes, the camera stayed on the standing figures. They neither spoke nor moved. Maybe one scratched his head. Will kept checking the audio, but there was nothing to pick up. It got so long he wanted to fast-forward. He felt his composure clouding. He shut off the feeling. All the funerals he'd gone to over the last month for the fallen, each one brought back to him his odd luck. He'd never collected so much as a knife knick. He, who was a dumbass, the one who last weekend tripped on a soft trail with his son, got dirt grimed into his palms, his weak ankle made worse, mud on his knees. He missed—no, he walked right past, even though he was looking carefully for it—the home of a neighbor who needed a hand moving a table. He got lost at least a few times if he deviated from home to work and work to home. He was a beach ball, a milk shake, a pin-the-tail-on-the-donkey blind man, and one, it seemed so far, who survived. So why Hoseyn? How come the careful one?

Still more four guys standing in a row staring straight ahead. One was taller than the other three. The guy seemed not so good at freezing, now that Will looked. There—the tall one shifted his center of gravity from one foot to the other. Two of the men were standing close. They were checked out. Inhuman, in a way that spelled drugs to Will. It was one of the ways to bankroll an insurgency. These two didn't know about not using. Then again, in most uprisings, the discipline was rarely there. Or maybe it was all wishes. He liked to think they needed numbing to do this.

He leaned forward on his elbows. Waiting.

There was an adjustment in them he couldn't pinpoint but recognized. It was beginning. If this was Prophet, if this was the easier battlespace, their intended victim would shape-shift into their own father, son, or uncle, and they would back off, wondering: How could we slaughter our loved one? Who put him here and stole away the kafir? Are we mad? Are we lost?

One figure knocked the hostage over like a bowling pin; another kept the hostage's head on the floor. Another had the knife. It was not large enough for the task. When Will saw it, he felt emptied, no one location. It was his stomach, his head, both heels, the fingers overweighted, his upper chest a sick, weak sail. It began—the sawing motion too slow, one figure immobilizing the hostage's body, hands of a second figure over the dying man's eyes, hand of another figure over the dying mouth, from which a sound came unlike any sound except the sound that came from this way of killing. Finally, the head lurched free of the body, and the figure with the knife took it by the hair and held it in the air. His partners began chanting. The figure placed the dead head on the prone body, but the head would not stay upright. The figure molded the body so it would better cradle its head. He turned the head this way, then, wanting the eyes, open, to face the camera, he made his final correction. The cameraman zoomed in and rested there.

Will's jaw was stuck. He put his tongue against his locked molars. He had ground top and bottom teeth into each other. He opened the hinge of his jaw slowly. His tongue moved across the top back teeth. Were the edges sharper, or was he imagining it? He put a finger and a thumb in his mouth and tugged on a tooth. No slippage—it was anchored and stable. He looked around the room. It was still there, as he had left it. The boxes stacked against the wall, the sound of others working, computer keys like toy wings flapping. His eyes were gelid. Could anyone see him like this? He felt skinned. He swiveled to see. There was no one.

Don found Mabel in the garden at three in the morning. She smelled sober. She was breathing. He couldn't feel her pulse. The only thing to think was that she was alive, her pulse shallow, or that he just couldn't find her pulse. But then she revived. Sat up, though she didn't want to stand. Weak pulse, he said to the dispatcher. Hasn't been drinking. Yes, she's breathing. Sir, the dispatcher advised, I believe your wife fainted. This is not, strictly speaking, an emergency, and I will have to recommend to you at this time that you convey her to the nearest emergency room or consult your personal physician during regular hours.

So Don carried Mabel to their Volvo. He drove to Georgetown Hospital, about six blocks. He parked the car, and they walked slowed into the emergency room, where they waited their turn. When the nurse asked his name and he said, "Don Grady," she laughed, but only a little. "Right. And I'm Queen Latifah."

She looked at his health-insurance card.

She asked for his license.

She looked at him, and the license, and the insurance card.

She got up and walked away and then opened a door and went through it, closing it behind her.

Don looked at Mabel. She had wanted to lie down. He had put her on three chairs moved together in the second row of the rows of chairs. Her nose was pointed at the ceiling, one of her arms flopped down and away from her body so that the back of her hand rested flat and casually on the floor. Even like that, he thought, she looked like a beauty.

There was a boy who kept pushing his chair sideways in a rough circle against the wall. Don wondered if the boy would hit Mabel; he was getting more agitated each time his chair hit the wall. A woman holding a baby had started to cry.

A doctor came back with the nurse.

"Mr. Grady," he said, "I'm sorry about the misunderstanding."

Don looked at him and said, "Fix that boy and help that woman and her baby. And let me carry my wife to a bed, so she'll be next."

Vera drove across the Potomac with Baby wrapped in a blanket she kept in the trunk. There was also a box of Snickers back there; she gave Baby one. They took the George Washington Parkway north and found the parking lot, just like Baby said. Then there was a walking bridge across the Potomac, the island's only access from land. They hurried over, past the sign that said *Park Closed After Dark*.

As they walked, deeper into Roosevelt Island, Baby was on her second Snickers. She thought it would be a good idea for Vera to have some, but Vera said no. She was in a state. It had never made sense that Baby saw anything from the Amoco.

Baby hadn't been anywhere near the Amoco. She'd been back here, with a date who was paranoid, and Baby didn't know and didn't care who he was or why he was jacked up. All she knew was, he gave out like he was scary mean, but he wasn't, and, besides, he paid bigger than she had asked. For a little while, he had been a regular.

"Here, here!" Baby was shouting to Vera all of a sudden. They were definitely alone. Funny how they felt this was *their* island. Vera had to go running, because Baby was way ahead of her. Now Baby had her own flashlight, Vera's backup from the car, and Vera could see the beam dancing in the trees ahead. Then it stopped.

When she reached Baby, Vera lost her footing. If she had wanted to find the tree, put her palm on its trunk, it wasn't going to be here. There were no trees. The ground was black. There was a stack of sod, behind it another one and another. Bags of topsoil made a wall to the right of charred land. A backhoe, a trailer, a hulking of equipment waited in the background. Baby was running her hands along the sod's brightest-green feathery grass.

"See," Baby said. "Need to come up on it like a surprise."

Vera felt uneasy.

"I seen this first, I had to lay down," Baby told her.

Vera shook herself. She was trying to get herself staunch again. This might be one of the last nights to see this exterminated parkland, this earth before the sod.

"Baby, thank you for showing me this."

"Hmm-mm."

"But the night of the crash?"

"Different." Baby whistled.

"What was it like? Tell me."

"I got your tickets. Come on to the show," said Baby, walking back into the trees.

Vera followed, and soon they came up on a rock the size of both of them.

"This where he like it. Right here," Baby said.

Vera shone her flashlight into the clearing. She could see it perfectly from this vantage.

"We here," Baby said. "We done. We hear it. He fall flat on this ground, right here. But I see. Three. Like Batman. First guy takes a stereo out. Other stereo, now three stereos, only the stereos are phones too. Talkin' on 'em. Numbers. Ninety-two. Twenty-eight. Five. Forty-four. Eight. Eight.

"Then this, like, monster noise comes up, like, you know, when the train comes in the station? It's here, right *here*.

"Next thing I know, Batmans gone, stereos gone, these here trees is all *burning,* but not like tree burning, more like metal burning or someshit. Leaves are, like, hissing, like *snakes*. My date, he's all gone. Me, I take off for the lot. But I'm, like, all turned around and shit—and *what do I see?* Not Virginia. I see the D.C. side. Lincoln on his chair.

"Then, true fact, I look up and there she is. White woman in a tree. She got this big parachute twisted all over and she's twirling—then, boom, she just stops. I say, 'Lady, lady.' But she can't hear."

Walking back, Vera saw the sign that said *Park Closed Until Further Notice*.

· · ·

There was no explanation for Mabel's passing out in the middle of the night in her garden. The doctors were stumped, and their tests were inconclusive. The best anyone could say was that she had suffered some kind of minor stroke. There was no evidence of it in all the neurological scans, but it was worth watching, because it could be a warning of a more serious stroke to come.

Mabel could have told them all about it. It was a version of death, one in which a person realizes that what they imagined about themselves, however unflattering, was not nearly as awful as how they were, by many other people, seen. She had thought that by making fun of herself she had inoculated herself against derision. Her fainting happened the night of the day she would always remember, the one in which she was standing in the lobby of the paper, the report in the boxes Jonathan Strasser had given her. She was trying to get upstairs to the Room, trying to flirt with the guard, which hadn't worked; trying to use Don Grady's name, which hadn't worked; trying to get Adam to rescue her, which hadn't worked and had hurt the most. She could have saved the day, but no one, including herself, had taken her as someone who could have anything to contribute. Adam, the nicest guy alive, someone she'd thought had a longtime crush on her, just wanted her to go away.

She couldn't tell Don what had happened. It wasn't because he would be upset that she was having an assignation in a bar with Jonathan Strasser in the middle of the day. It wasn't because it was a betrayal to have gone to the paper with the hope of getting credit for unearthing a report her husband had had all along and she had actually had dumped in her lap. It was because each time she tried to tell Don, really and truly tried, he didn't understand what she was saying. She had long ago stopped listening carefully to anything he said. To be met with her own attitude, to feel the loneliness of needing to tell something integral to who you were and where your life had been and where it was going, and to receive in return distracted apathy of the kindest sort—it killed her.

REFUSING REASON
ITS REASONS

The church made one of its sounds. It had something to do with a pew, the old wood of it, creaking. Adam was still. Stanley looked around for someone or another, and his eye rested on chrysanthemums, pots of them, at the pulpit. There were harvest colors: ocher, cinnamon, hyperactive yellow. There wasn't much room in his thinking for the spectral. He did like the echo.

But Adam wasn't listening. He was thinking about what Stanley was thinking.

"Why do I get the feeling you don't think it matters who I pick?" Adam was laughing a little, but uneasily. His throat felt dry.

"Because that's how I feel." Stanley smiled, but he didn't feel like his smile. He would have to talk about the managing editor—that was clear enough. The church was cold, almost too cold. Then he said, "Not entirely. I think it's a question of who do you want to spend most of your days talking with, who it is you most can't do without on that front."

"It's important because of the message it sends to the Room," Adam said, a little irritated by Stanley's weak attempt at interest, but he meant this—this observation mattered to him. "It's important because I feel we're slipping."

Stanley knew this perennial problem had to do lately with the White House surveillance story the other paper had managed to get. In Adam's mind, Martina had been responsible for that, because she hadn't argued with Adam about placing trust in Mitch Pendleton, an old head. She should have fought. Stanley knew that if she had fought Adam—that would have been wrong too. Her elbows would have been deemed too sharp. It was impossible not to get on the wrong side. They should have just seen that. Why didn't they? If Stanley had written the management tomes that no editor studied (they had no training; they reported, then edited), he would have made a diagram with pale yellows, greens, and pinks mapping this phenomenon. Instead, in real life, the wrong side you got on in any interoffice battle was judged a character trait. In Martina's case it was: not assertive enough. No one considered what the other side of wrong would have meant.

The clobbering had continued. That got said. Often. The other paper had been pushing out driblets of new information that were termed *staying on top of the story*, forcing television to follow, blogs to fizz, columnists to insist and dismiss. Stanley paid it little mind. But Adam, he did. Adam cared deeply.

"It'll break Martina's heart" was all Stanley could think to say. "She deserves the job. This latest foul-up—it shouldn't dominate your thinking. There's only so much she can do."

"Gordon inspires people. He's a gifted, aggressive journalist with a keen eye for a story, a masterful sense of history and politics."

"I wouldn't know about that."

"Stanley, you really are biased."

Stanley resisted the impulse to shrug. What he really wished was that he could tell Adam what Vera had been finding out about the pilot. But it was too early. She needed to learn more. Right now, what she had was not much more believable than a UFO sighting. Oh. He realized now. Wood contracted and expanded, didn't it, with temperature changes? The pew, the cold, it made sense. The church's floor of stone would magnify the least reverberation.

"He's immoral," Stanley said with what he hoped was restrained emphasis. Yes, he thought, Gordon Bray radiated this.

"Gordon is not immoral. What on earth are you talking about?"

"It's the feeling I get," Stanley said.

Adam felt awful, and without warning.

"I'm not amused by this," he found himself saying, more coldly than he had expected it to sound. He looked at Stanley's suit vest and his brown jubbah. There was his customary headgear—always the baseball cap. Today it bore the insignia of the U.S. Park Police. He was sitting there, Stanley was, tearing the cuticle of his left pinkie. Adam looked a little more closely. In the church's dim light, it looked as if the sides of both Stanley's thumbs were scabbed over. Adam's poor, challenged daughter had that habit. She wore five or six Band-Aids almost always on her fingers. But a grown man—Adam had never seen one do such a thing.

You couldn't explain many a thing, or even understand one thing at first. As Vera understood scripture, meaning was a light that shone from certain angles on certain days and that could only be taken literally after great study, if at all. So she tried not to rush the word according to Baby—to wit, that she had seen men in black clothing setting up electronic equipment, causing a fire, disappearing, and subsequently, at another location on Roosevelt Island, come upon a white female hanging from a tree. You couldn't make snap-crackle-pop judgments, as Vera was ever accustomed to do, if you expected to understand the unexpected. With certain events, the witnessing of them alone rearranged entire segments of known history. However improbable Baby's testimony might be, Vera vowed not to stick it under the category of vision. It could be under the category of fact. It could have happened. She repeated this sentence to herself on a regular basis. She began the patient consideration of the ways in which it might have happened before trying to prove it hadn't happened.

Part of this involved going back and photographing the park closure notice, the black ground, the piles of sod, and the tree, which she did put her hand on, a sensation that was not nearly as interesting or uncanny as she had thought it would be.

She printed the photographs and thumbtacked them to the cork on her side of the cubicle. Whenever she was put on hold, whenever she couldn't think of a lede on the many Metro cops stories she worked most nights, whenever she was tired, her eye rested on the black ground, the sod, the sign, and the tree. Her early attentions drifted to the tree. She got a book about the forests of North America and started putting thumbnails of various tree trunks against the photo. Then she realized the leaf was the obvious easy thing to match, not the bark—why hadn't she thought of it sooner?—and immediately she learned that the pilot had fallen into an oak tree. She had a small rush from this, a private triumphant attitude that she carried around with her into the ladies' and down to the cafeteria for some coffee and back to her desk, where, before she quite sat down, she saw her deskmate, Marcus, talking to an attentive and respectful Adam Sanger, until Adam walked into a meeting and a National reporter stopped to talk to Marcus. The National reporter, named Graham Matthews, didn't even know Vera's name and would have no reason to talk to her about anything, and so, as her phone rang and she picked it up, she hoped by the end of the call she could once again learn from the example of Mitch and hide, even from herself, her nonstatus.

Not too long after that, one day on the phone—giving her number to a cop in the Seventh District, looking idly at the sign, her least favorite of her quartet of photographs—she saw it. There, on the bottom of the sign, so small she couldn't read it, were some letters. It looked like three, four, maybe five letters.

She took the tack out of the picture and walked over to the Photo Desk. The Photo editor was a seriously friendly person with nothing but good mood and good energy all the day through, even though it was getting near crunch time, five or so, but that never stopped him from saying, "Miss Veraciously Vera Hastings!" So he said that, and she asked if she could look at his magnifier, and he put the photo on the light box and, like a jeweler, Vera put her eye to it.

And looked. Her eye just went deep down into it, couldn't acclimate right off, but then there was the sign, the top—no, the bottom—no the top edge, over here, there, to the right on the bottom; before she even got to it she prayed her eye would be able to see it. *M* something. There was an *S* at the end. It shook and blurred. Her eye was tearing. She lifted her head up.

The Photo editor was on the phone, his feet on the desk, throwing a yo-yo. After a while, he hung up. "What you got?" The yo-yo was still going.

"You have good eyes?" she asked him.

"No."

She nodded.

"But I tell you who does. Your boss. Mr. Stanley over there." He motioned affectionately to the Metro Desk. He picked up his phone's receiver, dialed, and invited Stanley over. There was talking and laughing, and Vera getting impatient. Finally, Stanley lowered his eyes to the light table and after a few seconds said, "Sure. MECS."

"MECS?"

"Can you perhaps blow this up for us?" Stanley asked.

"Do it to it," said the Photo editor, picking up the photo and handing it to a Photo aide. "Get thee the digital input from this scrap. Download, send to Miss Veracious, and behold, all shall become known to us."

Adam had had no idea. Martina had left his office. She was probably on the elevator now. He hoped she was. Though, given the shape she was in, she could very well be in the restroom. He put his hands over his face, his fingertips in his eyes, and pressed until he got the spangled black that was what his eye could see of his eyelid. He had missed it. Missed it and missed it and missed it. And from what she said, everyone but Adam Sanger knew.

It was inconceivable to him. Even now, knowing, he didn't want to know. He would be going over his contribution to it for months— though, to her credit, she had not said he ever did anything to encourage— He stopped in mid-thought. He heard a sound. It was around eleven. The desk was gone, all the reporters, just the copy editors left. Was she at the door? Had he missed her knock? He was dazed, absolutely not thinking clearly. He waited.

"Yes?" he said this like a child, timid.

Nothing.

"Anybody there?"

Suddenly, more than anything, he hoped it was Stanley. It was only eleven, so Stanley was still here. He got up quickly and opened the door—to no one. Fast, he closed it, and, after locking it, stood still for a count of ten.

He edged his way along the plaster wall and looked out the glass wall. He saw Stanley's desk, but not Stanley.

Adam believed she had started with "feelings." That must have been the first word she used. Even at that he was too obtuse and had not detected anything amiss—because, goddamn it, they all had feelings for one another. They were in the Room day after day, week after week, year after year, he had never worked anywhere else, nor had she, the Room itself was the same room he had started in at twenty-one in the summer of '71, though of course they had changed the furniture, rearranged and made way for the gray-blue that replaced the Fisher-Price colors. Apart from his parents' home, apart from the two homes he'd lived in with his two families, his feelings were here, right here. The feelings weren't about closeness, he hurried to say, but reporting, it entailed feelings. Who could report without feeling? And your status, there was a well of feelings about your status, and your place in the Room, and how you were seen and how Adam saw you. But these were feelings from a group of public feelings, and naturally she had those kinds of feelings about him. He was the authority figure. He was Dad. He was in charge. *Do you have a feel for what Adam's thinking is on this? How does Adam feel about the top?*

"Crush" was the second word, and then, because it was in the past tense, as in having had it years ago, and because it was a "foolish" one, and because the funny—Martina *was* funny—stories she told about various things that had happened and he'd completely misunderstood, like the time the white flowers came and she'd actually sent them to herself in hopes that he might ask her about them—but no, no, that was later, that was recently . . . Adam moved away from the wall and found himself edging back to the door of his office, thinking if he were near the windows he possibly would be unseen from the Room. He slid his way along the windowsills, reached his bookcase, and somehow got into the chair behind his desk.

"I have to face that I have fallen in love with you." From the safety of his chair, he could replay it in his head. It was possible he had sneezed when she said it. How does a person want you to respond when she says such a thing? It had to have been obvious, by that point, toward the end, that he did not share her—her—regard. He sounded like a prig. He was a prig. He was going to sneeze again. No, he wasn't. Yes. He couldn't find a tissue. He hadn't been able to then either.

He thought she had gone out to get him a tissue. But she hadn't. She'd just . . . left.

Baby took Uncle Asis out of his milk carton. She unwrapped the newspaper from around his fur head and took off the Kleenex covering his face. His brownie eyes peeped at her. She touched his wood nose.

A roach long dead was trapped in the newspaper around his feet. She wrapped it inside a scrap and folded the rest of the paper into a boat to hold its dried-out body. She put the boat on the windowsill.

It took her a while, but she pulled the stuffed chair from the other end of the room up to the window. She climbed up and found the hole in the screen with the tips of her fingers. Then she made a top for the boat with a cotton puff and wrapped a rubber band around it. "Jesus take you softly," she said as she put it through the screen.

She inspected Uncle Asis's backside. It was still torn. She thought for a moment. It was probably better to move the chair back against the door. Quiet as she could, she pushed a little every so often. In the meantime, she put one leg up on the bed and pulled the string between her legs. Out came the baggie she'd put up there that morning. Inside was a needle wrapped in a chewing-gum foil and a spool of thread she'd lifted from a 7-Eleven. She took some nail-polish remover from the dresser, and another cotton ball, and cleaned the bag before taking the items out. She put it in the bottom drawer, inside a beret.

She listened. It was quiet in the house. Earphone wasn't home. He was in jail. She thought it a good time and a bad time for this chancy behavior of hers. On the one hand, he wouldn't come pushing through here and do something. On the other hand, all girls were free without Earphone on them. That meant Goodie. Goodie was satanic. She had already done some things to Baby. One was setting her clothes on fire. Another was peeing on her bed.

Earphone didn't let any of them have a purse. He checked into all their wastebaskets. Time to time, he emptied drawers. He snuck under their beds, between the mattress and the bottom part. He once cut up a girl's pillow. He said they were thieves and would hide a nickel. No one had a closet. Cheats, all of you, he said.

She held the needle up to the light. She put the misty strand close to the eye of the needle and guided it through.

She placed him on his side. She slid the needle into the frayed fabric; it came right out. There was a sound downstairs. The stairs were loud, and here came the bang, and the knock on her door.

"Babee," whined Tulip.

"Babee Waybee," cried Goodie.

"Titty face, open the door!" Giggles came through.

She sat there.

"She playin wit' herself." Goodie made syncopations of exaggerated sex sighs.

"She stinkin up that room with herself," Tulip said. Banging and banging.

One of them jiggled the doorknob. Baby looked at the lock holding. It didn't hold for Earphone.

"I'll huff an I'll puff an I'll—"

A siren cut off Tulip. Baby heard scuttling down the stairs. She went to the drawer with the beret in it and pulled out a baggie with two fluorescent-orange earplugs. She scrunched one in one ear, then the other.

She settled back on the bed. It took her a few tries, but she got the fabric to fold and stay together, and then she got the needle through all four layers. It held. She sewed up the opening in no time. She took an earplug out and listened. Quiet again.

She put Uncle Asis up against her right shoulder and patted his back. "There, there," she said.

She turned off the light and, to be extra careful, closed the window. It wasn't that cold a night. She held him against her neck as she lay on top of the covers. She wanted to sing him a song. She couldn't risk it. She tried sleeping on her side with him in the crook of her arm. Maybe then it would come.

It was no use. The special feeling wasn't going to come. She turned the light back on. She'd feel better if he was safe in his milk carton. She needed to clean everything up too. No wonder she couldn't relax. She took what was left of the old newspaper that covered him and threw it in the trash. Then she took the needle and spool and put them back in the plastic bag in her silver beret. She took the new newspaper she'd gotten that day and looked through it for a pretty page. The Style section had the flag and a lady with her head bowed. That was no good, so she looked on the front page. There were some autumn leaves in a photo near the bottom. She put that aside. That might be good. She paged through—sofas, banks, cell phones—nothing personal. She turned to the Sports page. It was a Wizards game, a long, big picture of an impossible dunk. You could see everybody on the sidelines, their mouths open. They were tripping. There was one man, he looked like he wasn't there. He wasn't even watching the game. It took her awhile, but she realized eventually. She'd seen him. He was there the night that girl was in the tree. He was the white man with the face blank as bread.

PANJSHIR **JANUARY**

10. THE MOON SHINES IN MY BODY

Mary hit the switch for the battery. She hit the switch for jet-fuel start. She put the data-transfer cassette in the slot. Through the engine's maw, she heard Frank in her ear: "Grim 1, pick your tail up, give me a wave." She flipped him the finger. "Sugar Mary, mother of wingmen, give the throttle a split-tail wiggle." She ignored him, rested her left hand on the throttle and her right on the stick. She might as well stay that way for the mission. A turtle could steer this one.

They flew alone tonight, just the two of them. A Reaper, the newest drone, was busy in Helmand Province. Predators, the smaller drones, were available, but nutjobs wanted a big fire. She'd been pulled out of sleep, taken her go-pills, and thanked the air force once again for her approved Schedule II narcotic. A weapons loader she didn't recognize put his arm in the air. She raised her index finger, gave him the hand signals.

Just seconds, the wheels were up and ground was lost. The airlessness, how she needed it. "Grim 2, I'm falling in love," she told Frank. They'd turned off the com so they could only hear each other. "Miss X, you can't be serious. You need man love to put you right."

Her right multifunction display showed the geography in green. All it had were lines and swirls, bordered with numbers. Around her canopy were the actual stars, a thick night-rug of them. The one she almost bought last weekend in the Kabul bazaar, the bursts were scattered through with dollar signs, and diamonds too. Even tribes wanted more than heaven. There was the moon, tonight a crescent.

They were headed to Khushali Torikhel, a village in North Waziristan—tribal Pakistan, near the Afghan border. It was a short ride from Bagram.

"Grim 1, Bossman." It was the air controller. The coordinates were loaded, but they didn't want any missteps on this thing.

"Bossman, Grim 1 go," Mary said.

"Grim 1, Bossman double-checking coordinates with Kmart," he said.

"Copy that, Bossman."

They'd been in Afghanistan a month, flying missions like this one, but not often enough for Frank, and too many times for Mary. Snow had layered over the base since she'd arrived. First tour she'd done, it'd been winter too. She didn't remember being this cold. The B-huts felt like cardboard. All Frank craved were missions south, but not for the warmth, because there wasn't any. He wanted to be where the firefights were. Up here, it was impersonal. Shows of force, aerial assassination. Pilots didn't even read the intel, they just flew by a cassette to a coordinate the intel designated, dropped fire, went back, waited for the next run a week or so later, sometimes longer.

She didn't blame Frank for wanting Helmand Province. It felt better to incinerate bad actors pinning down trapped men. But when the numbers of men on the ground were so small, choppers did the job better than Vipers. He tried to change minds about that—as if a few decades of doctrine and wartime hadn't happened. He angled and argued until he figured out it wasn't anything pervious to suck-up or butt-kiss.

Lieutenant Colonel Avery Hood was their squadron commander, but everyone knew he was substantially pointless. This fight belonged to Special Operations Forces—nutjobs, as Frank called them. There was no more confliction stew, as there'd been her first tour, no more Tampa saying what her wing could do. After the Anaconda mess, even military saw fit to amend. So nutjobs decided where she and Frank flew. Nutjobs they'd never met told them what to smoke.

"Grim 1, Bossman. Kmart affirms coordinates."

She waited for the order.

"Grim 1. Bonzai debris." There it was.

"Grim 2, hold fire."

She looked down. There was debris, a green house in a green village.

"Coming, honey." Frank's voice came just as she pressed the pickle. He was trying to be happy for her. Even though he had nothing to do now but watch.

She had a five-hundred-pounder. She tossed it on a seed.

On her display, lime-colored smoke puffed. Looking down, she saw the same through the night-vision visor on her helmet.

"Debris destroyed," Bossman said after a while. "Grim 2, go home."

No need for Frank. He was backup, in case she missed.

It was detached, this war. It hung from the side of the country. Her part was secret, so mostly it didn't show. Some in her squadron bitched about this. We're out here risking our skins, they'd say, and no one back home cares. That was shit. She'd give them risk. She'd serve some stats. The highest danger to a pilot was friendly fire. Or doing something stupid like that Blackwater pilot flat-hatting through a canyon in a turboprop—he couldn't pull up fast enough when a mountain showed. Or having a malfunction, like her crash.

But, as with so many things, they still didn't know what that was. You walked in the dark with a whistle round your neck, and when you blew it to judge the echo, only dogs could hear it. They came barking to tell you what was what. You scratched around the dirt, wondering, what were the pups trying to say? That's what this war was. Maybe it took a girl on the edges to see the whole thing clear.

All that left were orders. She got them. She followed them. Predator drones were too dinky to match a Viper. Reaper drones were twice as fast as Predators, could fly twice as high, had nine times the horsepower, and carried ten times the payload. As yet, there were only four, and three were in Iraq. More were in production. Military was working to cross out Viper pilots for good.

B-huts slept six. There were plenty enlisted air-force females at Bagram, but not enough officers to fill a hut. Mary's had a medic, a Chinook pilot, and a media specialist.

The medic was a disaster jumper named Eve who went for officer training after Kosovo. Now she was senior airwoman, search and rescue. She had a bald patch on her head, where the hair would fall out and only partially grow back; she called it her stress mark. She tried to camouflage the spot with a nonstop brown tattoo to match her hair. It didn't quite work. Daylong, she looked as if she'd just sat up from bed or got drawn in a *Peanuts* cartoon. Eve had a habit of singing in her sleep, off-tune, too loud. Lately, Mary had been pulling a hat down past her ears to ward off the freeze, so it didn't matter.

The media specialist was ROTC from Purdue. She kept every press release she wrote locked in a tackle box. She complained about missing hunting. It was verboten. But base rules hadn't stopped her. It was the weather that upset her, closing up her favorite mountain grounds with useless snow. She hung out with a trio of army reservists not long out of college. They'd arrived scared and had gotten mostly loud. Mary couldn't always ignore them.

The Chinook driver was married, with two kids and a husband deployed at Balad in Iraq. Her mother was watching her babies in Carlsbad, New Mexico. She and the mom were on Skype almost always. After a while, Mary started talking to the mother too. She was a broad-faced Korean woman who seemed to have an oversupply of loving attitude.

The day after the nighttime run, Mary woke to a morning blizzard. Blankets of snow whumped against the hut. The plywood bowed and gave, too weak to split. Her hutmates were gone. The heater did what it could, which was never enough, since huts had no insulation. The cold poured in, pushed by the front coming off the mountains. Her sleep bag was for subzero temperatures, and her nose, just the nostrils and tip, stayed out for breathing. Inside the cocoon, she dozed and woke, the go-pills ruining real sleep.

A hut was the size of a singlewide, with six-foot-high panels making bedrooms not much bigger than a bed. The plywood hooches lined up in rows and columns as in trailer parks, only pushed closer to one another, with a central walkway made of broken rock running between them, which led to the main road. Across the road, but still in Bagram's air-force village, were the relocatable buildings, called RLBs. They were hollowed out, no panels, just a long corridor, like the belly of a whale, with bunks inside it. Frank lived in one. Most soldiers liked B-huts, because, unlike RLBs, they contained no shitholes. As Mary mushed the hundred yards to the female latrine, she wished she'd gotten the RLB: winter meant boots and parka for the first pee of the day.

On the way back, she ran into the weapons loader from the night before. She'd not recognized him then, and her eyesight through the splotching snow wasn't good enough to let her place him either. She'd not taken time to wear gloves, and her hands were jammed in her pockets when he offered his hand to shake hers.

"Tasty kill," he shouted into the wind.

She put her hand in his mitten. He was a big man. He put his other mitten around her hand and added, "Stay warm."

"Thanks," she said and pushed on. By the time she got to her hut, the snow seemed icier, and as dull razors of it hit her face, she thought this might be a day to avoid the Dragon and eat in. Microwaves weren't allowed, but she could open a can of tuna.

The Chinook pilot, Seri, had returned while Mary was gone. She was on her bed, laptop flipped open. When the snow howled in with Mary, she shielded her screen.

"No choppers in this scat," Mary said as she pushed against the wind to close the door. She pulled off her dripping parka and tried to shake it into a controlled puddle by an empty cot near the door.

"Snow day in Kabul," Seri said. "It's fifty degrees in New Mexico."

"Sleeping now, huh?" Mary looked at her watch. It was a little after eleven in the morning, their time. About half past midnight back in Carlsbad. Seri couldn't talk to her mom for another six hours.

"Yeah," she said. "We gotta clear off the roof like any second."

They listened to the plywood making its moaning whistles. They couldn't let more than a foot accumulate: huts weren't strong enough to hold it. A couple of slackers woke to an avalanche in their laps one night.

The snow had been wet, and Mary guessed by now it was starting to harden on top. Last time the crust got thick, they'd had to pickax it loose.

"What's the forecast?" Mary said.

"Base commander hasn't got one yet. Or did have one, but now it's not up anymore," Seri said.

Mary flopped down on her bed and crawled back in her sleep bag. She was hungry, but too cold from her trip outside to hunt around in the commissary food she kept in a box in the corner.

"They've got a cam on all these snics cleaning the airfield," Seri called from her room, which was next door to Mary's. "It's snowing as fast as they're plowing."

"Maybe if we heat some water in our coffeemakers it'll up the temp in here," Mary said.

Seri laughed. Then she said, "How was it last night?"

Seri didn't generally ask questions after a run. But, then, generally Seri wasn't snowed in with her after one either.

"Clear."

"T-Knee with you?"

"Yep."

"What kind of fire did you have?"

"Paveway."

"The enhanced ones?"

"Yeah, dual-mode. We used GPS, not laser."

Seri was quiet.

"Well, you should know that Purdue here is writing it up," she finally said.

"What?" Mary sat up in her bed. A press release from Purdue? These ops were secret, and last night's hop sure was. Seri must have misunderstood.

"You were sleeping this morning when she got pulled out of here."

"No."

"It's not so bad. It's happened to me. Your family—"

Before Seri could say sorry, Mary said, "Forget it."

They'd not talked about her mother gone, her father locked up. But

Seri had probably heard plenty about it outside the hut. Gossip was in no danger of dying at Bagram.

"I was going to say your family would enjoy it. They send the press release special-delivery. My mom was . . ." She stopped. "I'm a royal ass, aren't I?"

"You're fine," Mary said.

"My mom is gonna whup it up for you. She'll get Ricky and Lisa on Skype, and we'll sing some hip-hip-hoorays."

Mary closed her eyes. The bag had gotten warm, and she'd hoped to sleep again, but now she was too jazzed. She should welcome Seri's befriending her; she actually liked her. Instead, she felt impatient. Now especially, but often when with her, she found herself hoping for an interruption. The snow day was beginning to seem too long, especially without Seri's relatives to keep Seri occupied online.

A mechanical scraping approached and then passed their hut. It was the mini–off-roader plowing the main path. It always shoved the snow tight against the hut door.

"I'll dig us out," Mary said, pulling out of her bag.

"Let's just do the roof too," Seri said.

"May as well," Mary said.

They sat on the roof for a while after they'd cleared it. Mary balanced on the wire broom she'd used to sweep away the last. She enjoyed her quickened breathing, felt glad for metabolism heat. They hadn't needed the ax or the pitchfork, which they'd left on the ground below. Visibility wasn't great, but while they'd been up there the storm had cycled away from a gale into those free-floating, oversized flakes that always made Mary feel a little sedated. Others were on top of their huts too, shoveling, or jumping off into fluffed mounds. Mary and Seri watched a snowball fight a dozen huts away, and soon there was a crowd, and someone found a way to keep score. But every so often they'd see a pair or three like them, just sitting on a roof, looking at the white hushing the base.

"There's not going to be a press release," Mary said after a little while.

"Maybe not," Seri said. She just stared out, didn't turn to look at her.

"I don't enjoy it." "It" could mean the release, or last night's hop. She seemed incapable of straight talk, even with Seri.

"Release won't say you do."

"I saw the weapons loader from last night on the path after I peed this morning, and you know what he said? 'Tasty kill,' " Mary said, keeping her tone light, since her meaning was now unambiguous.

"He just wants to get in your pants," Seri said.

That made Mary laugh. "Bagram love," she said.

"It may be Bagram, but I wouldn't call it love," Seri said.

"Oh man."

"Oh boy," Seri said. "Oh boy, you mean. What is he? Eighteen?"

"No, he's full-grown," Mary said. "A few days older than Purdue."

"If she brings those reservists to the hut one more time, I'll ground them. Make them do their homework. Tell them to play Go Fish."

"If they know how."

The snowballing looked as if it was noisy—some getting pissed off, others taking sides—but the snow muffled all. It gave Mary a childish sense, as if she were in a hollow and anything wrong had been neutralized, sucked out of the air, and kept at bay outside a twinkling perimeter.

She was just enjoying when she heard Frank's voice below.

"X," he yelled. "X!"

She peered down at him. He was carrying sections of corrugated fiberglass, pale green skiffed with snow. He put them above his head and shouted: "Sleds."

"T-Knee, you know better," Seri said. She'd never much liked Frank.

Mary clapped snow off her ass and climbed down the ladder. Frank had switched his regulation parka for a blanket with a thick drawstring.

"What is that?" Mary said.

"Pashtun snowsuit."

"Why?"

"We're going off base, Miss X!" Frank was on his toes, jumping too.

"Not me."

Seri was standing up on the roof. She was about to say something when Frank said, "Come on, Extra. Rex and Jeff have an armored Land Cruiser. They're waiting for us right now at the gate. They're packing a bunny suit for you."

Rex and Jeff were sheriff's deputies who'd traded in amphetamine dealers and shoplifters for training Afghan police under contract to the State Department. They'd been here since before Mary and Frank's first tour. Some DynCorp contractors lived in villas—if you could call them that—in Kabul proper. They were unfinished concrete spruced with tipsy balconies and reflective windows that looked like mirrored blue sunglasses. Last year, after a convoy of DynCorpers got blasted on their way out of one of the villa neighborhoods, the company started scattering personnel. Jeff won the lottery when DynCorp put him up in the new Serena Hotel, in the center of town. It was like Bali in Kabul, no gilt crud, stunning plain, tranquil. Last week a suicide bomber got through the Kalashnikovs and the security walls to blast eight guests in the lobby and gym. Jeff had assisted on the investigation, worked straight through since, but today weather had shut down the city.

Jeff was divorced. He called Vermont home. He acted like he condemned flirtation. Rex was a weightlifter who missed his wife, home in Greensboro. Frank was the jester, and Jeff seemed to need the antics. Rex was a little more interested in Mary, mostly because he had a recreational pilot's license back home. He knew a lot about vintage aircraft, like she did. It was often she and Rex in a corner debating Taylorcraft history while Frank talked trash and made Jeff laugh.

It took a while to reach the base entrance, since the shuttle bus wasn't running. When they got there, the Land Cruiser, with its slithering antenna, was puffing like a smokehouse. They climbed in, and even Jeff was in a good mood.

"Here you go, Mary," Rex said, handing her some wool pants and a pile of red sweaters. They looked like Rex's.

"This?"

"X, you'll look like a lollipop," Frank said.

"Not a good idea to wear anything regulation where we're going," Jeff said from the driver's seat. He looked at Mary in the rearview mirror. "Though they might be a tad big."

"I forget how little you are," Rex said.

"That's 'cause she's a killer," Frank said.

"No, it's 'cause you're a dick," she said.

Frank whistled. "Testy."

"Somebody your way got more than testy last night, from what I hear," Jeff said.

Mary kept pulling one of the sweaters over her head.

"Over thirty dead, more wounded," Rex said.

"They took some of the injured to the ISAF camp near Khost," Jeff added.

"Why?" Frank said.

"One of the commanders over there is trying something different, that's all," Rex said.

"His own private detention center?" Frank said.

"Nothing like that. It's a clinic."

"They don't even have a medical facility there," Frank said. The International Security Assistance Force camps rarely did.

"He's got some mobile thing set up," Rex said. "A gift from some NGO."

"What do you mean by different?" Mary said.

"Oh, he's got this sub-rosa deal where if locals insist that civilians got plunked, like even though Special Forces says they're Taliban, he'll treat them," Jeff said. "Winning hearts and minds. Freelance."

"Fuck," Frank said. "He's crazy."

"We're trying to catch him at it red-handed," Rex said. "Then we'll send it up the chain. Right now it's rumor."

"It's happening," Jeff said.

"Not till I see it for myself," Rex said.

"If it weren't for this sky dump, I'd be over there," Jeff said. "Apparently, some of these people are going to the embassy about this one."

"They say it was an F-16," Rex said.

Frank and Mary didn't look at one another or say anything.

"For all we know, there wasn't even a run last night," Rex said.

"Guys, guys," Frank said, wanting the subject changed. "Where we going?"

"Nice little mountain up here," Jeff said, his tone saying, Not yet.

"Sorry, Frank," Rex said. They were putting Frank and Mary on the spot. And it wasn't like them.

"We're both sorry," Jeff said, but reluctantly. Mary kept her face fixed: apology neither accepted nor denied.

"Look, who knows, right?" Rex said, honestly sorry.

" 'Who knows' is right," Frank chimed.

"The other day, I'm on grievances," Rex went on, "meeting with your friendly lords of the locals and so forth. Saying some unnamed Afghan guys I'm training are, well, causing problems with some of the girls, little girls. I say, 'Okay, let's find the girls, let's get some descriptions.' He says no way. We go back and forth. Finally, he says, 'Okay, you send a woman, we'll let her talk to the girls.' Bring a nurse from the Canadian NGO up there, she spends the day in the village. Comes back. Says, 'These girls aren't girls. They're women. Plus, they said their husbands put them up to this, to say this.' "

"Fucked-up country," Frank said.

"Aw, come on," Jeff said. "How many times do you look into something only to figure it's not what it was sold to you as? I mean, really?"

"When I was in the army . . ." Rex began.

"Well, that's your problem right there." Frank bumped his fist on Rex's back.

"My wife, there's a better problem. Talk about not being as sold," Jeff started to say.

"Mountain have a name?" Mary asked. She wished she could press through the seat, whisk out under the chassis. She'd left base to avoid Seri, to miss Purdue's coming in the hut with the release, and here were Jeff and Rex with updates. She concentrated on keeping her chin level, her line of sight unbroken. Frank tried to catch her eye once and then gave up. She sensed Jeff checking the mirror, looking to see how she took it.

She could feel defensiveness, its brittle coil, threading and breaking through her.

You could kill civilians, as in carpet-bombing Japan, as long as it looked as if you were just on the brink of losing to Japan. But if you were kinda winning but not entirely, you better not touch a hair on any civilian head. When an enemy got that equation entirely figured out, which took, oh, maybe ten minutes, enemy would simply mix up soldiers with civilians. Best example of this was military honchos storing weapons under cradles. So, when she bombed the weapons cache, enemy lost his firepower, sure enough, but, more effective than that firepower ever would have been, he could say, Lookie here, I lost my wife and kidlets.

She was still fuming, but now at herself. Kiddiewinks, munchkins, babes in warland. Serpent, thy name is Mary.

They drove to the arrow. In the air, that's what Mary saw when she flew here. It pointed north and east, to the Hindu Kush. Four thousand years, land here had been contested. She was just the latest to visit. The snow under the Land Cruiser was packed, some of it slippery. She waited for the spin-out, a jackknife. The cold this January was killing Afghans. She'd heard hundreds had perished. She thought she saw one of them a distance from the shoulder.

"See that," Rex said.

"See what?" Frank said.

"Back that way, four o'clock," Mary said.

"Shit," Frank said.

"Is he dead?" Rex asked.

"We should stop," Frank said.

"And do what?" Jeff said, his speed steady.

"Earth too hard to bury him," Rex said.

"Maybe he's not dead," Mary said.

"We try to help, we get to be targets," Jeff said.

"PRTs up this way haven't had trouble," Frank said.

Provincial Reconstruction Teams. One of them had built a paved road from Kabul to the Panjshir Valley. It used to take five hours to reach the valley from Kabul. From the cockpit, the Panjshir Valley was the space between the index finger and the thumb on the hand reaching for the arrow. It seemed to come from China, as if grabbing for a spear.

They reached the foothills just as the snow tapered off. Mary couldn't find any signs of clearing, though. The sky was heavy gray, like wet concrete. Countryside was deserted. They were miles from the village she'd seen. The only manmade fixture was a grouping of pylons the PRTs had sunk into the roadway along the hairpins and dropoffs.

They slid the fiberglass boards out of the Land Cruiser, and each carried their own. At first she'd thought they'd have to lug the boards uphill before they could sled, but when they walked a few steps, she saw they were parked at the crest of a slope. Frank threw his down and pushed off. He lay on his belly, soles of his boots large in the air, then smaller and smaller until he reached bottom and coasted to a stop. He left a fluted track, as if someone had dragged a fork down a pile of salt. Jeff followed immediately, but Rex waited until he saw Frank climbing back.

She watched them skidding into the recess. She heard exclamations, and their dampened voices sounded as if they'd floated out of her memories from childhood. She fought the feeling that something was wrong. She told herself it was nothing more than the way she felt before she jumped into the first cold water of summer. Just go.

She went a little slower than she'd expected at first, but then velocity picked up, really exploded. Midway, Frank made to leap in front of her—he did leap and then leapt back, bellowing. She couldn't tell what he was trying to say. For the first time in months, she felt magnificently careless. Like any June lake that she'd first dived into, the speed encased her, cleaning her out.

Rex was at the bottom, waiting for her. They ran back up the hill like kids. Frank was on his way down when they got near the top. He steered right for them, and Mary stood in his way with her arms folded and feet planted, then sidestepped at the last moment.

"X!" Frank hollered. His hand reached out for her ankle. He missed. "I'll get you next time," he wailed, his voice winding down into a shrunken sound near the bottom.

When they reached the top, Rex went down feet-first, toes up. He batted his hand against his open mouth, whooping like an Indian chief. Mary whooshed down just after him, a dolphin.

The hill was broad. After a while, they trudged west to find powdery portions untouched by their careening. Frank tried a standing run and flipped instantly. Sometimes they hurtled down simultaneously, trying to bumper-car each other. They moved for better snow a few times, then decided to pair off for more momentum. It didn't work for Rex and Frank, who split apart off their sled and tumbled like cylinders downhill. Somehow Frank's boot catapulted out from under him and shot in the air like foam off a geyser.

Mary got set to ride with Jeff, and he pried his weapon out from its shoulder holster and tossed it aside. "Potential projectile," he said, laughing. The denseness of it sank out of sight into the snow, and she put her arms around him like a girlfriend.

At the top again, Rex took her and lifted her over his shoulder, and she bent at the waist, her arms down his backside, which she smacked and punched. She was kicking too, and they were laughing so hard he staggered, but then he got her down on the fiberglass and pulled her into his chest. She was thrilled for it. She pulled up snow as they flew down the hill, smashed it back in his face, as junior-high as she could be.

At the bottom, Frank gave her a hand up off the fiberglass and said, "X, play nice."

She had a stab in her, and then, as if her babyish hurt had appeared in the landscape, she pictured a boy at the ridgeline, crouching to fish Jeff's sidearm out of the drift. She looked up a little too fast.

"Jumpy," Frank said, but he wasn't teasing.

"Just a—" She stopped.

Frank's eyes followed hers up the hill. Rex was already halfway up, tramping on a slant to get closer to Jeff, who was on his knees. Mary scanned, her vision skipping and sliding along the pylons, the double-back line of the next pass, trembling lines of mountains behind it. All she saw was Frank tearing up after Rex.

She heard a footfall. She turned, and the white blinkered her in a shout. She tripped forward, leaving the fiberglass behind, scrambling up with both hands, crabbing the hill when she backslid from trying too hard. She didn't look up. She put all of it into scaling the height. She rasped out Jeff's name. She called for Rex.

"Frank," she tried to shout when she reached the ridge.

They were gone. She ran, crisscrossing, disbelieving. She stood and waited, listening. A frantic sensation like a river rushing filled her ears. She searched again, looking for tracks. She found the scuffled snow. She moved her gloved hand across the indentations she was sure they'd made. There was the Land Cruiser but not where she'd thought it would be. She looked for markers, but she hadn't thought to settle on them earlier, and now it was all a repetition of harshening frosted shapes, the road like the sloping of the shoulder, pylons duplicating against mountain views, the sky that uninterrupted shade of cement.

She didn't have a cell phone, but the willowy antenna of the Land Cruiser came to her. The radio. Or maybe Rex or Jeff had left a mobile in the glove compartment. Who had the keys? Her mind was moving along a syncopated path, and she was walking toward the tailgate, try-ing to remember if the door got locked after they pulled out the fiber-glass boards, when all of a sudden her foot turned, an ankle twisted, and she pulled herself away from a backward slip. She fell flat on the ground, but her chin was in air.

Her belly and chest were on the ledge. All she could see was so white, so without shading of any kind, that at first she had no depth of field. It was only when her eyes could detect the most delicate grays that she sensed her position. Her face hung over a great distance.

Shocked, she pushed back, or tried to, and then she saw them. They were faceup—Frank's legs and arms extended, Jeff bent, Rex in a sprawl. At the heel of the sheer drop where they lay, so steep it was brown and free of snow, she could make out the beginnings of the return of the storm, a sifting of snow shaking once again through the air.

She arched herself away from the cliff. Her ankle was tender but didn't seem broken. She saw it now—they had each watched one of the others disappear and gone to help, only to make the same plummet. She was convinced they were knocked out, not dead. There was no blood she could see, even from this height. The snow had to have cushioned them.

She crawled slowly, paying heed to any icy silver on the surface. She was going to stand and try limping for the Land Cruiser but thought it safer to stay low. Her sense of the incline seemed inaccurate, and theirs had been too. Everything was so white they'd lost their bearings. When she reached the bumper, she pulled herself up and pushed the tailgate's switch pad. The back windshield floated upward with a spring-loaded gasp.

She hoisted up and through the opening. She levered herself over the back seat and sidled through the front seats to avoid the gearshift. It sapped all of her wits, but she found it, a mobile phone in a plastic well under the radio. She stared at it a few seconds before locating the key-pad, as if she'd only just then encountered a cell phone. She should take off her glove. She pulled on the fingers and placed it on the dashboard, making a mental note of exactly where she put it. She was about to dial 911 when it hit her. She was in-country. There was no 911. The importance of reaching someone came whamming into her, the memories of her mother with it. It numbed her into confusion. She felt the raised touch-tone buttons. It was like reading Braille, because her eyes were closed, shut tight, and she moved her finger down—two, five, eight, zero. She pressed. The ringing gave way to a voice that kept breaking up, then a British accent came on the line, then another voice, also breaking up. The aggravation of misunderstanding helped wake her some. She told the fourth person on the line, "We had an accident; we're on the road heading north from Bagram, right at the arrow to the valley; tell the pilots. They'll know it." The words helped her. She sat upright, opened the passenger door and got out.

She started tracing squares in the snow to inspect systematically. In seconds, she found Jeff's Beretta, checked the safety, and secured it with an ankle holster she found in the Land Cruiser. There were some Turbo-Flares and good rope too. She set up the flares so the choppers would see them. Rope was strong, extra long. She tied a figure eight around the ball hitch, looped the rest over her left shoulder, snaked it around her waist and between her legs. She took an end in each hand and eased to the cliff's edge. She pushed off deliberately but gently, staying close to the cliff, pausing often as she descended.

When she reached them, there was nothing to fasten the rope to, so she tied it to her good ankle to stop it from flying in a gust and knocking her silly.

Frank's eyes were open. Her dead mother's had been that way when Mary found her.

Mary folded over. Her face landed in snow. She forced herself up to half kneeling, then pulled forward. She grabbed on to his hand to get beside him, tight against him, her right arm over his chest, her right leg over his thighs, her pelvis straining against his flank. She cradled his head in her right hand, rocking. Her forehead was on his right cheek.

She stayed against him. Her mother had been dead longer; she'd been cold. She'd *exsanguinated*. The word stayed with Mary. Yes, Frank was warm. There—wait. Was she imagining? In the left corner of her lips, she felt a brief movement, the slightest possible. It stopped. She waited. There it was again, an upward bump.

He had a pulse.

She pulled back and looked at him. His eyes were fixed, the pupils dilated.

"Frank!" She shouted this.

He was catatonic—not any blink, just fixed.

Rex, though, moved. She heard it. Snow crunched. There he was, trying for an elbow to raise himself. His eyes popped open.

"Where's the fire?"

She went to him. "Rex, it's Mary." He cringed, not recognizing her, and then his eyelids fluttered down.

Right beside him, Jeff wasn't breathing. She saw it. She didn't even check for a pulse. She tilted his head back, took his nose, and pushed her breath into his airway until she saw his chest rise. She gave another breath and listened. There was nothing. She started compressions. She pumped and counted.

She didn't hear the Blackhawks. It wasn't until a medic took her hands off Jeff that she understood help had come. They had Frank on a stretcher. Rex was sitting up. The medic kept saying something, shouting in Mary's ear. Mary leaned closer to hear. She went too far, and the rope she'd forgotten around her ankle tripped her; she fell into soft snow, unharmed again.

11. WATCHMAN, WHAT IS LEFT OF THE NIGHT

t was near 0200 when Mary left the hospital for her hut. The mountains, ghost-alabaster from the half-moon, took up positions around the base, creating an outer cordon. Bagram looked like prison after dark, watched by guard towers, surrounded by barriers. Mary smelled salt and fuel as she walked.

Jeff was dead. Rex had a broken leg, broken arm, and busted ribs. Frank's condition was critical. She looked calm, so they let her keep up with all the steps. Ultrasound found minimal bleeding in his abdomen, CAT scan showed his brain was concussed, and surgery to relieve the pressure had come in the golden hour after first impact. An R.N., a major who'd served in the Balad hospital, sat with her during the operation and explained that Frank's brain in his head, hitting the ledge, had been like a melon in a cannonball slamming into concrete. Most this nurse had seen were from IEDs, but in Afghanistan, falls caused them too. Without the snow, Frank would have been smashed dead. They called it traumatic brain injury. On the best end, it was no worse than hockey or football. At the worst end, it was vegetative. Frank seemed to be in the middle. So much would depend on the next twenty-four hours.

As she took the turn into the B-huts, she remembered it was just about twenty-four hours since she'd been pulled out of bed for the run. Her ankle was sprained but not enough to need a crutch or a cane. The swelling was already going down. She was fine. She could feel the sleeping spreading out ahead of her, the huts contracted from the cold, plywood windows hammered shut. Everyone in those huts would call her lucky. Some would make her ashamed. They all had stories of legs blown from bodies by mortars, backs and chests shrapneled with ceramic crush, rock bits, and bone splinters from soldiers smithereened beside them. She'd seen them at Walter Reed.

Her day, this day, amounted to something else. They'd gone and got hurt sledding. It was pitiful. And more than a few would say it, not just behind her back.

She opened the door to the hut as fast as she could and closed it faster to conserve the little warmth inside. She stood still for a bit, to adjust to the pitchy interior. After a while, a spectral leavening gave out the hut's contents, and she made it to the door of her room. By the time she got there, Purdue was at her room's doorway, then Seri at hers. From another door over came the sound of Eve singing, something that might have been "Row, Row, Row Your Boat."

"You okay?" Seri asked.

"Good God," Purdue said.

Mary looked where Purdue looked but couldn't see.

One of them turned on the light. Mary blinked hard and saw blood, but hardly any, on the sweater Rex had given her. She touched her face, and it seemed as if the thinnest dried skin were covering parts of her own. She scraped a touch off and looked at her fingernail. It was yellowish, not blood. Something else. She had no idea how it got there.

"Get some water," Seri ordered Purdue, who just stood there.

"Now," Seri said.

"No," Mary said. "I'm good."

Seri shook her head, disappeared into her room, and returned with baby wipes. She drew Mary in, sat her on the bed, and started cleaning her cheek. "How could they leave you like this at the hospital? It's in your hair."

"Not important," Mary said. Adrenaline was still in effect. She was screaming-white awake. Her insides were one big overhead light.

"Take that off," Seri said after she'd cleaned all of Mary's face. Mary obediently unzipped and pulled, stepped out of her pants. She stood in her bra and panties, one powder blue, the other washed-out black.

Seri handed her a pair of sweats and a hoodie. Mary started putting them on while Seri laid a pair of socks on the bed.

"What the fuck happened to you guys?" Purdue was back, standing in the doorway to Mary's bedroom.

There on the bed beside the socks was the press release.

"No," Seri said, grabbing it away.

"You know what? You're fucked up," Purdue said and left.

Seri and Mary listened to the slam of her door. Eve had stopped singing. The silence rolled in to them.

Seri put the release on Mary's pillow.

"Lies," Seri said.

Mary was putting socks on her feet.

"Are they the interesting ones?" Mary asked. "Or the easy ones?"

"There's a whopper. The rest is the usual."

She reached over Seri and read. When she got to the end, she said, "So they're saying it was a Reaper."

"That's right. Someone in Nevada," Seri said. "Someone on a joystick at Nellis." All the unmanned air vehicles, the drones, were controlled—much like any video game—at Nellis Air Force Base in Nevada.

"Not a Viper," Mary said.

"There are no Vipers at Bagram—you should know that," Seri said. It was okay if a drone went into Pakistan and dropped a bomb. That Vipers were doing it—that was like Laos, or Cambodia.

"Killed someone named al-Libi," Mary said, continuing to read.

There was nothing about civilians. She felt strangled by that, remembering Jeff's talk about it, but it was more than this, some congruity, a mixing of her own hospital hours and those of the victims she'd made, as if someone had arranged this day to get her to see, to realize, for good. But she wasn't feeling it, not even close.

"Sleep," Seri said. "That's what you need."

Mary looked at her blankly. "I can't imagine sleeping right now."

"You want to raid Eve's stash? I'll bet she's got Valium, and stronger."

"Horse tranquilizer wouldn't touch me."

"Just lie down."

"I can't."

"All right, then. Well," Seri said, standing up, "maybe you need some alone time."

"Seri, do you have pictures of your kids I could look at?"

"Now?"

"Yeah."

Seri sat back down. "You don't like kids."

"I know."

Seri lifted her eyebrows, let out a stream of air. She was about to say something. "Please," Mary said. "I don't know why."

She watched Seri get up and leave. She rested her head against the plywood divider. Soon Seri was back, with a maroon photo album and a Tupperware box.

Mary woke with Halloween snapshots on her arms and chest. Seri was asleep on the floor, dirty laundry her blanket. Mary could smell coffee. She shifted her legs and heard what might be a crumple. She felt around her knee and pulled away some photos.

Eve looked in, her face bleared with the too much moisturizer she used in cold weather. Seri lifted her head up.

"This is good," Eve said.

Seri smiled. She put her head back down.

Mary moved some of the photos carefully. One kid, the boy, was a pumpkin. The girl was a strawberry. They were somewhere around two and three years old. She couldn't remember their names. She never did. Eve, unlike Purdue, knew exactly what to say about yesterday, which was nothing. Why ask about Frank when there was nothing Mary knew about Frank that Eve wouldn't hear within minutes of leaving the hut? Why inquire as to press releases about runs that were done and past? Today is today. Night was night.

"Put you right under," Eve said, referring to the kid photos and sipping at her coffee cup from the doorway. "Better than Ambien."

183

"Can I have some of that?" Seri said, pointing to the coffee.

Eve left.

"Me too," Mary said louder.

"Fuck, what time is it?" Seri's voice was husky from sleep.

Mary tried to judge the light through the shut plywood. "Maybe seven."

Eve was back with the two mugs. Caretaker, she knew their preferences: Seri's was black, and Mary's white with sugar. She was right about the kids. They'd put Mary to sleep.

"Thanks, doc," Seri said. "Lifesaver."

"Beauty Queen and Bringer of Life," Mary said.

Eve bowed.

"Time, please?" Seri asked.

"Oh eight hundred."

"Shit!" Seri sprang out of the laundry. Mary started shuffling photos into the Tupperware box.

"Is Purdue gone?"

"Of course."

It was warmer. She felt it. She could hear the drip dropping from the roof outside.

"There's messages here for you," Eve said to Mary.

She looked. Squadron commander. Hospital.

"You should of woke me!"

"Told me not to," Eve said.

"Who did?"

"Some private who came by with these."

Mary pulled on a uniform, grabbed her gear. She'd pee on the way. She looked at the mirror by the door. Seri'd cleaned her up good.

The path along Disney Drive was teeming after the snow day. The languages and accents gathered up, then flew off, as she went. Poles, Germans, French, Brits, Aussies, Kiwis, Egyptians, Turks, Koreans, Norwegians. The saluting whisked up and down, the snow melted, the sky had blue in it. She willed it to be a good omen for Frank. She tried calling the nurse from the previous night on her cell phone but got voice mail. Commander's message told her to go to the hospital first. That worried her.

On her way, she got a call on her cell from one of Rex's DynCorp buddies telling her Rex was already in Germany. He said Rex's condition was stable, but they were flying him to London for more testing. There was a memorial service for Jeff day after tomorrow, at the U.S. Embassy. He offered to pick her up at the gate. She told him she'd be there.

At the hospital, they ushered her into a room. Commander Hood came forward to her. She didn't like his expression. It was not the face of a man who was about to chew her out—that's what she wanted to see. Off-base nonsense has tragic consequences. His face should have beamed that.

"Sit down, Captain," he said, seeming as if he might take her hand. She could hear lowered voices in other parts of the room. It was a waiting room, like any hospital, but there was the regular MP posted at the door.

"Frank's the same," Hood said.

She waited.

"Can I see him?" she finally asked.

"Absolutely," Hood said. He looked high-minded. And his worst flaw, the perfection of his handsomeness, seemed more pronounced than usual. He needed to drink ugly, get beat on, come nearer to something bad for him.

Now it looked as if he was going to come in with her to see Frank. She really didn't want that. He followed close by, grazing her elbow. He was oversolicitous, momentous too. Saying about her crash, and now Frank's this, and how ironic, and you just never knew. But then some specialist came toasting in, all hot with important missives for him. They made earnest expressions, spoke flat-dramatically, that military specialty. Mary kept waiting, stared at a protocol poster on anesthesia, Hood every so often telling her to hold on, hold on. After too long, he said, Go on ahead; are you sure you'll be all right? Yes, she would.

Finally, she was in a corridor, wide and dormlike. A nurse she didn't know had come to escort her past soldiers on highly developed gurneys. Now the nurse was stopped, a doctor talking to her in confidential tones. Mary waited again, her eyes drawn to the men prone around her. They were so still, so shipshape, with sheets the color of blue scrubs, and tubes coiled importantly on their stomachs. This way station was a masterpiece of cleanliness, a sanctuary from expressed pain, or at least from any pain that caused cries or moans. Deep in technology's sympathies, these soldiers seemed little like past fallen. No mud came here.

She remembered what they'd told her the night before. They would be shipped to Germany promptly. The C-130 that took them would be an airborne ICU. It would land at Ramstein Air Base; from there they'd be rushed to Landstuhl Regional Medical Center and, as soon as possible, flown on another cargo plane across Europe and the Atlantic to Andrews and Walter Reed. The average length of time for transport of the injured from front lines to the States had been forty-five days during Vietnam. Now it was four days.

Just then the nurse from last night was at her side. "Captain," she said, any sentimental wet wrung from her voice. She guided her to Frank's gurney.

He looked perfect, purified somehow, without edema or bruise. If there was broken skin, she couldn't see it, his head white-wrapped. Everything wrong was hidden. His coma could have been deep sleep. The nurse stood there with her for a while. She was grateful for her stoic way, it gave Mary some room. She put her hand on one of Frank's hands.

"I take it your commander got with you," the nurse said after a little longer.

"Yes, as far as it went."

"I have a few things we should talk about," she said. "When you're ready."

Mary took her hand back. "I'm ready."

They moved a distance from Frank. The nurse leaned against a piece of medical equipment, something bulky.

"He'll be going to Landstuhl today. We've got a transport leaving in less than four hours. We have folks assigned to pack up personal effects, but Lieutenant Partnoy went to the trouble to make some binding requests we're duty-bound to honor. One of them is that you be the assistant to the sicmo—Summary Court-Martial Officer—that's designated to conduct the processing of effects. Normally, it's a supply soldier or clerk. He specified you. He also specified that under no conditions were any papers among his personal effects to be sent to the JPED—I'm sorry, Joint Personal Effects Depot. Those are to be kept in your possession. Apparently, he left instructions among them as to how you're to handle them."

"This has to be done in four hours?"

"No, the cutoff is three days from date of incident. The inventory is scheduled at his RLB at 0700 tomorrow."

"Understood."

"Frank also designated you be the one to call his wife, and we didn't want that to happen last night, for a variety of reasons I won't go into right now. But we need to call her ASAP. Are you able to do that now?"

"Yes."

"I'm the head nurse around here, so we have a specialist assigned for morale calls and notifications. The only thing I'd say to you is, there is a sentence sequence that they'll give you with some fill-ins for the blanks. I would stick to those—unless, of course, you feel Lieutenant Partnoy specified you because he didn't want that kind of formal communication. Did you know his wife?"

"A little."

"Come this way."

Mary followed her to the specialist, who explained the phone, how long she'd have—as long as she needed—and gave her the form for a VSI—very seriously injured—call. He told her he would stand by in case she had any trouble with the connection. Then he dialed the number. It was 10:30 in Maryland.

"Hello."

"Clara?"

"Who is this?"

"Clara, it's Mary. Mary Goodwin."

"Oh my God."

"Clara, he's alive, he's not dead."

"Oh my God."

"He's banged up, but he's going to be fine."

"Where, where is he?"

"We're still at Bagram."

"At Bagram."

"That's right."

"Can I talk to him?"

"Not right now." She was evading. And she thought: If I don't tell her facts who will? Someone she doesn't know. A doctor, someone better at it. But Frank had wanted it to be her.

"Is he in surgery?"

"He had one operation," Mary said. "To relieve pressure on his brain."

"Oh my God. His brain."

"Nothing got blown off. Nothing's missing."

"Thank God. Oh, thank God."

"It could be a lot worse."

"Are you okay? Were you injured?"

"No, I'm fine."

"You ejected."

"No. I didn't—we weren't."

"Oh. You weren't with him?"

"I was, yes, I was. We weren't flying."

"Tell me it wasn't an IED."

"It wasn't. Clara, it was a freak accident. To be honest with you, it was a stupid, dumb thing. We were sledding, and we shouldn't have been."

"Sledding? Did you say sledding?"

"I said that, yes."

"He got hurt sledding!"

"I'm afraid, yeah, he did."

"Oh, you should have said that right out!"

Mary felt abashed. Maybe she should have. She dropped her voice.

"It's embarrassing."

"It's wonderful!"

Now she saw what she'd done. She'd either have to leave her with this impression, of barely banged-up sledding Frank, or pull her back to traumatic brain injury, hockey or football but maybe vegetable. That's what she would have said to Frank, if it had been Clara injured: hockey or football but maybe vegetable. A surge of missing him knocked against her.

"I just thought you should know," Mary managed, throat tight.

"Well, they'll have him back in the cockpit in no time!"

Frank's wife would be an optimist. That made all the sense in the world. Mary saw she had to give her something straighter, though. People can handle it, they always can. Maybe that's why Frank wanted her to be the one to make this call.

"Clara, he's going to Germany, and from there to Walter Reed. It was a fall, and it was far. He's not regained consciousness since, which is not the best sign. He could be great, you know, football-concussion level of problems, or it could be bad. Vegetative. That level of bad. Or, as mostly happens, something in between."

"Oh, Mary."

"I'm sorry."

"I'm not sure I . . ."

"Clara, don't worry." Christ, she was saying the words "sorry" and "worry." She couldn't stand them. And she'd misjudged. She shouldn't have laid it out for Clara. Frank had wanted her to do this because she was a woman. He'd known all along her tough-girl pose was just that.

"I'm worried. I'm . . . I'm . . . I'm . . . I'm," Clara stammered.

"Clara, where's your mother?"

"In the Ozarks—you know that."

"Right. Right. I was thinking if you could visit with her . . . But look.

Just, you'll be getting some official communication about how to meet him at Walter Reed. I'm not qualified really to be making this—"

"Mary, I'm worried about you. It's . . . you . . . for you, this isn't exactly new. It's—I'm worried for you."

That wasn't right. How strange of Clara.

"I'm fine—really, I am."

"You're not fine. You should talk to someone."

There it was. The advice she always got.

"I probably will. Listen, they're telling me time's up here."

She hated to lie, but not too much.

"Mary, thank you. Thank you for making this call."

"Frank wanted me to."

"He'd told me that," Clara said.

"Uh-huh."

"Well, he asked me who it was I'd like to hear from. And I said you."

That surprised. Her thinking stopped cold. Finally, she said, "Clara, you know my e-mail, right?"

"It's on the refrigerator."

"Well, you know how to find me, then. If you need, you know, any-thing." What could she give her that she needed? She would have liked to say something more true, something perhaps about having no idea Clara felt close to her—in any way.

"I'm honored, Clara." That was military talk. What a mistake.

"Oh, Mary," Clara started to cry.

Mary tried one more time. "I'm moved, more the word—you—that you wanted me to be the one to call."

"Mary, you promise me you'll talk to someone."

Well, at least Clara said that again. That made it easier to say her goodbye.

All day and all night, the snow melted. Bagram had become rivers. The largest were slush. Mud spread everywhere, and at once. The sound of it clasping and unclasping her boots as she tried to move through it in the early morning made Mary tense. She could see that a grouping of Gators, their drivers attempting to lay down planks to make camp passable, had succeeded only in getting mired. A smaller truck brought to pull them out got stuck too. The tank sent to save them waited. Beside it was a sludged congregation of logistics officers and Afghan civilians arguing with an army sergeant who had slept with all three of Purdue's reservist friends. She watched him take the opportunity to grin at her, but then he looked as if he remembered the latest news about her. He changed from giving off that he was planning to wink at her and exuded a smoldering, sad seriousness that seemed designed to burrow through her toward the place where consolation could lead to desperado fucking. She looked down, furious and tempted and then mad at herself about that, then aggravated and clumsy in the silt slickness; when she looked up again, the group was out of shouting range.

She arrived late to Frank's hut, coated to her knees, mud splatted all the way up to her chest. His hutmates, men in her wing, pilots all, had stopped at the muck by the front door, which had a slash of red tape across it. She wished she'd missed them. They should have been getting breakfast by now. The mud had probably stopped them. They had the look of people trying to figure out the best path where there really wasn't one. The driver she liked least, Huck, saw her first.

"Extra," he said.

"Huck," she said.

Others wolfed out their greetings. She'd forgotten how deep men's voices together could be. Frank had to have been shortest among them. She felt comfortable near him, but these towered when they got close to her. They were unsullied by any bilge. They put out a hand, one by one, respectful, polite, each good enough or fine-looking, eyes unclouded, minds at ease. Their processing of Frank's escapade and injury had left all undisturbed. He'd done something stupid, which he often did, and paid a price, which might be high or low. As to her appearance to process his personal effects, it made sense, since anomalies such as her were often connected to anomalies such as Frank. These pilots were regular guys, the healthily dominant genes. She and Frank were recessive alleles.

They made room for her, and she went up the two steps to the hut's door, giving it a quick knock that sounded too soft. She tried again.

The sicmo was another giant. He had to bend his head to put it outside the hut's door to greet her. They exchanged salutes, and she followed him inside.

He led her to Frank's bed, in the back, on the left. The empty foot-lockers were open on the floor beside it. Piles of freezer bags, garbage bags, permanent markers, index cards, reinforced tape, bubble wrap, padlocks, and serialized metal seals were piled on the bed.

"Captain, as specified by Lieutenant Partnoy, you are to take possession of all documents. I am to verify that it is documents only that you are removing."

"Understood."

"In addition, you'll be placing all other personal effects in these lockers while I take inventory of each item. Each item will be identified and taped with its box and item number. Do not attempt to sort out or destroy what may or may not be pornography. List it and ship it. JPED has the manpower to screen and remove. Do not attempt to clean soiled clothing. We will remove war souvenirs, illegal drugs, or alcohol."

"Yes, sir."

They began with gear. A laptop. A DVD player. There were only two DVDs. One was *Full Metal Jacket* and the other, *Apocalypse Now*.

Seemed as if every man on base had these two. Their first tour at Bagram, some went around repeating choice lines from the films. Fire-fights were *the real shit*. Infantry liked to come out with *I have become death, destroyer of worlds*. Marines favored *Though I walk through the valley of death I shall fear no evil because I am the meanest mother-fucker in the valley*. This tour, guys had watched them too many times over, and no one re-enacted favorite moments anymore. Killer talk, nihilistically shaded, had been in your face. Now it was the valley of cheesy.

She picked up the red MP3 player that wasn't an iPod. She remembered him talking about winning it in a beer-cap contest. She gave the sicmo the brand and model number of a digital camera about the size of a pack of cigarettes. She'd been with Frank when he bought it in Doha on leave. There was the camera-battery charger he got at the airport. She folded the earbud headphones that he'd always cussed for falling out of his ears. There was his cell phone, one that flipped open and had a ringtone like the theme from a game show. She saw the two cell-phone chargers—he'd lost one, bought a new one, and then realized he still had the old one. A USB drive. A portable printer. Two radios. A compass, GPS, optics, night-vision periscope. She examined his clock radio; he'd written something, looked as if he'd carved it with a scissor tip, but she couldn't tell what it said.

His clothes and shoes came next. He had three pairs of clean socks, three dirty; six pairs of boxers, all dirty; six T-shirts, all clean; the regulation uniforms—physical training, airman battle, and camouflage. He had a pair of running shoes, shower flip-flops. He'd worn his combat boots.

After that, it was photographs thumbtacked to the wall. Three of his new baby boy, Trevor. Another of his daughter, Angela. Another of Clara holding Trevor. Their wedding photo. His sister and her kids. His brother. His parents. She'd heard Frank talk at length about his sister's husband, who left her six months ago with no explanation. She knew his brother was a telephone-company manager who didn't get along with Frank's father. This father was a strict disciplinarian and retired army. She knew his mom was a substitute schoolteacher but was artistic and had started trying to change one of their bedrooms into a studio so she could paint, but his dad didn't like it. They'd been fighting recently. She remembered in particular Frank saying his father's moods were steep and treacherous. They'd laughed at that.

"You all right, Captain?"

"Sir?"

"This can't be easy."

"He's not dead, sir." She shouldn't have said it, but, there, she did. His solemnly sympathetic tone grated. It was treacle-phony. It combined with his self-congratulatory implication in every bodily tic, unintended move, and breath taken. Each denoted something like: Poor asswipes like us are here while la-di-das back home go shopping. He wanted her to get with him on this—what was it?—oh, that this personal-effects processing was sacred duty for gritty people. All it was, in fact, was something someone dreamed up to prevent family claiming the air force lost or stole something. And Frank didn't give a damn about any of these so-called personal effects. He didn't consider any of them personal. Family photos, he used to tell her, were so overexposed, so military-endorsed, so encouraged to be promoted in any public setting, that any authentic meaning had been shrink-wrapped away. Everyone agreed that everyone could agree: We're supposed to be fighting for them and wanting to return home to them. That's the only emotional experience we're supposed to be having. It's universal. See, they love their kids, these Afghans, just like we love our kids. What if you hate your wife? What if your mother up and left when you were three? Everybody loves who they're supposed to love. We're all the same. *The Great Same.* That's what he called it. She'd heard him hold forth on it more times than the days they'd spent together.

"He was your wingman."

"Still is."

"That was a pretty stupid stunt you and he pulled."

She wasn't sure it even rose to the level of stupid stunt. Stupid stunt would be picking off the turbans of locals with a sniper rifle from a secluded promontory. Sledding—what was sledding?

"Uh-huh," she said.

"He may never fly again because of it."

"He may not."

"You were outside the wire for no good reason."

"That's correct."

So Frank still had the photos above his head, first thing he saw every morning. She'd wondered, since she'd never seen his quarters, if they would be here.

Finally, they were done with everything else; it was time for the documents. She turned to the shelves at the foot of his bed. There was a stack of file folders. She pulled them out and sat down on the bed to look at them.

They were filled with sealed envelopes. Each had a date on it. After opening a few more folders, she saw that the dates went back to their first tour. She looked at the sicmo.

"For inventory purposes, we'll just put 'X number of folders, Y number of sealed envelopes,' " he said. "Let's divide the folders and count the envelopes. No need to open them. They're for your eyes only."

There were fifteen file folders and 103 envelopes. She put them in one of the empty garbage bags and carried them back to her hut.

Her mobile rang almost as soon as she'd stepped inside. It was her group commander. He told her to report to the Joint Forces Special Operations component post immediately. The Component requested conventional air-support sorties for Special Operations Forces on a mission-by-mission and priority availability basis. Was she being taken off the roster? If so, why'd they have to meet with her? Her CO could have alerted her.

She grabbed some of the letters, including the one Frank had stapled to the earliest file folder. *Start here,* he'd written on it. Maybe they'd make her wait and she could take a look at it. It was still warming up, so she threw her hat on her bed.

Back through the mud she went, although by this time the planks and blocks were down. The boards were already grimy, but it was nothing like the boot-sucking ooze surrounding them. While she was walking, she tried to call to Landstuhl to check on Frank. After more than a few failed attempts, she decided she needed to check with someone at the base hospital. There might be a better number she didn't have. She was ready to dial the hospital when she realized she'd not been paying attention to where she was going. The component post was never easy to find. Now she was lost.

She backtracked, feeling daffy. She remembered how some sailor she'd met had broken down the branches: Air force was too sensitive and squishy. Army was too conservative and Christian. Marines were too serious. Navy was just right—how'd he put it?—for a fella who likes drinkin', fightin', travelin', and chasin' women. Frank's take was simple: Squishy. What did "squishy" mean? Every so often, Frank would intone, "Give me your sensitive, your squishy and love-tossed."

She tried another right turn, and there she found it. She hurried into the post, reported to the clerk, got told to wait, and sat down with Frank's first envelope. She was about to open it when she noticed the clerk hyperfascinated and not even trying to hide it. Mary stared back, blatant and offended. The girl looked away but maybe only because the phone rang. What was it about an envelope? Precious on any base, she knew that. There was a country song Purdue loved about letters from home. It was more than that. An unopened envelope had an alluring tang, a whiff of momentous. An olden aura too, like riding through base in a chariot. She put it back in her leg pocket. She'd not wanted to read it in the hut either. She'd have to think of somewhere else. Luckily, it wasn't too long before the senior NCO came out of his office and told her to step in.

"Understand you and Lieutenant Partnoy had a serious accident," he said when she sat down. "Sorry to hear about it. Terrain here is dangerous. Simplest thing can turn ugly."

"We shouldn't have been out there."

"Probably. But not definitely. I've seen *much* dumber moves."

She smiled a little. He tilted his head as if he were saying, Ease up on yourself.

"Captain, this is the situation," he began. "Special Operations has a need for a fixed-wing pilot, specifically a female. They've evaluated your accident out of Andrews, and there's no pilot error. Think you handled it well, given the systemic failure your aircraft exhibited. This one, this accident, there's a process there, but all I can say is, this is a request of such a nature that they—they want us to proceed from this end. And there are some other parameters, details I'm not even privy to. Suffice it to say, you fit these parameters, along with about two other pilots. Both of them happen to be in Iraq. There's a selection process. Part of it takes place here. The second stage, if you make it through the first, would suspend your deployment. We'd have to ship you back home for a while.

"This is a special-access program, and right now, that's all I can say about it."

She'd heard about these. Not known anyone well who'd gone through any. Some assignments could last a week, others a year. Or more.

"Would the mission be based out of Bagram?"

"I don't know."

"Any time frame?"

"That I don't know either."

"Can I opt out?"

"Yes, at this stage in the process you can. Though, apparently, if the two other pilots don't work out, you may be sitting here again with me."

"How much time do I have to say yes or no?"

"Forty-eight hours. But, Captain, security on this is need-to-know. So, if you think you're going to have time to discuss it with anyone, think again. You can't. On the other hand, if you want to think it over carefully for yourself, that seems to me to be a good idea. No need for you to give me an answer right this minute."

She stood up.

He did too.

"Please convey to Jeffrey Watson's colleagues over at DynCorp my sincere condolences."

"I will, sir."

She climbed into the cockpit. She watched her crew chief walking back toward the morning light. Years of kindness to crew gave her this time alone at the back of the hangar with no mission. It wasn't allowed. It wasn't strictly disallowed. Actually, no one to her knowledge had ever thought to do it, or, if they did, gotten caught. Sometimes things wigwagged out of notice that way. She put her head back and closed her eyes.

For a while, she imagined the feel of a ride. She flew a split S, barrel rolls, more than a few chandelles. She wished she were at Red Flag, the sky all hers except for one opponent. She wanted to box in the sky. The pilot who trained her, a Gulf War veteran, he'd have said she wanted a knife fight in a booth.

Frank was still unconscious. Landstuhl had put him on a flight to Walter Reed that afternoon. Clara's e-mail said there was nothing to do but wait. Mary remembered the nurse saying so much depended on the next twenty-four hours. It was now the fifteenth hour of the second twenty-four.

She imagined pulling the stick back, the great sick of gravity. The first time her 110-pound body weighed a thousand pounds, she wanted more. Come here, she called to it, see what you can do. She'd been told it pulled the blood from your head. But you really couldn't imagine it until it happened. Only a few things were like nothing else at all. The slamming force of Gs was one of them. Frank, gone but not gone, was another.

She wasn't past praying. She was no churchgoer, yet difficulty often brought a holy time. The plea came easy. Bring him back to me. She could have said it everywhere she went, to everyone she knew, for the rest of her natural life. She suspected it would be the background track of most days coming.

She looked at the first envelope. The glue to seal it had dried out. It was closed but pulling open. She pushed her finger under the flap. Inside were a standard sheet of letter paper and a glossy clipping, folded up tight, maybe from a magazine. She put that on her lap.

For Extra
Dec 4, 2001

Your hard to talk to. Did anyone ever tell you that? Well its true. Drive me crazy 9 times out of 10. But you're my flight lead. The day I got told it was a woman, won't ever forget it. I said what are the chances? And why me? I realized it was like I'd gotten cancer. Because that's what people ask themselves. (I know from what happened to a friend of mine.) And that got me to thinking.

There's got to be a reason I got you. Maybe a way to teach me something about my usual pastime which since this is for posterity I'll call skirt-chasing. I do have a daughter now and that's caused some changes in my way of life. (Though to be honest not that many.)

I don't know if I'll keep doing this could be just a whim. I've been thinking about it for a while now. Today what got me to put pen to paper or fingers to keyboard was all this business about the Afghan girl in National Geographic. Here's why. This girl— the eyes mostly—had a hold on me from the time I was a kid. I used to see it in the diner where my old man took me on Saturdays. I saw it all over the place really. She was just there, one of those things like Its the Real Thing Coke, or Ghostbusters, that you can't stop seeing. But it wasn't til we deployed that I even got that she was Afghan. I was something like 7 when the 1st photo came out. I mean, I think I thought she was an indian. As in cowboys and indians. Then I saw this National Geographic while we were here about how they tried to find her. And they couldn't and couldn't. But they did. And when I saw what happened to her—it blew me sky high. You know they had to use iris scanning technology to make sure it was her. That's how much she changed. But she was only 27! X, she was your age. She looked older than my mom.

I can't tell you how long I stared at those two pictures. I still do. I don't keep them lying around for anyone to see. But I put them in here so you could take a look. Unbelievable isn't it? Tells you a lot right there about the difference between life here and life back home. And you know what else? She liked the Taliban. (Said something about how it brought peace.)

The other thing that got me going is the feeling I've had ever since we first deployed. The feeling that we lived through something that people will be talking about after we're gone. But today one of the flyboys got me going about how it was going to get to be like Veteran's Day 30 percent off sale, Memorial Day no down payment extravaganza at Chrysler. One day, there'll be stuff that makes us want to puke about it. They won't remember this feeling I am living right now that we have something in our lives that means something.

You know of course cause you're looking at these photos of this girl, that she looks a lot like you. Creepy isn't it? I wonder if anyone besides me ever told you that. Not the old one but the kid one. And you know she's an orphan like you. I know, I know, your old man is alive but to me based on what I know it would have been better if they fried the bastard. One day I hope to talk to you about it. You won't now, so be it. Me, I'd be yapping my head off about it. It's something to have lived through. And I respect you for having come out the other end. You're a survivor Mary Goodwin through and through. I never saw anybody man or woman with your level of determination.

The plan here is that I'm going to write and you know I was going to do a blog and password protect and all that but I just couldn't deal with worrying about someone hacking into it. Some things paper is better. For one its only in one place. For two you can protect it and tell if anyone got to it with that super duper invention, the licked shut envelope. And three if anything happens to me you'll have these letters right in your hand to hang onto. I don't know maybe your too hardass but I know if you went down I'd want to have something that would tell me for real what you've been thinking. Cause I honestly don't know. And I honestly would like to know.

She wondered if Frank even recalled these words by the time he wrote her the last letter. She'd checked the dates on the envelopes, and the last one he'd written on the day of the accident.

Some things hadn't changed. She hadn't told him anything more about her father—maybe he realized that would never come. He'd never mentioned this Afghan girl, or her resemblance to her. It seemed as if he were living a parallel life, and she felt absurdly miffed. Who was this Mary he wrote to? Why didn't he tell her, the living Mary, that she was hard to talk to? Why didn't he tell her, the person he saw every day, that he resented being assigned a woman as his lead? She knew he did anyway.

At first she thought she'd only take one envelope with her. She hadn't been sure she could read more than one. She feared what? That she'd break down? *Chuck a spaz?* That was a Frankism. With Seri and Eve and Purdue, privacy was zero. Crew, though, they would get how she needed to sit in the bird alone after her wingman got hurt, even if it was sledding that socked him. But the hut girls knew she got no letters, had no boyfriend. They would, out of concern in Seri's and Eve's case, explore and push, and sooner or later word would circulate that Frank declared secret passion in stacks of love letters. Right now, the envelopes were in her ruck, a place of nil interest, under a blanket, under her bed. She'd have to buy a tackle box and lock, like Purdue's. The covered-over byways of Purdue rose up—the story of press releases in the box suddenly sounding truly unlikely.

Your mind heated up fast. Mary'd had all kinds of ideas about what

Frank might have written. Maybe an Afghan woman he'd been hooking up with had gotten pregnant, and he'd left directions to an isolated village. She pictured the perilous journey, the grateful woman, tearful in Mary's arms when she learned Frank was injured, possibly—but then the tape burned in the reel, film snapped; he wasn't dead. No matter how bad you wanted the dramatic tale, they were so hard to make plausible, even in your own head. The heroic sped ahead, just out of reach.

She looked at the other envelopes she'd grabbed. She was going to read them in order but couldn't resist picking the most recent ones. He'd written it just before they'd gone sledding. It was a different envelope, probably from the base commissary. It was thicker than the other one; there were lots of sheets of paper. He'd reinforced the glue with tape.

There were at least a dozen pages, maybe more. As she unfolded them, she saw Internet addresses in minuscule print at the tops and bottoms. But where was his writing? With some effort, she flattened the pages out.

The first one was a map of the run they'd done that night. It looked as if it was from Google Earth, but it might have been DOD. There was North Waziristan. She looked closely at the circled star that was Khushali Torikhel. She went to the next page.

It took her mind a few seconds to make sense of it. There was a girl. It was a photograph of a girl. She wore a locket. It could have been a clover shape. Plackets of sheer ruffles crossed her chest. The sleeves had more of the same. She was wearing a nightgown, and it flared into more ruffles, wider and stiffer. Everything she wore had been white. In the extravagant debris, she finally saw. The bomb had taken her legs.

There were more of these girls in white. She pushed the pages aside— one, two, three, and a fourth. Her hand felt filmy, superlight. She was sitting but losing balance. The nightgowns—identical, as if someone got a discount buying in bulk. They were donations, charity. They came that way. As they'd come to her, after her mother's murder. She had twelve brown dresses, same size, same style—overstock.

She put her forehead to her knees and her hands on her ears—trying not to listen. As the sole witness, she had to say it. They made her practice. She walked through days repeating it: *Pax huic domui, pax huic domui, pax huic domui.* On the stand, they asked her, "Janeta, do you know what the words your father was saying meant?" She shook her head. The judge reminded her to say the word "no."

"No, sir," she said.

"What did you think it meant?"

She was afraid to say.

"Now who's the dummy," she said into the witness-stand microphone. At the defendant's table, her father sat in his air-force uniform, his eyebrows near solid over the bridge of his nose. They'd bolted him to the floor and his chair. He tried to rise up after she spoke. Sighing from the spectators traveled from the back of the courtroom into the jury box. They had told her not to look at him, but she couldn't help it. He was straining to stand. The judge was banging. The people were craning. She put her head in her lap. She put her hands on her head. She covered her ears. It got quiet. The lawyer translated the words for the jury. "Peace to this house."

She'd been the one who insisted on her name change. Her aunt thought it wasn't right. Your mother wanted "Janeta" for you, she told her. It's only up to God to change it. But Mary thought a court and a judge could do it just as easily. She chose a pretty, fresh name, nothing like the most important thing that had ever happened to her. Janeta Enriquez became Mary Goodwin.

She sat up to get back to now. Her eye found the far end, the daylight. She listened to her breathing a few minutes. Then she saw it, a figure in the hangar, coming her way.

It wasn't the crew chief, a wiry dude. It was a bigger man. The ladder was on his side. The sound if she jumped on the other side—too loud. She could just go down the ladder. But she so didn't want to talk to whomever. She sank down in her seat, the top of her head below the rim of the cockpit. Maybe this guy hadn't caught sight of her.

Within seconds it was there, the rap on the fuselage like a knock on a kettle. She stayed down, hoping. Maybe whoever it was would get that she wanted to be left alone. But no, but no, but no, she could hear steps coming up the metal ladder.

"Extra."

It was the weapons loader from the run, the congratulator on the rock path in the snow.

"Drew," she said, trying to push the envelope and papers behind the flight-control-systems panel.

"What's that?"

"Some orders."

"You got orders?"

"No, I mean, well, not . . . uh. I—Drew, I'm supposed to not be talking about it." She could be referring to the special-access assignment. She could.

"No problem," he said. "Sorry." Then his eyes got different. Seri's joking came to her.

"Do you need any help? I mean, I'm sorry about Frank." He put his hand on her shoulder.

"Yeah, I was just, you know, thinking about that."

"Here?"

"Seemed as good a place as any." She needed to get out of the cockpit. She started to stand up, but his hand stayed on her shoulder; actually, it traveled, and it was holding her arm, then her wrist.

"Let me help you," he said.

She looked nervously down the hangar. It was empty.

"Sure, thanks." That was better. Refusing, confronting—best avoided.

But this was the man who complimented her "tasty kill." Through the interference of all the emotions that had followed his words, she'd forgotten them and saw she shouldn't have, because now he was carrying her down the ladder, saying something, but doing too much mumbling. She felt a little like the bride on the threshold, a little like the injured party. On the hangar floor his kissing was tender. He seemed to be pushing for something from her that was sex but more than that. She wasn't fighting him. She'd been wanting wrong kisses since that night at

Walter Reed. The dead, those Tinker Bells, they made her want this even more. Let's get lost. This man was taking her. She hung back in the strength of him; she was going to have to balk at some point, but he was so insistent she started thinking she wouldn't have to be the one to stop him, the crew chief would appear, the hangar would get busy, as it always did—and sure enough—"Get the fuck away from her, you sick fucker."

Her crew chief sounded as if she had the look of defenseless *chica* brutally attacked. Wrong, she wanted to tell him. Not me. But he would avenge. His face was blotchy. She expected her new love to swagger, to respond in keeping with his physical might, but he didn't; he wiped the wet of her mouth from his and, without a backward glance, said, "Sorry, sorry. It won't happen again." He disappeared behind a Viper next to hers, his steps a petty echo until he reached the mud at the hangar's far end.

On the new road to the embassy, Rex's friend was driving along the Hesco barricades smack in its paved middle. The barriers forced a multi-ton to weave like a drunk. Mary saw Karzai's palace, its third-floor balustrade sagging into what had been a grove of trees, now a clearing of stumps.

The U.S. Embassy was orange and mustard, a combination only a little more ugly than the structure itself. A sign instructed, *Dim Lights Drive Slowly When Approaching.* They drifted slo-mo past gates, guns, guards, roadblocks, living quarters on the left, café on the right, planters that doubled as blockades topped off with the last of the unmelted snow. When Mary had first arrived they'd held a few straggling roses.

They finally reached the main building. There were hundreds of dirt-scumbled vehicles in the parking lot. She was surprised to see so many participants in what until now had seemed her own bad dream.

Two days after the accident, Rex was stable. His friend really wanted to know about the sledding. He kept saying the word—sledding this,

sledding also, sledding maybe—scoffing, but maybe she had the problem; she was in one of those states where who it was that brought the
mess was unclear, but, regardless, she wasn't giving any more than
monosyllables to scrub it up. He didn't like that, so, after more questions got more variations snootier than not, they dropped into silence.
She needed to be more pushy, more back-in-your-face, especially after
Drew, whom she disliked, maybe invited, the feelings going guilty,
unwelcome, and back to craven, circling like that, until, as usual, she
ordered herself just to shut it off. What came in place was parading
angels, frills in white, locket like clover, and, soon enough, now who's
the dummy. Close by the childhood diagnosis floating up: Occasional
emotional lability. No cognitive disorder. Affect flat. She held on as they
walked into the embassy.

They were early. But so was everyone else. People had begun filling
up an auditorium on the first floor. It was almost all men, the baritone
hum of them filling the lobby. A good many were carrying M4s and
wearing thigh holsters, looking, with their bulletproof vests pushing
their chests out, intently virile. They would be.

Man-hate was insinuating. Head was unstringing. She excused herself and found the restroom. She didn't need to use the toilet; she just sat
on it, the stall door locked. She had to get through this thing. She had
to. She repeated it: Affect flat. She listened to the world going on outside
the bathroom, the many human interactions, so many and so varied as
to be almost dignifying. They carried on. They went about. They just
did.

After a few minutes she felt less overloaded, more her customary
pissy biggity. She got out of the stall and went to the mirror over the
sink. She looked nothing like that Afghan girl. It was nothing to do
with—Fuck. She realized with a start she'd left the *National Geographic* clipping—hell, the letter! the fucking angel shots!—all of the
letters and enclosures were there in the Viper. The thing with Drew had
completely distracted her. The crew would find it. She was so fucked.
She'd tried to keep everything from her hutmates, and now, now—she
had to tabulate her missing tasks, get organized, shut down this trilling

brain romp. Oh—she needed to tell her group commander her decision about the assignment. She'd hardly given any thought to it. No, she had completely fucking forgotten about it. She started to wash her hands. Fuck if the soap in the dispenser wasn't that bismuth-pink, color of gagging and itty bikinis.

A woman walked in, neatened in a dress and low-heeled boots. She was also wearing makeup, something Mary hadn't seen in months. Either her eye shadow was sloppily applied or she'd been crying. When she went for the toilet paper and started blowing her nose, Mary saw she could get out without either one of them getting too embarrassed.

"Mary Goodwin?"

Mary stopped.

The woman walked away from the stall, toward the hand dryer Mary had tried to slink past.

"Are you Captain Mary Goodwin?"

"Yes."

"Health Attaché Holly Fitzsimmons." She offered her hand to Mary, then, looking at the toilet paper balled up in it, changed her mind.

"Head cold," she said, worrying Mary had misread her tears. "The worst." She bent to start washing her hands. "Listen," she said, turning to look up at Mary, who'd reinstated inching away. "Wait," she said. "Wait, I'm so sorry."

"I should get going," Mary said, weighing how bad it would be to bolt.

But now this embassy woman was sliding her palm into Mary's, saying, "I am sorry, truly sorry, for your loss."

"Thank you," she said, monotone.

"You shouldn't be here by yourself."

"Actually, I came with . . ." She couldn't remember his name. Had he even told her?

"Let me get you seated properly. There's space reserved at the front."

"I'd rather just go in and, you know, sit down."

"No, no, no. Come with me," she said.

They went into the lobby, now even more crowded, the voices sounding almost contentious. Mary guessed she and this Holly were the only women on hand. But then she saw some Afghan women—or perhaps they were Pakistani—carrying a large poster board through double doors. They couldn't fit. There was a scurrying, and the crowd bunched, then all movement stopped, and there was no way to fan out again. It was like a crowded elevator as the doors close, people trying to rearrange their bodies to cause the least offense by the way they held themselves.

She heard Holly say something she didn't catch to a man standing next to her. He had longish hair and a beard. At first he looked like Jesus or a washed-up rocker, but then she saw that his hair wasn't nearly long enough for the biblical likeness and he was too powerfully built to qualify as ex-druggie. She was trying to remember if she'd met him before when the embassy woman said, "Captain, this is so amazing. But this is Will Holmes. He's—well, I'll let him explain it."

"Captain," he said to her, offering his hand to shake. His grasp was so strong she thought he was playing with her, but this was hardly the setting for the kind of grip that certain military types tried out on her before introducing their low opinion of women in the armed forces.

They were so close, a few inches from cheek to cheek, it seemed after the fact to be making introductions. "Hello," she got out. Had Health Attaché Holly said what or whom he was with? She guessed DynCorp, maybe management. He had no vest, no visible weapon. He was wearing a topcoat or blazer, but she was packed so against him she couldn't tell if he was in suit pants, khakis, or, for that matter, blue jeans. "I'm sorry," she said, "I didn't hear—you're DynCorp, right?"

"Mr. Holmes is with DOD."

He looked beaten down, and yet also, though it was so hard to put together, alert, acutely, strangely awake to her, to what was going on around them, but mostly to her eyes, to the crankpin disjoint coming from she didn't know exactly where, to Holly Fitzsimmons's examination of how long and just how he looked at Mary. And when he couldn't get away with looking at her any one second longer, he stopped, and in a knucklehead way, something just on the line between afterthought and dopey, said, "Sorry for your loss."

The crowd flooded forward before she could respond, and Mary got hurried down an aisle and across a row to make sure she sat in the front with DynCorp regional executives and the deputy ambassador. It wasn't until the memorial service was over that she recalled how Holly Fitzsimmons had said, "This is so amazing," and that she would "let him explain it." As Mary got into one of the embassy Humvees—Rex's friend had left to report for duty—she realized that this man from the Defense Department, this Will Holmes, hadn't explained anything.

ROCK CREEK MARCH

13. NIGHT FIST, QUIET KNIGHT

Washington's winter was snowless and mild, signifying mankind's interference and indifference yoked, biblical scourge misinterpreted, glaring alarms unnoticed, and still Stanley hadn't called Mabel. It was early March, too much like May, and still her cell-phone number on the stray piece of paper sat in his top desk drawer, numinous souvenir, dearest diamond, untouched.

He looked at it daily. It sat there in a nest of rubber bands. It winked at his bad nights. It teased on his worst afternoons. When the announcement came of Adam making Gordon Bray managing editor, it went neon. But Stanley couldn't use it. The spirit in which it was offered seemed gone, gone utterly, when Martina quit. He hadn't met Adam in church for months.

His sole link to hope was Vera. She was insensate with hardworking industry. He had never seen such a searcher. He wondered if ballet, that branch of dancing dedicated to body-deforming practice for perfection, had made her immune to dead ends. She tunneled to them and through them. All she needed was an ear to hear of her raging disappointment and she was back in shape for more. That part was easy. He enjoyed her stories of how, when she got to one version of events, or just before she thought she got it, it changed to something else.

She had determined that MECS—the acronym on the *Park Closed Until Further Notice* sign on Roosevelt Island, where the pilot crashed—stood for Media Exploitation Component Services. There were only a few mentions of it online. One said it was the National Security Agency's analysis program for documents and data seized in Iraq, Afghanistan, and other locales. She found a company Web site or two that described contracts it had with MECS. One sold a linguistics platform-server to MECS, to process and extract information—people, places, phone numbers, addresses, and other "entities"—in the native script of forty different languages. A national-security blogger said West Virginia Senator Jay Rockefeller, of the Senate Intelligence panel, secured six million dollars for MECS. The blogger, a political-science student at Georgetown, said MECS was established in late 2001 to coordinate efforts among the FBI, CIA, the Defense Intelligence Agency (DIA), and National Security Agency (NSA) to analyze and disseminate information gleaned from millions of pages of paper documents, electronic media, videotapes, audiotapes, and electronic equipment seized by the U.S. military and intelligence community in Afghanistan and other countries.

Vera found a MECS job listing, for an Audio Video Exploitation Specialist. She found a 2004 House Armed Services Committee statement by Lowell Jacoby, director of the Defense Intelligence Agency, who said that DIA was the *executive agent for Media Exploitation Component Services . . . whose mission was being moved to lower tactical levels so that forces can take advantage of documents and other media found on the scene.*

But that was it. There was not a single story in a major newspaper. No television transcript contained it. There were a few mentions buried in appropriations bills, but they were short, and told next to nothing, except that MECS did exist. The Pentagon reporters told Vera they'd never heard of it, but when she shared what she knew, they shrugged and called it a data-management office. What exactly was she thinking was newsworthy about it? She told them it was strange that such an office would have anything to do with an F-16 pilot's crashing. What does Pentagon Public Affairs say about that? First they said there was no such sign on Roosevelt Island. She faxed them the photograph, and the following day they came back to her and said it was not a Defense Department sign—it lacked some numerical coding all such signage had. What was it, then? Off the record, the spokesman told Vera— some prank, kids probably.

Vera was beginning to see that her search faced a wall she'd not anticipated. Many had worked to build it. They rightly saw that the world must have its expertise. They believed it was too complicated for the common man, and for those beings with uncommon attributes—ghetto ballerina and passing mulatto—occupying lowly denominators—night cops and night editor—it was as narrow as pencils in fat, angry oceans. Stanley told Vera the obvious, how there were beats—night cops, Pentagon, White House, courthouse, legal affairs, Redskins—because there had always been beats. They predated the summer of '71; they were contemporaries of hansom cabs. Like a trotting horse pulling a woman in a petticoat, Stanley believed, beats kept the Room hidebound. And so Vera labored, trying to reach Jupiter on a pogo stick.

Vera tried to play it back. She'd been walking to the bike rack on the second level of the parking garage. Whispering the Marian litany of Loreto: "*Mystical rose, pray for us. Tower of David, pray for us. Tower of ivory, pray for us. House of gold, pray for us. Ark of the covenant, pray for us. Gate of heaven, pray for us. Morning star, pray for us. Health of the sick, pray for us. Refuge of sinners, pray for us.*" It was dark; one of the garage lights was out. She couldn't remember if she'd heard the footsteps behind her—there were so often people getting their cars around then, just after the first edition closed. He was on her so fast. She did remember the scent of him clearly, because at first she'd thought it was Stanley, but this wasn't the smell of cigarettes. It was the smell of chalk.

She knew that smell, because her father liked a pool hall near home. She didn't remember much else about him, really, except that whiff of the gentian block he ground his cue into and got on his hands when she was, oh, maybe only four, the last age she would have been when he was still around.

But this chalk wasn't Daddy; it was Gordon Bray, the new managing editor. She'd seen him here, getting his sea-green Vespa. He grinned at her with the glissading confidence she imagined she'd have had if she'd been him.

Her memory eddied right there. Did he say, "Baby says 'hi,' " in that Euro accent of his, or was that said later, after he told her he had gotten to know Baby. Gotten to know Baby—her mind took more than a few turns to bring that twirler down to earth.

He took a cigarette and offered her one. She remembered how wrong it seemed that Gordon Bray smoked Salem. She remembered lying, saying something along the lines of "Menthol, menthol isn't my thing." He was lighting up anyway. He took in all of her when he inhaled. He said—what was it?—"Isn't my thing either." Or maybe "That's not what I hear." It was the sound of a car on the ramp, a car with worn brakes, that she remembered well. Because she thought that he would leave, that he wouldn't want to be seen talking to her. But Bray didn't care. She got on her bicycle and felt his eyes on her back until she'd turned the corner to the street.

Mabel?"

"Yes, hello."

"Mabel, this is Stanley Belson."

"Stanley!"

"Stanley, from the paper."

"Stanley!"

"I know I waited a long time to call you." He looked at the words he had written down to say to her. He'd added, *Please forgive me,* but now that he heard out loud what he'd written, he felt that was too formal, so he left it out.

"Oh! That's—"

"That day you came into the paper, when you walked over to my desk . . ." He'd decided he needed to remind her of this, because she might not remember.

". . . I was so surprised," he finished.

He sounded like an audio recording. He paused. *But it's been so long*—what was wrong with this? It felt false now, though he meant these words. He'd chosen them carefully so he wouldn't leave anything out.

"But it's been so long that I was hesitant."

She wasn't saying anything. He waited, in case she did want to reply, though he'd envisioned this as a longish set of sentences.

"Maybe it was spur-of-the-moment," he continued. "Maybe you thought better of it when you got home."

"Oh! No!" She stopped there. He wished she would elaborate. But she didn't. He waited a little more.

"But the other day," he finally went on, "I was looking in my desk drawer and came upon your number, and I realized I wanted to know how you were—how all these years you'd been. So I picked up the phone today and just called."

There. He'd done it. He'd actually done it.

"Stanley, are you . . . finished?"

"Well, the day is starting just now for me. Though tonight I won't be staying until two, the way I normally do, because I'm switching with someone. But I'll tell you what, it's very hard to find anyplace that's open at that hour. I've tried. The best thing is to meet before I go in, but for most people that means tea, or coffee, but rarely a drink. I suppose you entertain quite a bit."

See, he shouldn't have done it. He should never talk unaided on the phone. He needed more notes. Notes for when the conversation took an unexpected turn. But how had it? He couldn't remember.

"I think we should try for a day you have off. When is that? Next. The next day you're off."

"That's not until next week."

"Monday?"

"Sunday. It's Sunday night. Well, it's Saturday night too, but you, you will have some kind of gathering, and Sunday, generally . . ." He was acting like an ex-lover or a bumbler with a crush. He was neither.

"I think we could sit in my garden on Saturday. If this crazy warm weather keeps up."

"In your garden?"

"Yes. It's a quiet weekend. Five would be good."

"Don—he . . ."

"Don is home; he'll say hello at some point."

It couldn't be. He tried to summon the quiet Saturday of Mabel Cannon and Don Grady.

"Stanley?"

"I'm here. Yes, here."

"I'm so happy you called."

"Oh."

"I'll see you at five on Saturday."

Georgetown was dollhouses. Similar little trees and similar little houses lined up. Don and Mabel had found an irregular block canopied with oaks. The house was Victorian brick with Romanesque trim and mansard roof. It was a folly of a place, a bait-and-switch of a home. You thought it was small on one side, only to find it was huge. A large view gave way to a confining corner. The oversized edifice sat back from the sidewalk on a minor rise. There was a pair of Volvos in the driveway, one navy, one black.

At the door, he expected help to answer. But Mabel came. She was slim in dark-green flats, narrow pants, and mock turtleneck. She led him through a long hallway, past a cerise-painted living room, baronial dining room, kitchen made for catering the fêtes. They walked through the thickest glass doors, set into walnut frames, onto a porch that turned at right angles, screened, extending into a garden of still-bare ginkgos and year-round magnolia. He saw she'd been sitting on a cushioned armchair. A glass of white wine rested on a low table beside it. An overlong table, slim against a wall, carried wine bottles, glasses, liquor. Refrigerated shelves of wine took up another, smaller turn of a wall.

"What would you like?"

"The best wine you can give me." He was at ease in this setting. It was where he was from, this profusion of no-cost-spared, of everything considered to the last beveled edge. In the Room, she was empress to his footman. Here, they were equal members of a damned elect—those who feel fiercely.

"You grew up in Kalorama, didn't you?" she said.

"You remember."

"You were always kin to me, Stanley." She looked out into the garden. "Kalorama. Airless embassies. To think you came out of *that*."

She got up to go to the wine bottles but stopped midway. "Remember the time I interviewed the parents of that Tenleytown triple murder for you?"

She had. She was younger, and she'd rescued him. Saved him from the misery of making how-do-you-feel calls. She'd sensed he couldn't face them. He'd forgotten that. He'd been too busy fretting ever since she'd hugged him and given him her number. And, like a freshman in love, he'd put off calling her; it was as if taking up her invitation might expose how little she'd meant it.

"Red or white?"

"Red."

She put a finger on one label, then another. Stoney's—not the Stoney's of her Jonathan Strasser debacle, but from her earliest days—came back to her: the after-work drinks, bartenders from earlier closers, pushed-together tables of firemen, a night girl or three breaking for the cheeseburgers, the majority, even the hookers and excepting the water throwers, looking like mid-managing government types with fringe habits and family issues. There was a table of Newport-chaining cops, brothers in plainclothes. She handed Stanley his glass.

"To kin," she said, raising her own.

"What were you thinking of just now?"

"Oh, Stoney's. In the old days."

"It's closing, you know."

"No."

"Yes. They got an offer on the building—it used to be the worst part of town; now, with the Convention Center, it's all changing."

"That makes me so sad. Sadder than I thought I could feel—about Stoney's."

"So much went on there. So much."

"You still have those oak boxes?" She remembered his filing system.

He was embarrassed, but only some. "Yes I do. Yes."

"They were *amazing*. What Don wouldn't give to get his hands on *those*. 'Course, he'd never admit that."

"He knows this city better than I do."

"You don't believe that for a second."

He suppressed a smile and then laughed. "You're right," he said. "I don't."

"He's always wondered about you."

"We're talking about your husband, Don Grady?" He was teasing, but also wanting, not a little desperately, to hear more.

"We all wondered about you," she said. "Talked about you at Stoney's. Is he straight? Thai royalty? Senator's love child? For five minutes someone had the idea Nixon sent you to spy on Don. But they couldn't tally that with your crying jags. Yet you weren't entirely soft. When Janet Cooke fabricated the eight-year-old heroin addict, you didn't believe her. Don did. But you didn't. It ruined him, you know. For running the place. That's why he had to write these . . . these books."

Janet Cooke was a Swarthmore graduate, mocha and pretty, a Metro reporter when Don Grady was assistant managing editor, AME, for Metro. She impressed white editors with her ghetto reporting— "gritty," "real," they said. Midway through her second year on the job, she came to them with a story about an eight-year-old heroin addict. Don believed her, they published, she won the Pulitzer. Then someone at Swarthmore read the Pulitzer coverage with her bio in it and remembered she'd failed to graduate. They called the paper. The editors questioned her. For two days she held firm. Third day, locked in a glass office, surrounded, she confessed: she'd made all of it up. Her résumé, the story. The paper had to give the Pulitzer back.

"Why didn't you believe her?" Mabel asked him. "I've always wanted to know."

"It was just a feeling I had. I had lots of feelings that, well, went the other way, that were wrong."

"Did you? Somehow *I* don't believe *you*."

"She was easy to see through," Stanley said.

"I've often liked to envision alternative universes. Ones where, you know, the bottom dwellers are the treetoppers and vice versa. Think of it. Adam as the night editor. You as the executive editor. You would have let the stories be the stories they were," she said. "Instead of shoe-horning them into the same old stories."

"But that's what Don wanted when he believed Janet Cooke. He wanted a new story. He thought her story was. An eight-year-old. My God, it was shocking."

"There was nothing new about it! It was the same story, dressed up a little different: they're depraved, even when they're eight years old. Wasn't that the oldest story of all? Didn't Janet Cooke tell every white man what he'd suspected? She played to their worst fears. If she hadn't lied about herself, they'd never have found out little Jimmy was a lie."

" 'Jimmy's World,' " Stanley said. "I'd almost forgotten about it."

"In this house it's never been forgotten."

How odd that Don would have wanted to run the paper. It put into a new perspective his relationship, such as it was, with Adam. Adam had bested Don. Stanley frowned.

"What's that for?" Mabel said. She got up to pour another glass of wine.

"These titans."

She didn't get it. "Which?"

"Adam and Don, of course."

"And?"

"Their long battle."

"Oh, please. A bloodless maneuvering only the Room gives a shit about."

"Yes, you're probably right about that."

"Am I? I was hoping you'd argue with me."

"Oh, Mabel! You know more than I ever would about—about both of them."

"Not Adam."

"He's always been . . . affected, yes, affected—by you."

"Really?"

"We often talk about you."

"No!" She pushed forward on her stuffed chair, her knees almost touching his. He realized with a thumping downturn he'd done something he'd never done before—share one of Adam's confidences. He rarely spoke too long to anyone in the Room except Adam and whoever was his cherished night-cops reporter of the moment. The temptation to let slip had never come up before, and here, his first outing, he'd spilled in minutes.

"What does he say??" She was bouncing a fraction on the edge of her chair.

Stanley sank back in his and shrugged.

"That's the most unconvincing performance I've *ever* seen," she said, turning threatening, not even in a joking way.

He pulled in a long breath and looked around the porch.

"Stanley," she said, drawing out the last syllable.

"Reminiscing about . . . earlier . . ."

Mabel's jouncing stopped. "Oh," she said. "Oh." She took a sip of wine, a ladylike one, and inched back into the easy chair. Then he saw her concluding, finishing the thought. She sighed and let down her shoulders. "He thinks I'm ludicrous. I knew that. Already."

"He takes you seriously," Stanley said. His eagerness to please her had taken over within seconds again, and now his sin was not betraying Adam but misleading her. Or had he? He tried to remember what Adam had said, instead of what he, Stanley, had felt about what Adam had said. But then he glanced her way and saw she didn't believe his "seriously" claim anyway. She was back deep in the chair, staring into her wineglass.

"You know," she said, "I had a little episode. With him."

He leaned forward. "When?"

"Oh," she said, despondent still, "it was last fall."

"When you came in about the managing-editor job."

"You know about that. God. What a fiasco. Don is such a buffoon. But it wasn't when I came in that one day to let Adam know Don—how did he put it? Oh, 'throwing my hat in the ring'—was off-base, that I knew, for Chrissakes, I wasn't qualified. Jesus."

"Wait. What wasn't?"

"The episode. It wasn't that day I told him no, I don't want to be managing editor. The day I spoke to you. It was after that. I tried to come in, and I had, well, something I thought was important, to give him, and he, he wasn't—he was busy, just understandably busy. He blew me off. Basically. He just left me down in the lobby. And I just, well, I left."

How many times had Adam treated Stanley thus? Too many to count, but for Mabel Cannon, this was a blow. He felt terrible for her, because it was a wound practically no one would understand. A first-world problem, as he often put it, but no less painful for its seeming triviality. So whom could she share it with? Not Don. He wouldn't understand its sting at all. Stanley put his hand on her arm and said, "I am really sorry he did that to you."

She lifted her eyes to him and said, "Silly. It was silly."

"Yes, but . . . not."

She nodded. He saw her stripped of delicious fun—wild, absurd Mabel on a folding chair in an empty gym.

"I've made a ruckus of my life," she said.

He didn't rush in to correct her. He felt he owed her more. He wanted to go back to the day—in its details were better things.

"You know, no one ever gives Adam a gift. It doesn't surprise me he was obtuse about it. He is, mostly, obtuse about—anything like that."

"A gift?"

"What you brought him that day."

"It wasn't a gift."

"What was it?"

"Like a present? A bow and wrapping? No. It was nothing like that."

"What was it?" Stanley persisted.

"It was a report."

"A report?"

"The Sissy report."

"You had it!?"

"Well, sort of."

Stanley was confused again.

Finally, she said, "I had the thing in hand, but I hadn't really *gotten* it. It was, sort of, dumped in my lap. So it wasn't like a coup, a reporting coup. It was dumb luck."

"But we didn't have it," Stanley said. "And the other paper did. It's been crucial to Adam. Do you know Martina Welk?"

"Uh-uh. I don't know any of the reporters anymore."

"She was AME National. And she was in the running to be managing editor. And our getting beaten on that report, all through the fall and most of the winter—it meant this Gordon Bray, instead of Martina, got the job. That's an abridged version of things, but, well, close enough."

"I've heard Don mention that name. Gordon Bray. Well, you know," she said, sitting up a little, "Don's had that report too. But it's not just about White House surveillance. But who cares? I mean, do we really give a shit about it? You and me don't. But I thought Adam would. I had it, right in the lobby, but, well, you know, he thought I was coming up to flirt with him, no doubt. Which I was. But still."

Stanley sat, digesting all of this. It was fairly amazing to him. Then he said, "Poor Martina."

"Is she good-looking?"

"I thought so. An unusual beauty. A complicated bearing and inner life. I've always thought she was exceptional."

"Well, she wouldn't have been managing editor, then. At that level they only tolerate horsy women, matron mamas, bucket-face bags. Semi-fatties do well too. Face it: a brainy woman of any beauty is dead meat in the Room. It's the Jamesian effect."

Stanley was trying to get over the word "fatties." His eyes were unblinking. "Jamesian effect?" he finally got out.

"Anyone worthy of being a Victorian heroine is unworthy of success in any male pecking order. For one, their wives would flip: Here I am, staying home raising your kids, and you're promoting *her*! For two, they'd be too distracted and tempted to do the conforming to one another's ideas they expend so much energy doing. For three, they're all a little afraid of being risible, like Lev and—who's that intern he married—Meg. It's a category: husbands with intellectually embarrassing wives who are too pretty to be unobtrusive.

"No, the dirty little secret is these liberal men, these anti–sexual-harassment, pro–women's-rights lip-service providers, they all opt for wives as wallpaper. They're more in love with ambition than love. So poor Martina. Yeah. She never had a chance. What's that great, great, great Madonna line? *Could you be a little less.* That's what girls come to know in our enlightened times. *Could you be a little less.*"

James and Madonna. A range new to him. He thought of Vera—being a little less. His face fell.

"What?" Mabel said. "What?"

"Oh, I have high hopes for a young woman. A night-cops reporter. She's, she's—"

"Isabel Archer."

"Actually, I was dreaming of her being the African-American version of Don."

"Early Don, you mean."

"Well, yes. Yes. Not what he does now. She's religious. Not that that matters. It's just she has a devotional side, it makes me feel—I don't know—as if she brings to the mundane something no one in the Room does. Fervor, I guess."

"Not exactly welcome in a newsroom, fervor. And not exactly like Isabel Archer. 'Course, she never had anywhere to go. But we did. And yet, well, you know how it goes. I don't need to tell what goes on to a black man who passes."

He glanced up fast. She knew. They had not once discussed it. He had always assumed she was like everyone else—unaware. But, like Vera, she had known all along.

"I didn't know you knew," he said, looking at his shoes.

"Stanley," she said. "Oh, Stanley." She got up, he thought, to get more wine, but she took his glass and knelt on the floor in front of him, and placed both of his hands in hers. It was now impossible to see his shoes. He tried to look at her hair, a place on a woman he usually chose to study in such close quarters. She let him do that and said, "I love you. And if the world had an honest deity, you'd be its best king."

Vera was bugging about Armedia. It had an office in Virginia, in the suburb called Vienna. It was a company that specialized in content management and content-related solutions. She wanted to stick her eyes with pins when she read such words. But Washington wasn't East Knoxville. Facts didn't come in screen doors and walking sticks. They came in encaustic—so gunked with wax jargon and government pigment you couldn't even guess what was underneath. *Armedia's mission is to provide world-class solutions for clients to automate the creation, capture, organization and presentation of their intellectual assets,* a press release said. "Capture" was the best word in that bunch.

She'd found out that Armedia had a contract with MECS. She'd gotten a copy of the contract from a guy who'd made a consulting business out of keeping track of intelligence contracts. The address of MECS was the gold in the gravel of legalese. It was 2070 Chain Bridge Road, Vienna, Virginia. The next step was to get out there and see if she could buttonhole an employee or five in the parking lot.

Driving, always tricky for a city girl, went sour fast. Northern Virginia was the devil's development zone. So much shopping and too little roadway made Vera take the Lord's name. Buildings weren't big on having numbers on them. Further, everyone already knew where everything was but couldn't, when asked for directions, explain how to get there. She felt like tape-recording what instructions she did get; they were too jumbled with landmarks, too light on street names to jot down. Worst of all, she often couldn't make a simple right or left; she had to get in the proper lane, which usually managed to be five lanes away. So she was forever passing the turn and looking harder to make a U-turn. St. Jude, patron saint of lost causes, couldn't lift her. U-turn was miles ahead, and the traffic to it had a glowworm pace. She would have been better off walking, but that was no go, because sidewalks had gone endangered. The population of parking garages was fine. She found them all too often before she found her way home. Sometimes she just sat in a space to get calm.

The issues she had with Chain Bridge Road were typical. It was otherwise known as Route 123. This and other bottlenecks took her a visit to Virginia to get straightened out. But today, her second try, she was almost certain a building that had its back to the street, its main entrance in what should have been its rear, where it abutted a parking garage, was the one.

As she approached from the north, she again counted the buildings before and after it. It had to be 2070. She took the right turnoff, but too slowly; a Nissan gave a ferocious horn. In her fluster, Vera twisted wrongly along a service road, got trapped in a Pier 1 Imports lot with no exit leading the right way out again. She stared at the building, unreachable beyond a long, low wall. It had a fugly entrance. It looked like a gigantic—five-stories-high—toilet seat.

She had to drive out the way she'd come into the lot. Now she was headed in the wrong direction, at least for a stretch. She banged the steering wheel. As if to punish, her cell put out its cheep-cheep. She looked at it. It was the Metro editor, not Stanley, which was not good.

She'd been tempted to turn off her cell to keep interference to a minimum, but she knew that would only make them more slamzonied for her. Night cops, her beat, never had business in Tysons. Beats, as Stanley always said, kept her from roaming. She pulled over. She seemed to be a magnet for hurry-up drivers, two of whom were now honking her. She ignored these road racers, clicked on the emergencies, turned on her cell, and dialed the desk.

She hoped it wasn't anything in Trinidad. The neighborhood had been homicide heaven in December. Fifth District had messed around with checkpoints, gotten war-zone metaphors up and running. She'd been so swamped with shootings, police-state yak, she'd had trouble getting traction on her pilot. She looked at her watch. It was 7:30 p.m.

"Hastings?"

"You texted me."

"Where in God's name are you?"

Confession would be long this week. "Out in Northeast, walking Trinidad with some ACLU guy."

"Oh. Okay. Good idea."

She shook her head at herself. The lies of the other paper's bad black reporter burbled up at her. At least she wasn't in a bar. She glanced at the brick boxes of Tysons II, Neiman's squiggle on the largest building's corner. She wondered where Stanley, her usual protector, had gotten to.

"One of the copy aides noticed the scanner's got a shooting, 200 block of C Street Northeast," the Metro editor barked.

Vera was relieved: not in Trinidad. What a blessing. Lord loved her. "Thank you," she whispered.

"What?" he demanded.

"Nothing, just getting with somebody out here."

"Oh yeah. Right. So smash on over there. It's not Trinidad, but it's something."

"I'll do that."

"Good. Okay. Stanley's coming in later. I think he said nine."

She considered the traffic and closed her eyes. Body would be on a bus and tagged by the time she got to D.C. What was the point of going? She could so easily phone it in, and no one would be the wiser. She looked longingly at Chain Bridge Road. She was so close. Was it really going to take three rides out here to get to the MECS parking lot? Seemed so. She was stinging with frustration, but she pushed it away, checked her mirrors, and pulled out into the screaming horn of another motorist she just hadn't seen.

"An officer was sent to the 200 block of C Street NE to check on a person staggering in the road. Police said the man grabbed the officer's collapsible baton and hit him on the head several times. The officer, whose name was not released, then fired once, striking the man in the shoulder, police said."

Vera paused until she heard the keyboard stop. She asked Stanley to read it back. When he was done, she said, "Oh. That one was 7:30 p.m., okay? Just stick it up there after the word 'sent.' 'An officer was sent at 7:30 p.m.,' and then the rest, like I had it."

She heard him type it in.

"Ready?" she asked.

"Go ahead," he said.

"An 11-year-old boy was shot in the wrist about 10:20 p.m. in the 1500 block of 45th Street NE, police said. About 10:50 p.m., three men were wounded in their legs in a drive-by shooting in the 600 block of Park Road NW, police said. Officers found one man on the scene, and a short time later, two other men hit in the shooting arrived at a hospital, police said. Investigators do not know of a motive."

Finally, he stopped typing.

"Okay, new graph," she said.

"Right, new graph."

"Then, just before midnight, a woman was shot in the back in the 5100 block of Fitch Street SE."

"That's it?"

"Yeah, that's all I have on that one," Vera said.

"There was another shooting there last year," Stanley said.

"For real?"

"It was a woman too," Stanley said.

"I'll ask them about that."

"No, no, don't. This is taking you away from your pilot."

"I have one more," Vera said, a little ticked off at Stanley, though it wasn't his fault, not at all, this annoying night. But she still wanted to find out where he'd been earlier. "You ready?"

"Yes," Stanley said.

"The busy night continued at 12:05 a.m., when a man in his early 20s was wounded in a shoulder as he left a carryout in the 2100 block of Alabama Avenue SE, police said."

She stopped, scanned her notes one last time. "Okay," she said. "That's it."

"Vera, this is just, well, heroic. It's heroic. Thank you," Stanley said. He was about to ask her a question when her beeper went off. She looked. It was one of her detectives. "Stanley, this is my guy. I gotta go."

When she got to the 2700 block of Douglass Place Southeast, it was July 4 and Juneteenth come together. One in the morning, and children were hanging out on the eastern side of fabled St. Elizabeth's, built expressly for the mentally ill, partly shut down, still standing like an abandoned plantation house. Over here two of the worst, Douglass Dwellings and Stanton Dwellings, maybe army barracks but maybe pride of one unknown Negro architect, once sat on this hill. It was the highest place in Southeast. Frederick Douglass's homestead was near. Now the dwellings were down and something called Henson Ridge, built-fast townhouses, stuck up right and left. There were still too many empty lots.

"She up in there," said a slack girl sitting on a wall with two sisters, banging heels on bricks.

Vera took the advice and walked toward the apartment building catty-corner to the townhouses. A skein of boys jerked around behind her. "What channel you wit?" sang out one. "You ain't fornever coming back here," another boy mock-warned.

When she called Stanley, one kid was pressing his face into the glass of her car window. "You tole her you love her," said another boy. "Oh no, I ditent," said the face pancake.

She read from her notebook. "At 1:15 a.m., officers raced to the 2700 block of Douglass Place SE and found a 19-year-old woman with a graze wound to her head. A group of gunmen attacked her and a man, authorities said. The couple ran into an apartment building seeking safety, but the barrage of gunfire pierced the outer walls, police said. Police found shell casings from two handguns and a shotgun in the apartment complex's parking lot."

"I'm trying to tie all this together," Stanley said. "This isn't normal. This—I don't think we've had this since before Clinton."

"But you can't say that."

"No," he said glumly. "You know I would if I could."

The boys were gone, and her detective was tapping on the windshield. "Stanley, I gotta go," she said.

A half-hour later, she called him one last time, knowing it probably wouldn't make the last edition. He was still there, though, waiting for her.

"Shortly after 2 a.m., a victim walked into Greater Southeast Community Hospital with a gunshot wound in the back. The victim told D.C. police that he had been attacked at the Southern Avenue Metro station, in Prince George's County near the D.C. border."

GO VIEW THE LAND, EVEN JERICHO

The first man Vera approached was one of those white guys with no expression. She gave her name and the paper's name. She said both slowly. Then, "Sir, do you work for Media Exploitation Component Services?"

"This some kind of joke? Media Exploitation?"

"No, sir, not a joke. It's a part of the federal government headquartered in this building."

"I've never seen it on the directory. I'd remember that."

He told her he'd just left a meeting at the Northern Virginia Technology Council in Suite 150. He looked too shaggy for that, she thought. Almost a longhair, but he did have a suit on. "I come here every month," he explained. "And I always forget which floor it's on, so I look. Come on. I'll show you."

They stood in front of the tenant directory in the lobby, checking entries under *M*. "See," he said. MECS wasn't there.

He turned out to be the friendliest. Many veered sharp, not even letting her near enough to introduce herself. One muttered, "Not interested." Another announced, "I don't have anything to do with the media." Disdain at her effrontery was common. "This is a place of business," she got told more than once. A trench-coated woman struggling with purse, luggage, and briefcase said she would notify the security guard if Vera stepped any closer.

So she tried to choose based on dress. A man in T-shirt, sweater, and backpack—less corporate—might be more relaxed. "I don't speak to the press," he said. Still hopeful about his spiky haircut, she pushed a little with him. "I understand that, sir, but I could really use your help."

He walked—ran—into the parking garage, banged his head getting into a Prius.

She felt as if she were a little better than a panhandler, but not much. She knew black was a disadvantage, especially when it came to the women, who solidified into freezer-cold when she came their way. She had been careful to wear the middle-class uniform—small earrings, hair straightened in a bob, nails squared, short, and palest pink, heels so low they were almost flats. But for a certain type, it didn't matter.

Finally, she saw a brother coming from the glass double doors. It was getting to be eight, and most of the building had emptied. It was dark. Her feelings had been bruised, and her notebook was empty. It wasn't like her to be a pest. Yet she'd been excited, certain this address would be a breakthrough.

"Hey," she said to him instead of "sir," thinking being too formal had been her mistake.

"Excuse me?" he said.

"How are you?" she said, giving him her largest smile.

"How am I? Do I know you?" he asked.

"Well, no, but I'm Vera Hastings, and I work—"

He cut her off. "You're the newspaper reporter that's been down here."

She brightened. "Why, yes, yes, I am."

"You know," he said, stepping toward her, "I don't know where you get off thinking you can just set yourself down here. There are ladies who work in this building who are afraid to come down here because of you. Do you realize that? Do you? This amounts to harassment. You need to vacate the premises. Immediately."

"This is public," she started to say, but it was too late, she was near tears or near outburst or both. So she just walked away and tried to find her car, but, naturally, for a good five minutes couldn't. At last she did, got in the front seat with its sweet smell of cigarettes, and lit up, locking the doors too. She wished she had window shades. She wanted to pull them down and cry her eyes red. "Fuck!" she said, too loud. "Fuck."

This was just, just so— She looked. He was talking to a woman in a maternity dress by a car only two parking spaces away from her. Another man joined them.

She began searching for her keys in her purse. This was unbelievable. These people were seriously entitled. And it sure didn't matter that he was a brother; he was one of them, and he was proud, pleased, and puddle-drunk with earning white folks' approval. There, there were her keys.

She started the engine. She began to back out timidly, afraid in her state she'd hit something or someone. The trio stared at her. She could feel their eyes on her near-weepiness. She finally cleared the cars and garage columns, then wound around the driveway. In her rearview she could see they were still watching her—oh, come on, was one of them writing down her license plate?

From his window, Will could see her driving away. She was so close, but way too far. He'd been there. He wanted to tell her why she kept missing. He felt for her.

One of his linguists said they should have had the security guard escort her to her car. The guy was typical. Will asked him why use a hammer when all you need is your fist. The fist is free. The hammer has to be purchased and stored.

And this too: always let the inadvertent ally do for you. Those other tenants in the building—they were shooing her away. They did more to discourage and demoralize her than any security guard.

Always practice strategic thinking. How many times a day did he have to say it?

His linguist got it. But he'd never have thought of it on his own. Aggression and leverage were not a word man's specialty.

They surely weren't hers.

She'd found him, though. That was impressive.

'Course, she found only his address.

She found *him* but didn't know it.

How he'd loved expressing amazement at the name of his component. How he'd loved helping her, taking her to the directory in the
lobby. See, he'd told her, Media Exploitation Component Services isn't
there. She'd looked right in his eyes and not seen him for what he was.

These were the subtleties of his life. The ones he enjoyed.

The rest of it—farming out hard cases to Egyptian or Jordanian elec-
troshock, humiliating the captured at Gitmo, scooping up the innocent
with the damned—these were strategic, but the dead opposite of subtle,
and never satisfying. They were only sometimes effective. They could be
useful, but only as long as they were hidden. These days, there were too
many grunts with digital cameras, too many cell-phone photographers,
too many happy-at-home moralists. He didn't blame any of them. He
rarely hated them. He just wished they were a little bit more like this
Vera Hastings.

He could still see her taillights. She was turning onto I-66.

She was an appealing example of the worthy opponent, the by-the-
rules adversary.

He used to be that. Then he only advocated for it. Now he preached
its setbacks. In a better world, he would still be just like her. In today's
world, he could only recognize his values from a distance and remember the reverence he once had for them.

There, the last red lights had vanished. As if synchronized, his phone
burst into loud rings. He looked at the readout. It was the vice-
president's man, Rood Joseph, undersecretary of state for arms control.

"Will."

"Rood."

"We have news."

"Wait. What's the NIE situation?" The National Intelligence Estimate on Iran.

"It's still circulating."

"Good. It should be."

"Losing your asset made monkeys out of us. But that's why my
news—listen—I . . ."

"The solution is to declassify the key judgments of the estimates."

"Will—that's right, that's what we agreed. But—"

"But what?"

"My mole at NSA," Rood said. To get through bureaucracy, the vice-president's staff and confederates had moles, what they called "trusteds," inside key agencies. He got information quicker than through official channels. Having information before you were supposed to have it was equivalent to having power. Will didn't always approve of it. He didn't much like the vice-president. He certainly had problems with everyone on his staff. Rood Joseph—merely a vice-president believer, not his staffer—was the least objectionable acolyte of the Mean Man. Mean Man—that was what most everyone at MECS called the vice-president.

"There're some intercepts out of Tehran," Rood continued. "It's quite clear now. Your asset is very much alive."

Hoseyn.

"They heard him talking?"

"They heard chatter about him that made it virtually certain he was alive," Rood said.

Chatter. Oh, that.

"That's better than before—but it's, it's not *news*," said Will, trying to modulate his robotic delivery into something more human, but failing. "It's not 'very much alive.' It's not very much anything."

"You are too much."

"I may be."

Rood laughed, but a little unpleasantly. He'd wanted a bigger react. He wanted Will to believe Hoseyn was alive and kicking.

"There's going to be fallout," Rood said, his tone turning officious.

"Fallout?"

"The vice-president sees this as a reason to go back in."

"To Iran?"

"Absolutely."

"With what?"

"With you."

SLASH RUN   JUNE

Summer enervated the government, told homeowners the sea could renew them, and left the rest their city. The air conditioner in the window broke, or the bill climbed too high, and a fan did enough. Arguments reached sidewalks and drifted through open windows. There was comfort in knowing you were not the only one in lost, mad hell. In Blagden Alley, Stanley could hear a harmonica one night, the tenor from church practice on Saturday, a baby's whelping beside the cinder rage of rap.

Washington was as louche as any city; it just hid from itself until the heat set it free. Those who made the city's daily bread—accusation—slowed in high temperatures. This year, the judgmental faculty wanted cold weather. Pundits withdrew to Chilmark. Reporters took mountain camping trips. Elected officials were in Missoula for barbecue. The president had a place he always went, and he went there. Motorcades slept. Diplomats went to the mother country while their daughters stayed behind for *liebe* with men their fathers' age. The children of whores played outside at night and policemen too drained to give chase befriended them. Drunks bearing stolen rakes knocked on doors after sundown to sell gardening for cash money. The Black Rose, the consensual and legal bondage club, attracted gentle, amorous women. Only a few anywhere tried to quit smoking.

There was an undertow of bayou among the junior lawyers and investigators left behind by their vacationing betters. Trickery was deemed decent. Finding the lover scorned became as righteous a technique as finding the document that damned. Seduction had its uses. In each past, there was something dirtied, thrown away, and unreasonable to loving ones. That something was recoverable. It was not a breakfast thing. It was a midnight object.

The midnight lantern in Blagden Alley was Winnow. She was fourteen. Stanley had heard her mother scald mad at johns for years on the corner, under a streetlight. She taunted more than one cheapskate with his own cell phone, her finger light and ready on the speed dial to a wife in White Flint or College Park. This summer, Winnow mystified her mother. The illusion wasn't that Winnow would be better than her mother. The illusion was that Winnow wouldn't poach her johns. Yet Winnow was practical first and second, daughter only third.

To minimize conflict, Winnow started working Fifth and L Northwest with the tykes. She'd been hitting it for a month now. She'd busted through more dates than any of the missies. She had a new friend too, Heidi. Heidi worked a club. It was tight. This place attracted professional athletes, television personalities, that level of clientele. Heidi had what she called a referral service. As yet, Winnow couldn't safely estimate what her take would be. She had to be doing this for free straight out. Certain relationships come to pass; money would come into it.

Heidi was Chinese, or at least not black, Spanish, or a white girl. She had an accent like a kung-fu movie, and she could have been a stripper. But she had a scar that was not healing right, and that wasn't all. She was missing her thumbs. Club let her work hostess wearing long gloves with a clothespin taped to each palm underneath to make her look normal. She didn't have to bang bare on a bar, hold tight to a pole, anything needing five fingers.

Winnow, with her limp, felt she knew Heidi, really knew her. They had injuries. They'd met because a date came to Fifth in a taxi with Heidi, looking for another girl to make it three. The other tykes were dippy dumb about how to make proper love to another woman. Winnow knew how to look like she was pleasing girls, and it was not too far from the truth to say she felt more gentleness for Heidi than she did for any person, male or female, Stanley even maybe. Stanley was her every-so-often father. He was the one who asked her. Winnow had to think about it, was she or was she not a lesbian? Come to find out, she decided, she wasn't. She just had a special situation with Heidi. Winnow could hang out with Heidi and stay away from Blagden Alley, not have to go home and listen to her sick mother, who was in bed with one bad cold or some ache or some drug that wasn't making the grade to get her over.

Tonight the tykes on Fifth scowled at Winnow, slouched and jutted hips. Girls were swarmed up. Had to wear serious faces. Winnow, she had to laugh. Been in the world not long, girls have ideas that nasty faces make girls juicy looking. This market out here, this here is a sure grocery for pink. Instead, black jogging bras on these tykes. Jogging!

She took their business. Just now, a car full of brothers had stopped, rolled down a window. Winnow could feel a foot come off a brake, going on a pedal slow. What did her mama always say? "Evening, handsome. Looking for understanding?" She fixed that. "Evening, player," she whispered to herself, practicing just before the headlights, silver-blues, marked up on her. For them, "Evening, players. Need understanding?"

One says, "Come on." She hears the crease-crack of the car door. They put her in the front, on a lap. They weren't all brothers. One, he's driving. Says, "We understand you have a friend."

Something about the tone, it makes her say, "Oh yes, sir. I have a friend."

"Little friend. Small little friend," he says. She notices he has a beard, long hair. Another thing: sober.

"Little?" she says, but it's not a real question.

They wait too, a carful of men—she can smell their hair gel and shoes, a rubbery scent.

Tykes would have said anything, something. Winnow, what she does is remember. How, one night, Mama in the living room, three men, maybe more, through a keyhole. How it was soft. You remember a soft like that in Blagden Alley, when Mama was home with her circumstances. Business, in point of fact, but at the time, Winnow couldn't put a name on it. Mama's things at night—that's what Winnow would have called them if she'd told anyone about them. She didn't.

Her head's back in the car with the brothers. "Over here," she hears one say.

The car door opens from the inside. Something must have gone down, but she missed it, maybe while she was thinking of that keyhole. Could they have said something? Even asked her another question? Could she have answered?

She didn't know what made her snap out of it, but she did, the moment she heard the engine hesitate. It was a sound like they'd put wrong gas in it. She knew that sound too. Her mama only ever had low-test for the cars that need high-test. When the police came the first time in her life, she was surprised she couldn't describe a single one of the men she saw through the keyhole that night. This night, she got it. It was a dark-blue Grand Am, Virginia plates, T9P 112.

Mary arrived at National Airport from Nellis at 0800, after taking a commercial red-eye. She'd completed months of training, seven days a week, from first to last light. She was six weeks from deployment and finally set to meet who she'd be paired with—most likely, they'd informed her, an operator from Intelligence Support Activity. One of the other pilot candidates had dropped out; she couldn't hack it. The other was scary. Bigger, stronger, and tougher than Mary, she seemed the one that would ultimately qualify.

The mission was to infiltrate Iran with the ISA operator under a husband-and-wife cover, find a lost or maybe dead Iranian asset, and get out by foot, vehicle, or bird. She preferred the foot option, but, as ever, she wasn't in charge. She was, in this assignment, a little better than chauffeur, most valuable as plausible spouse.

They'd taught her more about Iranian airspace than seemed possible. And she'd mastered craft she might be called upon to use to ferry operator and asset out. There were commercial planes—Airbus, Boeing, old Fokker, ancient Tupolev. She was hoping the asset would turn out to be once and for all dead, and all she'd have to do would be fly below radar on a little Sky Arrow with the ISA operator in the back seat.

They'd done what they could to learn the new Russian S-300 anti-aircraft system Iran was rumored to have in place. It was laughable, really—they needed a fighter wing for an escort if they were genuinely expected to get out of Iran in a jacked Boeing or Fokker. The best thing would be being lucky enough to find a two-seat training MiG. Maybe the Iranian asset could sit on the operator's lap.

It had all taken on a hapless quality. Maybe it was because she didn't believe she'd be chosen over the other pilot. The woman was a punishing competitor. Whenever Mary accomplished a milestone in the training, this girl was sure to tell her that she'd completed it weeks before. When they were at Fort Bragg, it was obvious her rival had passed the eighteen-mile all-night land-navigation course carrying a thirty-five-pound rucksack in record time. Mary had to do the forty-mile march with a ruck lighter than the normal forty-five pounds. She was just too small. This girl could handle the male-required weight. She didn't let Mary forget it.

A car and a private named Jeff Halliday met Mary at National. She was in full dress uniform. Even after five hours in a seat, the uniform felt stiff and unforgiving in the sun. It seemed hot for a June morning, and, unlike Nellis in Nevada, heavy-clammy.

She'd been occupied much of the flight with thoughts of Frank and her last telephone conversation with Clara. She planned to stay with Clara and the kids tonight, and, depending on her orders and the outcome of this meeting, they'd all visit Frank together as soon as possible. Clara didn't want Mary to be alone when she made her first visit to him in all these months.

Clara said he'd come in and out of the coma a few weeks ago, but each time he appeared mostly unaware of his surroundings. It wasn't clear if he could hear. It seemed his sight was intact. But he had not spoken. His motor coordination was poor. He was tube-fed, and his overall condition was guarded. He weighed less than Mary or Clara. "Angela calls him 'baby daddy,' " Clara had said. "It sounds awful, I know. I can't get her to stop."

Mary knew all this—they spoke often. Yet knowing that she would see him in this condition, and soon, within the next day or two, minced her. Her feelings were about to emerge from the cold storage she'd had to force them into to get through the training. She looked out the car window. They were on I-66, heading west toward Tysons, and, sure enough, they took the exit for the shopping mall. They ended up passing it, though, and turning into the parking garage of an office building that looked, for all she tried not to see it that way, like a toilet seat. There was an Applebee's on the first floor.

To her surprise, Halliday led her toward the restaurant. She thought he'd turn for the building lobby, but he pushed through the taproom door into the smell of lager and fries. The hostess seemed to know Halliday, and at that hour, almost three before lunchtime, it was empty except for a table in the back with a customer drinking from a white mug that shone out from the bearish dark. Jeff pointed at the man, shook her hand, wished her luck, and said, "Don't let him scare you. He's a lot nicer than he gives off."

She walked to him; his back was to her. It seemed strange that he would sit that way, and it forced her to insert herself into a narrow space between him and the next booth. It placed her hips dab in his face. This was about to make her angry, just a touch, but then he stood up to make room for her. At first she recognized him from her dream life, but in moments it came to her: he was the man at the embassy in Kabul. Her reaction was suspicion, and he caught it—"We meet again," he said in military laconic. "I apologize for taking advantage in Kabul."

"Advantage?"

"I got a look at you before you knew why I wanted one."

Something was going on for him, something he was easy about suppressing, but she could sense it, a thin whistle at the edge of her hearing.

She would have liked a cup of coffee, and he seemed to read that, because he turned around, and the hostess saw him. He pointed at the cup—"You'd like some coffee?" he said to Mary.

"Please."

He raised two fingers to the woman, and they talked weather and chitchat until the coffee arrived. She drank it black, which wasn't her favorite way, but she worried that diluting it suggested mildness she didn't want to convey. Then she noticed that his cup was blond, and after the hostess had warmed it, he poured in more milk and an envelope of sugar.

"Look," he said, noticing her noticing. "You have no reason to pretend with me. And," he added, "that uniform isn't necessary from here on out."

She looked at his rolled-up shirtsleeves and bad tie, a rodent-brown with butter zigs.

"My CO—" she began.

"You don't have a CO anymore," he said. "You don't have a uniform. And you aren't going to be living with your wingman's wife and kids."

She tried to cover her surprise at the mind reading.

"It's you," he said. "The other candidate was let go this morning."

"But—"

"It just wasn't a good fit," he said.

She held back a few times, questions hard to stifle, to get him to say more. But he was done. He stood up. "Halliday will explain some things to you," he said, looking at his watch, a drugstore cheapie. "And, Mary," he said, his fatigue lifting at her name, then slumping back, "next time we meet, try to be more talkative." He smiled at her, poor boy's mouth of bad teeth not reaching, in its effort at warmth, his eyes, unsold. And in that moment it started—her interest, small at the very first, in getting to him.

Walter Reed had Velcro-cuffed Frank's wrists. His muscles had smoothed flat. His milky head was shaved. One side of it was dented like a dropped can of soup. His cheeks had thinned down, so his ears got big. His chin seemed collapsed; now he had an overbite. In wheezes, support hose inflated and deflated on his calves, to aid circulation. The mattress cover, waterproof, air-filled, made a similar panting to stave off bedsores. A bag of urine hung on a hook on his bed's chrome bars.

Clara was on a chair upholstered in banana-yellow vinyl, reading a crafts magazine. Angela, wedged into the same chair as Mom, was watching *Idol* on the high-mount television. Trevor was knocked out in a stroller, quilted baby bags looped on the handgrip. Mary wished she were a believer, she so wanted to pray them into disappearing, especially the moppets. Please, please, she entreated, could you just get out?

Hold up. Take it easy. *Play nice.*

"Mary." Clara dropped the magazine and inadvertently dragged up Angela, who popped out a whine, turned up the sound on the set, and woke Trevor, now snuffling. "How long have you been standing there?" Clara was about to come hug her, but she stopped mid-room. She clasped her hands together in front of her waist like a nun.

"Long enough," Mary said, the words coming out cooler than she intended.

Angela turned her head from the set and worried her gaze to Mary. "Mommy," she said, pulling it out in a ticky-tacky crescendo.

"I wish you'd called," Clara said. "I wanted to bring you up here."

"Day went different than I'd expected it to," Mary said.

"Oh, Mary."

"Clara, I don't think—"

"All right, you're right. You're so right. Angela," Clara said, stern. "Angela."

The girl slid off the chair. Clara took the remote from her and turned off the TV. "Take your brother to the cafeteria. I'm right behind you."

Angela pushed Trevor through the door. Clara followed, inching past Mary on the way, then couldn't help herself. Clara whispered, "I'm a boob."

Mary took her hand, touched her back a little. "Thanks," she said.

"I'll let them know you're here." Clara moved toward Mary and then thought better of it. She closed the door behind her. Mary had tried to explain on the phone earlier that she just wasn't sure she could do this first meeting with family entire present. But Clara, sweetie pie, couldn't imagine a world in which anything wrong got handled alone.

Mary moved closer.

In such short time, so much was lost. Minus his animating fire, Frank's body was exposed for what it was—not enough. This was the place for talk of a soul. It seemed to be pinpointed in something Clara had said doctors called the distal projections of axons, which another something called excitotoxicity from the fall had caused to degenerate. Mary put a hand, unaccountably, on his foot.

The cotton blanket had snags in it. She pulled at one a little.

"Frank," she said.

He lay there. So much for the miracle she wanted. After a few more seconds, it was official. The sound of her voice brought no response.

A knock came on the door. She stepped back a little and opened it. A nurse was standing there in aqua scrubs. "Captain," he said, "sorry to barge in, but Mrs. Partnoy wanted us to take care of . . ." He paused. He was carrying a plastic pouch. "I'll just be a minute."

"Of course," Mary said. She went into the hall and away from a view through the doorway. But she hadn't had to—she heard the silvery sound of rings traveling the rod as the nurse pulled the bed curtain around Frank.

Ward 58. The neuroscience unit. Her time at Walter Reed, one consolation on the gimp floor was, at least you weren't in 58. We may be Frankengrunts, but God help the brain bleeders. Frank might have said it too. She took a glide over that. Irony was just too easy. Dull, really. She didn't think this war was good for it. It suited Nam. They'd tried to force global war on terror into that old boot. What had Will Holmes said? It just wasn't a good fit. He'd been referring to her rival, but it meant another thing to her now, what with her back against a wall at Walter Reed all over again.

She knew what Frank would have said about Holmes—that she should be careful, much more suspicious. That she should talk to someone—not in the way Clara and everyone else meant it, but in the way of checking things out, finding what you could, protecting yourself.

You act like military loves you, Frank often warned her. It ain't your daddy. Well, he once corrected, maybe in your case it is. She had to laugh. Even at that. Even with Frank in this bed in the shape he was. She recalled one of his letters. *X, you have no skin sometime. Grow some. I'm not going to be around forever.*

In another time, in another war, they might have called her brave. "Reckless" was the word Frank used in his missives. Yet wasn't he the heedless one? Look at this. Ward 58. Look at how it played out.

Here was the nurse. He couldn't hide the sack of urine. His hands in latex were splodged with some of it. "You can go in," he said over his shoulder as he headed down the hall.

She went in. The bag on the bed bars was clear and empty. But now her cell was ringing. It was Clara.

"Mary, I have to get these kids to bed," she said, her voice still lapping with her caring tone.

"I know. Long drive to Bel Alton."

"You sure that condo they found you is going to be okay?"

"It'll have to be."

"Call me if you want—I'll have my earpiece in so I can talk and drive."

"Don't do that. Really. I'm okay."

"I'm doing it anyway."

"Clara, thanks. And, and, sorry to be so, so—"

"You just be yourself, Mary Goodwin. That's all you can be anyway."

"I—I appreciate . . ."

"Don't forget to tell them to put lotion on his wrists. Ever since they put those restraints on him, he's been getting a rash from them. I tell you, it infuriates me. He barely moves. I mean, aren't we supposed to be hoping he moves?! Oh, he could suffer a fall. Oh, he might pull out a tube. Oh, oh, oh. I tell you, Mary, it's so wonderful to have you here; maybe you can scare some sense into them."

"I don't generally . . . scare—"

"Well, now I've got an ally on the scene. So, anyway, look, I gotta run."

Mary closed her phone. She stood there watching Frank's heartbeat barbing along on the monitor. She recalled her time in that bed. The space-age deformity of her hip socket had fed her ego. All she'd been was crazy lucky. Just the way she'd been in the snow.

The light blinked. In the hallway, it dimmed, went out, dimmed, and then was gone. No, she thought, it couldn't be a power outage. Must be some kind of test. She looked at her watch. It was close to eight-thirty. She looked out there but couldn't tell if it was brownout or what until the nurse, now carrying a flashlight, appeared a few doorways down. He was speeding around and called out to Mary, "Something wrong with the nonemergency generators. Just sit tight. There's a flashlight on the wall in there. Just, just take it down and make sure it's working."

Mary went back and found the red plastic wall mounting. When she pulled down the flashlight, it made a spatting sound. She saw that punctate bits of red had chipped away. She switched the flashlight on and off a few times. No use, it was dead. The fluorescents were blazing in the room, though, and, most key of all, the monitors were bright and working. She was glad Frank wasn't on a ventilator. But others in this ward were.

She went into the hall to see what she could do. Another nurse rushed her way. "Can you," she said, "can you take this and Scotch it to the door?" She was carrying papers; some said VENT and some said NO VENT. She gave Mary a NO VENT and pushed the tape dispenser close to her finger. "Take it," she said. Mary pulled off some tape and watched the nurse go to the next door. "Here," Mary said, "I'll help."

"No. No! You're not authorized. Please, just, just go back into your husband's room. We need to get these soldiers out of here in case, and the halls, we can't have unauthorized personnel in the halls. Please. All NO VENTs need closed doors. Okay? Just close the door and go inside."

She was frantic, and it was natural to mistake Mary for a spouse. Mary left it alone, taped up the paper, ducked into the room, and closed the door.

She sat down on the yellow vinyl chair. It looked as if Angela or somebody had drawn a lot of suns with crayon on construction paper and decorated the room with them. There was also a mobile made out of hanger wire that carried Styrofoam stars painted red, white, and blue above Frank's head. She got up and looked out the window. They were on the fifth floor. She could see lights had gone out elsewhere. Some buildings—nonessential, she hoped—were in darkness. This was a messed-up situation. And they were supposed to have made some changes after the paper wrote up the lousy care here.

She'd almost forgotten the skin lotion. Maybe it was on the nightstand; she could see containers and bottles there. She walked over, bent, and looked. The stand was crammed with so much—a box of gloves, wipes, something called "perineal cleaning fluid," alcohol-swab packets, wrapped syringes in a carton, tissue box, emery boards—she scrammed them around on the small surface, but she couldn't see it. She opened the top drawer. There was some Eucerin.

She pulled the vinyl chair as close as she could to the bed. Somehow she didn't want to sit right on it, with its huffing mattress cover.

She pulled apart the Velcro and opened out the cuffs. Raised red bumps stressed and broke the skin. She thought she might recoil, but she didn't, just realized that Eucerin probably wasn't the lotion. It wouldn't be enough for this kind of thing. She stretched over to the nightstand and opened the second drawer. It was empty except for a little tube of ointment. She read the microscopic print. Altabax, for infections, not on lips or near eyes, 1 percent in petrolatum. Apply with Q-tip. She'd just put it on with her finger.

She pressed out a squirl of it. The lights flickered in the room, but righted themselves again. She looked at the monitors. They were off now, but, wait, they were rebooting. She could see the cursors flashing and, yeah, they leapt back to life.

Clara said he'd opened his eyes just two days ago and had been doing so for a couple weeks before that. Now he seemed as if he'd never woken. "Frank," she said again. "Frank, it's Mary."

Maybe she should have brought some of his letters and read them to him. She only had the one she carried with her everywhere. It was from the envelope with the photographs of the dead girls from her last

Bagram run, the day of the accident. She'd gotten back to her Viper after the embassy memorial and retrieved the printouts and envelopes from her crew chief. He'd taken them out of the cockpit and put them aside for her in a plastic sack like ones for groceries at the supermarket. He'd looked at the pictures; he couldn't help doing it. But he'd tied up the bag in a double knot for her. When he handed it to her, he didn't pass any judgment, just said, "No one saw this."

She kept the photographs. Looked at the girls' faces, and often, anytime she felt like dropping out of the Nellis training. She took them out whenever she felt she wanted to get out of the Guard, find an airline or some magnate with a jet to hire her. By now the girls weren't just any girls; they were *her* girls.

She was doing this, she reminded herself, for them. It could be the largest lie ever, and, sitting here with Frank, she saw it probably was, because nothing lined up that evenly. The truth of it was, she'd killed those girls and maimed one of them. It was all nice to say going to Iran might in some twisty, turny storyline save hypothetical little girls who'd not have to be bombed to save theoretical little girls over here. In the end, it was just a story she told herself. A story that at least for a little while longer let her do what she liked best—fly.

That's what she always said. Maybe in this room she should try harder. It was more than that, of course—it always had been. So she admitted it. It began the afternoon she hid under the bed after she found her mother. Getting out from under was more important than changing her name from "Janeta Enriquez" to "Mary Goodwin." It was the way she'd always imagined she could fix herself. Weaklings under rocks wanted wings. She'd found a way to get them.

Irony, oh yes. She saw it. Near-victim of violence now makes violent victims. But she'd gotten caught up in something more powerful—the richer sweetness of knowing she'd been able to outsmart her own nature. She had no innate talent. She forced herself. She berated and stomped and insisted her life into the cockpit, keeping in mind the way any combat jet lifted straight up and the menace it made when it did. Maybe, here in the honesty room, it was also time to admit she wanted to sonic up to the maximum-security prison in the village of Grater-ford, in the Township of Skippack, Pennsylvania, and bunker-bomb her father at the speed of heat. That's what flying did for her. Even if she didn't ever make that scramble, she knew she could. He was, in the dead half-acre they would always share in her mind, subjugated.

She looked at Frank's wrist. She'd been sitting there with the oint-ment on her finger, doing nothing.

Frank was doing something. His eyes were tracking rapidly beneath the lids. It was probably REM sleep, but she couldn't help thinking it was almost as if he'd picked up on her rage, was following it closely, running around with her racing thoughts. His heart was faster; she looked at the monitor with some alarm. And his feet, down at the foot of the bed, were pedaling.

She wiped the blot of ointment off on the blanket and stood up. "Frank," she said. "Frank!" She yelled it this time. "It's me! It's Extra!"

His eyes opened wide in one abrupt movement. She was right at him then. "Frank, Frank, it's me. Frank. Frank. Frank. Frank." She wasn't going to stop. She sensed he was going to recognize her. He was trying to clench her hand. She looked into his eyes. She saw him seeing her. It was Frank. He was there. She saw he knew her.

In another moment she saw in his still-open eyes that he was retreat-ing, and she understood she was looking at him looking at her, but he was no longer assuredly present. She tried to coax him back again. She willed it to happen. She begged for him with her eyes, looking in his to find him again. But Frank was gone.

They were home for summer break. Mabel's sons draped—long limbs folding over settees, fingers tapping sonatas of text into cell phones, private tattoos peeking out from undersides and torn shirts. She could see not one was in love. She doubted their interest was where it should have been—in fullest randy, chasing girls. They would be on the prowl for her.

But no. They let her be. Her youngest, lion of outrage, snarled at

Don. Dad did not nag Mom enough. Dad had not destroyed wine and spirits. Dad joined Mother in cocktails. Robert couldn't see why shame and its cousins, pride and continence, eluded his father.

Don soothed and condescended, praised and agreed. As usual, he did nothing afterward, causing Robert, after five days of perturbed piety, to announce he was going to work for the students organizing to fire the president of his university. He would head back to New York, had no use for the hypocrisy of Washington, and on the deepest level feared for his parents' marriage. But there was trouble finding an apartment in Brooklyn—he eschewed all things Manhattan—and so his exodus stalled.

That brought George, once the proto-environmentalist, to center stage, where he advised he had become an antiwar activist. There was a petition—he felt strongly they should sign it. Mabel asked how Don— the objective, fair-minded author—could do such a thing. How could Don—moral voice of his generation—not? "I cannot take sides," Don said affably. "You are taking a side by not taking one," said sweet George. "I could sign it happily," Mabel offered. That, her offspring informed her, was because she had no real principles.

She signed anyway. And still George was not still. One night he had friends over, fellow objectors. Mabel and Don served them dinner, the party spread into the yard, there was a joint of marijuana, Don had to leave.

"Why? To protect *his career*? A career of appeasement and col- laboration," George told Mabel, Don being absent. Her son's assem- bled friends watched with sullen solidarity. "Is that a career worth protecting?"

"He can't accuse people of wrongdoing and get caught doing any himself," she said, rejecting her usual irritation with Don's hyper- upstanding ways. He'd made an endearing exit from the party, opting for refuge in the 7-Eleven on Wisconsin for a Slurpee. She was supposed to call him on his cell once the cannabis was gone. Don hadn't asked the offender to leave, after all. She said that. Among the youth she'd just fed, the eye rollers outnumbered the impressed.

"When did he last accuse?" George wanted to know. "He's never even been to a secret prison!"

Harriet, the seasoned Pentagon reporter, had broken that story, though she hadn't actually visited the premises of any of the CIA prisons. To prove something existed, you didn't have to see it. Mabel could have reminded her son of that. But young George was right. No one Don talked to would have told him about the secret prisons. His sources were men who found themselves high up the chain of command. They were committed to keeping Don far from their failures, even their most well-intentioned mistakes. Everyone knew a gaffe in Washington could broil you alive as easily as a premeditated, elaborately organized system to scourge the guileless.

It was easy to be mad at Don. Watching one son frothing at him showed her how convenient, how comfortable it had been—for her. Meanwhile, there was Stanley, who could have left the Room moons ago, sticking it out. He was willing to be nastily misconstrued for the sake of—what?—right now it seemed for the sake of a night-cops reporter he believed was the polar opposite of Janet Cooke, who might be, in her own way, what Don had been at first, but long ago stopped being.

Although this night was for her sons, she was sitting in the middle of still another one of her parties, oddly not interested in a drink, or, which was entirely in character, interested in her children. She wondered. Maybe Stanley's night-cops reporter was the Room's unplanned daughter, a youngest last child cursed with a passionate nature, that trait the Room mistook for bias. She was probably someone who ruled nothing out, who went for the concealed and tough-to-prove. She'd have trouble speaking in the Room's preferred language—written reports from government men.

Mabel drifted away from the action, watched as the boy who'd had the marijuana fell asleep in a stuffed chair, and headed up the stairs to Don's office. She sat at his computer and looked up his file of home addresses for newsroom employees.

When she had what she needed, she called him to let him know the weed scare was over. After he got back, she told him she had a hankering for a Slurpee too. He didn't question why she got in her Volvo to reach a 7-Eleven two blocks away.

Don was always preoccupied, and for once she was going to put it to decent use.

The drive seemed to take forever. It took a while to find the number on the front door, backing up and pulling forward, wishing she had a flashlight. Finally, she found it and ran up the stairs, her car still running. After she pushed the last of the DVDs containing the Sissy report through Stanley's brass mail slot, she dashed off a note on the back of a blank check.

For your hopes, and mine, Mabel.

She pushed it through the slot. He'd be at work now, but he'd find it when he got home sometime after midnight.

She thought of his happiness all the way home.

Vera didn't see Baby. She parked on the side of the Amoco, near the restrooms. For a while she sat looking at nothing. Then she decided to buy a pack of gum from the man at the register. But it was a different one from the fall. The other guy had a lisp. He was easygoing. Luckily enough, this new one, clean-shaven with a deep voice, also liked to talk. She leaned on the counter and watched television with him. He had on a Nationals game.

It was only his second or third night, yet he'd already noticed "some pretty odd stuff." Vera nodded and smacked her gum. "Well," he said, "there's some whores here."

She felt he wanted her to be shocked. But when she went outside and starting talking to Baby, he'd think her shock was phony. So she said, "Well, actually, I'm here to meet up with one of those girls." And then something about the way he looked at her, she worried he'd think she was one of them, so she added, "I'm a reporter."

"Not supposed to talk to press," he said, pulling away from the counter. The air reformulated. The television was suddenly blasting.

"No problem," she said. She let the tense moments pass.

"Full count," she said, trying to change his mind. She eased against the glass door.

He resumed his stance against the counter but didn't say anything.

She looked at her watch again. It was completely like Baby to call her and insist on a time and then be late. She really missed the previous guy, though she couldn't quite remember his name. Maybe it was Phil. Or Glenn. He had a scrunched-up face, almost brown from freckles too. He'd been in a bad fight in high school that messed up his jaw. Changed me, he'd told her. She remembered that clearly. He'd not mentioned Baby at all at first. After more than a few visits, and after he'd seen Vera with Baby outside, he finally mentioned how worried he was about her. At first he'd given Baby free cigarettes, hoping he could persuade her to give up the life, get back home, stop being a runaway. One night, a cop paid a visit because he'd gotten word about a minor. The cop warned the guy about selling her cigarettes, which struck him as ridiculous. Cop said he'd overlook it if the guy called next time she showed up. The guy was so affronted by this blowhard he started hiding Baby in the employees bathroom when any cops circled by the station. That had been last fall.

It was close to midnight. It was like Baby to not show up, but Baby had never called her before. Vera decided to buy a pack of cigarettes from this jumpy newcomer and head outside.

Baby had said the boathouse first. Maybe she was there. Maybe she forgot about telling Vera to wait at the Amoco. It was so swampy, way too hot even at this hour to walk. She was already muggy with sweat when she got in her car. She turned the key in the ignition.

It wouldn't start.

She took the key out, studied it. Yeah, it was the right one.

She put it in, turned it just a little, and then turned again. Nothing.

Could the battery be dead?

Lord, cars and her did not at all mix. She'd just bought a new battery. Or maybe not. Since when was buying a car battery memorable?

She hunted for her cell phone. She'd just have to call Baby to make sure she wasn't by the boathouse. She probably should have just done that anyway.

Good, she was answering. "Baby," Vera said.

"Huh?"

"Baby, it's Vera."

"I'm sorry, but you've got the wrong number."

Vera pulled the phone away from her ear and looked—no, it was Baby's number. Her phone's contact list had put out plain: Baby.

"Who is this?" Vera demanded.

"Who is *this*?"

"This is Vera Hastings."

"Well, this is Kayla, and I don't know you." She hung up.

Vera called again. This Kayla must have taken Baby's phone away from her. Maybe Baby was standing right there.

Whoever Kayla was, she wasn't picking up this time. Damn, she probably stole it from Baby. Not all that surprising, really, come to think of it. It had to be Baby's pimp's phone, not Baby's. He could have taken it from her and handed it to another of his girls.

She looked at the television flickering behind the register. She needed to ask this new guy for a jump. It was an Amoco station, wasn't it?

"Hey," she said as she walked in. She heard cheering from the television.

"Zimmerman homer!" The guy said. "Hot damn."

"What's the score?" she asked, though she couldn't care.

"Tied at two–two," the guy said.

"Say, when the inning's over, could you give me a jump? I think my battery died on me."

"I'm not permitted to step outside after the garage closes," he said choppily.

"You can't? Really?"

"I can't leave this register unattended."

"Do you have any cables? Maybe somebody might come by and—"

"You'd have to ask them. I'm sorry. This being right by the highway ramp and what have you, they've got some strict rules."

She couldn't quite believe this. What a jerk. What a . . . Hold on. Please, hold on. There was no need to lose it. No need. She looked out at Virginia Avenue. Empty. This was a candy city. Flat out, it wasn't a city at all. It was a town that had some city people in it, and not one of them was where she was standing.

She had to call Stanley. But her phone was dropping the call. Actually, it couldn't get past the ringing part of the call. She started moving around to different parts of the gas-station lot. She stood by pump one, and then pump seven, and then—she got his voice mail the third time. He wasn't there. Or he wasn't picking up. Where was he? Okay, okay, so smoke a cigarette.

She sat on the edge of the Amoco cement, sparked the match, and realized: of course, that's where Stanley was—smoking a cigarette. Goodness. She sure needed to relax. She concentrated.

Get it in shape, Vera, get it under control.

She said that more than a few times. Cars came around the corner, and she thought they might turn in for gas, but no, straight for the on-ramp. It was now ten past. She ground out the cigarette. Okay, Stanley would have to be done with his smoke now.

"Night desk." Hallelujah.

"Stanley, it's Vera."

"Vera. I thought you were off tonight. This is a surprise."

He had that right.

"You know that Amoco right near the Watergate, where you make that turn to get on Sixty-six? Well, that girl whore I told you about—I was supposed to meet her here, but she hasn't shown, and I can't find her on her cell, 'cause I called and some other tyke answered, and then I get in my car, and the thing won't start, and this guy at the Amoco is no help, he *refuses* to give me a jump. . . . So . . ." It was so good to explain the whole thing, she was so happy, but somewhere in all her explaining she felt as if Stanley wasn't listening.

"Stanley? Stanley? Stanley?"

The call was dropped.

She wanted to squeeze the life out of the cell phone. She wanted to stomp it. She imagined a truck tire flattening it. This was turning into the kind of night that made her not so much frantic as feeling misunderstood, as if some kind of godhead she did not believe in, some gold calf in the desert, was testing her, taunting her, trying to see where she might just—oh no.

Her cell was making a consistent tinkle, doing so every three seconds. This was the warning that her battery was low. Not just low, as when the gas tank was on empty, but it wasn't quite empty. She'd gotten that warning earlier in the day. She remembered it now with agonizing self-pity. This was the final minute of her cell phone. This sound meant she was alone, abandoned, a black hitchhiker on a white planet. She watched the last screen tremors and then saw the display become a sonic purple, and then, in a shimmering dissolve, black.

She almost threw it on the ground, but she wasn't that kind of person. She pushed open the glass door of the Amoco.

"Can I use the phone here?"

"There's no phone here. They took out the pay phone. It was used for illegal activities." He didn't turn to her. He just stayed glued to the game. Except, she noticed, there was no game on, just a commercial, for a car dealership.

"My cell phone, it just died," she said. "And I'm a little . . . frightened."

He did turn then. He looked a little frightened himself. He *couldn't* be scared of *her*. Could he?

She saw he had a cell phone in his shirt pocket, and he saw her eye going to it. It was in that moment that she realized if she had been white he would have let her use it without hesitation. And after some seconds went by, she realized he wasn't going to let her use it at all. Dear Lord, she said, please keep my temper down. Please. She turned on her heel and walked out the door without a word. Her rage was a spluttering kind, a messy boil. It took her out of the Amoco lot, across Virginia Avenue Northwest, over Rock Creek Parkway, and into the woods around the boathouse. She might have been running. Images were blowing past, light blurring as if she were in a fast-moving vehicle with her eyes half closed.

She stopped. She just had to. She wasn't tired. She just wasn't sure—was the boathouse to her right or her left?

She tried to collect herself. She would have liked to sit down. But it was too warm to do anything. It was sticky. She took a deep breath.

The air had a weight. It was that humid. The trees felt too low. There seemed to be movement, though not exactly anywhere she could pinpoint. The undergrowth was leaves and weeds decomposing so minutely that it wouldn't be noticeable, except she was surrounded by the smell of slicked masses of dead buds, moth wings, seedlings, and things she didn't know the names of, flattened into the ground and each other. She heard a series of far-carrying hoots. The second and third notes were shorter than the others. What was that? She stopped. There it went again. From her Fresh Air Fund memories, tiny bits of them, Blue Ridge Mountains and forest-fire prevention, her mind pulled and tugged—

It was an owl.

She walked at a more even pace and was glad for the urban sky that gave her light. She'd gotten good at trees, studying them in her botanical guide during the time she wanted to find the tree her pilot landed in. There were many oaks—pin, post, bur, overcup, chestnut, blackjack, scarlet, black, white, shumard, chinkapin. Her pilot had dangled from a Northern red.

She was *her* pilot. Vera wasn't sure she'd given so much thought and feeling to any one person before. Vera often wished she could see her. Once, she woke up from a dream of speaking to her. She believed, without any reason, that the pilot was, in ways similar to herself, alone.

"Wait up."

She stopped her footsteps.

"Hello?" she called. "Hello!"

There was no wind and sounds had stopped.

"Baby?"

She took a step, turned around a few times. "Baby?"

"Baby!" She screamed this. She did it again. She was surprised at how hard she had to work to get a powerful yell out, so she half knelt and howled up with all her might.

"Baby!"

She heard scatterings of sound from it—boring animals like squirrels or frogs, maybe they moved—but the foliage noises were indefinite, and soon they subsided completely.

She stood there. Somehow the air seemed different because she had screamed into it. Now what. Then she realized: the boathouse was behind and ahead and left and right. She had lost her sense of direction.

She took a breath, a deep one, but the air was resistant; it was like trying to get oxygen from rock. She put her first two right fingers to her neck. She felt the beat in her jugular, a ragged, too-fast pulse. In the time it took her to get her unsteady arm back down at her side, they had materialized in front of her, all three of them on a cropping of moss.

Baby was carrying a flashlight. One of them, outfitted in pink jogging bra and marathoner briefs of silver spandex, was picking at the bark on a tree. An older one, wearing white opera gloves, had her arms folded across her chest.

"Mmm, mmm, mmm." The girl sounded like a sister, but she looked Asian. She was delicate, like a soda straw.

"Hi you doin'?" The jogger had lost interest in the tree trunk. She'd put her palms on her backside. She had no hips. Thighs and calves were pin-thin. Hair was in a severe flip, and all of her was as dark as a Tootsie Roll.

"Told you," Baby said.

"You gone up in the world?" the jogger snapped at Baby. "Can't you listen. We here. *We here.*"

"Now, hold up," the opera girl said to the jogger. "Baby."

There was a momentous pause, as if a film projector were gearing up for the first show at a full house.

"This here's my partners," Baby said to Vera. "Heidi and Winnow."

Winnow shifted to another foot and rolled her eyes. "And?" she asked pointedly.

"And this here is Vera, from Channel Four," Baby said. Her eyes burrowed into Vera as she said "Channel Four." Baby didn't want these lovelies to know where Vera really worked. So Vera took in her lie wordlessly. All muscles were motion-free. She stopped a blink just in case.

"How you doin'," Vera said to Winnow. "How you doin' "—she nodded to Heidi. Was this as goofy as it sounded? Or was she silly from stress and heat? She tried to keep her expression serious. She didn't know what she'd been so afraid of happening, but it sure wasn't this. The Lord had protected.

"We have a proposition," Heidi said. She unfolded her arms. What was with the opera gloves? This girl must be suffocatingly hot. Now that Vera looked closer, she saw the gloves were smudgy and gray at the tips. She'd worn them all day. What was going on with her?

"We have some clients. They busy, they this, they that. So they asked us to get with you," Heidi said. "In certain situations, come what may and so forth, you got to be direct. If you know what I mean."

Vera didn't know. Apparently, Winnow did, because she had put forth her lower lip in an expression of worldly fatigue. Baby was staring straight into Vera as if she might be able to supply an alternate to Heidi's words by force of thought. She was worried about something. Somehow Vera thought it best to agree with Heidi. "Sure," she said.

"We got some private information. About a man where you working. *The* man."

Vera was stumped.

"The boss of you," Heidi said.

"The green Vespa," Winnow said. She couldn't help herself; she had to interrupt.

Baby looked suddenly confused.

"You know!" Winnow said.

Baby nodded.

Green Vespa was Gordon Bray, the managing editor, and it was not one jot of a surprise these charmers knew of him, given her parking-garage encounter with him not all that long ago. "Baby says hi," he'd said to her that night. What had he gotten himself into?

"Vespa's a customer," Heidi said, frowning.

"You can't go at it that way!" Winnow exploded. She pushed herself out of Heidi's way and put her face up into Vera's. She had sheen for skin. Her lips were like big petals. "Now, look here, Lois Lane," Winnow said. "You report an army crash. The army don't like it. They tried to get your snippy nose out of it, but you too dumb to know it. That boss of you? He's all up the britches of every tyke out here. Could cause problems. For him. For you. So maybe that crash should stay crashed. That way, your boss, his private business, can stay private. Catch my drift?"

Adam had always suspected. There'd been plenty of suggestive coincidences. He'd just never had the correct sequence of events. As he'd hoped, Gordon Bray had picked up the details. Gordon got out more. He mixed in certain circles. He knew people on the inside track. One of them had brought home the goods on Don Grady.

The gist of it was simple. Grady often had information that the newsroom needed. Over the years, he'd agreed to share it with Adam. Adam and he would evaluate. Did the other paper have it? (The other paper was all Adam cared about. The lesser papers were lesser. Television was no serious rival, just village idiot in an overpriced suit that bumbled into news. Magazines were starlets, pretty to look at but demanding too much time and attention.)

So, if the other paper didn't have it, Don could save it for his book. After all, the publicity from Don's books was good for the paper. But if the other paper did have it, then the question changed. When and if the other paper published, would it so decrease the value of Don's revelation that there was no point in saving it for Don's book? If so, then Don would write the story for the paper. If it was too small a story, if Don was in the middle of great reportorial obligations, if he simply didn't care, then Adam could assign Don's information to a reporter. Don would not be mentioned at all. The paper would publish the scoop.

That was how it was supposed to work. It rarely did.

Most recently, Gordon Bray told Adam, it appeared that Don had had the Sissy report that contained the White House surveillance scoop. He could have called Adam the day the other paper posted the surveillance story on its Web site and Mitch Pendleton was fighting for air. He could have called Adam in the days and weeks after, when the other paper kept coming at them with scoops from the same report. Don had broken faith. Don had screwed the paper. He always did. But by the time Don's books came out with the revelations in them that would have been oh so pertinent for the paper to have had first, the milk was spilt, the cat from the bag, the sun long set.

There was just one step Adam had to take before he confronted Don. All he had to do was confirm this intelligence on Don's possession of the report with Mabel, who, on that funny day she came in to say she didn't want the managing-editor job, had seemed more than disaffected with Don.

He picked up the phone and dialed. She wasn't home. He didn't want to leave a message. It might fall in Don's hands. He looked at his watch. It was a little before 9 p.m. on a Wednesday in June. Were they at that country home they had? He went to the editorial staff's columnist directory in the system. They had Mabel's cell-phone number.

He dialed. It went to voice mail. He didn't want to leave a message. He got up and walked into the Room. Maybe this time he would banish Don Grady from it permanently.

She would meet him in Dumbarton Oaks. After gardeners were dispatched, after the two-story black-and-gold gate on R Street clanged shut and locked for the night, he'd know how to get in there. He'd say,

"We'll have all of it to ourselves." And they would lie down, faces to the sky, on the fleecy green of her favorite lawn, the one that sloped downward from the house and was edged with wisteria. Couldn't they go swimming in that slate-bottomed pool set high on a terrace?

Mabel was walking with her cell phone in hand on Thirtieth Street, telling herself she was going to Oak Hill Cemetery with the family key. She was going to visit her grandfather's grave, or that's what she'd told Don. What she wanted, more than anything, was Adam.

She looked at her cell. The display showed received calls, and the cursor was on his number from the time he'd called her.

He had called her. Stanley had to have spoken to him.

She could call him.

Her cell said it was nine, twenty-two after. She pulled her T-shirt dress away from her chest and looked down. She was wearing white bra and panties; save her, they were matching, and, yes, lace, a victory. They glowed a pale violet in the dark.

She pushed the green button.

It rang. But only twice. "Mabel," he said right away.

He knew it was her. He must have taken the time one day to enter her name and store it. Interesting. Also encouraging.

"How are you?"

"I'm fine, I'm fine," he said, as if they were daily, these calls.

"This a good time?"

"Yes, yes it is."

"Where are you?"

"In my car. I'm driving from the paper."

"Home for the night."

"Maybe. Not sure. I may have to go back in."

"Uh-huh."

"Where are you?"

"I'm in the Oak Hill Cemetery. I told Don I was taking a walk."

"I could meet you there."

She gasped. She hoped he didn't hear. This, this had been too easy. This was how it used to be. This was the old days made new. She had been using the tone of the woman with a brief to file, and she almost shifted her voice, but her forlorn apparatus was firing on some of its dendrites, and it said, Don't do it.

"I'll come to the gate," she said. "Opposite Twenty-ninth Street."

"I'm on Mass., just about in Sheridan Circle. So two minutes. Less."

"Okay."

She had been strolling around the three mausoleums at the entrance and was now near the circular path along the one farthest from the gate. She smelled her hands. Had she washed them after eating dinner? Hell, they smelled like pizza. She bent down and scrunched them around in the grass, working fingernails under fingernails, flicking out and pushing in and flicking out. There—she put her fingers to her nose—they smelled like a lawnmower. She was as alluring as antifreeze.

What did she think? That they'd grope in a cemetery? Was this about that? It couldn't be. He was not attractive, God knew, he was not attractive. She should go home. This was a dreadful mistake. Why had she called him?

She sat right down on the ground. Her head ached, and a cramping in the arch of her left foot had begun. She jumped up to step on it, push it out, and then it relaxed, and she slumped back down to reckon with her fantasy and its upcoming reality. Maybe it had been too long. Maybe this part of her life was over. Adam wasn't going to be the love of anyone's life. He was a steward. He had run the paper without imagination.

In a minute she saw his headlights. They were perpendicular to the gate. She could say they got their signals crossed. If she stayed here, he couldn't see her. He might be afraid to call her again on the cell—what if Don had unexpectedly joined her on the walk? Had Adam moved along these centimeters of deception, did he know how to stray? There was also this. It would ratchet his longing, wouldn't it, if the night didn't work? The next time would be sweeter. It always was when delayed.

When she looked up, the headlights were gone. The temperature might have dropped a degree or two. Maybe she'd been sweating, and by sitting she'd settled down enough to sense the coolness on her skin. She stood up to peer. No car was in sight. He'd given up. He'd left.

She was flash-sorry. The regret was deep. She rubbed her forehead. She remembered how he'd done just that during her visit to the Room. And look what she'd done—pulled him in to push him away. She didn't understand herself. She made no sense and was having no fun. She was a mime with a plaid heart, a poodle in a buggy, a vandal in a cemetery, a grown woman playing teenager, and not for much or for keeps. She sure didn't want to go home. The thought of the front door, the inevitable staircase, the climb up it—

She was sitting on the ground. He moved closer to the gate. He tried it. It was locked. He stood there. What in creation was she doing?

Now she was standing up. Walking, walking, coming his way— couldn't she see him? Apparently, she couldn't. He tried to figure this out. Then it hit him. He'd not explained. He was so excited about Gordon Bray waltzing in with the news about Grady. In his rush to fill in this one last color on the chart, he'd barely explained to her why he needed to see her. Good, now she was within earshot.

"I know this is awkward. I just couldn't wait."

"Adam!"

"You were hiding over there," he said.

"I was. I can't quite believe it, but I was."

"Why?"

"I was just trying to figure that out."

"Are you going to open the gate?"

"Yes," she said. "Yes, sorry. Of course."

She put the old key in the old lock, and the bolt turned back. The gate swung slowly open. Adam walked through.

"I'm consumed with this," he said. "I should have said more on the phone. I'm not good. Good at this."

"I understand."

"Do you? Do you know how long this has just driven me absolutely crazy?"

She seemed to shiver. Yet it was hot. The air in the dark had the intensity of unshaded noon. The city was equatorial this summer. He believed every prophecy of melting.

"That day I came in—"

"That day you came in! That was something."

"I know," she said. "I thought, am I crazy?"

"Not crazy. Not at all. Because I was thinking the same thing."

She seemed to be walking up the hill, getting farther away from the street. That was probably a good idea.

"Don—" Adam began.

"Oh, he, we can just—let's not talk about him."

"I think we have to," Adam said.

"You're right. You are."

"Of course."

"But . . ." Mabel hesitated.

"Let me say something."

"Go ahead."

"How aware are you, I mean, of what, you know, goes on for him?"

"He tells me everything," Mabel said. "Over and over and over."

"I thought so."

"I knew you would know that!"

"Look, it's what he's about."

"Adam. That. That is exactly, exactly, exactly how I think of it."

He could have kissed her. He'd waited a long time for this.

"The Sissy report," he said. "Let's go back to the Sissy report."

"I feel terrible about it."

"Why should you? It's not your fault. My God."

"I should have just called you directly."

"So he did have it."

"Of course he had it."

She was pausing in front of a tombstone. "Let's sit here," she said.

There was an arbor, an enclosure of greenery. She moved into it. He followed.

"You have no idea," he began, but before he could finish his thought, her lips were on his, and she was, what was it, she was intimating a way of moving that was, there could be no other way to— "Mabel." he finally pulled back. "What are you doing?"

Her lips were in a frenetic shape. He thought she might close her mouth, but that took longer, though her eyes had a sleepy, sideways look, so almost, yes, a crazed look, fever for eyes. He looked around at the bower they were in and then back at her and then at his hands, as if they might hold the answer to this overheated abyss he now found himself in with, with her.

In the old days, Stanley would have wheeled in luggage. One of the obit writers would have asked, "Vacation?"

The Sissy report would have filled at least two suitcases. He would have gone to the closet lining the length of the Room's interior wall, the one where he usually leaned his umbrella, the place he hung his winter coat these many years. He would have pushed the bags in there. All the hangers were empty in June, tangled in groups on the long pole. Still, he would have worried. Was it a safe enough hiding place?

Instead, he carried it in his man purse. All of the DVDs—fourteen, to be exact—fit nicely. He took the discs out and placed them beside his terminal. When he walked by his desk, his eye burned right to them. They glowed. Then he refocused, and they became an unobtrusive stack on his busy, messy desk.

We need to talk.

It was the first time he'd messaged Adam in months. Since Gordon Bray became managing editor, Adam and Stanley's church meetings had been suspended. It had happened before, these kinds of moratoriums, but never for this long.

Four. The usual place.

If he were a teenager, he would have gulped. He'd hoped to wait only a full day for a reply. He wouldn't have been surprised if he didn't get one at all.

Sure.

His own cool, in that one word, thrilled him. "Sure," he said to himself more than once over the course of the day. When he found himself saying it out loud, in response to any one of many questions put to him from this one and that one, he had to stop a wiseass grin.

Walking the short half-block to the church, he thought he might run into Adam. When he didn't, he reminded himself to be reasonable. No doubt Adam would be late.

He pushed the heavy doors into the smell of Sunday flowers.

His eyes adjusted to the dim. He walked slowly toward the pews. He felt his way to a seat on the far right, their usual place.

It took a few minutes for him to realize Adam was there too. He was sitting at the front of the church, in a pew off the center nave, staring at the altar. The hot afternoon coming through stained glass didn't quite reach him.

"Adam," Stanley said.

Adam popped up before the echo ended. He hurried back to Stanley. "I'm glad you messaged," he said. "Jesus." He put a hand through his hair.

"Me too."

Adam didn't seem to hear that. He looked at the ceiling, then put his hand at the back of his neck, wincing.

"You can't imagine what happened."

"I have some . . . some news," Stanley said.

"I really thought I'd nailed Don, I mean really proved it this time."

"I think . . . just before we . . . Don? . . . Did you say Don?"

"Don. Yes, Don." Adam was still standing up, and now he was pulling on a shirt cuff with the other hand.

"I . . . don't . . ."

"You don't, of course you don't, because I'm . . ."

"Just sit. Sit a minute."

"I can't."

Adam walked a little bit toward the pew in front of them, and then marched back as if he might forget what he wanted to say. "You remember, during the first Bush book, why, he had the National Intelligence Estimate and he never, he just never had the common courtesy to let me know. But that was—by no means . . . that was not the very worst. How many times over the years has he screwed us? How many? How many times have you and I sat here and just . . . just . . . been *amazed* . . ."

"That was terrible. It really was."

"I should have gone to . . ."

"But you didn't. And . . ."

"And I swore I would *not* let it happen again."

"But I have something . . . If you could just . . ."

"And then I heard from Gordon, who'd heard from one of his diplomatic buddies, one of those Council on Foreign Relations types, or maybe, hell, maybe at one of Don's damned dinners, that Don . . . *all along* . . . had the Sissy report. All the time we've been taking it on the chin . . . all the time the other paper had front-page news from that thing. And I said, Okay, okay, this is . . ."

"But, Adam . . ."

". . . the way to get this nailed down, no wiggle room . . . because you know and I know how he can wiggle. I said, The way to get him is to call Mabel. So I do. So I get her. So we—why I don't know, but we did—we set on this cemetery, you know, the one in Georgetown. . . ."

It was no use. It was best to let Adam tell it all.

". . . and I get there, I drive there, and I should have known. Oh, Stanley, I should have, because I get there and she is sitting on the ground. I mean, what grown woman sits on the ground in a cemetery? She's nuts. Not okay. Not someone you can trust. Not someone you should ever—no matter how driven to want to believe— But that's the thing, I still want to believe, so I get out of the car, and she stands up, and we laugh a little, and we walk some, and I'm telling her, but she, being nuts, being Mabel, she seems, oh yeah, she seems to be following exactly what I'm saying, and she's saying, although, now that I think about it, maybe she didn't say it—it doesn't matter. It doesn't matter because I'm talking to her, and she says, yes, he had the Sissy report, absolutely, and then . . . plunk, out of nowhere . . . *she kissed me*."

Stanley lowered his gaze. He was wearing sandals today. They were heavy brown leather. He could see his big toe clearly, thanks to a ray of white light from the June sun. It was really kind of monstrous, the skin a perilous thickness, a lot of it cracked. He moved the toe. It seemed almost divorced from him, but it was his toe, he was moving it.

"She hadn't even been drinking. But it wasn't like kissing your sister—it was a kiss kiss."

He seemed to have found a stopping point. Stanley gave him a few more seconds, in case it was just a pause.

"I can't believe I let this happen. I . . . just, I just can't. I've kissed Don Grady's wife at night in a cemetery. And she's so nuts, so crazy—she'll probably tell him."

"I don't know about that."

"Really? You don't think she will?"

"No. I don't."

Adam finally sat down. He looked at Stanley purposefully. He seemed to be checking for something.

"You've known her forever."

"Yes, yes, I have."

"You don't think she'll go to him with this."

"No."

"Because if she did . . ."

"She's a discreet woman, actually."

"Discreet?"

"I'd say so."

Adam stood up again. "Well I—you seem so . . . certain."

"She most likely chalks it up to a misunderstanding. Not much worth mentioning."

"But how, how in the world, could she mistake my . . . my reason for wanting . . . to talk?"

"You were excited. You sounded excited. She took it to be—

another—a different kind of excitement." Stanley felt his own ebbing. The early-morning adrenaline, his too many cups of coffee, some of their effects had not yet dulled away. To calm himself the last bit more, he looked at the church windows, away from Adam. He had never looked at them before. They were quite beautiful.

"I have got to be more careful," Adam said, sitting back down. "It—it happened with Martina too. Though not a kiss. Nothing that blatant. She's not a kook like Mabel."

Stanley stood up.

Adam stayed seated, looking confused.

Stanley checked his watch. He knew that would be all he'd have to do. Adam wouldn't remember that he had any news. He wouldn't recall that Stanley had been the one to e-mail him first. With a shudder, Stanley realized that if he'd told Adam that Mabel had given him the Sissy report, Adam might well have not believed, because it was from Mabel, that it *was* the Sissy report. And even if Stanley had been adroit enough to hide the report's provenance, Adam could very easily have taken it from Vera and given it to one of the national reporters. Stanley kicked himself for not having considered this earlier.

"I guess we do need to be getting back," Adam finally said.

Stanley would give it to Vera. At some point down the road, they'd tell Adam she found it herself—from a source, any source. He'd never done this before, but at the moment he felt like making up the source. Adam didn't ever have to know it came from Mabel, the kook.

As that last of his coffee buzz deadened away, he realized the Sissy report might not be as much as he'd hoped. Yet he promised himself he would make Vera feel it was. Wasn't that more important than any information contained in it? So what if it was stale? So the other paper had picked over it for months? They weren't Vera.

For the first time, Adam and Stanley returned together instead of separately, as they usually did, to conceal they'd been meeting. There would have been a time when Stanley would have tingled at such an emollient from Adam. As they walked past the elevators into the Room, Stanley looked around. Almost everyone was in a cold jitter—jaws to phones, eyes to screens, fingertips to keypads—locked in rapid talk and quick thinking. He'd always believed they rarely missed a thing, these insects. Yet the night editor walking with the executive editor—that was outside this hive's neural hum. Vera was there, though; she'd just come in for work. She saw them and gave Stanley a happy look.

Adam tossed off a "see you," and Stanley went to Vera's desk. He would have had a smoke with her, but he wasn't ready for her yet.

"A meeting in an hour or so?" he said instead.

"Since when do we have a meeting?" It sounded officious. Smoking room was their idea of a meeting.

"Just want to make sure you're not driving to northern Virginia tonight," Stanley said.

"Oh. No, not going," she said, a little brighter. But her face fell when she added, "There's something I need to tell you."

Stanley looked up from the budget on his screen. "How about now? I have a moment."

"Umm—later would be better," she said.

That wasn't like her. He wondered, as he read the wires, what she couldn't just say, but mostly he thought about how to tell her about the Sissy report. He wanted it to give her more than a boost. He wanted to send her, just launch her.

When the time came, he took her to a conference room and put the DVDs on the big table between them. He wished there were more of a flourish, something in the family of drum rolls or cymbals.

"What's this?"

She looked, as she usually did, alert but not impatient. At the ready— Vera's default state.

"This is going to change everything." It was absurd; he said it anyway.

"That would be nice," she said, but minus any snark—she meant it.

He slid a piece of paper across the table.

"Take a look."

She read for a moment, then stopped. "Stanley," she said, then went on reading. "It's about MECS," she whispered a little later, puzzling it out.

"It's one of fifty pages that mention MECS," he said. "I just printed one for you."

"Is this—what is this?"

"This is your pilot. This is what happened to her."

She had an intense expression. It was—concentration, categorizing, and, he thought, hope.

"It's from the Senate Select Committee on Intelligence," he said.

"The Sissy report?" She was bumped up now.

"The Sissy report," he said. "The one Mitch was trying to get that day."

"That," she said. "I felt bad for him. I can't believe it's . . . it's right here, right on this table."

"It is."

"How did you get this?" The admiration, he had wanted to see it from her, and here it was. He wished that his motives could have been pure—that he only wanted it for her, this unexpected triumph from the unseen corner.

"An old friend," he said. Mabel. He really could call her that.

"Shouldn't we tell Adam?" She looked distrustful, just somewhat, as if she wasn't convinced of Stanley's comportment at such a discovery.

"I met with him today."

"What did he say?" The hope in her—it was fully ignited now.

"He wants you on this. No distractions."

She seemed to lift up. "I will—I'm—Stanley, this is—he said that? I'm just—unbelievable . . . I just—I've had—but this—"

"And you had something to tell me." He hated to interrupt the burble. In the past he wouldn't have. He felt a calibration inside himself shifting. He felt stronger. He felt—what was it—that there wasn't as much time as he used to think there always was. Yes, he was more than serious. He seemed to have urgency.

She pushed her chair back a little from the table. The lights were too bright, as they always were in the glass conference rooms along the sides of the Room. And it was just after deadline, so he could see the Room emptying, reporters with shoulder bags over their backs moving toward the elevators, the Copy Desk editors beginning their thankless push to edit out ambiguities and blunders.

"Baby saw that night . . . of the crash—saw who was there," Vera began. "I hadn't really thought it through. But she might be able to see the same people coming out of MECS. I need to take her out to the MECS building. She might recognize someone."

"That's a good idea," he said, more absentmindedly than he intended. They had the Sissy report. How important would Baby be now? As soon as he posed it, if only to himself, the question resurrected hot shame—he blushed. Baby—definitely less than reliable in the Room's way of reckoning, but on this pilot story, proved right independently twice—he of all people shouldn't dismiss her.

"Is that what you needed to get with me about?" he asked gently, his humility ebbing back.

"Uhm. No." Now she looked embarrassed.

"Uh-huh." He gave her a warm smile. She was looking at him as if she wanted him to lean forward. So he did. He waited awhile.

"Gordon Bray is using," she finally said.

"Junk?" Stanley asked. He'd heard scuttlebutt that the managing editor was a heroin aficionado. He'd dismissed that out of hand.

"Tykes."

He was surprised and sank back in his chair. His eye registered that the Room had produced a frantic gathering by the desk of the executive editor's secretary. Someone was actually raising his voice—just who he couldn't tell from this distance. Nor could he hear a thing. But he could tell from body attitudes and one gesture or two that something unacceptable was going on involving sports reporters and an editor from the Business section.

Gordon Bray patronizing child whores inserted itself back into his thinking; so strange, its appearance in his mind apparently needed to be neutralized by the bickering scene near Adam's office.

"How do you know this?" He was stern now. Like the heroin, it could be bunk.

"I know because he told me," she said. "Though not in so many words. And I also know because some older girls came and told me."

Better than rumor—better than he would have imagined. Yet he tried to look tough to Vera. He tried to think.

"How long?"

"I don't know that," she said in a resigned tone. "I wish I didn't know any of it."

"This has been discovered more times than there's gray hairs on my head," he said, giving his jaded expression all he could. "Maybe not this high up the food chain. Though I'd have to give it some thought."

"But tykes? This isn't just whores. It's girls. Girls."

"That's not unusual," Stanley said, but he was lying.

"It is illegal." Vera, upright.

" 'Course it is. This all was built on illegal." Now he was sounding like an old head, bitter, cranky.

"They're only fourteen," Vera argued.

"At least they're not twelve." He was saying what he knew Adam would say. It sounded arch. It was baffling to Vera too. He saw her face blank into consternation.

"Don't we have to do something? Report it?" She was giving up as she asked, he thought. Stanley, the giver of the career-saving Sissy report, had morphed into tooth-and-claw exponent, ugly cynic, Room defender.

"We could," he said. He was acting like a dervish dolt today. He was all over the place. But he was through—he had decided in the church with Adam—with his ineffective decent ways. "We may yet. For now, I'll handle this in my own way. Sometimes, Vera, you can make the world shine in the way you like it to shine."

They were all there. It was a little less than a month since Vera had gotten the Sissy report from Stanley. It was around eleven in the morning. Adam sat behind his desk. Gordon Bray lolled on a leather armchair. Martina Welk's replacement, a zaftig in a black skirt, sat on the tweed sofa. Anne, the newish Pentagon hire, kept one hip on an armless chair. Harriet, senior to Anne, just in from Berlin that morning, was immobile on an identical seat. The assistant National editor in charge of national security had a knee against the zaftig. The National projects editor had a knee against him. Stanley was sitting on a side table. Vera had left the one empty chair alone—it was for Don Grady, who hadn't shown up yet. She chose a wall by the doorway. She leaned there, watching all heads bent to her story. Every so often one of them would turn the page. She saw a few staring at the five-column photograph of a slam-dunk at a Wizards game.

Gordon Bray laughed and whispered to Adam, "I was at that game. Killer shot."

Vera felt him look at her. She wouldn't look back. She'd come ready. She began the humility litany. *O Jesus, meek and humble of heart, hear me.*

The Metro editor sauced through the door. "Sorry, sorry," he sang. He gazed around for a chair, saw what was to be Don's, and said, "Taken?" Adam, looking over his half-moons, said, "That's for Don." Metro editor did an eye bounce around the room, casting about for another wowzer glance. He got one from the National projects editor. Then he found the printout of Vera's story on a table and pushed his backside onto the windowsill.

There was a hoot from outside the door. Vera made room. Tabitha's head came in and said, "We just have one set of contact sheets."

Adam frowned. "Where's Joseph?"

"He says he doesn't want to come in here or you'll yell at him."

The Photo editor was suddenly nattering in the center of them. "See, you're not smiling," Vera picked out from what he was saying.

Adam pouted a smile.

Tabitha handed the sheets to Adam, along with the glass piece. "This will be good enough," he told her, then, "Go." He looked down into the images, then added, "Tabitha, call Don on his cell phone, please."

From the desire of being esteemed, deliver me, Jesus.

Gordon, claiming his intimacy with Adam, leaned in to the contact sheet. They back-and-forthed a few comments Vera couldn't hear. Bray seemed amused by one of the photographs. Adam's one smile was tight. After a while, it got plain Adam was unwilling to adopt Bray's air of cheerio disdain. Bray lounged back, doubly bored, now by Adam's probity.

Tabitha, at the door again, said, "Don is stuck in traffic coming from the Pentagon. Terribly sorry. At least another ten minutes." The rookie Pentagon reporter looked aggrieved. Don Grady encroaching at the Pentagon might always be happening, but it usually went unannounced.

"We'll start, then," Adam said. He pulled his lower lip upward. Could he be trying to look like an eagle?

"Remind me," said the Metro editor, slumped on the windowsill. "Who is it that says this Wizards fan is some kind of a spook?"

"Let's not. Let's have some . . . I don't want that kind of discussion just yet," Adam said sternly. It seemed as if the diction, not the question, offended him, but Vera couldn't be sure. *From the desire of being loved, deliver me.*

"I am having a great deal of trouble following, but maybe it's just me," said the zaftig, whose name was Constance. She spoke out of her nose, scanning and reading. "Oh yes. That's right. Never mind."

From the desire of being extolled.

Harriet, the seasoned Pentagon reporter, cleared her throat. She took a sip of coffee. "How much of the report did you get?" she asked Vera without malice. Vera liked her calm face.

She could feel Stanley draw himself into an invisible snit on the side table. He'd wanted Vera to be vague about this, and here, best reporter in the Room had of course asked the question, clearly and affably. "She has all the pages relevant to Potomac Pilot," Stanley told Harriet hurriedly. She looked at him as if he were a spaniel. "Potomac Pilot?" she followed up.

"We need Don. You see, this is why Don should be here." Adam glared, putting down the glass piece on his desk.

"Vera," Harriet tried again.

"I have the report," Vera said. She wouldn't lie. She'd made that promise to herself. She was sticking. *From the desire of being honored, deliver me.*

"Vera and I," began the National projects editor, wanting to mark out his territory, which was Vera, in all her iffy new importance. Stanley had been consigned to nosebleed seats weeks ago. Vera's reporting and writing were now under the hot-ticket supervision of this man, who'd spent the last many weeks apologizing for not talking to her. "Vera and I had to make a decision early on, which we did, and that was that we would be creating more problems than we could solve if we tried to fully parse the report."

"I'd like to see it," Harriet said. Vera knew that would happen. How Stanley had imagined it would not, she failed to see. *From the desire of being praised.*

"We'll get to that," Adam said. He seemed to want to have a certain kind of exchange take place but had no power to begin it on his own. It was as if he were helplessly waiting for someone previously instructed to bring in the elephants.

"Where did you get it?" That was Anne. "Why was this source of yours on the ground the night of the crash?" Anne's questions seemed backed up inside her.

The door opened, and Don Grady walked among them. "My apologies to everyone," he said in his voice that Vera had only heard on television. He glided to the empty chair. Almost instantly he twisted at the waist and gave Harriet a smile. "Get with me after this," he mouthed at her.

From the desire of being preferred to others, deliver me, Jesus.

Adam put down the glass piece and sat up.

"Good morning, Don," he said. Don sidled back and sat down. "Good morning, Adam," he said, surveying all of them with distracted chagrin. "Gordon!" he whisper-exclaimed. He was about to say more but stopped himself. He started scribbling on a notepad, tore out a sheet, and passed it, folded, to Bray. Bray opened it and did a silent rocking laugh.

Adam stood up.

"Vera's written a story about a crash we all didn't pay much attention to when it happened, almost a year ago. I'll tell you all now what I felt I couldn't then: I was contacted by the White House about the crash, and told not to publish any story we might write about it. I wasn't quite sure why that happened. That's one thing. The other thing is that Vera's been able to get her hands on a report that we were unable to obtain, and got beaten on, over the course of the last year or so. She's written something here that shows how that report contains some pertinent information about the crash. Interesting stuff.

"But what we're here today to do is talk about whether this story is ready for publication. I've called on all of you, and any ideas you might want to have." Vera wasn't sure that tracked. She saw Adam wasn't sure either. "But before we do that, I think we need to talk about something that's pretty much on everybody's mind, and that is this report." Vera could see the Metro editor watch-checking. He couldn't care less about this report. Stanley looked faintly electric. So did Anne, the rookie. Harriet was drinking her coffee steadily, nose in Styrofoam mug. Vera's new editor looked proudly complacent. The assistant National editor looked as if he saw an opening to be the first one talking, but Vera couldn't see how, because he was the most out-of-the-loop person on the story. Bray shot Vera a worried look.

"We could have used this report," the assistant National editor said, moving his knee away from that of Constance, his boss.

Constance, too new to know if this was so, nodded authoritatively.

"Certainly is," Don Grady said, clearly only half listening.

"What?" That was the Metro editor. He didn't care who played Don in the movie, he would not let such shit mar this scene. "Certainly is what?"

"Why, old news, of course," Don said.

"That's not what he said," the Metro editor said.

"I'm sorry. What did he say?"

"That we could have used this report," Adam said.

"What report, just to make sure, is this?" Harriet's lips had lifted, but just a tad, from her cup rim.

"The Sissy report." "White House surveillance report." "The puppet report." "Family Jewels II." "Black ops." Gordon didn't venture a title. Neither did Don. He looked momentarily snookered. Vera tried not to stare at him.

"What did you call it?" Adam directed the question in a straight line to Don.

"I didn't," Don replied.

"Why not?" Adam shot.

There was a noiseless tick as more than three people gained the understanding that something besides Vera's story was at issue.

"I don't think, just yet, just now," Bray was saying in some kind of continental, faintly Brit way, "that this particular"—drawing out each syllable—"piece of journalism"—again each sound articulated and isolated—"is ready for the newspaper." He fanned the pages of the book he'd been toying with on Adam's desk as a punctuation mark, lifted his chin, and grinned, mouth closed.

From the desire of being consulted.

Constance whirred up. She narrowed her eyes at Gordon. "Gordon," she said, "Gordon, since you think it's not ready, which I wholeheartedly agree with, by the way, but could you, would you sum it up, put it in a nutshell for me."

Gordon looked at her, semi-horrified.

"What in a nutshell?" whispered the Metro editor.

"The story."

"This story?"

"This story right here on our laps."

"It's not on my lap."

"Vera's story. What's it about? Is it about a plane crash? A secret military program? A Pentagon—what did you call him, spook tasker?—gone renegade? A deeper problem in our military system?? What? It seems to be about too many things."

From the desire of being approved.

"I don't see a nut graph. I just don't."

"It begins, *The program raises questions about the creation of a new, sub-rosa military command,*" protested Vera's new editor, truculent.

"Who saw this guy the night of the crash?" Gordon Bray's voice cut through.

"I think you know the answer to that," Stanley said, standing up. He was off the side table, but holding on to it for support.

Gordon looked at Stanley. Vera could see he didn't know who Stanley was. *From the fear of being humiliated, deliver me.*

"That's really between Vera and her immediate editor, and myself," Adam said to Gordon. He'd let this get too heated too fast. He smiled at Stanley. But Stanley wasn't looking at Adam.

"It's a young streetwalker named Patrice Edwards," Vera's new editor said, apparently unable to hear Adam over the energetic trading of sentences between Constance and her two Pentagon reporters.

"Streetwalker?" The Metro editor tucked his chin. "What is this? Busby Berkeley? This pye-pup is a *ho.*"

"How young is she?" This from Stanley, now a full step away from his side table. "Don't you think that's of some import?"

"The source on the renegade is a whore?" Don harrumphed. "Since when?"

"Please." Adam didn't bellow, but it was as if he had. All talk dead-ended. Don seemed inordinately satisfied, as if Adam had cleared the decks because of Don's unanswered query.

"Don, could you just set my mind at ease?" Adam poked out.

Don looked at him with stillborn happiness. He sensed this was not tending toward a crowning of his unanswered question after all.

"Do you have this report?" Adam asked a little too softly. Vera saw Adam entirely alive. He was on a promontory.

"No," Don said.

"Vera," Adam said, everyone mesmerized to see him address her head-on. "Where did you get the report?"

"I got it from Stanley, who got it from Mabel Cannon."

Don almost stood up. "You what?"

Constance had listened carefully but was lost. Who was Mabel Cannon?

Stanley pushed himself forward, herky-jerky, toward Gordon.

"There are two young women in serious jeopardy here," Stanley said. "One is fourteen. The other is a fighter pilot. We have forsaken them."

From the fear of being despised. From the fear of suffering rebukes.

"You know my wife?" Don Grady looked at Stanley.

"They grow up fast these days," Constance said in a tone both knowing and distressed. She leaned forward on the sofa and almost got up to referee.

"Is Mabel Cannon the whore? Or is that Patrice Edwards? I'm confused," said the Pentagon rookie. Vera watched Harriet suppress a smile, then saw her catch Vera catching it.

"Can I just ask one small question? Who is this guy at the Wizards game?"

"That's the guy they call the Chair."

"Who the whore saw?"

"Who the whore saw at the crash."

"Who she also saw at this Media Exploitation Component Services."

"Who we got calls about on the desk," said Constance, light dawning. "We actually brought a hooker to a government facility!? I said they had to be wrong! And *I* was wrong. I lied to those callers."

"We should be kept in the loop," said the assistant National editor for national security.

From the fear of being calumniated.

"You will not stop this story from running if I have anything to say about it," Stanley told Gordon Bray. They were a foot apart now.

From the fear of being forgotten.

"You need to explain what they were trying to do to this pilot."

"Is this like the Tuskegee Airmen?"

"No, you're thinking of the Tuskegee experiments."

"I think it's a little of both."

"Not treating for syphilis. First black fighter pilots. I mean—"

"Look, it's right there in the fourth graph. Request For Proposal for avionics intercept, blah, blah . . . in an effort . . . blah. Oh, here. *The government sought technology to bring down an aircraft without the pilot being able to stop it.*"

"So this pilot was a guinea pig."

"Almost died too."

"But, shit, she didn't die."

"And there's just one of them. It's not like they snuffed a battalion."

"Aviators do not belong to battalions," Harriet said. "Squadrons, groups, wings. No battalions."

"She calls it a battalion here."

"No, she does not."

"You have paid for sex with a fourteen-year-old," Stanley said. Did he have tears in his eyes? Vera started across the room for him.

"This Chair—almost maybe wasting a pilot, I don't know. Now, if he's hiring just one shortie with government lucre on Uncle Sam's time—*that's* a story."

From the fear of being ridiculed.

"The point, I take it, is that this Chair runs things unchecked."

"That's right."

"He could be experimenting with the pilot some more."

"Pilot may not even know it."

"But nobody died here!"

"So the pilot—was it a he or a she?—okay, she. She. She never signed off on the program?"

"So what does this prove about covert operations?"

"In all honesty, my wife has never had anything leaked to her."

"Vera hasn't either. She got it from *her editor.*"

"I did not give her the report," said Vera's new editor. "I had *nothing* to do with that."

"Stanley," Vera said, taking his arm. *From the fear of being wronged.*

"Stanley?" Gordon asked.

"This is not the time or place," Adam was saying to Stanley.

Gordon Bray studied Vera. She studied him too.

"They're just girls," Stanley said. Until this moment he'd forgotten Winnow's peanut-butter kisses, how she spooned Jiffy on top of Hershey's and lined them up like frosted brown hats on his back-porch window.

"They're teenagers," Adam said. "I mean, really, Stanley. I—"

"They're fourteen at most," Stanley said. "They say they're fourteen. That means they're probably thirteen, or twelve."

Vera knew Winnow was fourteen. Baby—she was twelve. Vera had ordered her Maryland birth certificate. It was sitting on Vera's desk.

"There was a misunderstanding," Adam was saying. Vera couldn't tell if he was talking to Don or to Gordon.

"Baby."

"Baby what? Does she have a last name?"

"This other one, the one who saw the Virginia plate. How old is she?"

"Stanley, these are streetwise, worldly-wise—"

From the fear of being suspected.

"How old is your youngest?"

"My daughter Rebecca?" Adam said. "She's thirteen."

"Okay," Stanley said.

"You know how old I was when I lost my virginity? The ripe old age of fourteen. Now, *that* really *isn't* the point. The point is, these are street-smart, calculating individuals. They have seen it all and then some. This is not anyone corrupting some tender blossoms."

Mabel looked over at Don. He'd come back from a meeting at the paper ruing the demise of journalism. He said the Room was filled with young reporters, unfortunately too many of them hired to fill quotas, who had no understanding of the mechanics. Here he was in bed now, cross-laced with the mechanicals for apnea. Black straps under his chin and above his forehead kept a mask over his mouth and nose. A tube from his mouth pronged to a machine on the nightstand. Its motor and electronics combined to make a noise equal in decibels to his snoring. The difference was forcing air through his pathways. Unaided, a flap at the back of his throat blocked his breathing once the relaxation of sleep began. He would gasp. He would struggle. He would bat around the bed. The few times he hit her, she got bruises. After a while, he went to the sleep clinic and came home with the REMstar.

The doctor said they would sleep better. In theory, she did. She probably, over time, got more hours than before the snoring machine. On the nights when she couldn't sleep for her own worries, she viewed the device as intruder. It sat there, casting into the future, the ventilators to come, the minor ills and never-too-serious procedures that precede them, the night as night. She would try to talk herself out of it. He looked, with his tubing, like a supersonic pilot. She should imagine him in training for astrophysics.

She didn't know about the end of journalism. She knew she was reading obituaries more than before. She went for age first. Headline usually told that. No matter the age, she read the cause of death. If the deceased was under fifty, she read the whole obit. If over, she got picky. Her favorites were actresses. Many of them were names she didn't recognize. They'd been famous in their day. That always humbled. So too, at first, did the stories. Then she saw. These ladies so often shared the same trajectory. The hard times, the trying and trying, the one big chance, the breakthrough, the prime, the height, full powers, maturity, mastery, a falling off, last revival, advancing decline, last song, final appearance, usual obscurity, sometimes ruin, survived by some. The statesmen were less regular. So too royalty, business owners, artists, and famous wits. Though the last of these she saw less often. It had once been a something to be. Now in its anachronistic dotage, being a wit was as sad, sad as night and the mask and the tube and the straps.

She took her medicine, which was to walk the house.

Don didn't hear her leave bed. He couldn't. Once she did a tap dance—though she'd never learned tap and, being barefoot, lacked metal. It was a jig. Her emancipation, without divorce, could be here now if she saw it thus. She would just have to re-see her life. All was the same, but all would be different if only she could re-see it. Out in the hallway, she imagined not being.

All took death badly. Wasn't *being* at least as bad? Here's the liver. Not the organ, but the woman who lives. One day, she doesn't want to *be*. No one lets her go. It's a tough exit, little lady. You'll regret it, sister. No chicken she. No shrinker. Or shirker. She makes her plan, she fights her nights, like this one—"like mine," Mabel whispered into the stair-way. It takes a life of living to get to not being. What if I want it now? Rewrite, send me Rewrite. Mabel dipsy-doed on the stair. Okay, she couldn't sing, but anyway: I could have danced all night. I could have spread my wings and done. Done and done.

Would anyone here, she asked the dining room, care to think?

What was his sin, damsel? Tell us his wrong.

She approached the kitchen table.

He erred not.

No? Then how your travels?

She'd get to that. She was sleepy enough now. She climbed those always stairs. She entered the master bedroom. She climbed in. She fell asleep by the diode light of the REMstar.

The story didn't run. They needed Vera back on night cops full-time. The situation in the Trinidad neighborhood was ongoing. Harriet and Anne were systematically combing the Sissy report; they'd cull nuggets if any were left. The pilot piece was interesting, but it wasn't all there yet. There might be a magazine story in Media Exploitation Component Services; Harriet would take a look.

Trinidad would settle down. At some point Vera could team with Anne on a profile of this Will Holmes. It was easy to misunderstand his role, especially for someone like Vera, new to all this. The word Harriet got back on this guy was that he was some geek trying to make out he was more than he was. That might be wrong. They could check further.

Vera met up with Gordon Bray one more time in the parking garage. It was a few days after the meeting in Adam's office. Gordon was in his car, not the Vespa. He eased down the ramp and stopped when he saw her about to unlock her bicycle.

"Vera."

She waved, working the combination.

He stayed.

The lock came open.

"These stories," he said. "Tough."

"Yes."

"You did great work."

"Thanks."

"Next time."

"Next time."

One by one, Will fired them. First the bozo that came up with the idea. Then his chief supporter, the linguist who'd wanted to get Security to escort Vera Hastings off the premises. Moron hadn't learned a thing from that day. Why use a hammer when a fist will do? Third was the idiot who thought national security was involved.

Hadn't they always done what needed to be done?

Mostly, Will said. Not always.

They all thought they'd stopped the story about MECS with this caper. Underage prostitutes had nothing to do with Vera Hastings's being taken off the story.

They didn't believe him.

We didn't fuck them, the bozo insisted. We just promised to get Earphone off the street and out of their pockets. Earphone?

Their mackdaddy. Their pimp.

Pimps, anything at all to do with pimps, on his watch.

They'd been more than wrong. They didn't know how much he wanted the story to run. If it had, Mean Man wouldn't have been able to send him looking for Hoseyn. If it had, Goodwin would have known what he'd done to her. She would have learned he'd flubbed her out of the sky. And then, knowing that, she surely would have pulled out of the Hoseyn mission.

He wanted them to run his photo at that Wizards game. Blow my cover. Come on now. Blow my blue sky.

You didn't need a hammer when Mean Man had a friendly in that newsroom. Was it Don Grady? Was it Gordon Bray? These names got tossed around. For once, Will didn't know. He knew he was tired. He knew Goodwin wasn't. Every day they worked together, watching her bright and true reminded him. He wasn't the Chair. He was the floor underneath it.

GIHON **AUGUST**

17. THE UNMAPPED TUMBLED REGION

They crossed the border west of Bazargan under a gibbous moon. Turkey lay flat behind them, Iran short ahead uninhabited. The pack on Mary's back was light, her vest heavier. Will's ruck weighed easy on his shoulders. They'd depend on Kurd itinerants, their sense of terrain, and useful caravanserais. They would move at night and sleep the day.

She expected no trees but they were here. Cypress was prevalent. In the Iran she'd imagined it would be oven-hot. Instead, she was walking through an improbably agreeable August. Not far north were the mountains of Armenia, west was Turkey's peak called Ararat. Noah was said to have landed there. They would travel south to the Karun River, once called Gihon. The Garden of Eden was its headwater.

For now fields roved the hills before them. They used a trail along flowering wheat. She liked the rustling of stalks, a shimmer sound that created a trance. The deal was, no communication until they were close to the truck. Now, about twenty kilometers in, Will's back turned for the first time and he stopped. He took her hand and traced the number two on her palm.

He guessed two minutes until they reached it. She nodded, and they picked up the pace.

Soon enough, there was the pickup, an old Khodro. It was parked against an outbuilding she couldn't see too well. Up closer, it looked as if it might house a threshing floor. So this was it. They both surveyed the surroundings to find nothing. Will opened the driver's door. She unfastened the key from under the passenger seat and handed it to him. The old engine tracked up.

She watched him drive, imagining his mind along the memorized directions. Here was the stand of ash and oak. Four clicks to the next on the right, followed by an intersection: take the left. They hiked a series of hills; count them: one, two, three, four, five, and six. On the seventh, slow down. She looked across a valley, into its shifting plains. Wedged in the corner was the ruin.

It took another hour to reach it. They took shelter in what once were stables and found the water left for them. Mary opened the cardboard box. She gave Will an apple from it and took the peach. She opened the bag of nuts and the container of cherries. She placed these between them. After he finished the fruit, he left to piss, and she found a private fortress under what had been a watchtower. As she squatted, she held her weapon with both hands. When she returned, Will's head was on his ruck, his legs long. She took a handful of cashews and leaned against the half wall overlooking the courtyard.

The silence between them made certain they'd not miss any sound. Problems could come infinitesimally for them. In the time it took to say your sentence, your ear got compromised, because it was hearing your own voice more than any other noise. Like the deaf, they had shapes to trace in one another's palms. You couldn't do conventional sign language, because in the dark it was too easy to miss a motion made in the air.

She wondered if his eyes were open. She could tell he wasn't out yet. She already knew, from when they mocked this up at Bragg, and later near Nellis, the sounds he made when sleeping. They'd done twenty days straight outside at night, just them, in steam-room Carolina weather, then repeated it again in stropping desert. Now, here, she wanted to pull out one of the letters from Frank she'd brought. She didn't want Holmes to see her do it.

As close proximity as they had been in during training, all she knew of him came from direct observation alone. He told no stories about his past. He didn't mention a wife, though she'd heard from her Amazon rival that there'd been one. Mary did as Will did, but, given she believed he knew everything about her, she tried to best him at withholding even the most trivial comment. On occasion, that made him smile.

She thought about walking in the courtyard for more direct light from the moon. She could get out of his eyesight that way. He might think she needed a shit and leave her be. The letters were in her vest, which was on the ground. She stooped and felt in the pocket. She took out two of them. She had a total of six. She'd wished she could have stowed more. She'd chucked the envelopes to make everything more compact. Before she stood up, she pushed the pages inside her shirt.

She went to the caravan entryway for camels, now disintegrating. The brickwork was bad, crumbly lattice. But it provided enough cover and enough of the moon. She slid down so her back was against the inner wall.

This is how you fly. You are shortcutting pathological. That's right. You heard me. See I know you have an idea that you're the careful one and I'm the crackpot. I'll let you in on a little secret. I got the word on your call sign. How it went down when the TOs took the powwow to mull over the choices. First out was Psychette. Mary "Psychette" Goodwin. That's right. Couple of reasons. One, you never opened your mouth. Nothing scares an aviator more than a stoic individual with a rack. Sorry, that was disrespectful. You're kind of flat up there, really. But that's the trippidy on you. Second up, one LT points out, she Swazilicrashed every single time she landed first week of training. Except you never washed out. I don't mean a little trimming on the edges. I mean a controlled crash to where each on ground watching is saying: She's goner, she's crispy.

But someone got the idea that this was sexist, this –ette business. The air force is no way the navy. So bombs away on that one. (Squadron already had a Psycho.) Next came Awful. That had a lot of variations. Very. Can you imagine? Mary "Very"

Goodwin? Definitely. Truly. Highly. Really. Mightily. Majorly. But they seemed too namby-pamby. So someone said, what about Mega? Ultra? Real? Way? It almost was Way. Almost. But someone said that was Wayne's World and that's tired and there was a vote, and Way lost. After the tally, objectors shout out there ought to be some Evil Knievil in your handle. We got it. Mary "Banging" Goodwin. (This was judged by all concerned to refer too clearly to the nasty.) Slamming and Ramming were offered up. (Ditto.)

Suddenly it's all quiet over the beers. A song goes up. It's one of those World War II pilot ditties I cannot stand. Natch, it's "Mary Ann Burns."

> She's a great big Son-of-a-Bitch, twice as big as me,
> With hair around her asshole like branches on a tree.
> She can swim, fish, fight, fuck, fly a jet, drive a truck,
> Mary Ann Burns is the girl for me!

And some joker says, but Goodwin's not X-rated. And in the middle of this tripe, they all stop. Right there. And say that's it. Extra. We'll just call her "X." They high-fived. Mary "Extra" Goodwin got born. Dumb story, right? But wait. Did I tell you there's a rumor Goodwin's not your real name?

Here was her favorite part.

Something made her look up. Will was standing there.

She folded the letter into its smallest size and scrambled to her feet. Will looked like he didn't know what to do. He came a stitch nearer, as if going for her palm, then reached for her shoulder, as if he might whisper in her ear. She stepped off and away from him. Her eyes asked, What the fuck?

Then he looked at the dirt. He waved for her to join him as he knelt. She watched him trace it out across the ground.

Can't sleep. Come back.

The smell of warm bread woke her. It was early evening, not yet dark. A boy had smoothed a tablecloth on the ground under the far squinch supporting the dome.

There was a bucket of water by her head. The boy made a face-washing motion. He was wearing *I Dream of Jeannie* pantaloons. They were black-blue woven cotton, mended with red thread. Will was up already, his bucket missing. She carried hers back to the fortress of the previous night. The sun had set, but there was light. Once again the air was its surprising cool.

After she was done, she turned over the bucket and sat on it. She'd found from Bragg and Nellis it was good to go over the hours ahead. Frank was right. She'd been shortcuts and screeching when she started out. But you went around and you learned. Tonight they'd cover a minimum of three hundred kilometers. Will was probably inspecting the truck right now. The kid would travel with them, just in case there was a language situation. Their goal was to reach Takab in two days' time. They planned to camp with the boy's relatives, then at a shrine called Takht-e-Soleiman, remote from the major roads, far from a village. The kid knew it well.

A stone tossed into her chamber. It was Will saying, Let's go. She got up and followed him, already farther ahead. Sure of her, he didn't even turn around to look at her. She decided to play and ran up behind him, catgirl soft, tagged him, and scooted. See if she could get one slip-smile out of him. But there was no happy face, just him chasing back at her, and her faster, and her knowing he had that bad foot and could he, and, yeah, he knocked her rump with the heel of his hand, and then she got the grin, but only in his eyes. She put her hands up for surrender.

She could see the boy watching them, his arms folded. He was narrowly made, with bushy bangs, ears under more waves of hair, a capable expression like that of a miniature grown man. He wore grape-green plastic mold slip-on sandals a size too little. She could see him trying to read their horsing around. When they got closer, he went under the dome, back into the hidden corner. The light was graying down fast, but she could make him out, crouching, and pouring from a thermos. When she sat near the tablecloth, he handed her a snag of bread torn from what resembled a flopping pita two feet long.

It didn't taste as good as it smelled. The tea was too tannic, and as she forced it down she started thinking about the headscarf. The kid sensed it, because he picked it up and nodded at her. Was he going to put it on her? She shook him off. No help needed there. He wobbled up and brought back from a plastic bag what looked like a short black raincoat. She stood up, took it from him, and put it on. She folded the black scarf in a triangle and tied it under her neck. Will wasn't watching this fashion show. Sometimes he did that—just disappeared in full sight, lost in thought.

But now the kid was hopping around, tidying up and emptying their cups, and when he got done, he bowed with a flourish in front of Will. That got Will from his funk.

So they loaded up the Khodro with a cooler, containers of gasoline, a bicycle that the kid had come on, along with some baskets he'd saddled on its fender. He climbed in the back seat, lucky he was little, because it was more of a half-bench than a place to sit. He fit just right. Will put the truck in neutral and drifted away from the entryway, waiting until they reached the dirt road to get in gear and slowly accelerate. The kid's chin was on their shared front seat, anticipating.

"I am Baz," he said as the truck picked up speed.

"*Madar,*" Will said to Mary. The Farsi word for "mother."

"*Pedar,*" Baz said to Will. Father.

"I am honored to be your guide," Baz said in English to both of them.

"How old are you, Baz?" Mary asked. She guessed he was nine.

"I am thirteen years old," he said.

"Are you okay?" Will asked her, his eyes on the road.

"Yeah. You?"

"Good."

"Good."

"The map?" he said to Baz.

"I have it, mister."

Will put his hand up for it.

"It is here in the head of me."

The boy won a genuine laugh from Will. Mary wanted to tell Baz: Jackpot. Don't count on another one soon.

"My uncles are wanting you."

"Are they?" Will said.

"They are wanting you to the *yaylaq*."

"I understand," Will said.

"I will take you."

"Good," Will said, and then, turning to Mary, "Summer pastures."

She nodded.

The truck strained. Here began the climb to the highlands. She remembered studying satellite images—filaments of roads along the Turkish border. Now they were on them. The last light was tricked out to her right as they threaded south. Some of the meadows were gloaming carpets of green. The peaks far away on her right were now a blunting white. They were covered with perforated ice and frozen slag, even in August.

This boy, recruited from among the radical, those who insisted on the restoration of Kurdistan, a separate nation stretching from Iran through Iraq and Turkey south to Syria, would help them retrieve Hoseyn. Nutjobs, Frank always said, were cavalry for the normally damned. Here were the unlikeliest hussars: Baz would pose as their son. Mary would be his seeming mommy. Will, wife gone, children alienated, was dad.

This family's home would be emptied Iran. Two-thirds of it not even nomads walked. This basal margin, the bottommost in population density, hosted mountain ranges made from cooled magma. As the last light gave out, Mary could just see the folds of olivine basalt ahead. Hidden among them were encampments and goat flocks. In the north, their tenders were Kurdish, like Mary and Will's pseudo-son. Farther south, the shepherds were Bakhtiari or Torkashv.

"We are giving thanks to you," said Baz, irrepressible.

She looked at him in the light from the dashboard. He looked as if he was shaking to speak to them, his eyes moving constantly, his alertness a pinball. Will took no note of it. He studied the rearview with menacing reverence. He read the road with ossified concentration. What he really looked like was submerged. If you talked to him, he might come up from the deep, but maybe not.

"You okay?" he asked her. Like the mirrors, she needed constant checking.

"Yeah," she said, but she wished Will would direct more of his concern toward Baz. "We appreciate your thanks, Baz," she told him.

"I am from *peshmerga*. My father's father died under the Baathist hand. My uncles lie in Al-Anfal."

Peshmerga. Those ready to die. It was the self-given name of the Kurdish guerrillas of northern Iraq. They were America's only unquestioning fan club, the still-grateful few in an international of disbelievers. They could even count Frank among their majority, if she read his letters right.

"Your bravery is important," she said to Baz. "We couldn't be here without you. Do you know that?"

His smile swept the truck cab.

"Al-Anfal is a sad place," she said. "I am sorry your family lost loved ones there."

They saw only one vehicle that night. It was a silver Paykan. *I'm the supplicant of Fatima* was written on the rear windshield. Fatima was the prophet's daughter, the mother of Shia Muslims, the majority in Iran. At first Mary thought she was the Virgin who appeared to three shepherds. Baz told her no.

She was cold when they reached camp, near four. They were at the highest elevation so far. The thinned air was damp. Baz's father greeted them. A grouping of men stood at a distance. Mary's shivering made

Will insist she sleep before the talking Baz's relatives wanted. Through her fatigue and the mixing languages, she understood they wanted her to join unmarried women a small way from Will's place among the men. Will wouldn't agree. They would bunk together or they would leave.

He took her by the arm to get in the Khodro. It offended her, really, his possessiveness. She could walk to the truck herself. But she yielded. He was tense, perhaps anxious. Stubborn when uncertain, he needed her indulgence. She leaned against him as if weak and felt him relax. It was no problem this way; they could sleep in the truck bed.

Baz's father came running as they reached the front bumper. Here, he said, take what is ours. They straggled back with him, Baz a sitting Buddha before his family's tent. When they came near, he rose and pulled back the flap.

"I thought we trusted them," she said to Will once they were inside, not wanting to challenge him but doing it out of leftover pique, and something else maybe; she was almost too tired to know.

"Not that much," he said, unholstering his HK 23, his voice unfriendly. "Here," he said. "Clean it for me. I'm too tired." She thought, "Why? We're not in a sand squall" but said nothing. She just dropped to the ground and started. She sure wasn't going to clean her own.

He sat down and then lay down after a bit. He watched her go through the rote motions.

"Okay," she said, handing back the pistol, laser module, and silencer.

"You're gonna have to piss in front of me; I can't let you out of my sight," he said.

"All right."

They waited for the last sounds of the men to go away. She took a look through the flap. Smoke creviced above a far tent. Otherwise, nothing.

They walked to rocks near a stream. She pulled down her pants and used the water. He stood next to her, looking over her head at the embankment. When she was finished, they put their backs together and he pulled out his cock and pissed. They went a little upstream and splashed the frigid water on their hands and faces.

"Listen," he said as they rolled a massive rug to the flap to block cold. She sat back on her heels. He looked alarmed. She knelt forward to him and traced signs in his palm, asking him, "No talking?"

He nodded. He went into his ruck and pulled out twine. He took her hand and tied one end of it around her wrist. He cut off another end with his knife and tied it to his own. Their heads rested at the flap, and the string went between them across it. That way, any intruder would trip. The cord would break or tug, waking them. They'd practiced this at Nellis.

It made sleep difficult. He was a thrasher and had awakened her more than once during the last training run-through. She didn't think they needed this precaution. But he was in a mood she knew enough of not to push much. Sometimes when he saw her consistently surrendering it calmed him to relent. So she lay down.

He lay as far away as the length of twine would let him. She tried to stay still, hoping he'd drop off quickly. She wanted to see how he settled, what position he finally took. Then she could get herself into a place least susceptible to any flail.

He just lay there—none of his sleeping sounds, no jerking twists.

Her mind tried for what might have irked him. When they drove into the encampment, something got him, all of his subcranial signposts from years of this she didn't have. She couldn't sense any of them. She kept coming back to Baz's face—a bad hurtle for him, this contention. She regretted her gender so often, just the thorn of it.

She looked at Will. She began to toy with her end of the string. She could fractionally move and tug. She spoofed it into moving without moving. She fell off, playing with it, finally asleep.

Baz hung back. She could see him mooching himself into the smallest size. They were pushing through the higher ridgelines. He looked seasick. That wasn't possible. Will was irritable, as per usual, in the driver's.

"Baz," she whispered. She turned toward him and put herself almost in the back of the truck cab.

He looked up with his chin down. His eyes were swimming, or was it the dark?

"Baz," she tried again. She tapped his knee, got no response, then put her hand on it more firmly, gave him a squeeze. He was so slight.

He produced a paper bag, a small one. He had rolled it up and written something on it she couldn't quite see. They had gotten a later start than anyone had wanted. There'd been too much to go over with their Kurd hosts. A costume change too: Mary's manteau and scarf were too citified. She now wore the loose kameez and hand-woven dupatta of Kurd nomads.

"What is this?" Still she was whispering. She didn't want Will to get pissy.

"For you," Baz said.

"For me?"

"Please," he said, wrist up, bag perched on his palm.

"What's going on back there?" Will's brows were visible in the rearview.

Mary returned to the passenger seat with the bag in hand.

"A gift," Mary said. "From Baz. For us."

Baz shot forward. "*Madar* only."

"*Madar* only, huh?" Will said.

"Thank you," Mary said. "May I open it now? Or should I wait."

"Now," Baz said. She could tell he wished Will would not have to witness opening the present.

She peeled back the bag, a brown paper but flimsier than back home. There was the immediate aroma of roasting, and then, in browned handfuls, pistachios. They had all been shelled. She felt the graininess of the salt slathered with cooking oil. Her fingers were slick, and she was hungry at once. The smell filled the truck.

"Baz," she said, her voice a chime. "This is the best gift."

Will dipped into the bag. "Good, really good," he said through his munching.

The sun fell down, and they ate. There would be rain. They were also approaching roads more traveled. Mary needed to practice Farsi, just in case. Will didn't think the Kurds were right about police stopping them—why would they? In bad weather, though, accidents were an issue. That was the only thing that would get them out of the car that would call for play-acting. Filling up the tank was a quiet stop, one they'd done the other night at an isolated turnoff.

"I understand," Will said.

"*Mifahmam,*" Mary tried.

"*Bale!*" Baz exclaimed. Yes.

"Don't understand," Will said.

"*No . . . no. Nomifahmam.*"

"*Namifahmam. N-A. Na-mi-fah-mam.*" Baz went slow.

She tried again. Muffed it. Third try, success.

"What is that?"

"*Ooncheeah.*"

"*Bale!*" Yes, from Baz.

"Careful."

"*Beppo.*"

"Shortcut."

"*Raheh kootah.*"

"Where is my husband?"

"*Shoharam kojust?*"

"Where's my son?"

"*Pesaram kojust?*"

"I'm sorry."

"*Bebash.*"

"I didn't realize I was doing anything wrong."

"*Nafahmidam ke kar e eshtebahi mikonam.*"

"*Doroste!*" Correct.

"We're innocent."

"Ma bigonah im."

"Can I call someone?"

"Mitunam be kesi zang bezanam?"

"How old is your son?"

"Pesar e shoma chand salesh e?"

"Response," Will said.

"Un sizdah salesh e." My son is thirteen.

They went on with it. "Help us." "Leave me alone." "My husband is injured." "We are mountain people. We are not far from home." "My father expects us." "Are you all right?" "Does your car start?"

Just as they reached the wider road, the first thunder boomed to them. Mary felt the distances around them. They were small, wayward, in weather that went for miles. She saw the moonbeams of rain ahead, and then they were in it, the plumpest water beads smearing on the windshield.

"So what's the golden one?" Will looked at her, actually smiling.

"Golden?"

"The get-out-of-jail-free?"

"Akh!?" Ouch.

"I don't think so," he said.

"Lotfan be man ye bihess konande bedin."

Baz laughed.

She'd asked for an anesthetic. Politely.

Will fished in one of his pockets. He brought out a khaki-colored curl of plastic. Baz looked at it, dumbfounded.

Mary started laughing and pulled out her own, tucked in her old pockets.

"Nashenava hastam," she said—I'm deaf. *"Hastad shekaste,"* she said, pointing to her hearing aid—It's broken.

18.   TO EXERCISE MY DEPLETED FURY

They reached the crater lake at dusk. From its sinter shore they could see another dormant volcano. Baz said that cone was dry. This crater's water, underground-fed and mineral-glutted, was too dense to swim in. It had sucked men down. Mary watched one of its tight waves. It looked like mercury lapping.

They were adrenaline. This was the leg of the mission that required driving past night into day. They had been on the road eighteen hours. Baz went to work in a courtyard north of the fire-shrine redoubt. Mary thought they should help him stake the tent. Will said talking was more important. They were now one day from Ahwaz.

She knew the sequence. They would go to Ahwaz for the maid. Those who talked to her believed she might have helped Hoseyn, but she refused to talk to any Iranians the Sacred Sons sent her. Someone, possibly Hoseyn, had instructed her to talk only to an American.

Will believed Hoseyn was dead. He thought the maid's role was simple. She was a trap designed to deliver Will to the regime. He would pursue the alternative scenario as long as safeguards were in place. He reviewed them with Mary one more time. As always, he asked her if there was anything she thought they were missing. Just then Baz came running.

"Someone," he said, breathless.

They followed him to a colonnade on the north side of the plateau. He pointed to the curling road they'd used to reach the lake. They saw a convoy of trucks—four of them—along with two motorbikes and a car.

Will shrugged. "A road people use," he said to Baz. "Farms—orchards."

Baz pulled out binoculars and handed them to Will. "Look," he said.

"Okay," Will said. "Okay. The truck."

Mary looked for an explanation, but he wouldn't give it. He'd been tense the last hours of the drive. He hadn't laughed since the hearing aid.

They dismantled the tent and reloaded, then pushed the truck into a leafed-over gully near the tin roof protecting the southeastern gate. They hiked to a bluff and camouflaged behind scrub. It seemed they wouldn't have enough time, and then they had too much. The waiting kept lengthening. Then the first nose of a motorbike came through.

Now she saw. One driver in fatigues opened a door. Then another. Their passengers ducked out with assault rifles.

"Safirs," Baz whispered, naming the tactical jeeps.

"Basij?" Mary wondered. A young man's paramilitary force.

Baz shook his head. "Haqqanis."

Haqqanis were a secretive Iranian military detachment.

Again Mary tried for Will's face. His eyes were lost in the binoculars. "Get the weapons," he signaled in her palm.

She went to their rucks and pulled out the components. She handed Baz the grenades, the launcher, a semi pistol. She began to assemble the sniper rifle.

When Will took it, she shouldered her M4, set up her spot scope, and lay on the ground behind him. She watched the Haqqanis establish a perimeter. The site was larger than she'd realized; the men started marking off square segments.

They'd find the pickup. If they didn't, they were pretenders. She timed their searches for each segment. First they went slowly. By the fifth segment, having found nothing, they speeded a fraction, and by the next, they were ten seconds faster, then twelve, then sixteen, their impatience building.

Will touched her hand. They smiled at each other; there was no question the men were hurrying. They both knew it. In her palm he told her, "Not us."

They'd never vary segment-search time. They trusted automaton precision.

There were twenty-four men in all. Just as she considered that, Will's fingers came back. "I take the head." She saw the one in charge, his mouth in a radio. "Then ears." She saw a radio operator by one of the jeeps. "Then arms." The tall one smoking with the other tall one— neither doing the segments searches.

She began punching in the variables on the handheld.

Will's fingers were back again. "Go ahead."

She took her time. She got the calculations squared away, then realigned them. Okay, done. She checked Baz. He had the binocs. He lowered them and looked at her. He was afraid. She had no time to comfort him.

She code-punched the Prophet system case, and it flipped apart. Will's eye still in his scope, her fingers flew on the flexed keyboard. She got the satellite. She started talking to it. All of the number strings poured in and out of her, the setup in progress, yes, no, not yet. Done. She retyped the passwords for this part of the sequence.

Her mind greased through the delicate intercepts. One was enough— no, two—get past the last, onto the other. Right. Right. Right. Right.

She'd finished. She dived for her scope and hoped to see it.

There, in the crepuscular deepening, it began. The commander was listening to his radio, and listening longer, and longer, and longer. She swept to the operator below. The music of his motions—how it shaded into her. He was talking on the com. Just talking and listening and talking and listening.

The commander motioned to the deputies. The deputies radioed the men. The men began returning, walking up the plateau or down it, wherever. They slung their carbines behind them; the assault rifles went casual on their backs. They gathered in a semicircle around the commander, nodding and talking.

Soon they began walking to the vehicles—down the pathway they went. One opened a door, another; soon they were closing them, starting the engines, the two men astride the cycles, the sedan backing up along the dirt. Once turned around, they went away orderly to the main road. Mary watched the last bumper slip out of sight. Prophet, Will's invention, had worked.

You're reading his letters to you."

Mary looked up at Will. She was sitting in a ruined hall, farthest in, flashlight on Frank's last missive. They were so far from the main road, there was no harm in talking. Plus, they'd run off the goblins for sure.

She put down the letter.

"I miss him."

He was near, standing over her.

"Can I?" The light was on Frank's page.

"Why?" she asked.

He sat down. Okay, she'd misunderstood. He'd been asking if he could sit. He put his flashlight at the arch over them. Now they had a cathedral.

"Felt good, didn't it?"

"Today? Oh. Yeah. Yeah, it did." In Mary's hands, Prophet had sent a signal to a satellite, and a satellite had sent the Iranians signals that sounded like voices they knew. The voices told them to go away. And they did.

"You were good."

She dropped her head so he couldn't see he'd made her happy.

"Done it enough times," she downplayed.

"Training," he said. "Not in-country."

"It just worked."

"No, it didn't. You got it to."

"Like you couldn't have."

"Not the point."

"Thanks. Thanks, but . . ."

"But what?"

"I wasn't so calm once, almost cost me."

"Seems to me you saved two men on that mountain. The other man—no one could have saved."

It was just after sunset. She pulled the flashlight back farther from

Frank's letter so she could see Will's face. She couldn't read it. She heard something in his words—the tone—what was it?

"My crash," she said.

He moved his face away to look up at the old hall's steps and where they led—the arched opening and, beyond it, the dark-violet sky.

"That," he said. With his face turned, she could just hear him.

"I still don't know—"

"Malfunction," he said.

"—what happened."

"Why won't you—"

"—let you read it?!" Her voice was raised.

"No, no," he said. He'd turned back to face her. He looked—could it be?—abashed. "No, Mary, I respect that."

She floated down slowly to a nicer mood. "For that—I—I thank you."

"He was your wingman." Will said it so fast. She'd counted on a long pause.

"Had my back," she said, a little too quickly—hoping to match his snap delivery—and then she was in trouble, for first ever with Will she sensed the back of her throat smaller, her eyes dampening.

"You ended up having his."

"Not enough." Tears fully threatening, she cut the words shorter. They came out sounding wrong, choppy and clammy at once.

"You have to hope he improves." His words were perfunctory, but he said them with a luster of kindness unusual for him.

"I look at him in that bed," she said, giving up. "I just—I just . . ."

"Challenges everything you thought you knew."

"Exactly." She turned to him. He was searching her face. He moved his hand to her forehead and pushed aside a piece of her hair.

They talked a little more, none of it as difficult. After an hour or so, they got out of the old hall and back to Baz without anything else passing between them.

. . .

Mary walked through Ahwaz as Will's wife, son Baz trotting between them. The heat sagged her. She had a step in the mission coming, a particular task assigned to her. She succumbed to forgetting it. All along the city avenue, she gave up, into the office building, to the elevator, Will pushing the up button. There was air conditioning, but it was flagging.

Oil-industry men were here. They waited for this elevator, murmuring of refining, service, supply. In Ahwaz there were no longer just Iranians, but European and Asian businessmen, united by petroleum, speaking schoolhouse English, the only tongue they could half manage between them all. Baz wanted Mary to think of the ancients. This, he'd told her on the drive, was the lower extension of Mesopotamia, just east of the Fertile Crescent, the Iranian portion of humankind's earliest civilization. As their Khodro motored south, the temperature of the highlands burned away, and their unseasonable August had turned soupy.

The elevator had come. Mary, Will, Baz, and the businessmen tried to fit. Will, last to enter, pushed four. Nothing happened. He hit the doors. The gears caught above them. Nothing moved. He hit more floor buttons—five, six, at eight they started going up. They got out at seven and walked down to four.

They found the office. Will told the receptionist they'd arrived for their appointment. His Farsi must have worked, because she handed him a clipboard. He was filling it out when a man walked out. This way, he said. Mary took Baz by the hand.

They came upon a doctor in a white coat, who ushered them into a room. A woman followed them in and handed each of them an ice pack. No names were exchanged; no greeting was necessary.

"I apologize," the doctor said in English. "It's fifty Celsius. The government should be shutting down the city. Instead they lie and say it's forty-four."

"Where is she?" Will asked. They had come for the hotel maid.

"One moment," the doctor said. He went to the door and spoke to someone waiting there.

The ice pack was already warming. She wanted the scarf off, the manteau too. Will was glazed with sweat, his color reddened. Baz looked groggy.

The doctor came halfway into the room. "There's a delay. This heat. I'm afraid she's not here yet."

Will stood up. "Then we have to go."

"If you could just wait a few more minutes."

Mary and Baz were standing too.

"This makes everything so difficult," the doctor said.

"It does," Will said. "But it can't be helped."

She and Baz followed Will through the door and down the hallway.

Halfway through, the maid appeared. She was a teenager, Mary saw through her own wilting. At home she would have been a creature of long hair and stretch jeans, cell phones and iPods, texting and down-loading, but here she was dignified, mysteriously fresh in long sleeves, navy jumper, matching veil.

She came at them with fast bubbles of Farsi, bursting to tell and tell. Baz through all of it was saying, *"Bale, bale, bale"*—Okay, okay, okay. Will tried to stop her outpouring but it was a cascade. As she got to the end, she took both Mary's hands and kissed her on each cheek twice. She kept holding her hands and smiling, tilting her head to Will, beaming into his eyes as only a person who didn't know him at all would do.

So much for second-guessing and elaborated precautions, Mary thought. All the preparing for this moment had redounded to flawless clarity. This girl was no trap.

"She says that your friend is alive," Baz translated. "She says that he waits for you always. She says he is at a place, where she knows. She says he wants you to visit. She says you are a good man. She says there is a good way to go. You must help her—to, to . . . to go there. Can you do this thing?"

Will took the girl by the hand, and they walked a little farther down the hall, away from Baz and Mary. To her surprise, she saw them talking. Yet Will's Farsi—it wasn't good enough for such a conversation. She strained to see.

After a while, the girl slipped a paper to Will, and he had it hidden so quickly, Mary questioned what she'd just seen. Had she imagined the paper?

In the next moment, the girl's back was all Mary saw, and Will was walking toward her and Baz. She had never seen him look this way. He was—there was no other word for it—lightened. He didn't smile. That would have been too much. But he was unclouded, clean almost.

"Let's go," Will said to Baz. "We need to meet at this place." He had a piece of paper with a map; surrounding the grid, the rest of the page was covered in numbers.

They sped from the maid to the Caspian Air service hangar. The maid's missive, perhaps her words, seemed to have made Will accept that Hoseyn was still on the American side, his loyalty extant.

Even so, from just outside the hangar, they watched to make certain no strike force, no disguised commandos, no bustling laborers—no one, really—intended to ambush. Mary spied the craft she was to fly, a Tupolev 154-100, the upgraded airliner, this one with blessedly familiar Western avionics. All she had to do was fly it fifty-four nautical miles, to Iraqi airspace. Iran would be unprepared to shoot down a commercial airliner. They wouldn't scramble fighters in time. They wouldn't get surface-to-air missiles in time. By the time they did, if they did, Will, Mary, Baz, and Hoseyn would be on Basra tarmac. Baz would slip across the border back to Iran later without them.

She checked maintenance-crew activity. After an hour, she concluded that one of the planes was still in the help shop. But the other two, they were good to go.

Will was setting up. Now she joined him. They checked weapons, decided on positions and access, alternative egress. Yet Mary couldn't help gravitating to Baz, glancing at him, worrying. She could see him sobering, counting down the final minutes to the great adventure's end. Will was missing Baz's hurt.

When she got a moment, she knelt where he was leaning against a wall in his boy crouch. They were hiding behind what looked like a construction trailer, in a narrow space in front of a small one-story station of white concrete.

"You will return to your family," she whispered

He nodded glumly.

"They will be proud of you."

He didn't smile.

"Your mother will celebrate. Your uncles. Everyone."

"You will stay my mother," he said.

At full dark, she saw for certain the sky was cloud-free. This was true boon. Her crash, so many months ago now, was the reverse of this night. As the men at the lake had disappeared, so would devils. So had, she saw, her cooler self. She wasn't tender, but she felt, perhaps for the first time, the worth of kindness. Had Frank begun this warming and Baz finished it? There was so much when this thing was over that she wanted to talk about with Will.

Just then, a man appeared. She saw him about a hundred meters from the trailer where they were hiding. Baz didn't see yet. She pushed away from him closer to the wall. Will was by her side, and he leaned in to the wall too.

Hoseyn was walking toward them. She saw he was taller than she'd expected, and thicker, not the reedy scientist in the pictures she'd studied. She was supposed to be reading whether he was friend or foe. He looked bloated to her, and what did that mean? He was not in a hurry—was that a sign he'd turned against them, or did it mean he was here to welcome their offer of escape? She tried to feel wary, and she did, almost instantly, but it dipped just as fast again as the momentousness of his arrival kept hitting her.

Will was immune to it, she could feel it. Her usefulness at this red moment was slack-poor. Why did concentration fail when it did? All she could sense was drama, and that was something to do with her softer self, this basket of happy hopes she'd so recently gotten. She decided to trust Will on this, let it go to his judgment. He was the one who knew this man. He could read him, couldn't he?

And Will seemed to be deferring, because he wasn't moving, just watching and waiting, and it wasn't until Hoseyn was almost confused, not sure what or whom he should be approaching, that Will looked at Mary. He put his fingers in her hand, saying, "This is not okay. Not yet."

Hoseyn called out his name. He put his hands in the air, as in westerns, and he started turning clockwise, step, step, another step.

Will watched him, letting Hoseyn's cinema surrender continue. After a while, Hoseyn put his hands down, and then he stopped turning.

For many moments, there was no movement, no sound, nothing but the thinking—all of it Will's and Hoseyn's—and then Will pulled his fingers out of Mary's palm, stood up, his weapon on Hoseyn. He walked out from behind the trailer. Hoseyn's back was to him. He didn't see Will.

He crouched at Will's touch. His hands flicked up, but Will didn't let that happen, he said something, she couldn't hear what it was. They went to the ground, an awkward scrambling; Will seemed to pat him down, to half hit him, but she might have imagined that. Baz was breathing so fast she almost put her hand over his mouth.

They rearranged themselves, Will and Hoseyn, sitting on the pavement near the hangar, Will's hand on the back of Hoseyn's neck, speaking directly into his ear, as if to avoid lip readers, or to feel with his hands Hoseyn's reaction to each word he said. They talked like that and talked some more; Mary kept Baz quiet behind the trailer.

Finally, she saw Will stand up, gun still on Hoseyn, but now Will did the tilt to the towline truck that was the signal that Hoseyn was leaving with them, that he was, in the next moves at least, to be trusted.

Mary went to the hangar station that controlled the bird's doors. Within seconds she had the staircase down.

She just walked up it. Baz followed. She went to the cockpit. She started the engines. She pulled up the stairs.

Will, Hoseyn beside him, drove the towline truck. They led the bird out of the hangar by the nose.

When they were clear, he disengaged the towline.

She released the stairs. They climbed aboard.

She pulled up the stairs. She closed the door. She began her checks.

Hoseyn stood behind her. Will was behind him. Baz had the copilot's seat, eyes merry. She took the bird along the apron of runway, slowed for the pivot. She came to a full stop. She began the turn. The wings swung. The engines rumbled slightly. She had completed the arc on the ground when Hoseyn seemed to lose his balance.

They tried to catch him. But he was past them, his fingers strong on her pistol, the barrel to Baz, then the bullet through him. His next was Mary, and he pulled her, his forearm a bar on her neck, her gun at her temple. Now he talked to Will, threatening her life, advising his moves, that he should put the gun here and do it like that. She heard him talk of his wife, that he had to do this because the government had her. Mary first had in mind her father, who'd had a knife but never reached her. She next felt the fist of shock in her gut, the rawest for Baz. She heard Will tell Hoseyn that Hoseyn could kill her. She heard Will insist she was nothing to him. He told Hoseyn that they wouldn't get anything out of her, that she knew less than nothing. Then, his eyes in hers, he took his gun to his own head and fired.

In the cockpit's small space, the blood punched over all of them. She would have staggered. Hoseyn did. His grip got loose, and she poured out from under him, reaching for Will, crawled, and as she was crawling for him got her hand on his. She pulled herself up and closer to him. He was still warm, possibly in the last seconds. But then Hoseyn was on her, pulling her up, and she was yanking herself free, him pulling. She slam-whacked for his nose, felt the cartilage suck and crack away from his face, but no sound came with it, it was gone, they moved in silence, slow-eyed motion coming in and out of the range of her deteriorated thinking. He sank back; she felt Baz's body come between them, his boy foot in the way. She tried to feel for the metal Hoseyn had to have in his hand.

He was down. She saw that now, the gun lying in a black sparkle in the cockpit lights. She swooped for it and found another hand, not

Hoseyn's, then another on her waist, around her neck, someone, and then another, getting what her crash and mountain ice had not yet: her.

For many months in Evin Prison, Mary couldn't tell. Now she knew it. The chair in this room was wood. She was not the first to sit in it. She felt the oil on the underside. It was ever so faint, but it was there. Our fingers gave out just the most insubstantial film of it. They could not take that away. She had that now.

In their white dresses, her victims were her instructors.

They said she was to be forgiven.

They said she was never pure, but she could be chaste.

In not many days, they took her to the trees to hear the leaves.

ACKNOWLEDGMENTS

Thanks go to my friends in Iran but most especially Amin and Hamid, to the many generous people who assisted me in Afghanistan and Pakistan, to those in the military who shared insight and suggestions, and to my tireless editor, Robin Desser. Deepest love goes to Richard Price, who wooed me from fearsome independence into several gardens of zooming, blooming light.

A NOTE ABOUT THE AUTHOR

Lorraine Adams is a novelist, critic, and Pulitzer Prize–winning journalist. Her novel *Harbor* won the *Los Angeles Times* Book Prize for First Fiction, was a finalist for the Orange and Guardian First Book prizes, and was selected as a *New York Times* Best Book, a *Washington Post* Notable Book, and *Entertainment Weekly*'s Best Novel of the Year. She is a regular contributor to the *New York Times Book Review* and *Bookforum,* and was a staff writer at *The Washington Post* for eleven years. She lives in New York City.

A NOTE ON THE TYPE

The text of this book was set in Sabon, a typeface designed by Jan Tschichold (1902–1974), the well-known German typographer. Based loosely on the original designs by Claude Garamond (c. 1480–1561), Sabon is unique in that it was explicitly designed for hotmetal composition on both the Monotype and Linotype machines as well as for filmsetting. Designed in 1966 in Frankfurt, Sabon was named for the famous Lyons punch cutter Jacques Sabon, who is thought to have brought some of Garamond's matrices to Frankfurt.

Composed by Creative Graphics,
Allentown, Pennsylvania

Printed and bound by Berryville Graphics,
Berryville, Virginia

Designed by Soonyoung Kwon